The Stolen Dead

MJ White is the pseudonym of bestselling author Miranda Dickinson, author of twelve books, including six *Sunday Times* bestsellers. Her books have been translated into ten languages, selling over a million copies worldwide. A long time lover of crime fiction, the Cora Lael Mysteries is her debut crime series. She is a singer-songwriter, host of weekly Facebook Live show, Fab Night In Chatty Thing.

Also by MJ White

A Cora Lael Mystery

The Secret Voices
The Silent Child
Leave No Trace
The Deadly Echoes
The Unspoken Truth
The Stolen Dead

MJ WHITE
THE STOLEN DEAD

hera

First published in the United Kingdom in 2025 by

Hera Books, an imprint of
Canelo Digital Publishing Limited,
20 Vauxhall Bridge Road,
London SW1V 2SA
United Kingdom

A Penguin Random House Company
The authorised representative in the EEA is Dorling Kindersley Verlag GmbH. Arnulfstr. 124, 80636 Munich, Germany

Copyright © MJ White 2025

The moral right of MJ White to be identified as the creator of this work has been asserted in accordance with the Copyright, Designs and Patents Act, 1988.
All rights reserved. No part of this publication may be reproduced or transmitted in any form or by any means, electronic or mechanical, including photocopy, recording, or any information storage and retrieval system, without permission in writing from the publisher.
No part of this book may be used or reproduced in any manner for the purpose of training artificial intelligence technologies or systems. In accordance with Article 4(3) of the DSM Directive 2019/790, Canelo expressly reserves this work from the text and data mining exception.

A CIP catalogue record for this book is available from the British Library.

Print ISBN 978 1 80436 713 1
Ebook ISBN 978 1 80436 712 4

This book is a work of fiction. Names, characters, businesses, organizations, places and events are either the product of the author's imagination or are used fictitiously. Any resemblance to actual persons, living or dead, events or locales is entirely coincidental.

Printed and bound in Great Britain by Clays Ltd, Elcograf S.p.A.

Look for more great books at
www.herabooks.com | www.dk.com

For my readers.

Thank you for believing in Cora, Minshull and the South Suffolk CID team.

This series is yours.

Past reason hunted, and no sooner had
Past reason hated as a swallow'd bait,
On purpose laid to make the taker mad.

Sonnet 129, William Shakespeare

One

THE COLLECTOR

I've been waiting for this for a long time. Now it's here, I can hardly contain my delight.

The *perfect find*.

The crowning glory of my collection.

I think of the boxes I've already catalogued and stored. Filled with discarded things nobody ever saw the value of. But I saw them. And now they're mine.

My torch beam quivers as it traverses the dark beach, the damp shingle brought alive by the light. Like shadowy diamonds lining my path, welcoming me. I'm shrouded in mist, the sea hidden somewhere beyond, the sound of the waves muted as if in reverence to me.

My mouth goes dry.

The knife, heavy in my palm, slips.

I catch it a moment before it falls.

If it isn't perfect, it doesn't count, I scold myself.

Nerves swell within me, but I kick them aside. I have prepared too well to fail now.

I'm inches away. My fingers close around the knife.

And my perfect piece opens his eyes…

He tries to move but the alcohol in his bloodstream roots him to the shingle. His voice cracks as he throws back his head. I've never heard a man scream before, but the sound sets my blood pumping. Purpose. Determination. Strength. A building fire, searing as it rises.

I step over his squirming frame, raise my knife. And strike.

The force of it brings my face level with his. The stink of his breath fills my nostrils as it's punched from his lungs, the hot, sticky blood bathing my hand around the hilt of the knife where it meets his chest.

A single wound, just like I planned it. Swift and clean. The perfect specimen.

I stare deep into the whites of his eyes as blood bubbles out from his lips, my own heart pumping fast as his bleeds out.

'I found you,' I soothe, holding firm until the fight leaves him. 'You're *mine*.'

Two

CORA

'Slow down!'

Dr Cora Lael laughed as she maintained her pace. 'If you can't keep up, you can always meet me there.'

'I *can* keep up, thank you very much,' DS Rob Minshull puffed, his running shoes sending up showers of shingle from the beach as he followed her. 'I'm just saying, it's a Sunday morning run, not a race.'

'You keep telling yourself that,' Cora returned, breaking into a sprint. 'Slacker!'

Minshull groaned but Cora heard his steps increase behind her as they raced along the beach.

It was good to be out after weeks of rain and sleet following the Christmas break. Cora had spent the last few weeks at work gazing out of the single window of the South Suffolk Educational Psychology Department's office, willing the driving precipitation to stop. Nothing beat being out in the wild, untamed beauty of the South Suffolk coast. And today, with its bright, brave sunshine and surprisingly pleasant temperatures, was the perfect day to return to her favourite route.

Shingle Street Beach was quiet and still, the unique lagoon at its heart reflecting the gentle passage of the clouds above. A favourite place with locals and virtually unknown to tourists, it was smaller and quieter than any of Felixstowe's beaches or the wide shingle beauties of Orford Ness and Aldeburgh further up the coast. Cora had fallen in love with it when her late father, Bill, had taken her there with her younger brother, Charlie, to birdwatch and skim stones as kids. And she loved it still. Minshull, a recent convert, was quickly discovering its charms, not least the coffee shack that had recently opened at its northernmost point. Nobody quite knew what the opening hours of the coffee shack were, but a dog walker they'd met at the car park this morning told them she'd seen the owner, Eric, arriving to set up for the day.

Which was all the incentive necessary for their Sunday morning run.

Having Minshull alongside her (or, to be precise this morning, several paces behind) was an added bonus. Since the major murder investigation they'd worked on together just before Christmas, she hadn't seen much of him, the CID team investigating a spate of farm thefts that had so far proved fruitless. Added to that, recruitment had been slow for their new detective chief inspector, the position remaining stubbornly unfilled since the sudden removal of the former incumbent. The delay in securing a replacement was causing headaches for Minshull and his team, all weary of the vacancy. Cora knew what it would mean to him to be away from the ongoing drama, if only for a few Sunday morning hours.

'What time does Eric's open?' Minshull called.

'Nine a.m.' Cora checked her watch. 'We have ten minutes to get there.'

The promise of hot bacon rolls and home-roasted coffee was enough to inject pace and enthusiasm into Minshull's progress, the detective sergeant drawing level with Cora within seconds.

'Loser buys breakfast,' he said with a grin, sprinting ahead.

'Oi!' she laughed as she dashed after him.

I... found... you.

The voice severed the salt air like a knife.

Cora skidded to a halt, the sudden intrusion of sound cutting across her path. The shingle ebbed behind her like a stone-studded tide. Where had the voice come from? Cora scanned the beach for its owner, but aside from Minshull still running ahead, she was alone.

I found you...

It was close: too close to miss if it had come from a fellow beach visitor.

I found you...

Insistent. Proud. A slight edge to the tone that Cora couldn't quite pin down. Was it a warning? A jealous claim? A threat?

Rooted to the beach, Cora leaned into the sound. Her every sense told her this voice hadn't been spoken. It was an audible thought, an emotional echo, recent and insistent – and *close*.

'Rob.'

Minshull didn't hear at first, heading towards the wooden beach café a little further up the beach, spurred on by the promise of breakfast.

'*Rob!*'

This time, he turned, his smile vanishing.

'What is it?' he asked, running back to her.

'I heard a voice.'

It was testament to the years they'd known each other that Minshull immediately understood. Cora's ability to sense emotional echoes from objects – audible fingerprints, as she'd explained it to Minshull and the CID team she worked with as a specialist consultant – wasn't always easy for others to understand. But Minshull did.

'Where?'

'I don't know – but close.'

Together they began a search of their immediate surroundings. The shingle beach stretched emptily ahead and behind: to the right leading down to the soft grey sea, to the left heading into the long, rough grass of the low dunes bordering the beach.

I found you...

Cora closed her eyes and let the thought-voice lead her.

I found you... You're mine...

Instinctively she began moving, back towards the line of dunes, until a sudden hiss right in front of her caused her eyes to open.

Not an object, discarded, bearing the thought-voice of its last owner.

But a person, lying motionless in the shingle.

'Here,' Cora called, her thudding heartbeat clashing with the still-repeating voice.

The body lay in a slight indentation a few steps from the curve of the dune. A bearded man, lying on his back, his glassy eyes open to the pale March sun, pupils wide, unseeing. A filthy sleeping bag covered his feet and legs, his hands clenched in fists at his sides, the skin turned blue by death, matching the shade of the tattoos across his knuckles. A deep bloom of red stained one side of his pale grey fleece jacket. But the bloodstain wasn't what caused Cora's breath to catch.

It was the large pile of beach detritus covering the centre of his chest.

Strands of seaweed, fraying blue rope, shingle stones, white shells and shards of cream-glazed sea pottery that her mum loved to search for whenever they visited the beach, gathered together. They had been placed with care, each piece infused with the same insistent voice that had summoned Cora to the man's resting place. From the side, it appeared as if the beach-combed finds were bleeding, their sharp edges stained by the congealing blood of the dead man, as the voice continued to stake its claim.

I found you... You're mine...

'Don't get any closer,' Minshull rushed, scrabbling in his pocket for his phone. 'Yes, hello, this is DS Rob Minshull. I'm on Shingle Street Beach, not far from Eric's Beach Café. We've found a body...'

Three

MINSHULL

'It's a weird one.' Chief pathologist, Dr Rachael Amara, crouched beside the dead man, scanning his body. 'And you say there's a voice attached to the beach stuff?'

Beside her, Cora nodded. 'It's coming from the items as a collective, but I can hear identical ghost-echoes of one voice, which suggests that whoever piled it there did it all themselves.'

'Fascinating.' Dr Amara observed Cora with a smile. 'Loving your work, Dr Lael.'

'Can you tell the cause of death?' Minshull asked, standing beside Cora. He'd been watching her since the discovery of the corpse, ready to support her if she needed it. She said she didn't, of course, but she'd accepted his embrace once the call to Control had been made. They'd held each other for a long time, and it was impossible to tell whether the reverberation between them was his body shaking or hers.

Considering all the deceased victims Minshull had encountered over the course of his police career, this was only the second body he'd discovered – the first not on duty. Shock was already pulling at his frame like an insistent child, demanding attention.

'It's impossible to say, until we can get that little lot off his chest,' the pathologist replied, looking over to the chief scene of crime officer, who was inspecting the body from the other side. 'My guess is the wound itself is beneath it. Brought your tweezers, Brian?'

Brian Hinds gave a grim smile. 'Should have done. I wasn't expecting a game of Jenga so early on a Sunday morning.'

'How will you remove it all?' Cora asked.

'Bloody carefully,' the chief SOCO replied. 'There could be prints on any of the pieces. I think we'll need to edge it with something first to prevent any fragment from falling and getting lost. But it'll have to be slow and steady: there's no way we can take that pile off him intact.'

Minshull and Cora stood back as the SOCO team converged at the scene, carefully photographing and recording the body, their heads bent in hushed discussion. There appeared to be some debate over how exactly to contain, and then remove, the beach detritus.

'Should we stay?' Cora whispered to Minshull.

'I'll wait for the okay from Joel,' Minshull replied, glancing at his phone and willing his superior, DI Joel Anderson, to call at that moment. 'Shouldn't be too long.'

They watched their colleagues at work, as the SOCO team positioned themselves around the body. Despite the strengthening wind and first spots of rain beating against them, they moved with painstaking care, edging millimetres at a time to support the pile of beach finds as a clear Perspex sheet was slid slowly beneath it.

Frustration itched at Minshull, so unused to being an onlooker at a crime scene. His gaze remained on the operation to remove the beachcombed finds, but his mind was already racing through possibilities, facts and potential lines of inquiry.

So many questions presented themselves.

Who would have travelled to such a remote spot to murder someone? Why this beach? Was there significance in the location? Had it been chosen for a reason? Had the victim been killed where he now lay, or somewhere else and dumped here? Did the dead man fight back? Until they could examine the body, it was impossible to tell. Deep ruts in the shingle around the body suggested movement of some kind, but were they signs of struggle or evidence of a body moved into position?

The body was situated a considerable distance from the road, the shingle beach slippery enough to walk on without the literal dead weight of a corpse to carry. Were more people involved? Had the victim been chosen or was it merely a tragic case of being in the wrong place at the wrong time?

How long had the deceased man been there? Judging by the dirty, stained sleeping bag and dishevelled clothing, he could be a rough sleeper – you got them on the coast, many drawn to the beaches to be away from everyone else. But was it that simple? What if the body had been arranged to give that impression? To dissuade anyone from considering the man's identity beyond him being homeless?

And why this beach?

Why here?

Did the killer intend the body to be discovered, or might they have hoped it would lie here undisturbed for some time? The beach was far from deserted around the clock, but the infrequency of visitors might make it a perfect dumping ground.

Except that didn't explain the pile of stones, shells and rubbish on the dead man's chest. Why place it there? And what was its purpose?

Beside him, Cora was quiet. Minshull saw her flinch as the pile shifted onto the Perspex sheet. What was she hearing from the blood-tinged shards of stone and shell?

She hadn't seen the body. She'd *heard* it.

Even now, years after first encountering Dr Cora Lael's unique ability, Minshull struggled to understand the magnitude of it. How loud must the emotional echoes have been around the deceased to summon Cora's attention over the thunder of the incoming tide? Without her insight, they might have passed the body completely.

He shuddered. Cold seeped through the thin fabric of his running gear, a chill as cold as a grave. There were warm clothes in his car, but that was down at the other end of the beach – and until his superior gave him orders to stand down, he was stuck here.

'Are you cold?' he asked Cora, his voice low.

'Freezing,' she breathed, a brief smile offered in reply.

'As soon as the Guv gets back to me, we can return to the car.'

'It's okay.' A line appeared between her brows as her gaze drifted back to the SOCO team. 'I don't envy them that task.'

'Me either.' He paused, uncertain whether to ask the question. 'How loud are the voices?'

'They're whispered, but they're magnified.'

'How so?'

Her breath shuddered as she exhaled. 'It's like there's a copy of the voice attached to each piece of that pile. Like a recording of the same voice, repeated hundreds of times in unison. They sound… possessive.'

'What do you mean?'

'Like the speaker is staking a claim. *I found you… You're mine*. It's threatening, almost. As if the stones and shells and body might argue back.'

Minshull made to reply, but jumped when his mobile phone buzzed in his hand. Offering an apologetic smile, he answered the call.

'Rob, how's it going?' Anderson sounded out of breath, as if he'd sprinted up several flights of stairs to reach a phone.

'Slowly,' Minshull replied, his heart leaping into his mouth when the pile of debris suddenly slipped a little. The shouts of the team cut through the rumble of the tide at his back.

'What's happening?'

'A slip, while they're extracting the pile of detritus from the body. They've got it now.'

A rush of air sounded on Anderson's side of the line. 'Nerve-wracking, I imagine.'

'You have no idea, Guv.' Minshull forced his gaze away from the salvage operation, moving a few steps from Cora as he lowered his voice. 'I don't think they need us here. Until they can move the stuff off the deceased and get him away from the beach, there's nothing we can do. And Cora's clearly in shock…'

He didn't mention his own shock, sick-cold and creeping up his spine.

'Then you should both get back here,' Anderson replied. 'I'll ask the medic to come and check you both over.'

'Thanks, Guv. It's for Cora, you know.'

'Of course.' Anderson paused. Had he heard more in Minshull's reply? 'But you should get yourself checked as well. To be on the safe side.'

'I will,' Minshull assured him, keen to move the conversation along. 'I just need to get us back to my car…'

'You'll do no such thing!' Anderson's bark severed Minshull's sentence.

'I'm fine to drive.'

'You've just found a body. You're in shock.'

'Honestly, I'm okay.'

'I won't hear of it. You're witnesses to the discovery of a body. You need bringing in like anybody else.'

'But my car…'

'Tim Brinton's there with a Uniform patrol. Tell him I want you and Cora brought back to HQ, then give him your keys. Someone'll drive your car back.'

Minshull bristled. The last thing he needed was being escorted back to Ipswich in a patrol car. But the chill was setting into his bones now, his concern for Cora overriding his natural inclination to argue the toss. Besides, Anderson was a mountain not to be moved when he was in this kind of mood. 'Okay, Guv.'

Sergeant Tim Brinton was already jogging his way over to them when Minshull ended the call.

'Sarge, Dr Lael.' He nodded a greeting, reaching them in a shower of gravel. 'If you'd like to come with me?'

'DI Anderson wants us escorted back to Police HQ,' Minshull said, apology flooding his tone. Brinton had enough to do, securing the area with his small team, without having to provide a taxi service.

'Of course he does. And rightly so. I've got Ted Fletcher grabbing you both a strong tea from the beach shack and then he'll get you back.'

'Appreciate it, Tim.'

'My pleasure, Sarge. Chuck us your keys and I'll get your motor back, too.'

'Thanks. I'm sorry you've been lumped with this.'

'No need to be sorry about it. Always in demand, me.' The uniformed sergeant's wry smile spoke of many years of similar requests. 'I don't expect you get the chance to be chauffeured all that often. If I were you, I'd make the most of it.'

Leaving the developing crime scene felt like skipping a test, as it always did, the urge to remain with his colleagues strong. But as Minshull and Cora climbed into the back seat of the patrol car, he found he was glad of the release.

Cora didn't fight the decision to return to Police HQ in Ipswich with Minshull, as he'd thought she might. She was quiet beside him as they drove towards Ipswich, PC Ted Fletcher's kind chatter filling the space where conversation might have been. Fletcher had given Cora his police jacket when he'd seen her shivering. Minshull made a note to find her a jumper when they got to CID.

Wincing at the overpowering sweetness of the tea Fletcher had apparently heaped several spoonfuls of sugar into, Minshull turned his mind to the act of drinking it, a necessary focus to steady himself. There would be much to do when they arrived in Ipswich: the journey was a chance to breathe, to gain some sort of perspective on what they'd found.

Anderson was waiting for them on the ramp by the fire exit overlooking Police HQ's car park when the patrol car pulled in. Concern was etched deep into his features, the DI making no attempt to shield his response. Oddly comforting, in a strange way.

Thanking Fletcher as they left the patrol car, Minshull led Cora to the ramp.

'Guv.'

'Come inside, both of you. No offence, but you look like crap.'

Supressing a grin, Minshull followed Anderson and Cora into the building.

Four

ELLIS

They were clearly shaken, despite both Dr Lael and DS Minshull's protestations to the contrary. DC Drew Ellis wasn't fooled by any of it, but he kept his smile kind and his questions gentle and respectful as he guided first Cora and then Minshull through the formal statement process.

Even in his relatively short police career, Ellis had seen some awful things. But he couldn't imagine discovering a body off-duty. That must be a nightmare: finding yourself faced with a crime, but having none of the tools and securities you relied upon every day. Especially a murder.

Not *officially* a murder, he corrected himself.

It hadn't been declared as such yet, but the victim had hardly stabbed his own chest and covered the wound with beach rubbish himself, had he? Ellis and his colleagues in the South Suffolk CID team had already accepted what the pathologist would no doubt confirm.

Anderson had tasked Ellis' fellow detectives with finding the identity of the man. Ellis felt the itch of irritation that they'd have a head start on him. DC Kate Bennett particularly. She was the first to start a race when research beckoned – the most competitive person Ellis knew. He suspected her need to succeed came from years of battling to be seen. Every female colleague in South Suffolk Police had faced the same fight, the Force still unofficially geared towards male colleagues, despite all the training and PR insistence to the contrary. But as South

Suffolk CID's only female detective, following the dramatic departure of their former DCI, her battle was far from over.

Ellis liked going head to head with her the most. The sooner he could be back in the CID office, racing against her to find the identity of the body on the beach, the happier he would be. Not that he'd ever admit it to her, of course...

'So the first indication of the body was Dr Lael's observation?' he asked, carefully. While the CID team were all comfortable with Cora's unique ability, recording it for evidence presented a problem. How did you report that a body had been discovered because a witness heard voices from the beach finds piled upon his chest? Ellis recorded the details, careful to remain faithful to the accounts while leaving no room for question of Dr Lael's testimony.

'Yes,' Minshull replied. He looked weary, stubble lining his chin and his running gear giving him a diminished appearance. Ellis had seen his superior out of his chosen work uniform of a dark grey suit, white shirt and tie, but today the sight of him so out of place in a building he was so much a part of was startling. He was always clean-shaven, always impeccably turned out. Ellis felt scruffy beside him in the CID office. The change today was unnerving.

But then, Ellis was unaccustomed to seeing Minshull on the opposite side of an interview desk. His heart went out to his superior, even if the situation made him uneasy.

'And are you okay, Minsh?' Blanching, he quickly corrected himself. 'Um, DS Minshull...'

A gentle smile met his consternation. 'I'm a bit shaken, as you would expect. But I'm fine, DC Ellis. Thank you for your concern.'

Ellis offered an apologetic grimace, met with a raised hand of dismissal from Minshull. Grateful for the gesture, he pressed on.

Twenty minutes later, he was released from the purgatorial task, accompanying Minshull back upstairs to the blessed familiarity of the CID office. As they reached the door, Ellis held back.

'Sarge.'

Minshull turned. 'What?'

'I just wanted to say... I get it. The shock thing. And I know we don't mention it *in there*...' He nodded at the CID office door. '...but if you need to talk – or not – I'm here.'

Minshull observed him for an uncomfortable moment, his expression difficult to read. 'Appreciate that, Drew. Thanks.'

As soon as the moment had arrived, it vanished – Minshull heading inside the CID office with Ellis shuffling in behind him. But its briefness was immaterial: its implication was seismic. Minshull rarely dropped his professional mask with the team and Ellis had rarely challenged it. That he had now and Minshull had received it meant more than Ellis could express.

'How did it go?' Bennett whispered as Ellis returned to his desk.

'Weird,' he returned, watching Minshull and Cora walk into Anderson's office, the door firmly closed after them. 'But, you know, okay.'

Bennett shuddered. 'Rather them than me. I can't imagine finding a body on my morning off.'

'Me either.'

'How were they both?'

'Shook up. Minsh didn't admit it, but I mean *look* at him.'

'Odd they were together,' Bennett mused, glancing at DC Dave Wheeler and DC Les Evans, who were both working. 'Not the first time, either.'

The scent of gossip made Ellis forget some of his earlier unease. 'They've seen each other a lot outside of work. Dave reckons they run together most Sundays.'

Mischief danced in Bennett's eyes. 'Tenner says they get it on before the summer.'

'What?'

'Shh! Keep your voice down!'

Ellis wheeled his chair closer to his colleague. 'You can't bet on a thing like that.'

'Well, who else's love life can we speculate on? They're most likely to get together out of anyone in here.'

'I can't see it,' he replied, surprised by how defensive he sounded. 'Tenner says they don't.'

The quick handshake to seal their bet passed under the radar of Wheeler and Evans. How long their colleagues would remain unaware of it was anyone's guess.

'Any news on the deceased?' Ellis asked, keen to return to safer ground.

'Couple of names have come up,' Bennett replied, consulting her notebook. 'Both rough sleepers, both pretty well known in the area. Although neither has been seen sleeping on that particular beach. I don't suppose he had any ID on him?'

'Currently unclear. Until they get the pile of stones and stuff off him, SOCOs won't be able to check.' Ellis watched as Wheeler walked over to the whiteboard beside Minshull's desk to put up three photos from the scene. 'It's an odd one.'

'It is. If they want volunteers to go down there, I'm going to offer.'

'Me too,' Ellis replied, instinctively. He'd learned that where Bennett went, he should be also.

'Okay, so what are you two plotting?' Wheeler grinned across at them.

'World domination,' Ellis returned.

'Bit ambitious for a Sunday, but fair enough. Any news on the deceased's ID?'

'Two names so far,' Bennett replied. 'Lee Braunton, forty-two, and Steven O'Halloran, forty-six. But they've only been raised because neither has been seen in the local hostels for a while. They could be anywhere.'

Wheeler nodded. 'It's tough for people right now. More rough sleepers than I've seen in a while and the local council being less than helpful finding safe places for people. But sleeping on the beach in all weathers? Can't be good for anyone.'

'Definitely wasn't good for our deceased.' Ellis spoke before his common sense engaged, a rush of blood to his face when he saw Wheeler and Bennett's expressions. 'I mean… Who goes out looking to kill rough sleepers? And why pile the beach stuff on his chest? It's odd.'

'It's evil.' Evans raised his head from his work. 'Kind of crap you see in telly thrillers, not real life. Better hope the press don't get hold of it. We'll have every deluded true-crime nut flocking down here.'

The thought chilled Ellis. 'Then we'll just have to make sure they don't find out.'

Five

ANDERSON

The pathology lab was a cool balm to the mind after the noise and bustle of the CID office. All the same, DI Joel Anderson wished a visit here hadn't been necessary. His sternest warning had been required to dissuade Minshull from accompanying him – the DS would need to be involved in the investigation into the body he'd discovered, but Anderson could allow him a day to process the discovery. Despite Minshull's protestations to the contrary, he would be of no use here. Not today.

At least Anderson could spare him this.

'Joel, what a lovely surprise.'

Dr Rachael Amara greeted him like an old friend, which he supposed he now was. They had worked alongside one another on many cases over the past eight years and were well versed in each other's idiosyncrasies. Dr Amara's much acknowledged dark humour and eccentricity appealed to Anderson's sense of humour, and her expertise as chief pathologist had his utmost respect. Meanwhile, Anderson suspected his Caledonian deadpan humour and self-professed world-weariness were what Dr Amara liked about him most.

It was a surprisingly gratifying exchange.

'Always a pleasure, Rachael, even in these circumstances.'

The pathologist dismissed this with a wave of her hand, a new small red rose tattoo at her wrist catching Anderson's attention as she did so. 'It's *always* in these circumstances. Occupational hazard, I'm afraid.'

'New tattoo?'

'Yes! Isn't it a darling? Found a new artist up in Lowestoft. Criminally young, of course, but gorgeous work. I could pass on his details if you're ever tempted?'

Anderson felt the blood desert his head. 'Not likely. I get dizzy at a blood test. No way I'd willingly allow a needle anywhere near my skin.'

Dr Amara's boom of a laugh bounced around the clinical white-tiled walls of the lab. 'I see. Maybe Ros and I should get you riotously drunk and ink you in your stupor.'

'That's about the only way you could make it happen.' Anderson could just imagine his wife's glee at that sort of devious collaboration. He glanced over at the slab where the body from Shingle Street Beach lay. 'So, what have you found?'

'Once we removed our friend's collection of pebbles, quite a lot.' She led the way to the body, patting its shoulder gently when she reached its side as if reassuring the corpse.

Anderson hid his smile. No wonder younger officers were freaked out by the enigmatic pathologist. 'How long did it take to remove it?'

'The best part of an hour. And Brian's team were cataloguing the pieces for almost two. In the end, we had to divide the pile into five to have any hope of bagging and transporting it all. But beneath it we found this.' She indicated the bruised line just to the left of the upper chest. 'Knife wound. Clean and precise. One stab, straight to the heart. My guess is that whoever did this knew exactly where to strike.'

'Any signs of a struggle?'

Dr Amara shook her head. 'None at all. Which suggests to me that the victim was struck while they were sleeping. Or unconscious. Fast, accurate dispatch. Boom!' She mimed a single stab to the chest. 'Our man had consumed a significant amount of alcohol, so my guess is that he was either passed out or sleeping it off on the beach when he was attacked.'

'Do you think he was killed on the beach? Or was he just dumped there?'

'Ah, now, that's an interesting question. Look here.' The pathologist moved to the right leg of the body, Anderson following her. 'You can just about see scratching and bruising here – crouch down a little and you'll see it better.'

Sure enough, a line of abrasions was visible where the underside of the thigh met the mortuary slab. 'Aye, just about. Drag marks?'

Dr Amara clicked her fingers. 'Exactly!'

'So he was dragged where? On the beach? Or from another location?'

'He was dragged a short distance across the beach, concurrent with the marks we found in the shingle leading to the body. The thin fabric of his trousers was abrased – torn in a few areas – and we found shingle and sand fragments in the material. The lines led from the direction of the sea to the body at the edge of the shingle. My guess is he was sleeping or passed out nearer the waterline and dragged into place post-attack. Had he been dumped there, I would have expected to see drag lines in the opposite direction.'

It made sense. Unless the body had been transported to the beach from the sea, there would be no reason for drag marks to follow that trajectory.

'Right. So he fell asleep on the beach – or passed out – and was attacked as he lay unconscious?'

'That would be my best guess, yes.'

'Any ID found on the body?'

'Would that we were so lucky, Joel. From the state of his clothing I would suspect he had been sleeping rough for a while. We did, however, find this…' She moved to a table behind the slab and picked up a clear plastic evidence bag, which contained what appeared to be a creased and scuffed small rectangle of cardboard, with one of its edges torn off.

Anderson headed over for a better view. 'A business card?'

'It once was. We found it in his shoe. It had been taped over a hole in the sole. Most of the print has been lost to water damage, but look here...' She indicated a faded, broken line of text with one gloved finger.

Anderson squinted, hearing his wife's admonishment in his mind as he willed the stubbornly blurred letters into focus.

You need reading glasses, you daft man. Make an appointment to get it sorted.

No fear – he retorted, blinking quickly to get the desired effect. He didn't need glasses. It just took his eyes longer to function than before.

The letters that reluctantly swam into view formed a two-word name:

HALYARD INN

'It's a pub, about two miles up the coast,' Dr Amara said. 'It changed its name a couple of years back to *The Wayfarer's Arms*, but my colleague Jim, who lives nearby, says most people in the area still call it by its original name.'

It wasn't the conclusive ID Anderson had hoped for, but the lead was more than welcome. 'This is brilliant, Rachael,' he said, his own smile mirroring that of the pathologist. 'Thank you.'

'My pleasure. Apparently the landlord has been there for years, just changed the name when the brewery wanted to refurbish the place. He might know more about our man on the beach.'

'We'll check it out. Any idea when the beach stuff will be processed?'

'Your guess is as good as mine.' Seeing Anderson's grimace, the pathologist relented. 'I'll ask the question, but I can't guarantee a fast-track. You know how stretched resources are...'

Anderson held up a hand. 'Anything you can do will help.'

It was the same for everyone working for South Suffolk Constabulary. Budget cuts, belts tightened far beyond the point that anyone had anticipated, rumours of more to come. Anderson suspected the limited budget excuse was partly to blame for the delay in recruiting a new DCI after the debacle of the former incumbent's departure. Ros was adamant he should relent and submit his application. Anderson would rather personally pick through every pebble found on the dead man's chest. As thankless tasks went, he'd get more satisfaction from the latter.

The DCI position was a poisoned chalice.

There was no way Anderson was going to accept it.

Six

WHEELER

There was something uniquely satisfying about walking into a pub in the daytime, DC Dave Wheeler thought, as he entered *The Wayfarer's Arms*. Even when you were on a shout and technically not supposed to be partaking of the tempting range of ales displayed across the ornate pulls that lined the old oak bar. The scent of beer, the way it hung unhurriedly in the air, the sense of a slower pace the moment you walked in – there was only one word for it: magic.

That it happened on a Sunday afternoon during a shift was even better.

Even if the purpose of his visit was far from congenial.

Beside him, DC Les Evans appraised the beer selection with greedy eyes. 'Maybe just the one, Dave?' he suggested. 'Support a local business and all that.'

'I don't reckon the Guv would be too happy if we did,' Wheeler replied, despite his own desire for a cheeky Sunday afternoon pint.

'Oh, I don't know,' Evans argued. 'I reckon he wouldn't mind. It is Sunday after all.'

Wheeler chuckled. 'He *wouldn't mind*? How long have you known Joel?'

'I'm just saying…'

'So we rock back up at CID stinking of beer and he'd be fine with that, yeah?'

Evans' slump was all the reply needed.

'Exactly. Be thankful he sent you out at all, Les. You've been chained to that desk in the office since you returned.'

His colleague had to grumpily concede the point. In the months since his return from serious injury sustained on the job, Evans had been placed firmly on desk duties, Anderson refusing to consider anything else. That he'd suggested Evans accompany Wheeler out on this shout was tantamount to a miracle.

The pub was the kind fast vanishing in Suffolk, furnished with good, honest wooden tables and chairs, and a single run of red velvet upholstered bench seats along one wall. While smoking had been outlawed years before, the suspended dust in the air gave the impression of layers of smoke, a slight fog illuminated by streams of sunlight through the bullseye glass windows. The only concession to the desires of modern-day pub-goers was a flat-screen TV in one corner, the muttered burble of Sky Sports News playing mostly to itself.

It was Wheeler's kind of pub.

Shame they weren't here for the ambience or the beer.

The man behind the bar raised an impressively bushy pair of eyebrows in welcome as Wheeler and Evans approached.

'Gentlemen. What'll it be?'

Reluctantly, Wheeler showed his warrant card. 'DC Dave Wheeler and this is my colleague, DC Les Evans. We're investigating an incident on Shingle Street Beach…'

'The body.' The matter-of-fact summation took Wheeler by surprise. 'We heard.'

'What did you hear, sir?' Wheeler asked, carefully. It was never a good idea to assume what a member of the public knew. He'd made the mistake before, early in his career, where he'd given more information than was necessary, earning him a proper dressing-down from his then superior.

'Assume all they know is gossip,' his old sergeant had admonished him. 'Hearsay. Fantasy. Never confirm anything it's not their business to know.'

'Coppers all over the beach. White suits and white tents. Body bag coming out.' The man sniffed, as if he'd relayed this information so often he was bored of it now. 'My missus was down there, walking the dog, early doors. Saw the whole thing. Murder, is it?'

'We're treating the death as suspicious,' Wheeler replied. 'Are you the landlord, sir?'

'For my sins.'

'You had this place long?'

The landlord blew out his cheeks. 'Going on twenty year now.'

'Can I take your name, please?'

'Ted Allward.'

Wheeler made a note in his notebook, then produced a photo of the business card discovered in the dead man's shoe. 'The gentleman we found had this in his shoe. *Halyard Inn* – I believe that was the previous name of this establishment?'

'It was. Name they all still call it now, despite the best efforts of the brewery to stop 'em.' Allward gave a chuckle that displayed the smallest hint of nerves as he took a closer look at the image on the bar. 'And it was in his shoe, you say?'

'That's correct. Taped over a hole.'

The landlord's smile vanished. 'Hm. I wondered if it might be him.'

'Who's that, Mr Allward?'

'Ron Venn. Ronald, though nobody called him that. Good bloke, if you overlooked all the crap.'

'Regular, was he?'

'You could say that. Everyone knows Ron. Used to see him in here most evenings, nursing a pint for hours. He sat over there.' He pointed to a table with a single stool beside an unlit fireplace. 'Liked to see what was going on, but preferred to be left alone.'

'When was the last time you saw him, sir?' Wheeler asked.

'Eight months ago.'

The landlord's definite reply caught Wheeler's attention.

'That's very specific.'

Allward hefted a sigh that spoke of a story yet to be shared. 'That was when I asked him to leave.'

'Was there trouble?'

'Not the sort you'd think. Ron lived here for a while, in a spare room out the back. I let him stay because he'd had a rough trot, poor sod. Lost his home, couldn't hold down a job, nobody seemed interested in helping him. Council bods were less than useless. My missus said I was making a rod for my own back asking Ron to stay. Turns out she was right.'

'In what way?'

'Chap had his demons. Things he should've had help for years ago. Only he was from that generation that never admitted they needed help—' he tapped his temple '—up there.'

'How long did he stay with you?'

'Couple of months. It was only ever a temporary thing, just to help, you know? Would have been longer, if it were up to me, but he made it impossible to keep him here.'

'What made you ask him to leave?'

'He nicked a bottle of whisky from the stockroom, got himself blatted and started throwing punches. Scared my missus. I couldn't have that. So I told him to go. Haven't seen him since.'

Wheeler nodded as he took notes. 'Did Mr Venn have any family?'

'None that he spoke of. None that ever helped him, at any rate. We didn't know much about him, only that he wasn't born here. There were plenty of people looking out for him, though, back before the trouble. Last I heard he'd found somewhere else to sleep, but I didn't ask where. You don't when someone's caused you grief. I wished the bloke well, you know, but I didn't want to get involved again.'

'Can I ask what the link is with the business card?' Evans piped up. 'How you knew it was Mr Venn from where we found it?'

Ted Allward's gaze swung to Evans, regret and genuine sadness in his stare. 'Because I taped it there. First night he stayed with us. It was only meant to be a temporary solution, just covering the hole until he got a second-hand pair from one of the regulars who'd offered. But by the time they brought the shoes in, Ron had slung his hook.' He shook his head. 'Terrible how it turned out for him. I wouldn't have wished it on the fella, even after everything.'

'Did Mr Venn have any enemies? Anyone who might have wished him harm?'

'Only himself,' the landlord replied. 'That's the tragic thing: everyone liked Ron. He was decent, you know? Kind and funny. Got on with most folks if he was in the mood. Reckon he could've had an easier life if he wasn't hell-bent on battling himself.'

Wheeler's heart went out to Allward. 'I hate to ask, sir, but if we needed someone to identify the body—?'

'Of course.' The reply was so fast it stole the end of Wheeler's question. 'I don't bear him any ill will. Least I can do for the poor beggar now.'

Seven

MINSHULL

Anderson would be the death of him.

Minshull knew why his superior had refused to allow him to view the body, but that didn't mean he had to like it. The DI had been all for sending Minshull home – after all, he wasn't scheduled to be in today – but Minshull had dug his heels in. There was no way he was going to be banished to his apartment, twiddling his thumbs, while his CID colleagues dealt with the crucial early hours of a murder case.

In his mind he was pacing the crime scene, seeking out details, looking for links. At the earliest stage of an investigation, so much felt like casting about in the dark, but he'd learned to value the search. Before your mind became set on theories, before a firm sense of a perpetrator emerged, much could be gleaned that could so easily be missed later.

Little shiny nonsensicals, DC Pete York called them. The night detective who covered the CID office when the team were off-shift was a big believer in small details. 'The pieces of the puzzle that call to you,' he'd told Minshull during one early-morning shift handover, 'that's where the magic is. Where your instinct first fires into action.'

What did Minshull know so far? A body on a beach, suspected to be a rough sleeper, minimal signs of struggle, although some suggestion that he had been dragged into place from a location a little further towards the sea, evidenced by abrasions along his legs; the extreme precision of a single stab wound to the heart, and the strange pile of beach finds placed deliberately on the chest. Blood had not yet been identified in the drag marks found in the shingle where the body had been dragged, the current theory being that he'd been dragged soon after the fatal blow had been delivered and had bled out in the location where his body had been found. Forensic tests were ongoing, the wait for results now underway. Everything else was unconfirmed, the threads frustratingly unconnected. But better to be here, in the CID office, waiting for them to connect, than spinning out alone in the silence of his apartment.

Even if that meant sifting through endless missing persons files.

He unsuccessfully hid a sigh as he flicked to another entry, the hollow eyes of a middle-aged man observing him from the misper photo. Not the man on the beach, but another soul lost to the fringes of society, stepping out of the rigours of everyday life into an unknown realm.

What made someone disappear? Leave everything they knew and vanish?

Minshull had pored over misper files many times before during his police career and today's journey through the misplaced, displaced and forgotten would be far from his last. But what struck him every time was the intense sadness of lives lost. Whether by choice or circumstance, the sheer number of people missing in Suffolk was staggering. It had become worse since the coronavirus pandemic, when the boundaries of everyday life were loosened further, allowing more souls to slip through the net.

'Any joy, Sarge?'

DC Kate Bennett was by his desk, a mug of coffee in hand. Minshull hadn't heard her approach, so consumed was he by the task he'd been assigned.

'No sign of him yet,' Minshull replied.

Bennett nodded, carefully moving the papers strewn across Minshull's desk to place the mug safely between them. 'Thought you might need this.'

'Cheers, Kate.'

'How are you doing?' She lowered her voice, despite only the two of them being in the CID office. With Wheeler and Evans chasing a lead from something Dr Amara had found on the body and Ellis sent downstairs to get an update on the Uniform team's operation on Shingle Street Beach from Sergeant Tim Brinton, the quietness in his workspace was another kick to Minshull: proof again of the deliberate distance he was being held at by Anderson.

'Getting there.' It was a lie and they both knew it. Relenting, Minshull offered Bennett the briefest of smiles. 'I'm trying to keep busy. You?'

'Oh, you know, enjoying the unexpected joy of being called in on my day off.'

'Sorry.'

'Not your fault. We all know the job. Besides, being here is saving me from the endless delights of flat-pack furniture.' Her wince spoke volumes.

Minshull knew a little of Bennett's current home life – the recent end of her marriage and relocation to a new house. Wheeler had alluded to some of the details. Minshull hadn't pushed for more. It was her private business, not titbits of tantalising gossip to be shared at whim. He'd seen the change in her, though, despite her best efforts to conceal it. Her determined focus, her quietness between the bursts of office banter, the moments when the mask slipped. It was no wonder she'd recognised the same battle in him today. There was only so long you could box everything up.

'Sounds like a treat,' he replied.

'You have no idea. Some of the instruction sheets are crimes against fact.'

'We have a name.' Anderson strode into the office, phone pressed to his ear.

'Guv?'

'According to Dave and Les, our deceased is looking likely to be Ronald Venn, sixty-four. Landlord of the pub they went to see has agreed to ID the body.' He nodded at the files on Minshull's desk. 'You might find him in there, but sounds to me like he wasn't missing, just sleeping rough.'

'When will the ID be?' Bennett asked.

'I'm arranging it with the good doctor now,' Anderson replied, a broad grin appearing as he paused to listen to his phone. 'She says hello.'

Both Bennett and Minshull raised their hands as if the eminent pathologist had just walked into the room.

'They say hello back. Yes, I will. Thanks, Rachael.' With a final nod to his colleagues, he headed into his office.

Minshull turned to the 'V' section of the files, flipping past more unclaimed souls to look for the name. But where Ronald Venn's entry would have been, he found nothing.

'He isn't here,' he said, a chill unexpectedly laying siege to his shoulders.

The first sign of the numbness of shock retreating. A reminder of what was to come...

He'd powered through on adrenaline alone since waving Cora off with a uniformed officer several hours before: now he knew it was a matter of time before the reality of the situation would hit home. A wave of nausea traversed his stomach, the grab he made for the mug almost sending it flying.

Bennett averted her gaze as he drank messily, hot coffee stinging his tongue and throat. She understood as everyone in the Force did. Minshull used the pain as an anchor to grasp back control.

'You could always head home, Sarge,' she offered. 'Now we know who we have.'

'I'm fine here.'

'Okay. But if you change your mind...'

'I won't.' It was a bark of a reply. Glancing up at his colleague, he offered a weak smile. 'Appreciate it, though.'

It was enough. Bennett returned to her desk.

Ronald Venn, 64. Minshull typed the name into a web search, scanning the lists of results. Apart from one random match with a former American high school sports coach, he found nothing.

No online footprints, no mention of his existence bar whatever the pub landlord had told Evans and Wheeler. Sixty-four years of life and nothing to indicate he was ever here.

And now, thanks to someone else's actions, no chance he could change the course of his life.

Minshull had encountered homeless and displaced people from the earliest days of his police career, more than there ever should have been. But it never failed to make him sad that anyone should be reduced to a life like that, and angry that other people should be complacent to see it happen.

Despite the chill in his bones as the events of the day sank in, Minshull felt fire fill his belly: determination that Ronald Venn would not be a faceless victim of an unknown killer. He made a silent promise to the name he'd written down in his notebook.

I'll find who did this to you.

He rose from his chair and made for Anderson's office.

The detective inspector looked up from his call, beckoning Minshull in.

'Yes, I will. Keep me posted on the rest, okay? Talk soon.' Ending the call, Anderson dropped his phone onto a wedge of papers on his desk. 'ID has been set for tomorrow morning at eight.'

'No sign of him in the misper files, Guv.'

'Thought it was unlikely. Thanks for looking.'

'No problem.'

The DI observed him for a moment, the scrutiny uncomfortable. 'No offence, Rob, but you look like shit.'

'And *that's* the kind of compliment I came in here for.' Smiling hurt, but humour helped. 'I checked with Tim Brinton. His team are chatting to everyone attempting to visit the beach. Cora reckons it isn't really a tourist draw: most of the visitors are locals. Someone must have seen something – at the very least to give us an idea of how long our victim had been sleeping on the beach, and if he'd been seen talking to anyone.'

'Best leave them to it.' There was an edge to Anderson's reply that Minshull couldn't quantify.

'I – intend to, Guv.'

Anderson let out a sigh and rubbed his temples as he slumped back in his chair. 'I mean, these questions can wait for you until tomorrow.'

'We need to work out for certain if he was killed there, or somewhere else and dumped on the beach,' Minshull protested. 'His killer could be close to the location still: someone might have seen him.'

'All true,' the DI replied. 'But there's little for us to do until the ID tomorrow. Go *home*, Rob.'

It wouldn't stop Minshull's mind from turning over every piece of the puzzle, or working up lists of potential strategy. But his body had reached the edge of what it could stand, begging him to surrender. 'You can manage without me?'

Anderson gave a wry smile. 'We could've managed without you hours ago. Go. Get some food and sleep. You look like you need both.'

Minshull's car was waiting where one of his uniformed colleagues had returned it from Shingle Street Beach. Tiredness bore down on his frame as he eased behind the wheel, but when he drove out of Police HQ's car park, he took a right turn, away from the road that led to his home.

Anderson was right: he needed food. And sleep.

But first, he needed Cora.

Eight

CORA

Alone in her apartment in the former Bartlet Hospital building in Felixstowe, Cora allowed the after-effects of the morning's discovery to register in her body. It began with numbness, ice-cold and remote, the emotion she knew would follow imprisoned behind thick walls of nothingness.

She was no stranger to shock, but the chilling sensation of it still felt alien and raw. As if she were being controlled by someone else. In her time working as a police expert with South Suffolk Constabulary, shock had become a necessary aspect of the job. Cora accepted this, but that made it no easier to navigate.

The gloom of the afternoon surrendered to the fast-encroaching shadow of night beyond her window. It was only when the door entry phone buzzed that Cora registered the darkness of her apartment around her.

Snapping on the lights, she made her way to the receiver on the wall, her fingers cold and stiff as she pressed the button to answer.

'It's me,' Minshull announced, adding, 'Rob,' uncertainty edging his words.

'Come up,' Cora replied, surprised that he was here at all.

It wasn't the first time Minshull had visited her at home. Many of their Sunday morning runs began and ended at Cora's apartment. But his unexpected arrival this evening brought a rush of nerves she wasn't prepared for.

When she opened the door to welcome him, she instantly understood why he'd made the journey from Ipswich to see her. In the deep lines of his brow, the paleness of his skin and the tell-tale purple smudges beneath his eyes she saw her own experience mirrored.

'I didn't want to call…' he began, his words faltering as Cora instinctively gathered him into her arms. Instead, his own arms replied, encircling her body, his breath warm against her ear as they held one another.

Slowly, the persistent shake that had been present in Cora's body began to subside. She felt the tremor in Minshull respond in kind.

'Okay?' she whispered against the warm skin of his neck.

'Yeah…' The word travelled out of him on a sigh as he stepped back.

They traded weary smiles, both a little flushed.

'Come in and sit down,' Cora offered, closing the door and ushering Minshull towards the sofa.

'I grabbed some stuff on the way over.' Minshull raised a carrier bag. 'I haven't eaten anything today. I wasn't sure if you had, either?'

Now that he mentioned it, an ache registered Cora's stomach. 'I haven't.'

'Ah, well, good job I brought supplies.' Minshull began producing packs of sausage rolls, pasta salads, crisps, biscuits and a handful of chocolate bars from the bag, spreading them across the coffee table.

'Did you raid a petrol garage shop?' Cora asked, amused by the impressive stash of snack goods.

'Something like that. Go on, help yourself.'

Cora watched him as they ate, wondering how much the feast was there to service their hunger and how much it served as a distraction from the subject of the body on the beach. In the years she had known Minshull, she'd seen how often he stuffed his own emotional response away behind busyness, procedures and humour. Their discovery this morning had clearly had more of an effect on him than he'd admitted earlier. Cora sensed it as a tension around his frame: when he discarded empty wrappers on the coffee table his thought-voice attached to each piece simply stated *No* – a single word, sounding as if it was spoken through gritted teeth.

No... He wouldn't talk about it.

No... He couldn't address the issue, for fear of losing all control.

Cora had seen him blindsided in the earliest days of murder investigations before, but this felt different. Personal, even.

She waited until a natural lull in their eating before she dared address it.

'This one's a bad one, isn't it?'

Stung, Minshull dropped his gaze to the remains of a Scotch egg in his hand. 'Yeah.'

'Want to talk about it?'

'No.' A verbalised version of the thought-voice still insisting its position from the discarded food wrappers. Then, his shoulders dropped. 'Yes, I think I do. But I don't know how...'

'What makes it feel different from other cases?' Cora asked, her training kicking in – perhaps as much of a deflection as Minshull's late-night-garage feast.

'I don't know. Closer to home, maybe? More of a shock because we weren't prepared?'

'Whereas with a crime scene you're summoned to you already know what awaits you?'

Minshull looked up, his gaze searching Cora's face for – what was it? Reassurance? Understanding? A shared emotion? 'When I'm on a shout I know what I'm heading for. And even when the reality is a shock – like with what we found in Evernam last year – I've had that moment to prepare. To arm myself, mentally. This one came out of nowhere. I have no form of reference for that.'

'I know what you mean.'

'How are you doing with it?'

Cora brushed pastry flakes from her lap. 'Just suffering from shock, I think. I'm letting it work its way out. Any news on who he is?'

'We have a possible name. And we think he may have been sleeping on the beach. The landlord of a local pub knew him and has agreed to ID the body tomorrow morning.' He glanced at Cora. 'The voice you heard on the beach: could you make out anything specific about the person or persons speaking?'

The events of the morning had played on endless loop in her mind all day, the voice that had summoned her to the dead man as strong in her memory as it had been on the beach.

I found you... You're mine...

'It was a whisper,' she confirmed. 'No defining sound or tone around the words. I had the sense it was an adult, rather than a child, but the possessiveness in the shape of the phrase was childlike.'

'In what way?'

Cora recalled the urgent, jealous words, casting her mind around them like a net to capture their shape and pace. How best to voice what she sensed instinctively? She was better able to express this to Minshull now, several years into their working relationship: even still, her own words sounded cumbersome and stilted as she did her best to explain.

'Much of our pain, our panic and our anger are seeded deep in our psyche from our earliest years, so when we're challenged or put in situations where we feel vulnerable, the "child's voice" will reappear. It's why adults you would expect to be rational can display wholly irrational responses when they're stressed or anxious. You'll hear it during arguments – as I'm sure you've heard at work.'

That summoned a smile from the detective. Cora accepted it as a reward, pleased by the connection. 'Oh just a bit. When Joel gets going you can practically see his inner child yelling beside him.'

'I'll bet.'

'So this voice was under pressure? Or angry?'

It was the logical reply to Cora's theory, but she hadn't yet considered it. Was the speaker angry, cornered and lashing out, or proud?

'There was hurt there – wounded ego, maybe. But pride, too. Stubborn pride. And defiance.'

'So could the murder be an act to make a point?'

Cora observed Minshull carefully before she replied. 'I think the body – the way it was arranged on the beach and the pile of stuff on his chest – was designed to be noticed. Proof that it could be taken. Ownership, even.'

'Protecting the body as a possession? Or as the killer's work?'

'Both,' Cora replied. 'Whoever did this intended it to be seen. They want people to know they've taken a life and to demonstrate what they're capable of.'

As she voiced what her instincts had insisted all day, a cold shiver passed across her body. A murderer, now at large. Stalking the beach. Killing for notice.

Nine

EARLY MORNING NEWS BULLETIN

[**News anchor**]: We're getting reports of a body found on a Suffolk beach yesterday morning. According to several tabloid newspapers, the body of a middle-aged man was discovered on Shingle Street Beach, south of Orford Ness. Our correspondent, Ben McAra, is there for us this morning. Ben, what can you tell us about this discovery?

[**Reporter**]: Good morning, Joanne. The answer to your question is, not a great deal. The section of beach where the body was found is still cordoned off, as you can see behind me. Officers guarding the scene are remaining tight-lipped about what might have happened here. But several national tabloid newspapers are this morning insisting that a body was found here and that police are treating it as murder.

[**News anchor**]: Have the reports offered any names of who the deceased might be?

[**Reporter**]: Not yet, but there are rumours that the man was a regular on the beach. It's popular with a range of visitors, mostly local people, who walk their dogs, run, birdwatch and fish here. But there's one aspect of this emerging story that's generating much speculation from assembled press and locals alike: the manner in which the body was found. It seems the dead man was discovered with a pile of pebbles, stones and sand piled onto his chest. This bizarre detail is causing most concern with the people I've spoken to here today. I must stress these are unconfirmed reports, as yet unverified by police. But worrying, if true. For now, this is a developing news story and we'll bring you more as it comes to light.

[**News anchor**]: Ben McAra there, on Shingle Street Beach in Suffolk. In other news…

Ten

ANDERSON

'*How?*'

The gathered detectives of South Suffolk CID jumped to attention as DI Joel Anderson burst into the room.

'How the *bloody hell* did these *utter scrotes* get those details?'

'There were other people on the beach, Guv,' Ellis offered, instantly shocked into silence by one furious stare from his superior. It was a good point, as much of the DC's observations were, but Anderson wasn't about to be calmed by reason.

'There was a bloody police cordon, too, but that didn't seem to bother them.' He brandished a pile of newspapers, throwing them to the floor like incendiary devices as he spoke the name of each one. '*BIZARRE DEATH OF UNKNOWN MAN* – The Sentinel. *DEATH ON THE BEACH* – Morning Post. *BEACH MURDERER STILL AT LARGE: POLICE FOXED* – Daily Messenger. And the *Daily Call* has dubbed the killer The Beachcomber, for crying out loud! They've named the perpetrator already! Never mind that the bastards don't have a bloody clue who he is. They've just granted him infamy.'

'It's cheap and it'll pass, Guv,' Wheeler offered, ever the oil on fractious waters.

'It's a title that could encourage more killings,' Anderson retorted, not wanting to hear it today. 'Because you can bet your life he'll be watching. And anything we say now will look like a weak deflection.' He groaned and stared at the tumble of papers on the floor. 'It's a disaster. And I want to know who told them.'

'They'll never tell us, Guv,' Bennett risked, her colleagues nodding in silent solidarity around her.

'Don't you think I know that, Kate? It's why they're cocky as hell. They know full well they're safe from repercussions. They should be made to disclose the information...'

'What's the plan of action, Guv?' Minshull asked, clearly keen to divert Anderson's ire somewhere practical.

Sometimes his DS could be annoyingly professional. What happened to allowing the DI to rant like a bolshie baby in the office? It was one of the aspects of the job Anderson most enjoyed. And when his mood was as thunderous as it was now, a good old tantrum could soothe a multitude of frustrations.

'The body ID is happening now,' he replied, the fury that had powered him into the CID office slowly surrendering to a dull ache at his temples. 'Dr Amara will call as soon as we have confirmation. Then there's a press conference at ten.'

'Will Superintendent Martlesham take that?' Ellis asked, his colleagues all suddenly keen to avoid eye contact as they awaited Anderson's reply.

It *should* be Ian Martlesham's job. Especially as he and his colleagues in the upper echelons of South Suffolk Police had resolutely failed to recruit a replacement detective chief inspector for the department yet, despite six weeks of supposed interviews. By rights, Martlesham should be made to field all the invasive and frankly inane enquiries from the grubby little gobshites of the press. But the task was bound to fall to someone else: a lower ranking officer who lacked the professional right to refuse.

Anderson already suspected who that would be.

The creep of defeat already edging in, he sat heavily on the edge of Minshull's desk.

'I doubt it. I'm awaiting a call from him regarding arrangements.'

The collected wince of his team did nothing to lift his spirits. They knew the score as well as he did.

'Is there anything we can do, Guv?'

Anderson turned to Bennett, whose look of sympathy, while kindly meant, was still a kick. 'Not until we know where we're at.'

The buzz of his mobile summoned his hand to his pocket. Retrieving the phone, he answered the call.

'Joel, Rachael Amara here. We have a positive ID on our deceased. He's Ronald Venn, sixty-four, of no fixed abode.'

'Right. Thanks, Rachael. And thank your team, too, please.'

'Will do.'

He ended the call and faced his team. 'Okay, we have a positive ID on the body found at Shingle Street Beach. Ronald Venn, sixty-four years old. We know he lived in Suffolk, but beyond that we have no information. Dave, Les, what did the landlord tell you about Venn?'

'Only that he'd been coming into the pub for years and, when the landlord discovered Venn was homeless, the offer of temporary accommodation was made.'

Anderson turned from Wheeler to Evans. 'Any idea of how long Venn had been a regular there?'

Evans shrugged. 'He wasn't specific, just said *years*. Fella's run the pub for twenty years so it's likely to have been a while.'

'And Venn didn't tell him where he'd been living before he started sleeping rough?'

'No, Guv. I don't think they had that kind of friendship prior to the landlord offering him a room. I got the impression it was a significant change when he invited Venn to stay.'

'A familiar regular before, but not on a personal level?'

'Exactly, Guv,' Wheeler confirmed. 'Venn was part of the furniture, but the landlord said he liked to watch everything going on rather than participate in it.'

'Right. We need to build as full a picture of Ronald Venn's past as we can. Kate and Drew, can you look for any mention of him online, any mention in the press, any links to where he might have come from, please?'

'Guv.'

'Yes, Guv.'

'Thanks. Dave and Les, Uniform took some statements from people at the scene yesterday. Can you follow up on those, please? See if anyone remembers Venn, had any conversations with him, or heard any rumours about his life prior to sleeping rough on the beach.'

'No problem, Guv.'

'One question, Guv?' Ellis had his hand raised, a trait both endearing to his colleagues and a source of great amusement at his expense.

'Yes, Drew?'

'Could we be looking at a recent ex-con as potential suspect?'

Surprised, Anderson observed his young DC. 'Explain?'

'Well, Shingle Street Beach isn't far from HMP Hollesley. If someone had been released from there recently, chances are they might have stayed nearby while they got themselves sorted. Or if someone had escaped from there…'

A chuckle sounded from Evans. 'From *Holiday Bay*, you mean?'

'Holiday Bay?' Bennett frowned.

'It's what they call Hollesley Prison, owing to their impressive track record of losing inmates.'

Anderson had to admit it was an avenue he'd yet to consider. 'It's worth looking into. Check with HMP Hollesley for a list of recent releases, say in the last six to twelve months.'

Ellis beamed. 'I'm on it, Guv.'

'Appreciate that. Good work, everyone. Carry on. Rob, a word in my office?'

'Yes, Guv.' Minshull jumped to his feet and followed Anderson. He looked tired, Anderson thought, despite his insistence that he was fine. Had he managed to catch any sleep last night?

'Take a seat,' Anderson said, closing the office door. Some things were better discussed in private, away from the well-meaning concern of colleagues. And, knowing his DS like he did, Anderson was well aware that Minshull was unlikely to discuss his own personal state of mind when the rest of the team were in earshot.

He settled on his desk chair and faced the DS.

'How are you?'

Minshull's inaudible groan sounded from every inch of his posture. 'I'm fine, Guv.'

'Because if it would help to talk about it...'

'Really, there's no need. I just want to get on with the job.'

'Okay.' Anderson held up his hands, not wanting to prolong the already awkward conversation. It wasn't in his nature to press for personal information, being so averse to sharing it himself. But something in Minshull's response yesterday had worried him.

He recognised the warning signs. The trouble behind an expression that insisted he was okay. The shadow that clung stubbornly to him, visible in the moments he thought nobody was looking. Unmistakable. Dangerous.

In this job the things that got to you were never the ones you expected. You could encounter the grimmest, most gruesome crime scenes and remain unmoved, then go on a shout that appeared straightforward, mundane even, and be completely poleaxed by it.

The problem was the compartmentalising necessary to serve as an officer. Things swept under the carpet, hurriedly boxed and shelved away, the demands of the task necessitating forward motion beyond all else. You promised yourself time to process each knock, but the job was always pushing you on, refusing to relent.

It had happened to Anderson following the tragic end of a missing child case. While he was battling the practical and emotional fallout of that case, the recriminations in the press and the finger-pointing within South Suffolk Police, the next case he'd presided over had been the burglary of an elderly woman whose life savings were stolen at knifepoint. The distress of the lady sent cracks traversing the carefully constructed fortification around Anderson's memories. And everything crumbled.

He didn't think he'd come back from that.

It had taken every ounce of bloody-minded determination from him and fierce, relentless fighting on his behalf from his wife, Ros, to drag him back from the brink.

'Watch yourself, Rob. Take it from a stubborn sod who knows.'

Minshull's control flickered for a second. 'I – I will.'

'Talk to someone. Summon a defence team. Surround yourself with support. Whether that's Cora, or a professional, do it soon.'

He saw the battle in his colleague, the urgent need to escape this line of questioning.

'I saw Cora last night.'

'And how was she?'

Minshull stared resolutely at Anderson's desk. 'Good. I mean, she found the body, too, so she was shaken up.'

'Of course.'

'When we found Venn's body, I asked her what she'd heard. She said it was a whispered phrase: *I found you… You're mine.*'

'Any indication of age? Sex?'

Minshull shook his head. 'She sensed it was an adult, but no defining details beyond that. And she said it sounded as if the speaker were claiming ownership of the body, like a beachcomber admiring shells and pebbles they'd found on a beach.'

Anderson groaned. '*The Beachcomber.* I can't believe our friends in the press have called our perpetrator that. Infamy from the outset.'

Minshull said nothing, his head still bowed.

Anderson reeled in his frustration, concern for his DS resuming centre-stage. 'I wish I could give you some time, Rob. But this is going to blow up and I need everyone…'

'It shouldn't be a consideration—' Minshull's fingers worked angrily at the cuff of his work shirt.

Today was already turning into a day of tasks Anderson didn't want assigned to him. He didn't attempt to disguise his sigh. 'It's never rational, kid. That's why it throws you off. Doesn't have to be the worst thing you've seen. Just the thing you haven't armed yourself against. A kick in the balls you never saw coming. You don't expect to discover a murder scene on your morning off.'

A suggestion of a smile danced on Minshull's lips. 'I wouldn't recommend a career in counselling when you leave this place.'

It was the break in tension Anderson needed. 'Cheers for that.'

They shared a fleeting look.

'I'll be okay, Guv. I have good people looking out for me.'

The compliment came out of the blue, gone before either of them would acknowledge it. But it was enough.

The sharp trill of Anderson's desk phone saved them both from any further embarrassment, Anderson snatching up the receiver on the second ring.

'DI Anderson?'

'Ah, Joel, good. Martlesham here. We've called a press conference at ten this morning. Share the name and age only of the victim. Reassure the public that we have it in hand. You'll lead.'

Another kick in the bollocks, Anderson mused grimly, albeit one he'd seen coming from a mile off. 'Sir.'

'Excellent, Joel. I'll be watching.'

I bet you will, Anderson thought, as Martlesham rang off. *From the comfort of your office, far away from the bastards of the press.*

'Press conference at ten,' he told Minshull, gratified by the grimace of solidarity his DS sent back.

'What do you want me to do, Guv?'

'Chase Forensics on our pile of beach stuff, would you? As soon as it's released we'll bring Cora in.' He frowned. 'That's if you think…?'

'Cora will be fine,' Minshull confirmed. 'We both will.'

Eleven

THE COLLECTOR

'*...At a heated press conference this morning, a senior detective from South Suffolk Police insisted the hunt for the killer dubbed The Beachcomber is well underway. Detective Inspector Joel Anderson said the police want to reassure the public that Suffolk's beaches are safe, despite reports that some locals are staying away. He refused to give specifics of the investigation, only confirming the name and age of the Shingle Street Beach body: Ronald Venn, who was sixty-four and of no fixed abode. It appears he was murdered as he slept rough on the beach...*'

They *moved* him. Took him away from the beach! My best piece. He wasn't supposed to be moved. How can anyone admire him if he's not where I put him?

I stare at the news report, digging my left thumbnail hard into my right palm. It hurts, but I push harder. I shouldn't have left the piece on the beach. It should be here, with the rest of my collection.

The Beachcomber. That's what they're calling me.

They're wrong.

Beachcombers are amateurs. They just pick up whatever they find. Anyone can do that.

I planned The Collection. Curated it. I waited to find the right pieces.

It's *mine*.

The journalists are waving their cameras at the policeman in the news report. They keep asking about the public. What the public wants. What the public needs.

What about what I need?

'*I can assure the public that my team are doing everything possible to find the person responsible…*'

They don't need to find me. I'm here.

I look across the shelves of my collection, hidden from *the public* because I wanted to keep it all safe until it was ready to view.

But *the public* wants to see what I can do. That's what the reporter is really saying. They're all talking about it, the journalists say. It's in the papers, in the news, on TV. A trending topic on social media. Demand. Interest. Attention.

It hits me like a rock.

What's the point of a collection without an audience?

I slap my hand to my forehead, a warm drip of blood smearing across my skin from the place where I jabbed my thumbnail in.

I am so stupid.

Why didn't I think of this before?

My collection is so precious, so special, that people want to see it. Like in a museum. Like in an art gallery.

But the police took away my best piece. So I need a new one.

I'll go to a different beach this time. Find the right piece to show *the public*.

Then they'll see what I can do.

Twelve

CORA

'I've arranged cover for the next few days.'

'Tris, no. I'm fine...'

Dr Tris Noakes folded his arms as he faced his indignant colleague. Cora knew that look well: his mind was already set and nothing would dissuade him. 'It's sorted. So take some time and rest. You need it.'

Cora wished she'd never told Tris about what had happened on Shingle Street Beach. She'd informed him as a matter of courtesy, but his swift action to grant her time off from her job with South Suffolk LEA's Educational Psychology Team was an outcome she hadn't anticipated.

He was looking out for her, of course. She knew that. And, when she wasn't so annoyed with him, she'd appreciate it.

'I'd rather stay busy.'

'Then be busy. Just not in the office.' His expression softened. 'Give yourself a little time to process everything, yeah? You look tired. A shock like that isn't something you should ignore.'

There was no arguing with him, especially as Cora couldn't deny the weariness that had set into her bones. Reluctantly, she agreed.

Driving home from Ipswich in the second-hand car she'd recently bought, Cora listened to the lingering chatter of the previous owner, infused into the fabric of the interior. Her ability to sense audible fingerprints meant that the simplest of tasks – such as replacing her car after her last vehicle was damaged beyond repair – carried with them the echoes of strangers. The woman who had previously driven the red Ford Fiesta had apparently spent much time behind the wheel passing judgement on others.

What does he think he's doing?
She'll regret talking to me like that...
Scandalous, that's what it is...

The chatter would fade soon enough, but its presence was an irritation Cora would have to endure until then. It made her a stranger in her own vehicle, carrying passengers she hadn't invited, forced to listen to their relentless opinions as she drove across South Suffolk.

Reaching a road junction, a sign for St Just caught her eye. The village of her childhood, scene of her first case with Minshull and the detectives of South Suffolk CID, and home to someone she'd neglected seeing lately.

Indicating left, she headed for the village.

Sheila Lael met her at the door, wrestling a flowered apron from her waist. 'Cora! Am I glad to see you!'

She ushered Cora inside, the scent of baking as strong as the memories of growing up in the small house. Ghosts of her childhood giggled as they raced past her in the hallway, lurked by the doorway to the living room and lounged on the sofa. In the armchair nearest the window, she caught the sense of her late father, Bill, presiding over the noise and life of their home with his ever-present smile. The decoration and most of the furniture may have been replaced over the years, but this home would always hold more than its visible attributes for Cora.

Sheila, her mother, had undergone as much of a transformation as the bright and sunny living room in recent years, emerging from the too-long shadow of grief for her husband into the adventurous, bold spirit she now was. Her newly won social life included travel with friends from St Just WI and a view of the world that Cora could never have imagined for her.

Even the scent of baking was proof of her new outlook, an activity Sheila hadn't indulged in for years.

'I made a cake but it looks like someone sat on it,' Sheila confessed. 'Not sure what happened there.'

'I'm sure it'll taste good.'

'Maybe. I'll have to ask Jean about it. She's the baking whizz.' She perched on the edge of an armchair, a sense of restlessness around her Cora hadn't seen for a while.

'Everything okay, Mum?' Cora asked, her nerves suddenly on edge. Any suggestion that Sheila Lael was unhappy brought back fears of the dark period of her mum's life returning.

'Yes… No. I'm not sure.'

'What's happening?'

The flowered fabric of Sheila's newly removed apron folded and twisted in her fingers. 'Edith, one of the ladies from the WI, told me she saw Charlie the other day.'

The mention of Cora's brother was a surprise. Charlie Lael had been happily settled in Australia for several years, after travelling the world for almost a decade of his life.

'In St Just?'

'No. Up on the coast path, just off Hollesley Road. Buckanay Lane? She was visiting her daughter, who's an RSPB warden. She reckons Charlie was there with his binoculars.'

Cora had heard the name of the lane before, it being one of her father's favourite walks, leading through fields out to the coast. 'It couldn't have been Charlie.'

Sheila's expression was unmoved. 'She was adamant it was. Said it must be lovely having him home after all these years.'

'She's mistaken, Mum. He's literally on the other side of the world with Bethan, and their baby's due soon. There's no way he'd be in Suffolk so close to the due date.'

Cora dismissed the usual frustration that any mention of her brother brought. They had been close once, before Cora's ability manifested itself just after her sixteenth birthday. The moment it arrived, everything changed. It seemed that Charlie blamed her for the attention necessarily focused on her in the early years – endless consultations with medical professionals, the fight for any kind of diagnosis, the preoccupation of their parents with the radical change in their daughter. Charlie was twelve when Cora's ability came to light, seemingly incensed that his sister commanded so much of their parents' focus. At least, that's what it felt like to Cora.

Not that Sheila would ever acknowledge the rift. She'd told herself her children were close all their lives, a convenient myth she'd never relinquish.

'That's what I said to Edith, but she wouldn't hear of it,' Sheila said. 'Swore blind she'd seen Charlie. No mistaking him, she said. Her daughter was surprised anyone else was out there.'

'There must be lots of blokes in Suffolk who look like Charlie,' Cora began, but Sheila shook her head.

'Edith was so convinced that it made me want to check. So I called Bethan yesterday. Turns out they had a blazing row a week ago and she hasn't seen him since. When I said what Edith had told me, Bethan went through his closet. His travel rucksack was gone and when she checked for his passport that was missing, too.'

'But their baby's due soon…'

'I know! Two months' time. I know he and Bethan fight a lot – I don't understand their relationship at the best of times – but for him to go off like that… It's worrying.'

'Maybe he's just gone away for a while to clear his head,' Cora offered.

'No, not this time. I think it's more than that. Him and Bethan have been inseparable, ever since they found out she was expecting. I thought he'd found his home after travelling about for so long. Last time I spoke to him he was full of it: painting the nursery, getting everything ready. So why walk out and disappear when Bethan and the little one need him around?'

'Have you called his phone?'

'First thing I did. It says the number isn't available. I'm worried, Cor. If he's gone off somewhere, why isn't his phone working? And if it's true that he's back here, why hasn't he been in touch?'

'There'll be a logical explanation, Mum. There always is.'

Cora wished she could feel more confident in her assertion, her faith in her brother's apparent settled status marred by memories of his troubled teenage years. Because the Charlie who'd found love and a secure foundation in Australia was very different to the Charlie who had battled everyone and everything as a teen. Even Bill Lael, their famously steady and calm father, had been rocked by his son's countless run-ins with police, unexplained absences from home, school and college and thunderous moods that could exclude everyone from his world.

Charlie *had* gone missing before. Several times, in his late teens. Weeks with no contact, Sheila frantic with worry while Bill spent silent hours driving across the county searching for his son. Where Charlie was during those absences – and what he was doing – were never revealed.

What if the demons Charlie Lael battled then had returned? What if he had fled his seemingly happy life on the other side of the world to return to the shadows of his past?

Thirteen

MINSHULL

Having a name for the Shingle Street Beach body had set the wheels in motion, but raised more questions than it answered. It transpired that Ronald Venn had no family, no close friends beyond the kind landlord of the pub and very little on file anywhere about his life before he began sleeping rough.

The lack of detail was frustrating, especially given the hard work of the CID team in recent days. Bennett and Ellis had been the first to volunteer to join Sergeant Tim Brinton and the Uniform officers at Shingle Street, with Wheeler and a rather less enthusiastic Evans following suit. They'd talked to people at the beach, then followed up the initial inquiries Brinton's team had undertaken. Minshull had hoped that the surge in media speculation – now approaching fever pitch – might jog more memories and encourage members of the public to speak to police.

There were more people talking, but details remained frustratingly sparse.

Minshull observed his colleagues as they slowly converged in the centre of the office for a briefing. Each wore the same look – hope sparked by a step forward, thwarted by the weariness of inevitable dead-ends.

'Okay, thanks everyone,' Minshull said, summoning the meeting to order. 'Let's get an idea of where we currently are. So, Ronald Venn – what do we know?'

'He's sixty-four, but that's only according to what he'd told Ted Allward, the landlord at *The Wayfarer's Arms*,' Wheeler said.

'There's some suggestion he moved to Suffolk from somewhere else, possibly Ireland, a couple of decades ago.'

'Okay.' Minshull noted this on the whiteboard by his desk. 'Where did the suggestion come from?'

'Something Mr Allward mentioned. His wife had detected a slight Irish lilt in Venn's accent and he told her he'd spent some time near County Cork as a kid.'

'Might be worth looking into that, Dave, see what you can find.'

'No problem, Sarge.'

'Cheers.' He let his gaze travel across the faces of his team. 'Anything else?'

'According to a couple who'd seen Venn on Shingle Street Beach, he'd been a regular visitor there for a couple of years,' Ellis said. 'He was pretty friendly, by all accounts. Said hello, fussed dogs, spoke to passers-by. No mention of any trouble.'

'Thanks, Drew.'

'One woman I spoke to said he often smelled of drink, though,' Bennett countered. 'He was never aggressive or violent with it, but alcohol seemed to play a significant part in his day.'

'Did she ever see him drinking?'

'No. But she mentioned a dark green rucksack he carried with him that always had cans inside.'

'Was a rucksack found with him?' Anderson asked, from his perch on the edge of Minshull's desk.

'I didn't see one,' Minshull replied, the image of the dead man vivid in his mind. 'Guv, can you check with Forensics, see if one was brought in?'

'On it.'

'Thanks.' Minshull turned back to the team. 'Do we know anything more? Where he lived before he became homeless? Previous occupations?'

'There was one thing, Sarge.' The team turned to Evans who was, as usual, sitting as far back from the briefing as possible.

'Yes, Les?'

'A couple of the early morning dog walkers Dave and I went to chat to said they'd seen him walking on the beach recently with a younger man.'

'Description?'

'White male, dark hair, early to mid-thirties, a little taller than Venn, dressed in jeans and a red hoodie.'

Minshull added the description to the board. 'When did they see this man with Venn?'

'Several mornings last week. According to the eyewitnesses, the two men appeared amicable, talking and walking together.'

'Any idea who he is?' Anderson asked.

'No, Guv. One of the witnesses said he thought it might be his son.'

Ellis raised his hand. 'If it was his son, wouldn't he have taken Venn in? If he knew he didn't have a bed for the night.'

'Not necessarily,' Bennett returned.

'Why not? If I found out my dad was sleeping rough, I'd be there like a shot, bringing him home.'

'Not everyone has a good relationship with their dad, Drew.'

Ellis folded his arms in a huff. 'Something like that should transcend family problems.'

'You poor, sweet, idealistic baby…'

'I'm not idealistic!'

'Okay, enough now.'

Bennett and Ellis shrank back from their argument.

'Sarge.'

'Sorry, Sarge.'

'It's an easy assumption to make that a younger man might be someone's son,' Minshull said, his coolness extinguishing the sudden animosity between his DCs. 'And there are many reasons why someone wouldn't bring a parent into their home, even in hard times. Still, it's something we should look into. I'll check with Tim Brinton to see if his team have seen anyone matching that description. Let's keep looking, everyone. We need to build as clear a picture of Ronald Venn's life as possible. Anything to add, Guv?'

'Journalists,' Anderson growled, a collected groan traversing the team. 'It won't have escaped your notice that we have a little encampment of the bastards currently cluttering our front steps. They'll be after any scrap of information they can get their grubby hands on, so don't talk to any of them, even pleasantries as you pass. No doubt they'll write whatever they want about us, regardless of whether it's true or not, but let's not be the ones giving them fuel for their paltry little fires, okay?'

'Thanks, Guv. Right, team, back to it.'

Minshull returned to his desk as the detectives slowly filed back to theirs. The mention of the unknown man seen with Venn was intriguing. Who was he? Could he be Venn's son, as the eyewitness had assumed? Or was he just the latest kind soul to befriend the homeless man?

Wheeler had reported the strangely affectionate statement of Ted Allward, despite the friendship between the pub landlord and Ronald Venn souring after his Good Samaritan act. Ronald Venn appeared to attract kindness from others – out of concern or pity, maybe? Was his younger beach companion simply another concerned person drawn into his unfortunate life?

And if that were the case, what had made someone kill him?

The trill of the desk phone interrupted his musings. 'DS Minshull.'

'Sarge, it's Lyn Vickery at the front desk. I have a Ms Jones here who says she has information on the Shingle Street Beach case. She's adamant she needs to speak with you.'

'Thanks, Lyn. I'll come down.' Minshull pulled his jacket from the back of his chair. 'I'm going to see someone at the front desk,' he informed his colleagues. 'Is everyone clear on what they're doing?'

'Yes, Sarge.'

'All good, Sarge.'

'Great, thanks. And Drew and Kate? Try not to kill each other before I get back.'

—

Desk Sergeant Lyn Vickery's expression was pure apology as she indicated the woman waiting on the blue plastic chairs in Police HQ's reception. 'She swears she has vital information. Refuses to leave until she's spoken to you or the Guv.'

Minshull's heart sank as soon as he saw the identity of the visitor. Thank goodness Vickery hadn't called Anderson before him. That would have provided a spectacle for the waiting journalist posse that nobody needed in print.

He approached Maggie Jones, chief reporter of the *Suffolk Herald*, noting with dismay the look of triumph she wore. How had she wormed her way inside the building? And why hadn't Lyn Vickery chucked her out? Maggie was well known to the officers in Police HQ and certainly not for her glowing support of South Suffolk Police.

Ms Jones, indeed.

'DS Minshull, thank you for seeing me,' she said, rising to her feet.

Minshull ignored her outstretched hand. 'And now you've seen me, you can leave.'

'But you don't understand, I—'

'I understand perfectly, *Ms Jones*. You're not to enter this building again, do you hear?'

'I'm not trying to get a lead,' she protested, as Minshull began to usher her towards the door.

'Of course you aren't. That's why you gave my desk sergeant your surname only.'

'I *am* Ms Jones! She asked for my name: what did you want to me to say?'

'Out, now. If you try a stunt like this again, I will arrest you for obstruction.'

'Please, you have to listen to me!'

But Minshull was in no mood to play games today. He walked the journalist out, closing the door before any of her bored media colleagues lounging on the front steps could grab their cameras.

Bristling, he strode across reception, stopping briefly at the front desk.

'For future reference, that woman is the senior reporter at the *Suffolk Herald*,' he hissed to the reddening desk sergeant. 'She's not to be admitted again. Or any of her mates on the front steps. Clear?'

Vickery's apology was lost behind the slam of the interior door as Minshull stormed back into the heart of Police HQ.

Fourteen

CORA

'Charlie's turned up.'

Sheila Lael's hurried statement was little more than a whisper on the phone line.

'Where?'

'Here. At the house. Half an hour ago. He says everything is okay, but... I'm in the kitchen, making him a cuppa, and... I don't know what else to do.'

Cora glanced over at the clock on her kitchen wall. She had been unsuccessfully trying to pass the time of her enforced break from work, the hours dragging interminably slow. Confronting her clearly troubled brother unexpectedly returned home wasn't an ideal prospect, but a drive out to St Just would at least kill a few hours.

'Keep him there, if you can, Mum. I'm on my way.'

Questions beset Cora as she drove out of Felixstowe. Why was Charlie back? Why hadn't he called Sheila before flying home? And had he even tried to contact his pregnant partner, Bethan?

Even knowing her brother's past, Cora couldn't make sense of it. Had the imminent prospect of fatherhood made him run? Were more problems bubbling away under the surface that he hadn't admitted? Had Bethan asked him to leave after their row?

She supposed seeing him in person might provide some answers. Although being in the same room as her brother was never easy. Too much history filled the space between them: too many resentments on both sides, too many issues unresolved.

Questions about her family were part and parcel of every journey back to the village of her birth. A wealth of memories converged as the road led through the Suffolk countryside, both good and bad. A deep sense of loss for her late father; ghosts of her childhood and the sea change that occurred when her ability first manifested; more recent events with the missing child case in the village that first drew her into the working world of Minshull and the South Suffolk CID team. It passed over her in waves of warmth and chill.

Her mother met her at the front door, which was now painted a sunny orange after Sheila's recent foray into DIY. Worry was etched into her features, the wringing of her hands a sign that filled Cora with dread.

'I'm so glad you're here,' she rushed, ushering her daughter inside.

The moment Cora entered the hallway, the voice hit her:

I'm not hiding. I'm not...

Her brother's dark green travel rucksack was leant against the newel post at the bottom of the stairs, the insistent hiss drifting up from its nylon body and the pair of battered, sand-encrusted boots beside it. His voice was unmistakable, the tone a worrying throwback to the troubled teen he had once been. That insistence, that defiance, regardless of what his circumstances screamed to the contrary.

Was Charlie hiding from something?

And if so, what?

Her brother was seated on the armchair Bill Lael always favoured, the air muted around him. He offered his sister a weary smile as she walked in.

'I see Mum rallied the troops.'

'Good to see you, too.'

'Sorry. Hi, sis.' Charlie stood with a sigh and offered Cora a hug.

I'm not hiding... I'm not...

His thought-voice swelled around her, a dull ache registering at the centre of Cora's chest. Cora braced herself against it, relieved when Charlie broke the hug and slumped back into the armchair.

'I'll get tea,' Sheila muttered, hurrying into the kitchen.

'She'll drown me at this rate,' Charlie groaned, rubbing his eyes, revealing a new tattoo of a rising sun on the back of his left hand. 'That's the fifth pot she's made.'

'She's worried about you.'

'I know.'

'What's going on, Charlie?'

Charlie Lael observed his sister. 'I just needed a trip home.'

'You haven't been home for years. Why now?'

'Because…' He folded his arms across his faded red hoodie.

'Because what?' When her brother remained silent, Cora pressed on. 'Does Bethan know you're here?'

'She probably does now.'

'But the baby…'

'…will be fine with B. She has her mum and dad ten minutes away.'

'She needs you.'

'She doesn't. And I need to be in a better place before I become a dad.'

'You're already a dad,' Cora insisted, aware that her own frustrations were pushing too hard. She relented. 'Is the baby the issue?'

Charlie looked away. 'No.'

'No?'

'I dunno. Maybe. I just need to get my head sorted, and stuff at home was… I just wanted to touch base, you know? See Mum, reconnect with my roots. Is that a bad thing?'

'No. It's good you came back.'

'Thank you. Can we drop the interrogation now?'

It answered none of Cora's concerns, but knowing Charlie was here and not wandering on his own somewhere was a good thing.

'Are you staying nearby?'

'I was in an Airbnb in Hollesley for a week, but Mum insisted I move here. Better to be in the village, anyway, I reckon. Going to catch up with some of the old crew, go and hang out by the sea, probably check out the county's pubs. It's been too long.'

'Here we are.' Sheila breezed back into the living room, tea tray in hand. Her sing-song tone barely masked her rising panic. Cora sensed it around her like the slow build of a whistling kettle. 'Tea with my two babies. What a treat!'

Cora sat on the opposite armchair to her brother, while Sheila settled between them on the sofa. She busied herself with pouring tea into three mugs, then picked up a packet of chocolate digestives, her fingers nervously scratching and pulling at the packaging to find a way in.

'Blasted things… I can never get them open.'

'There's a tab at the side,' Cora offered.

'Is there? Oh, of course, here it is. Silly me!' Her chatter was too bright, strain showing threadbare just below the words, as biscuits tumbled out across her lap. She scooped up the escapees, piling them haphazardly on a plate. 'Take them, quick, before they run away again!'

Charlie reached over with barely concealed annoyance, grabbing a handful of biscuits and a mug of tea before returning to his slouched position.

Sheila's smile tightened.

The air in the living room cloyed with withheld questions, frustrations and fear.

'How come you're here, anyway?' he asked Cora, sounding bored already before the answer came. 'Thought you'd be at work.'

'I have a couple of days off,' Cora replied quickly, sending a look of warning to her mum. 'Annual leave.'

'Right. Still playing cops and robbers in your spare time?'

'Charlie! That's unfair,' his mother admonished. 'Your sister's a vital asset to the police.'

'Listen to their bins, do you?'

Cora resisted the bristle of irritation that Charlie's comment evoked. He'd never understood her ability, viewing the unwanted attention it brought her as a personal slap in the face to him. Where she had always looked out for him, putting aside her own feelings to make sure Charlie was okay, he'd been only too happy to throw accusations at her. As teenagers, he'd accused her of making it up for attention, which was ironic, given the attention Charlie commanded for himself at every turn. Cora wasn't altogether certain her brother didn't still view it this way.

'I assist them with serious crime cases. Like a quadruple murder, a while ago.'

That was a death knell to his mockery. Cora allowed herself the smallest moment of triumph. Where as a teenager Charlie's cruel words would have bitten at her skin, today they had no power. She owned her ability, so much so that she was actively pushing into it to see what her extraordinary mind was capable of. Juvenile jibes at her expense were no longer effective, from Charlie or anyone else.

'Oh... *shit*, sis... Sorry, Mum.'

Sheila glared at her son. 'I should think so, too. You'll watch your mouth while you're under this roof. And I won't have the pair of you fighting. I had more than enough of that when you were both living here. You need to be kind to your sister. She's had a nasty shock...'

'Mum...' Cora began, fear surging.

But it was too late. 'She found a body on Sunday. Murdered, most likely. So keep your clever comebacks and—'

'Murdered?' He was sitting forward now, his sullenness discarded. 'Where?'

'Shingle Street Beach,' Sheila rushed, before Cora could reply. 'Not far from where you were staying. So you're definitely moving here, where it's safe.'

'And this was on Sunday?'

'It's a murder investigation,' Cora managed to state, while her mother drew breath. 'I can't share details.'

'It's all over the news,' Sheila returned.

'Mum, don't...'

Her brother was watching her now, furrows appearing across his brow. 'I don't watch the news.'

'The papers, too.'

'I don't read them, either.'

Sheila gave a snort. 'Well, I don't know how you've managed to miss it. Your poor sis and her Rob found the dead body on the beach.'

'*Her* Rob?' Charlie's sudden amusement was the last thing Cora wanted.

'He's my colleague,' she began, but Sheila was already in her flow.

'He's a *darling*. Needs to get his act together with your sister, mind, but if they're going out for morning runs together, that's a good sign...'

Cornered, Cora rose from the armchair. 'Actually, I should be getting back.'

'What's up, sis? Embarrassed about hanging out with a copper?'

'Not at all,' Cora shot back, the impulses from her childhood rushing back. It had been so long since she and Charlie had been together in person that she'd forgotten the constant irritation their exchanges could bring. 'I just need rest before I'm brought into a murder case.'

Charlie's smirk vanished. 'How did he die?'

'Who?'

'The man on the beach.'

Cora blinked. 'I never said it was a man.'

'Mum did.'

'She didn't.'

'Maybe Charlie heard the news after all,' Sheila offered, the sudden tension between her children sending her to the edge of her seat. 'I mean, everyone's talking about it...'

'The first he heard about it was from you,' Cora countered, the air between them suddenly shrinking and constricting. Her brother's question – and the stung look he now wore – set her nerves on edge.

'It was just... I assumed, that's all...'

'Why? Why would you assume that?'

'Well... a body on a beach. Lots of suicides at the coast. Young men in the majority of cases...' He was blustering now, eyes wide.

Sheila's hand rested on Cora's arm, an audible buzz of panic surrounding her like a shield. 'See, Cor? Simple explanation. Sit down, love. Finish your tea.'

I'm not hiding...

The voices around Charlie swelled as he reached out to her. 'It's nothing, sis. Don't leave.'

I'm not hiding... I'm not...

'Why are you here?'

'I told you – I needed to come home.'

I'm not hiding... I'm not...

'You need to call Bethan. Let her know you're with Mum now.'

'I will.' His stare was unblinking, a panic Cora couldn't explain building behind it. 'I *will*, Cor. Just give me time, yeah? You don't know what I've had to deal with.'

'Sit down, love. I don't want my kiddies fighting. *Please...*' The wail from Sheila severed the tension at last between the Lael siblings.

Cora relented. She'd heard that tone in her mother's voice before, and it scared her. Sheila had come so far from the shadowy solitude she'd been trapped in following Bill Lael's death: Cora couldn't allow her to slip back there.

She resumed her seat, despite everything within her appealing for escape. Whatever Charlie Lael was dealing with had nothing to do with her. He was here and he was safe, for however long he chose to stay. His partner – and soon-to-be-born child – were his domain, not Cora's. She might not agree with his reasons for running away from them, but it was none of her business. It was clear Charlie was battling something major in his life.

The question was, what?

Fifteen

MINSHULL

It had been a long, frustrating shift.

A name for the deceased, but dead-ends all round for any details of his life.

A precise killing, with no apparent suspects or motive.

And a press pack already writing their own horror headlines, regardless of the truth.

Minshull reminded himself it was still early in the investigation, that loose ends invariably refused to be tied up at this stage. He knew this, as every detective in CID did. But it did nothing to lessen his frustration.

He said goodbye to DC Pete York, the night detective, who had just arrived for his shift, and made his weary way out of Police HQ. The evening was fast approaching, stealing what little light the day had managed to offer. He needed food, mindless TV and bed. Maybe a beer, to help him relax. After his sleepless night last night, he needed rest.

'You off, Minsh?' Oz Synett, Police HQ's car mechanic, grinned out from beneath the raised bonnet of a patrol car as Minshull passed. His cheery face was illuminated by an inspection lamp balanced on one side of the engine.

'Yeah. Bit of a late one for you, isn't it?'

The mechanic rolled his eyes. 'This bloody car'll be the death of me. Alternator's playing up and Sergeant Brinton needs it functional for the morning. Failed to tell me he needed it until half-seven this evening, of course, so here I am. My missus in't happy. It'll take a trip to that posh Italian gaff she likes to get me back in her good books.'

'Hope you get it sorted.'

'The car or my missus?' Oz chuckled.

Minshull smiled. 'Both.'

'Will do. Now, you get yourself home, son. You look like death warmed up.'

The compliments just kept on coming today, Minshull mused, walking to his car. He opened the boot and threw his bag and coat inside, the sight of his sand-covered running shoes where he'd discarded them yesterday sending a chill along his spine. He'd have to run again, soon. But the memory of the body on the beach was still too raw.

Maybe he should suggest a run to Cora – a restorative act for them both.

Was she avoiding going out, too?

He reached up and slammed the boot lid.

'Hi, Rob.'

Maggie Jones was standing beside the car, hands shoved into the pockets of her trench coat.

What the hell…?

'How did you get in here?'

'I've been waiting for you.'

'This is private property! You've no right to be here.'

'I ducked under the barrier. Nobody stopped me.'

So much for security, Minshull growled inwardly. It was no wonder South Suffolk Police were viewed with such disdain if they couldn't even keep their own car park secure.

'Get out.'

'No. I'm sorry, but you have listen to me.'

'You want a story, same as the rest of them.'

'If you'd just listen…'

'I am *done* with listening to you, do you understand? You're trespassing and you need to go.'

'I'm worried about my brother!'

Maggie's shout brought a flood of light from the direction of the damaged patrol car, Oz Synett raising the inspection lamp.

'You okay over there, Minsh?'

Maggie was breathing hard, her wild stare fixed on Minshull.

He should throw her out as he had earlier. But the fear in Maggie's eyes held him back.

'All good, cheers,' he shouted, waiting until the lamp beam retreated. 'What about your brother?'

'Not here,' she rushed. 'Can we drive somewhere?'

Against his better judgement, Minshull ushered the journalist into his car and drove quickly out of the car park.

She was quiet on the journey, her fingers wrapped around the belt of her coat. Minshull could see them working in his peripheral vision as the light from passing street lights washed over the car, twisting and pulling the fabric, the tension turning her skin ghost-white.

Thinking on his feet, Minshull headed for a small park on the outskirts of town. He swung the car onto the single strip of concrete that bordered a grassed area, silence rushing in when he killed the engine.

'What's happening with your brother?'

Maggie's sigh sent her body sagging back against the passenger seat. 'I think he might be The Beachcomber.'

Minshull twisted in his seat to stare at her. 'You're not serious.'

The journalist wasn't smiling, the same look of fear that had changed Minshull's mind in the car park present now.

'What makes you think that?'

'The location. The timing. The trouble he's been in. Just too many coincidences to ignore.'

'But you don't know all the details. Nobody does yet.'

'I know enough.'

'Ms Jones, I think you're mistaken…'

'*Maggie*. And I'm not.' She glared at him. 'I know you think I'm lying to get a story, but I'm not speaking as a journalist now. I don't want any of this getting back to my colleagues. I'm scared for my brother. Terrified for him.'

Taken aback by her assertion – and the change he saw in her – Minshull resorted to the safety of process. 'Was he near the beach?'

Maggie nodded. 'That's what made me ask the question. Hal's never really bothered with that part of the coastline until recently. He's been staying in Hollesley – birdwatching, he told me. That's why I asked him if he'd seen anything, when the news broke about the body on the beach. He'd mentioned Shingle Street a few times before that, so it set alarm bells ringing for me.'

'What was his response?'

'He freaked. Started yelling at me, accusing me of spying on him. Hal's had... *issues* over the years. He had to leave the army because of it.'

'How long ago did he leave the army?'

'Eight years. He had counselling and I thought it had worked. But his reaction scared me, Rob. Really scared me.'

'Why do you think that was?'

Maggie's gaze fell away. 'I have no idea. He's been doing so well lately, finding his focus again, talking more positively about the future. But the way he went off at me...'

Minshull considered this. Could the killer be found so easily? 'Would it help to bring him in for a chat? To rule him out, if he feels cornered?'

'You can't.'

'Why?'

Maggie fixed Minshull with a stare. 'Because he's gone missing.'

Sixteen

MINSHULL

'Missing man: Hal Jones, thirty-four, of Hollesley.'

Minshull stuck the photo of Maggie Jones' brother on the whiteboard as the CID team looked on. Even now, he wasn't convinced Hal Jones was the killer they sought. It seemed too easy, too simple, to join the dots.

'He may well turn up in a few days. According to his sister, he sometimes goes to ground when life becomes too much for him. He's ex-army, survival trained, and knows how to take care of himself in the wild. I've asked the Uniform team at Shingle Street to keep an eye out for him – apparently he's fond of birdwatching so he might head back there.'

'Is he a suspect, Sarge?' Bennett's question was one Minshull still had no answer for. He'd turned over everything Maggie had told him last night, but found no clear solutions. Hal's landlady in Hollesley had provided an alibi for the night Ronald Venn was murdered, confirming she had locked the front door and checked all her residents were in their bedsits. There was no way he could have gone out later, she'd insisted on the phone when Maggie had called her. She was a light sleeper and would wake at the slightest noise.

Even still, Jones' proximity to the murder scene and his army training kept him in the frame. Minshull still couldn't make it fit, but he'd dismissed people too early before in an investigation. At this point, every line of inquiry must remain open.

'At this point, I don't know, Drew,' he answered, dismayed by the fact. 'He doesn't have a motive as far as I can make out, but he has skills and proximity. And we can't check this stuff with him because he's gone AWOL.'

'Guilty conscience?' Ellis offered.

'Possibly. Who knows? Do some background checks would you, Drew? Find out anything you can about him. Especially his time in the army – where he served, why he left.'

'What about the pile of beach stuff, Sarge?' Wheeler asked. 'Did Maggie Jones mention anything about that?'

'It's the one detail she couldn't explain.'

'And, ironically, the one detail her mates in the press are having a field day with,' Evans wryly observed.

Minshull had to admit, this was the detail that caused the most doubt for him. The method of murder could easily be enacted by a former serviceman. His proximity to the location put him within easy reach. But the pile of sand, pebbles and beach detritus? Why would a skilled killer take the time to do that?

Minshull remembered the sight of the beach finds on Ronald Venn's body. They didn't appear to have been piled up in a hurry: and the small pebbles clearly weren't meant to pin the body down. Larger rocks might have suggested some kind of restraint before the man was killed. Piles of sand might have indicated the killer attempted to bury the body. But there was an order, a careful placing of the items on his chest. It was meant to signify something. But what?

'I think it's a ritual,' Bennett said. 'The pile of stuff thing. If Venn was killed immediately by the wound to his chest, why would the killer go to all the trouble of balancing all of that on him? If Venn was dead already, I mean.'

'So it means something to the killer?' Minshull asked, intrigued by the theory.

'Exactly.' Bennett confirmed. 'I don't know what, though.'

'Calling card?' Ellis offered. 'No coincidence the press dubbed the killer *The Beachcomber*. It's striking and it's different. It marks the murderer's work, makes it stand out.'

'Hell of a calling card,' Evans laughed. 'Maybe our killer's into jigsaws.'

'Or puzzles. To keep police busy.' Wheeler's suggestion caused a ripple of agreement across the seated detectives.

'Could the beach stuff be a clue they left?' Bennett asked.

'Explain?'

'A cryptic clue to their identity.'

'What, someone who likes picking up crap from the beach?' Evans interjected. 'Every bloody tourist and local picks stuff up on the beach. Hardly narrows down the suspects, Kate.'

'Why not?' she shot back, her irritation on full display. 'Maybe it means something to *them*. Maybe they think Ronald Venn is the same as the beach finds – a finders-keepers thing.'

'The ultimate prize...' Minshull considered the possibility.

'That's weird,' Ellis said, receiving a pointed stare from Bennett.

'The whole thing's weird, Drew. That's the point.'

Keen to avoid another argument, Minshull noted Bennett's idea on the whiteboard. 'We don't rule it out. At this point, everything is possible. We need to find as much as we can on Hal Jones. But we also keep an open mind. Let's look for anyone else in the Hollesley or Bawdsey area with a history of violence.'

'How did we get on with looking at recent releases at HMP Hollesley?' Anderson asked, his question reminding the team he was in the room. He'd been uncharacteristically quiet during the briefing, watching the back-and-forth of theory and conversation with his team.

'I have it here, Guv,' Ellis replied, pulling a sheet of paper from his notebook. 'Several of the former inmates moved out of the county upon release, but there are two who remained in the area – Jude Morris, forty-eight, who was in for aggravated burglary, and Alfie Gunnersall, fifty-two, who just served fifteen years for GBH.'

'Nasty bloody bastard, too,' Evans piped up.

Wheeler looked back. 'Which one?'

'Probably both. But specifically Gunnersall.'

'I thought the name sounded familiar. You put him away last time, didn't you?'

'I was in the arrest party.' Evans scowled at the memory. 'Little shite tried to bite one of the Uniform blokes.'

'Might be worth noting down everything you can remember about him, Les,' Minshull suggested.

'On it, Sarge.'

'Cheers. Drew, how close to Hollesley are Morris and Gunnersall?' Minshull asked, the emergence of two more potential suspects easing his discomfort about labelling Hal Jones so early.

'Still finding that out, Sarge.'

'Keep going, please. We need current addresses for them.'

'Sarge.'

A knock on the CID office door summoned the attention of the team, the detectives turning to see Superintendent Ian Martlesham striding in, a smartly dressed woman following close behind.

'Excuse the unscheduled interruption.' He beamed. 'I just wanted to formally introduce you to our new DCI.'

Minshull witnessed the smiles of the team tightening as one. He didn't dare look at Anderson. There had been no word of a successful applicant for the job – was the first they were all hearing of it after the fact? And what kind of message did it send for what Martlesham and the high-ups thought of Anderson's position that he was discovering this alongside his team?

A thought struck him.

Had Anderson been given prior warning of this appointment? Did that account for his unusual quietness this morning?

'This is DCI Fran Stephens. She's come to us from Essex Police, where she successfully established a new crime unit. We're hoping for big things from her in South Suffolk.'

Fran Stephens observed the CID office like something she'd just picked off the sole of her shoe. 'Good morning. I'm looking forward to the challenge of working with you all. My experience on a significantly larger force means I have a wealth of knowledge that will bring South Suffolk CID finally into the twenty-first century. I expect to have your full cooperation as I bring this department up to scratch.'

Shoulders bristled around the room, Minshull's included. Stephens seemed unaware of the tide of animosity meeting her words. Minshull had met her sort before: the ones who considered themselves above their position, who littered their conversation with thinly veiled insults and passive-aggressive observations. The kind of copper who thought the officers beneath them lacked the necessary intelligence to notice…

Stephens pressed on. 'I intend to hit the ground running, so I will expect a full CID briefing this afternoon, bringing me up to speed on the murder case. Changes may well be made. We can't afford another media embarrassment here.'

'O-kay…' Even Martlesham appeared taken aback. 'Joel, can we have a word in your office?'

'Sir.' Anderson's expression was set like granite. Minshull could only guess at the rage burning behind the DI's mask. 'Are we good here, DI Minshull?'

'Yes, Guv.' Minshull turned back to the team as Anderson led the way to his office for Martlesham and Stephens. He waited until the door closed before risking a grimace at the gathered detectives.

'Bloody *hell*…' Wheeler breathed.

Evans shook his head. 'High-ups strike again. Why can't we get a sane DCI? Years of utter idiots in the job.'

Minshull knew his own father was included in Evans' damning summation, but for once he didn't mind the mention.

'Because Joel didn't go for the job,' Bennett said, correcting herself when she saw Minshull's surprise. 'I mean, the Guv.'

'Why didn't he?' Ellis asked, his question just above a whisper. 'He would have rocked DCI.'

'Because he likes it here,' Minshull replied, his superior's refusal to apply for the post suddenly making sense. 'He'd be climbing the walls on the third floor.'

Ellis had to concede this. 'All the same, he would have been brilliant.'

'He would. But Joel's a copper and he always will be,' Wheeler offered. 'He loves being in the thick of it, even though the job rarely loves him back. I tried to convince him to go for it. So did Ros. This will be a kick, mind, even though he said he didn't want it.'

'Essex Police,' Evans groaned. 'They think they're better than us.'

'They have better budgets,' Wheeler said. 'Can't see DCI *Significantly Larger Force* is going to be too happy when she finds out how little we get.'

'True.' Evans gave a conspiratorial grin. 'Tenner says she walks in six months.'

'Can we return to the task at hand, please?' Minshull asked, stuffing away his own amusement. 'Do you all know what you're looking for?'

A chorus of affirmatives met his question.

'Good. Thanks, everyone. Back to it, then. And for goodness' sake, Les, if you're going to run a sweepstake, keep it out of view. The last thing the Guv needs is a dressing-down about your dodgy schemes.'

'Got it, Guv.'

Ignoring the temptation to wonder what conversation might be happening beyond Anderson's door, Minshull turned back to the whiteboard. He scanned the notes already written across it. The scattering of unconnected theories surrounding the case presented a frustrating puzzle yet to be solved. Until more was known about the names on the suspect list, there could be no way forward, no hope of unravelling it all until a clear motive came to light.

Beneath everything lay a stark, ice-cold fear neither Minshull nor his colleagues wished to voice: what if The Beachcomber was planning to strike again?

Seventeen

ANDERSON

Why did it have to be *her*?

Of all the officers Martlesham and his crew could have recruited for the apparently cursed DCI position, why had Fran Stephens come out on top?

And more to the point, why had she accepted a role in a force she clearly considered beneath her?

She was capable, of course. More than capable. Which is why what Anderson already knew about her made this new appointment nonsensical.

He'd encountered her before, just over a year ago, when a murder investigation led to a joint Essex and South Suffolk Police interview of a drug lord, whose minion was suspected of grooming young girls and had wound up dead in South Suffolk's patch. Fran Stephens was spearheading a groundbreaking Organised Crime Unit, in her shiny, disgustingly wellfunded headquarters that made Anderson want to weep with envy. After grudgingly granting him the interview, she'd made a point of acknowledging Anderson's skill, even offering him a job in her glossy, expensive kingdom before he left.

Why swap that for the chronically underfunded shabbiness of South Suffolk Police HQ?

Anderson smelled a rat.

There was more to this than the Super was admitting.

He saw it in the nervous slide of Martlesham's eyes between his confident words about Stephens and her appointment. In the hands fidgeting behind his back where he thought they couldn't be seen. In Stephens' own defiance, fizzing from her like sparks from a newly lit fuse.

What was the real story here?

'I expect to take a hands-on role in operations,' she was saying, seated at Anderson's desk like she was already sizing up both him and the office he currently occupied. 'Especially with the murder investigation. What's the op name for this one?'

'Operation Nautilus, Ma'am,' Anderson replied.

'Then I shall expect my team to refer to it as such in every instance.'

My team.

Anderson's hands became fists beneath the desk.

Two minutes in the job and she was already encroaching on his territory. He'd hoped for a jobsworth, a tick-box kind of professional, happier to do press stuff and be the face of South Suffolk CID than to get their hands dirty in the day-to-day. They'd just got rid of one interfering DCI – why appoint another?

'I will also be assessing budgets for CID,' she continued, casting a disdainful eye around Anderson's bright but admittedly tired-looking office.

He wondered if she'd seen the patched carpet in the main CID office, the broken blinds hanging limply from windows or the apologetic flicker of the outdated strip lighting. Perhaps if Stephens made tackling these issues her first priority, the thankless task could keep her out of his hair for a few months…

'But it's imperative we apprehend the person or persons responsible for Nautilus.' Stephens glanced at Martlesham, who responded like the ridiculous nodding dog Anderson's mother-in-law insisted on having on the parcel shelf of her car. No prizes for guessing where the power dynamic would lie between these two. 'We have to step up our efforts.'

Anderson had heard enough. 'With respect, Ma'am, *my* team has been active on this since early Sunday morning. In fact, it was *my* DI and our consultant expert, Dr Cora Lael, who discovered the deceased.'

'A civilian consultant? On a murder investigation?'

'Dr Lael has been assisting us for several years,' Martlesham interjected, the smallest hint of defiance in his tone. 'She is a significantly valuable member of the team.'

That shut her up, at least. Anderson would take any way forward as a win today.

Truth was, he'd been expecting this.

The irony he couldn't escape was that he'd finally reached the point of relenting over applying for the DCI position. They didn't have anyone and he'd made his point by not applying in the first instance. He'd woken early that morning, his mind resolved to finally follow the advice of Ros and Wheeler, the words ready to type. The application was in his email drafts, ready to be sent after the morning briefing.

So bloody close, Joel.

He cursed his own bloody-mindedness.

Had he acted when the position became available, chances were he'd be in the job now.

'You can't stop the past repeating if you aren't there to change it,' Ros had insisted, over and over, during the last six weeks. His wife's most frustrating quality was also one of the reasons Anderson adored her to his bones: her absolute refusal to drop a subject when she knew she was right. And she *was* right.

He'd hate the job, he knew in the very atoms of his being, but as DCI he could change the way things had always been done. DCI Sue Taylor and DCI John Minshull before her had made the job their own, so why not him?

That was academic now, of course. His gut, battered and bruised from years of experience, had warned him this was imminent. Why hadn't he listened before it was too late?

'Joel?'

Stephens was watching with a superior smirk as Martlesham's prompt brought Anderson back into his office.

Damn it!

'Sir?'

'Any questions?'

So many questions, but most of them too dangerous to ask…
'Just one, Sir.' He looked back at Stephens. 'I'm wondering what drew you to apply for this role, Ma'am?'

The smirk became a snarl.

'I was *headhunted* for the position.'

'Which must have been fantastic,' Anderson replied, going for broke. 'But what was it about South Suffolk CID particularly that made you choose us?'

Because you were a DCI in a major force before, he added wordlessly, indignation elbowing its way forward. *So why swap that position for one in a much smaller, lesser-funded, rural constabulary?*

Martlesham's stare warned him to drop the question. But it was a perfectly acceptable request, Anderson thought, refusing to relent.

'Well, I…' She faltered, the slightest widening of her stare evidence that Anderson had hit a nerve. 'It was time for a change.'

'To take on a rural force?'

'Come, come, Joel,' Martlesham breezed, just a hint of steel beneath his too-bright smile. 'You of all people should understand the appeal of working for South Suffolk.'

Oh, the irony…

'I'm just interested, Sir. There are challenges with South Suffolk that don't affect *larger forces*.' His emphasis was deliberate, a shot across Stephens' bow.

'It's immaterial,' she snapped, quickly regaining control. 'What matters is that I'm here now, and I'm ready for the challenge. I trust I can count on your full cooperation?'

'I will do my job, Ma'am.'

Anderson kept his smile in place until he'd seen Martlesham and Stephens out of his office, across the CID office and safely out into the corridor beyond.

Watching them leave, he finally released the artificial smile he'd worn, unleashing one carefully low growl as he returned to CID.

'Full cooperation, my arse...'

Eighteen

BENNETT

The beach stuff bothered her.

Bennett had already aired her theory that the beach finds were a clue to the killer's identity, roundly mocked by Ellis, of course. Maybe she'd shared it too soon. But at least Minshull had added it – with a careful question mark – to the whiteboard list. She didn't regret speaking up, though, regardless of what her colleagues might think. In this job you just had to jump in as soon as you had a theory.

Especially if you were the only female detective in an office full of blokes.

Bennett had long since reconciled herself to the fact that, in South Suffolk Police at least, she was destined to forever be a minority in CID. It didn't bother her: it had always been this way, from the moment she'd joined the team. But it meant she worked twice as hard, all the time, proving to everyone that she had earned her place and proving to herself that she was the best.

It was unfair and unnecessary, but it was the only way she knew to ensure she was heard.

She looked back at the scene-of-crime photos, taken in the misty light of Shingle Street Beach, the body in situ where Minshull and Cora had discovered it. The pile of pebbles, shells and driftwood on his chest had piqued her interest. Was it evidence that the killer had tried to bury the body? Or obscure it from view?

What Bennett couldn't reconcile with this option was that it looked deliberate. If not a clue to the murderer's identity, could it be some kind of marker? She remembered her Uncle Dan, a keen hillwalker, telling her about cairns, high in the mountains of Cumbria, where he spent every weekend he could.

'Sometimes they're just a pile of stones. A marker, to show you were there. But when the weather's bad and visibility is low, they can save your skin.'

What if the pile on the dead man's chest was meant do the same? Was the fog shrouding the beach that morning the reason for the cairn marking Ronald Venn's resting place?

Or…

Bennett peered closer, a new thought appearing.

What if the cairn was meant to lead the killer *back* to the body?

'Sarge,' she said, before she could think better of it.

Minshull looked up from his desk. 'Yep?'

'What if all that beach stuff on Ronald Venn's body wasn't to make a statement, or offer a clue? What if it was there to show the killer where the body was?'

Minshull stood and joined Bennett at the whiteboard. 'Would he be likely to forget?'

'According to Dr Amara, Venn was most probably killed late at night, or very early in the morning. Either way, the beach would have been dark. So what if the killer intended to return when it was light?'

Minshull's brow furrowed. 'Why? To revisit the body?'

'Or take it away.'

'A trophy?'

'Maybe.' Bennett shrugged. 'I don't think the killer was trying to disguise the body because clearly that wouldn't work. The pile of stuff looks deliberate to me, careful, even. Like a cairn on a mountain path. Something to mark the body's position so the killer could find it when they came back for the body.'

'And Cora and I disrupted their plan? By finding Venn's body before they could return?'

Bennett felt a rush of triumph. 'Exactly.'

'So, what does that mean for our search?'

'I don't know, Sarge. But I wonder if the killer never actually had a grudge against Ronald Venn.'

'A random killing? How does that tally with the carefully placed cairn?'

Bennett considered this. 'It doesn't. Because the identity of the victim wasn't part of the plan.' When it was clear Minshull didn't understand, she pressed on. 'What if the killer wanted a victim and Venn was unfortunately in the right place for them to strike?'

'So, they wanted a body but the identity was immaterial?'

'Yes.'

The moment she said it, Bennett understood Minshull's muted reaction. Because a motive-led murder that involved a grudge against the victim significantly narrowed their search, leading from family members to close friends to acquaintances. If her new theory was correct, Bennett had just blown the field wide open.

Anyone could have murdered Ronald Venn. And with no leads, an entire county of potential suspects and the sharp constraints of a rural force budget, how could they ever hope to find the killer?

'Sorry, Sarge.'

Minshull wrote Bennett's theory on the board in slow, determined strokes. 'No, it's a valid point. We keep looking. Random murders are rare. But if that's what we have here, we need to think beyond the obvious.' He looked back at Bennett, that jaw-set resolve she'd seen Minshull display many times before finally returned. 'I know we can do that.'

Nineteen

THE COLLECTOR

I should never have left him on the beach.

I realise that now. I should have moved him somewhere only I could visit. I'd planned it that way. I should have seen it through.

But I wasn't prepared for the *thrill*.

When you think of stealing a life – when you dream of it and plan it – you never consider what the experience will be like for you. Carry it out and it's done, you think. Move on to the next dream.

But the *thrill* – oh the thrill of it – like a million nerve endings firing at once. Like lightning electrifying your entire body. Heart beating so fast you lose your breath; laughter and tears and fear and elation balling together at your throat...

My hands were shaking so much I couldn't have carried him anywhere even if I'd tried. I went back to my digs to sleep it off. That was where I tripped up. Because, by the time I returned to the beach, it was swarming with *them*. Interferers. Filth. Busybodies trying to catch a glimpse of *my* star exhibit before it was ready to reveal.

I won't make that mistake now.

I look down at the shallow trench I've made in the beach shingle, digging down beneath an upturned rowing boat that's never going to float again. It'll keep my next acquisition safe from prying eyes until I can move them. Until they can be properly exhibited.

Dusk has already settled over the beach and the chill wind has emptied the place of visitors. It's exactly as I'd hoped when I checked the weather, hours ago. There's no mist, like the forecast suggested, but I like having a better view. It will allow me more control, being able to see further in both directions. Using the fog last time was a rookie error.

And then I see him.

Out at the water's edge, staring at the sea.

He's perfect.

I glance down at the knife on the top of my rucksack. I cleaned it especially. Used bleach, too. The wound must be as clean as possible, or else the exhibit will be ruined. Beneath the knife is a clear plastic bag of beach treasure. I don't trust this beach to provide what I need for the crowning glory of my display. Every pebble has been chosen for its size and its relation to the others. I scattered pieces of sea pottery in there, too, together with shards of driftwood. A curated mix to signify my unique collection.

I'm prepared.

My blood is rushing around my body, like before. Only this time, I'm ready for it.

And there he is: the piece that will make my name.

He's very drunk. A half-empty bottle of vodka swings by his side. He's ranting at the waves, like they're the reason he's trapped here.

That's why I know he's right for me.

He'll be happier when he's in The Collection.

Isn't that what everyone wants? To be part of something? To belong?

I watch and I wait. The beach grows darker, the air freezes around me and the wind drops. I don't know how long I wait, only that my toes pass from cold to numb inside my thick leather boots.

Finally, he drops to the beach, flat on his back. The bottle slips from his hand, the remains of its contents spilling down between the pebbles. And he falls silent.

I listen to the sound of the waves for a while, the rolling over of shingle where the land meets the water. And I wait, until I'm certain he's asleep.

Then I slip off my boots and press my stinging flesh against the stones. Pain dispels the numbness, the stabs of it sharp but necessary. It isn't a worthy collection piece if it hasn't demanded sacrifice from you to acquire it.

I used to hide from pain. Now, it guides me. Pushes me forward.

The movement of the sea over pebbles masks my careful steps. The knife rests in the cradle of my fingers, reassuringly heavy. He isn't moving, crashed out ahead of me. The collecting will be easy now. Like it was with the last one, only better.

A bubble of excitement arrives, almost pushing the knife from my fingers. I catch it as I push the sensation aside. I won't feel it now. Not yet.

Even in the dark, I can see the perfection of my new piece. He's younger than the last, skin supple and glowing in the emerging moonlight. No scars of life, even though he looks skinny. His eyes are closed, his open lips curled into a barely perceptible smile.

A welcome for me.

I glance back at the path I've taken across the shingle. It won't be far to drag him once he's mine.

I turn back.

I curl my fingers around the knife handle.

I feel strength surge through me, like it did last time.

Only *better*.

I brace my bare feet as best I can as I lean over him.

I raise the knife.

Twenty

MINSHULL

The short blast of the car horn outside his window was a starting pistol.

Grabbing his things, Minshull shut the door of his apartment and hurried down the stairs two at a time. He crashed out onto the street, the pre-dawn sky indigo-blue above him as he headed for the dark grey pool car parked alongside the pavement.

'Morning,' DC Pete York said from the open window.

'Is it?'

The joke was gratefully accepted, York grinning wearily as Minshull jumped into the passenger seat and slammed the door, wrestling the seat belt with sleep-clumsy fingers.

'Pressie for you on the dash, Minsh.'

The silver metal flask made the rude awakening worth it.

'You're a marvel, Pete,' he breathed, grabbing the flask as York accelerated away. The coffee was rich, smoky and the reason every detective in South Suffolk CID relished the handover from night shift to day when it was their turn.

He watched the darkened town slip by, dizzy still from the phone call that had dragged him from his bed.

Another body.

A different beach. Eighteen miles by road from the first, just up the coast. Three days after Ronald Venn was discovered.

He bit against the familiar stab of failure. They could have prevented this, if only they'd worked it out.

'Who's at the scene?' he asked, choosing procedure as the best form of defence.

'Steph Lanehan, Rilla Davis and some of Tim Brinton's crew. Dave Wheeler's going to swap with me after eight. I reckon Brian Hinds and the SOCOs will be there by the time we arrive.'

'The usual gang, then.'

York smiled. 'The dream team.'

'Must be a change for you, being out on a shout.'

'It helps when you're the only bod in the office. Been a few years, mind. Good job you never forget the ropes, eh?'

Slaughden Beach was less of a standard beach, more of a long shingle spit, marked by a series of sea-worn wooden groynes jutting out into the sea. The body had been reported not far from the Martello Tower, an iconic round tower known to everyone in the area. It might never have been discovered if a retired police dog, being walked before dawn, hadn't followed the scent from a dragged line in the shingle leading from the shore to an abandoned rowing boat, upturned over the body. The boat had been propped like a canopy between two proud hummocks of rough grass, the body lying in a trench about half a metre beneath it. The dog's owner had knelt in the shingle and, finding no pulse in the arm that strayed out of the cover of the boat canopy, had called 999.

Brian Hinds met Minshull and York with his trademark dryness. 'Can't say I'm a fan of these early mornings, chaps.'

'Us either,' Minshull agreed.

'Bet you had good coffee on the way over, though.' Hinds nodded at York, the legend of the night detective's coffee-making gift spreading far beyond the realm of CID.

'The best.'

'Ever considered a transfer to our side, Pete?'

'Wouldn't rule it out,' York replied, with a shrug. 'If the pay offer was decent.'

'Ah.' Hinds feigned embarrassment. 'About that…'

'As I thought.'

The conversation lulled, first light beginning to brighten the beach where they stood. Small talk could only sustain officers for a while at a crime scene – the serious nature of the job would always intervene.

Seeing the detectives' attention drawn to the team of white-suited SOCOs gathered around the boat, Hinds beckoned for them to follow him across the beach. They skirted the line of yellow marker signs flanking either side of the twin channels dug into the shingle, leading to the crime scene. Up close, the tracks were concurrent with a shape of significant size and length being dragged up the beach. The lines veered wildly from side to side, indicating some difficulty in moving whatever had caused them.

'Our deceased was discovered at the end of these markings, under the boat,' Hinds explained. 'Hidden pretty well, with the rowboat propped over the body like a makeshift roof. But what we discovered when we lifted the boat is significant.'

They edged around the working SOCO officers. Minshull saw it first, a groan escaping him.

A pile of beach pebbles, sand, driftwood and sea pottery in the centre of the victim's chest.

What had Bennett called it? A cairn. A deliberate pile of stones to mark out a location. Or, in this case, a body.

The victim was a young man, pale gold shoulder-length hair splayed out around his face. The right side of his jaw bloomed blue-purple and a dark line of blood ran from the edge of his mouth in a vertical line down his cheek. He was dressed in a black T-shirt and skinny jeans, the knees ripped to reveal blueing skin beneath, a double loop of silver chain loose around his neck.

'Same wound?' Minshull asked.

'We've yet to move the pile, but we're working on that theory.'

'What happened to his chin and mouth?'

'He's suffered a significant blow to the right side of his jaw, and it looks like that might have also split the side of his lips.'

'A punch?' York offered.

Hinds shrugged. 'Or a kick.'

'That's new,' Minshull said.

'It's possible he tried to fight his attacker. We won't know more until we can get him to the lab for a post-mortem.'

'Do we have the dog owner who found him?'

Hinds nodded to his left, where PC Steph Lanehan was deep in conversation with a huge bear of a man, his German shepherd dog enjoying fuss from PC Rilla Davis.

Leaving York with Hinds and the SOCOs, Minshull made his away across the wet shingle. The light was strengthening now, a milky glow in a sky streaked with pale grey and pink. Water danced in Minshull's eyes – from the cold air and the early start, he told himself. But an ache in the centre of his chest refused to be dismissed.

If they'd worked it out sooner.

If they'd found just one lead that connected.

What was it about this case that hit so close to home?

'Bit of an early one for you, Sarge,' Lanehan said, her own weariness visible behind her grin.

'Just a bit.' He turned to the dog owner. 'Hello, sir. I'm Detective Sergeant Rob Minshull. I believe you found the body?'

'Bolt did,' the man said, his dog's ears flicking in reply. 'Never would have seen the lad myself, not from the shore. But old Bolty caught the scent and he was off. Thought we'd left those days behind us.'

'Did you serve, sir?'

'Twenty-five years as a handler, Bedfordshire Police.' He offered his hand. 'Sergeant Jim Knowles, retired.'

They shook hands.

'Do you live in the area?'

'Aldeburgh. The missus always loved it, so I promised her we'd retire here when I left the Force.'

'Nice place to live,' Minshull said.

'It is. Quiet, or so I thought.'

'Do you often walk Bolt this early?'

'Every day. We both did earlies at work and neither of us can shake the habit. He wakes me up at half-four every morning. I bring him here because it's away from the main town beach.' Knowles looked over towards the SOCO team, his expression grave. 'Just a kid. And that stuff on his chest – is that what the Shingle Street body had?'

Lanehan and Minshull exchanged glances. When they didn't reply, Knowles held up a hand.

'I keep up with things. Hard to let it go when it's been your life.'

'I can imagine. Obviously, our investigation is ongoing,' Minshull replied, the knowing rise of the retired officer's eyebrows acknowledging the official line. 'But there appear to be similarities.'

'You checked the prison?' Knowles asked. 'I hear they're good at losing inmates.'

Minshull smiled. 'Nothing so far. But we'll keep an eye out. Would you be happy to give us a formal statement back at the station?'

'Of course. Ipswich, is it?'

'That's right.'

'I could come in later this afternoon, if that suits?'

'Perfect. And – not that it needs to be said – but can we count on your discretion regarding this, please?'

Knowles gave a grave nod. 'It's yours. Last thing you need is those press bastards swarming down here. Looks like you've enough on your hands.'

'Appreciate your cooperation, sir.'

As Minshull returned to the SOCOs, he wondered if the discovery of the murdered man would have as lasting an effect on Jim Knowles as it seemed to be having on him.

'Ex-copper?' York asked, when Minshull reached him.

'Yep. Bedfordshire, twenty-five years.'

'So he got the carriage clock *and* the dog? Can't be bad.' He offered a grin. 'What are the chances of an ex-copper being the one to find the victim?'

'We get everywhere,' Minshull joked. 'So, what's the plan?'

'Brian says they're waiting for the pathologist and then they'll move the pile of stuff off the kid's chest. At least they've had a bit of practice after the last chap.'

Minshull grimaced back, despite the unwelcome reminder that this might have been prevented. A second body, identical MO, different location but same landscape, so soon after the first victim was found. More than a coincidence. But the alternative was almost unthinkable.

A serial killer? Here?

There had been murders and manslaughters in the county before: more than the national press ever reported, being so fond of their 'local bumpkin' label for South Suffolk Police. But Minshull had never dealt with anything like this, nor could he recall a series of similar killings happening in such quick succession before, during his time in the Force.

At least they'd found the second victim before dawn, on a beach few people visited. And the ex-copper who'd reported it wouldn't broadcast the fact. Solidarity counted for a lot, especially with so few leads in the investigation.

Keeping a lid on this for as long as possible was now paramount. If the incessant media attention had emboldened the killer to take another life, Minshull and the team had to do everything in their power to keep the second death out of the news.

They weren't able to protect this young man.

But they could stop the killer being encouraged to strike again…

Twenty-One

VIDEO CLIP

A darkened beach.

Torchlight illuminating shingle and two feet wearing trainers, running fast.

The picture judders with every step.

The sound of heavy breathing. A distant yell.

Teenage male: 'What is it?'

A shout, soaked in panic. Words lost beneath the crunch of shingle.

A loud expletive. The steps increase, blurring in the shaky video footage. Tufts of sea foliage flash into view. The torch flicks ahead. Cracked wood, flaking paint, the bulk of the hull of a broken, weathered boat.

A scream. Followed by another, louder.

The camera view veers to the right. Flashes in the dark as the torch flicks around the old boat.

Teenage female: 'It's Ace!'

Teenage male: 'No... No! Ace, man! Wake up!'

The sound of violent retching. Tears. Screams.

The shaking shot zooms in on the body of a young man, lying supine in a shallow grave, the upturned rowboat a canopy for his resting place. The pile of pebbles and driftwood on his blood-soaked chest glistens in the torchlight.

The shot pans up to blue lips, grey skin. Blood from his mouth, staining his cheek. Terror-wide eyes staring lifelessly, straight into the camera.

The video snaps to black.

Twenty-Two

WHEELER

It was a disaster, on so many levels.

Wheeler watched the shock and horror of his colleagues become indignance and anger as the news broke across the media.

The video of the body discovery was everywhere, the number of press agencies, social media accounts and news reports reposting it multiplying by the hour. It had been sent anonymously to a news and current affairs account on TikTok with two million followers, which, of course, posted it for the world to see. The initial post was made at six fifteen a.m., the video quickly spreading before the CID team knew anything about it.

There was no question that it had been filmed hours before police arrived; before Jim Knowles and his dog discovered the body. That meant the crime scene was already compromised, before SOCOs had even had a chance to inspect it, potentially disturbing vital evidence that could have led to the arrest of the killer.

And worse, as far as Wheeler was concerned, was that it implied the kid's body had been found, filmed and then abandoned again on the beach. Failed by everyone, not least the anonymous video-makers assumed to be his friends.

While the makers of the video were yet to be identified, the internet busied itself with filling in the gaps of information for the body on Slaughden Beach.

The young man was named by the media as Alistair 'Ace' Avebury, a nineteen-year-old teen who had known his fair share of trouble in his young life. Trouble the papers and online news agencies were only to happy to pick over. Battles with drink and drugs, antisocial behaviour and several suicide attempts all documented, posted and commented upon, with no thought for anyone who knew him. Fingers pointed at years in and out of the care system, with everything levelled at the victim, from political diatribes about failing systems and angry incels bemoaning the emasculation of young men, to religious nuts warning that wrong lifestyles would inevitably lead to murder.

Poor kid got little say in his life, and precious little in death. That boiled Wheeler's blood. And what none of the bastard keyboard warriors realised was that they were doing the exact same thing the young man's killer had done: treating his life – and death – as expendable commodities. They didn't care about him any more than the person who stole his life, despite their public hand-wringing and fury.

'I want to know how we have an entire team dedicated to this investigation and yet the bloody media knows more about the victims than we do. How is that possible?' DCI Stephens eyeballed the gathered detectives, the temperature in the CID office plummeting in silent reply.

Wheeler glanced at Anderson, who stood like a rock beside Stephens. Joel would be *hating* this – not least the stealing of his thunder by his new superior. But he said nothing, even though Wheeler knew he would be burning with molten indignation behind his stoic stillness.

'With respect, Ma'am, the video was taken hours before the body was reported,' Wheeler risked, the act flying in the face of his usually solid compliance. She needed to know this team had worth, and that the posting of the viral video – and the internet sleuthing it had set in motion – was not their fault.

'That is not my problem, DC… ?'

Wheeler bristled. She knew his name all right. It was designed to belittle him, but it wouldn't work. He'd seen this tactic in operation too many times during his career for it to have any impact now.

'Wheeler, Ma'am,' he prompted, the slightest hint of condescension in his reply.

'*Wheeler.*' Stephens scowled back. She had a face like a pinched lemon and Wheeler wondered if she ever smiled. 'The point is, *they* shouldn't know before *we* do.'

It was a ridiculous point to make. The internet often knew about crime before police – hell, it was the first place he and his colleagues looked when incidents were reported. But Stephens didn't appear to be concerned with common sense, just needless finger-pointing. As first impressions went, this was about the worst introduction to the team who would serve under her. Berating everyone was a rookie error.

'Ma'am, we had no control over how this information got out,' Anderson stated, at last. 'But our commitment to this operation hasn't changed.'

'Whatever.' Stephens began to leave, face flushing. Had she realised her mistake? 'Get the formal ID on the body. And then find the persons responsible for the video. I will *not* have Nautilus fail, do you understand me? No more mistakes. No more excuses.'

The door slammed in her wake.

As one, the CID team sagged.

'Guv...' Minshull began.

'Stuff her.' Anderson's reply was a shock to everyone. 'She doesn't know what she's talking about. I believe in you. In us. And if *that*... if DCI Stephens chooses to throw her toys out of the pram over something so utterly beyond our control, let her. Maybe it'll keep her busy so we can get on with the bloody job.' He stopped, pinched the skin above the bridge of his nose and took a sharp inhale. 'You didn't hear me say that.'

'We all thought it, Guv,' Bennett offered, followed by a mumble of agreement from the rest of the team.

'Probably thought worse, to be honest,' Evans said, his wry addition to the discourse providing the lightness so badly missed since the morning shift began.

'Only with significantly more expletives,' Ellis offered.

Anderson received the comments with a rueful grin. 'You're all bloody marvellous. But repeat one word of what I said outside this room and I'll skin you alive. Now, does anyone have any leads for next of kin or close friends of the deceased? We need an official ID before we can proceed.'

Wheeler's hand shot up. He'd been about to share his discovery when DCI Stephens had burst into CID. 'Control received a call from an unofficial aunt of Mr Avebury, about an hour ago. She'd seen the news reports and was worried.'

'*Unofficial* aunt?'

'Not blood-related, but a close friend of the lad's mother. After the family disowned him, it sounds like she became his surrogate mum.' He checked his notes. 'A Mrs Alexandra Horton, lives in Barden. I spoke to her before the briefing. She's agreed to do a formal ID, later this afternoon.'

It felt good to deliver the news. Finally, a positive, in a morning filled with dismay.

'Dave, you are my new favourite person. Kate, can you assist?'

'Absolutely, Guv.'

'Great.' Anderson stood, pausing a moment to observe his team. 'I wish we weren't where we are. I wish we'd found the person responsible for the Shingle Street murder before another life was lost. But it is what it is. And now we know what we're dealing with, we double-down our efforts. Find the bastard, before he kills again. Drop any guilt you're feeling and channel that into determination, okay?'

There was a definite look in Minshull's direction before Anderson left the office.

Wheeler waited until his colleagues had returned to their desks, a new energy fizzing between them, before he made his way over to Minshull.

'Not impressed by the quality of the floor show,' he joked, studying Minshull's response. 'Think I might ask for my money back.'

'Good luck with that.' The smile was a gesture, a blink-and-you'll-miss-it concession. But it was more than Wheeler had witnessed in the DS since the news broke. 'Great work with the next of kin, though.'

'Cheers. Turns out the bloody hacks did us a favour. No way she'd have come forward if she hadn't heard the kid's name being bandied about.'

Minshull nodded, his gaze set at a point miles beyond the CID office wall.

'We need Cora,' Wheeler urged, his voice below the level of conversation between their colleagues. 'If she can hear from the stuff on the lad's body like she did with Ronald Venn, I reckon she'll be able to say if it's the same person responsible.'

'I think we both know it's the same person.'

'You know what I mean, Sarge.'

Minshull looked up, weariness meeting Wheeler's stare. 'Yes. I'll call her.'

'We should tell the team, too. About what Cora heard when you found Ronald Venn. Looks like we need all the allies we can get, with Stephens on the warpath.'

'You're right. We should do that, Dave. Would you phone Dr Amara and request a viewing of the beach detritus?'

'Won't it need to be processed first?'

'It will, but if Cora's not touching it, I can't see there would be a problem. If the good doc says no, we'll think of something else.'

'On it, Sarge.' Wheeler hesitated, debating whether to say what he'd crossed the room to express.

'Something else?'

'No... It's just... What the Guv said? I think you needed to hear that.'

Minshull said nothing, his expression stung.

Wheeler fought the urge to stop talking. This might be his only chance to share what had been on his mind for hours. 'Because looking back won't do anything for Ronald Venn, or Alistair Avebury, if that's who was found this morning. Best you, or I or anyone can do is look forward, Minsh. It's the only way.'

Twenty-Three

CORA

Heavy rain pelted the windscreen of Cora's car as she parked outside the Pathology Department, drowning out the last vestiges of its previous owner's voice. South Suffolk Police had a thing for bland, concrete buildings, it seemed, and the home of the laboratories was no exception.

She killed the engine and sat for a moment, watching rivulets of water cascading down the glass, blurring the scene into an impressionist painting in a muted palette of greens and greys. The pause was necessary, to settle her mind.

She'd been expecting the call, of course. The morning news had been ablaze with the news of a second body, the media frantically picking over any detail they could find. Putting aside her own emotion from the discovery of the first, she busied her mind with the task ahead.

At least she'd been able to come here immediately, still frustrated by the leave Tris Noakes had insisted she take from work. He'd texted her first thing, having seen the viral video that had announced the second body to the world.

> Go and help them find the killer. Here if you need me. Tris x

The more she worked with Tris, the more she appreciated the gift of his understanding. One of the few people who accepted her ability outright, revelled in it, even, Tris was a gem, both as an employer and a friend. It hadn't always been this way in Cora's working life. Employers had varied from being dismissive of her ability to threatened by it, placing her firmly in the 'other' category by their attitude and actions. And her previous employer – also, unwisely, her lover – had used her to further his own career, making her no better than a caged animal to be studied.

She shuddered in the chill of the car.

That was a lifetime ago, she reminded herself. Before Tris. Before South Suffolk CID. Before Minshull. She had come so far from the person she'd been back then. And her ability, once the thing that had othered and caged her, was the reason for her progression.

But would it reveal any secrets from the beach detritus she was here to inspect?

She left the car, pulling up the hood of her raincoat and sprinting across the rain-glossed tarmac to the Pathology building.

Waiting inside was DC Drew Ellis, his ever-cheery smile a welcome sight in the starkness of the surroundings.

'Morning, Dr L. Lovely day for ducks.'

The phrase reminded Cora of something her father would say, the old-fashioned British humour of it incongruous coming from the younger man.

'It is, indeed,' she replied, glad she had his company to view the beach detritus found on the two bodies. 'Morning, Drew. Rob said Kate and Dave would be here, too?'

'They're doing the ID at the mo, with the auntie of the chap from Slaughden Beach. I got the better deal, accompanying you.'

'Any news yet?'

Ellis shook his head. 'I reckon it's a foregone conclusion, though. Poor woman seemed resigned to it. I guess with all the press stuff there was little room for doubt.'

'Dr Amara won't be long,' the softly spoken young woman behind the desk informed them, as they signed in. Her smile was genuine, respectful. An occupational must, Cora suspected.

They took their seats in the waiting area, falling into easy silence. The room was bright and calm, painted in soothing shades of green, but Cora sensed the withheld breaths infused into the walls, the thudding hearts in the close air around the seats, the deep ache of loss where next of kin's greatest fears were confirmed. Sitting beside a potted palm she caught the gentle sobbing of a woman from a tissue discarded in the dark soil.

This wasn't a place anyone chose to visit.

At that moment, the door opened, a middle-aged woman holding a hanky to her eyes walking slowly through the waiting area, accompanied by Kate Bennett, a grave-faced Dave Wheeler trailing in their wake. The detectives traded grim smiles with Cora as they passed, Wheeler reaching out to briefly clasp her hand before they left the building.

'Dr Lael, DC Ellis, hello.' Dr Rachael Amara now stood in the doorway, a tired smile accompanying her greeting. 'Apologies for keeping you waiting.'

Cora rose from her seat. 'Thanks for seeing us.'

They passed through the entry door and walked along a pale grey corridor, the soft reverberation of their steps as muted as the air around them.

'Busy day,' Dr Amara said.

'I can imagine.'

Ellis glanced back. 'What was the verdict?'

Dr Amara gave a tight-lipped smile. 'It was a positive. Poor lady hadn't seen the lad for a few weeks. It seems they argued before he left. Always the worst, when someone passes unexpectedly. The shock of it. The regret.'

She said this with a sigh, the weight of it clear in the exhale.

Did the pathologist ever get used to seeing identifications? Cora couldn't imagine encountering them as regularly as Dr Amara had to. 'That must be hard to see.'

'Not my favourite part of the job,' Dr Amara answered, holding another door open for Cora and Ellis. 'But I like to think it's a privilege we have here. Providing proof of end of life, so that the grieving process can begin. The *not knowing* when a loved one is missing is the worst life sentence. Certainty, while heartbreaking and final, is key to healing.'

'Dave and Kate will probably stay with the deceased's aunt for a while,' Ellis said. 'I'll text the Sarge, let him know about the positive ID. Any message for him?'

'Only that the details have been confirmed. Alistair Avebury. Nineteen years old. Liked to be called "Ace".'

It was the name on the lips of every reporter, impossible to miss today. Cora felt the finality of the fact hit home. Such a young life, taken in the most horrific way.

They had reached the pathology lab, the cool quiet of the space startling. The chief pathologist handed Cora and Ellis masks and blue surgical gloves as they approached a bench that held two large bags of pebbles and sand, ready for inspection.

'Okay, here we are. Bag on the left is the pile found on Ronald Venn at Shingle Street Beach. Bag on the right is the pile we lifted from Alistair "Ace" Avebury this morning at Slaughden Beach.'

They were almost identical in size and type, the shingle from Slaughden Beach a little darker in shade within the clear plastic. Cora approached, Ellis by her side, while Dr Amara maintained a respectful distance.

'What will you be looking for?' the pathologist asked.

'Sound,' Cora replied. 'If, as we suspect, one person gathered all of the beach stuff, I should hear multiple copies of one voice attached. If not, I'm hoping to hear distinct voices, repeating in the same way.'

'Fascinating,' Dr Amara observed. 'And from this you can surmise…?'

'Thoughts, emotions, intentions,' Cora replied. 'It varies. But I can use what I hear to build a three-dimensional soundscape around the objects. It gives me an idea of the state of mind of whoever collected these pieces, their emotions while doing so and the conditions surrounding them.'

Dr Amara's eyes sparkled over her mask. 'Do you mind if I observe? I would love to see your work.'

Her question carried the same excitement Cora heard from Tris, an honest interest unencumbered by suspicion or fear.

'Be my guest,' Cora replied, her own smile genuine behind her mask.

'It's pretty cool, watching the doc do her stuff,' Ellis said, raising a hand in apology to Cora. 'Sorry.'

It was impossible not to like Drew Ellis and his enthusiasm. Cora knew it came from a place of complete dedication to the job, a factor that had come to her aid in the past. 'I'm glad you're impressed, Drew.'

She turned her attention back to the bags on the bench. Settling her breathing and her stance, she reached for the first bag, the older of the two.

The urgent whispers were as fresh now as they had been on the beach when they'd summoned Cora to the place where Ronald Venn lay. An unexpected rush of emotion rose, balling in her throat and stinging her eyes. Her own emotion, she knew immediately – a shadow of the emotional repercussions of finding the body on the beach.

Carefully, she pushed it aside, edging around her own response to investigate the sound beyond.

I found you...

The voice from before repeated from every piece of the beach finds, claiming ownership, defiant and adamant in its assertion.

I found you... You're mine...

A hoarse, urgent whisper. Impossible to decipher its gender as it had been on the beach, but the tones within developed enough to indicate an adult voice.

I found you... You're mine...

The same phrase, repeated by every piece. Cora expected the volume and presence of the sound-voice to vary throughout the pebbles, sea pottery, driftwood and sand, thinking of where hands might have connected with the beach pieces if they had been scooped up. But every single piece carried a strong sound imprint.

As if each one had been carefully selected.

It was more deliberate than a beachcomber picking up things from the beach that caught their eye. Strong intent laced through every hand-picked piece, a sense of purpose registering in Cora's body. Whoever collected these items had a specific criteria for selection.

She cast her mind around the sound-space, noting the uniformity of volume, the intensity of each phrase. The repeats tumbled over themselves as she turned them over in her mind, overlapping and melding together. But the whisper connecting them all was unmistakable: a single thought-voice, repeated myriad times.

Carefully retreating through the sound layers, she closed the evidence bag and opened her eyes. Dr Amara was watching from a few steps away.

'It's the voice I detected on the beach,' Cora confirmed, the familiar shake of her frame that always followed a thought-voice investigation jarring her words. 'One phrase, repeated over and over: *I found you… You're mine…* But what's interesting is the identical level of intensity and intent across the pile.'

'And that would indicate, what?'

'That each piece had been individually selected. A deliberate act.'

'It was planned?' Ellis had his notebook at the ready, watching Cora with care.

'I believe so.'

'So, a collector, then?'

Cora glanced at Dr Amara. She hadn't considered the voice character in this term, but now it made sense.

'Exactly.'

'Did they collect each piece to rest on the body at the scene?'

'I'm not sure, Drew. I think to go and find each piece, in the darkness, would have been too time-consuming. The greater the time to complete the task, the greater the chance of being discovered.'

'So, what? They collected it beforehand? Then brought the stuff with them to the beach?'

'I'd say that would be more likely.' Cora looked back at the bagged beach litter. 'The background tones behind the pieces sound like a beach environment, but I couldn't say for certain it was Shingle Street.'

'That would be consistent with the method of death,' Dr Amara observed. 'Practised, studied, even. A single blow, directly to the dead centre of the heart, takes either extraordinarily good luck or serious study.'

'It was right in the centre?' Ellis looked up from his notes.

'To the millimetre.'

'Bloody hell,' Ellis breathed, scribbling notes.

'So whoever did this was prepared,' Cora said, the details firming in her mind as she said them. 'They most likely arrived at the beach with the material for the cairn already selected and the strike required to dispatch their victim well rehearsed. They intended people to know the body was there and that it was theirs because of this pile of beach finds marking the body out.'

It seemed fantastical, the overblown stuff of lurid tabloid speculation, but here, in the calm stillness of the pathology lab, the details formed a credible line of explanation.

Dr Amara studied the bags of beach detritus. 'You know, I saw something similar, years ago.'

'A pile of finds covering a chest wound?' Cora asked, surprised.

'No. But tokens left with a body. It was when I worked for West Midlands Police, about seventeen years ago. My first multiple murder case, actually. Three bodies in total, over the course of eight months, same signature on each one. Children's toys – colourful plastic ponies that were all the rage at the time. They were placed in the hands of his victims. We found the killer's fingerprints on the ponies – the match was enough to link the cases.' She grimaced at the memory. 'Thank goodness the press never got hold of that one. I can't imagine how awful it would have been for the victims' families to have that kind of bizarre detail bandied about for entertainment.'

A *collector*. Was that who they were dealing with here?

'So the beach finds could be a marker left to indicate ownership of the body,' Cora mused aloud.

Dr Amara considered this. 'I'd say the motivation for their work to be seen and recognised as theirs is similar here, even if the type of marker used isn't the same. The plastic ponies in the case I worked on were brought to the dumpsite of the bodies, specifically to be left there as a calling card. Is that what you think happened with these?'

'Yes. Selected by hand, designed to be left with the bodies.'

'A similar motivation, then.' The pathologist added this detail to her notes. 'There could be something in that. Please, continue.'

Cora moved to the second bag, took a steadying breath and opened it.

I found you... You're mine...

It was instantaneous. Louder than the first, but identical in tone and urgency. Slowly passing through the layers of sound, Cora heard more: waves on a shingled shore, a lone gull's eery cry, stabs of determined breath. The newer beach finds carried a sense of chill that had been dulled in the first collection, as if each piece was cloaked in the dampness of sea mist. A pull registered physically at the centre of Cora's chest: a compelling urge to complete a task. She felt the laboured breath, the body shaken by adrenaline. The strong, all-encompassing desire...

Her stomach twisted, causing her to beat a hasty retreat through the layers of sound, the sickening closeness of the emotion fading as she travelled back. Emerging in the cool stillness of the lab, she opened her eyes.

'The same,' she confirmed, the burn of bile in her throat.

The scratch of Ellis' note-taking increased, the DC saying nothing.

Dr Amara's eyes narrowed. 'And something else?'

'The sound was fresher around these pieces. And the emotion... I can sometimes sense emotion attached to audible fingerprints as a physical sensation—' she tapped her chest '—*here*.'

'Incredible. Can you describe it?'

'A compulsion. A desire.'

'Sexual?'

It wasn't what Cora wanted to consider, but a valid question. 'I – I don't think so. But a strong compulsion, a total focus, to the exclusion of all else.'

'So we have a collector, compulsive in nature, staging a body post-murder, presumably, as what? A trophy? A statement? A piece of art?'

'A display,' Cora replied, the notion set as soon as she'd given it voice. 'A sign of ownership. *I found you... You're mine...* A childlike assertion, spoken by an adult.'

As she said it, a sudden memory returned, of their family on the beach at Felixstowe in her childhood years. Sheila Lael relaxing in a deckchair, her bare toes buried in the sand; Bill Lael beside her, snoozing behind the pages of his book; and her brother, Charlie, jealously guarding the sandcastle he'd constructed. Pebbles and driftwood picked from the beach with care, pressed with intention into the sandy walls.

You can't have this one, Cora. I made it. It's mine...

The warning in his tone. The firm set of his young jaw. The flare of temper if Cora so much as moved a muscle towards it.

Why was Charlie back in Suffolk? Why his sudden return, after so many happy years away on the other side of the world?

And why was she thinking of him now?

'Dr Lael?'

When Cora turned, Ellis and Dr Amara were peering at her.

'Sorry,' Ellis offered. 'We should call Rob – DS Minshull. He wants to know your summation of the examination as well as what I've observed. Can we do that from your office, Dr Amara?'

'Of course. If you'll both follow me.' Dr Amara gave Cora one last careful glance before leading the way out of the laboratory.

Twenty-Four

MINSHULL

She sounded worried. Minshull was worried, too.

'Can you come in?' he asked, more out of a need to check Cora was okay than to hear the report again in person.

'I should be getting back...'

'Twenty minutes. We can grab a coffee in the canteen.' Even as he said it, the offer sounded far from tempting. What was wrong with *I need to see you*? Why couldn't he vocalise it?

In the pause that followed, Minshull willed her to accept. The flood of work, stress and pressure in the intervening days had kept him apart from Cora; now, guilt lay siege to his conscience. She deserved better – as a colleague and as a friend.

He'd wanted to accompany her to the pathology lab, but Anderson had requested a meeting in his office. Ellis was a good choice to go in his stead, maybe even better than Minshull, having no prior link to the case. The DC was a magpie for detail and would find anything that had been missed. All the same, Minshull felt he should have been there.

'Okay,' Cora conceded, at last. 'But I can't stay longer than that.'

It was enough.

She was pale when she arrived in CID, her smile brief and weary as she was greeted by the detectives. His concern for her surged as he noted the laboured nature of her steps, the too-straight spine braced against an unknown battle.

Minshull led Cora into Anderson's office, the DI keen to speak with her about her experience at the lab. Graciously, she accepted Anderson's welcome, taking a seat at his desk. Minshull sat next to her, his attention drawn to her as she and Anderson talked.

'As you're probably aware, we had a positive ID on the body found this morning at Slaughden Beach,' Anderson began. 'And I understand Rachael Amara joined you for the inspection of the beach collection found on the young man's body?'

'Yes – and the original pile found on Ronald Venn. I talked Dr Amara through the soundscape as I encountered it, and compared it with the first collection,' Cora replied. 'Dr Amara said she'll send you her written observation of the inspection later today.'

Anderson nodded his appreciation. 'In your opinion, were the piles of pebbles made by the same person at the scene?'

'They were collected by the same person, with the same intent. The sound and whispered thought-voice were the same across the two piles, although the pile found with Alistair Avebury presented a louder version. But I don't think they were collected at the same time as the killing.'

'What do you mean?'

'The whispered phrase I heard was repeated by all the pieces in the piles,' she explained. 'But the amount of sound attached to each piece suggests to me that the beach finds were collected prior to the time – and, possibly, the date – of the murder.'

'In preparation?'

'I believe so.'

Anderson rested his elbows on the desk as he took this in. 'So, what are we looking at?'

Minshull caught the momentary pause before Cora's reply, noticing her fingers tightly woven where they rested in her lap.

'We're looking for someone organised. Someone who finds comfort in order. I believe the beach finds have been gathered individually, rather than scooped up together. Each one appears to have been selected for the task.'

'A beachcomber.'

'Yes.'

Anderson screwed his eyes tight shut, as if the air in his office had suddenly been laced with ammonia. 'The press will crap themselves over this.'

'It may work to our advantage, Joel.'

'How so?'

Cora's fingers unlaced, spreading wide as an offering. 'What's the one thing collectors crave?'

'More for their collection?' The prospect filled Minshull with dread as he spoke it.

'Or an audience,' Cora countered. 'Collections are supposed to be seen, to be admired, alongside the collector or curator.'

Anderson's eyes blinked open. 'So they're looking for attention?'

'Not just any kind of attention. Recognition. Acclaim. For their keen eye and their skill at curating.'

Minshull and Anderson let this sink in, the connotations of it impossible to ignore.

'But collectors keep collecting,' Anderson said. 'Does that mean more victims?'

'It might do.' Cora's answer was measured: bad news necessarily delivered. 'But now we know how they present their beach finds.'

'*Beach finds...*' Anderson muttered, clearly galled by the term.

'I think they see the bodies in exactly the same manner as the pebbles, shells and driftwood. Something on the beach that caught their eye. Something worth collecting. And what I heard was their territorialism, their determination to be recognised as the finder...' She broke off, swallowed hard, regrouped. 'Think of a child, defending a collection of pebbles on a beach. Or a sandcastle. Or anything they believe to be theirs. That adamance, that insistence that the items belong to them.'

Minshull held up a hand. 'If they're so determined to own the bodies, why aren't they taking them away? What use is a collection if it's incomplete?'

'Maybe the bodies were too big to be moved. Maybe this is a new phase of the collection they haven't yet figured out the logistics of. So, instead of adding them physically to their collection, they're marking them with the piles of beach finds. An indicator that the bodies are theirs.'

'A cairn...'

Cora and Anderson turned to Minshull.

It was what Bennett had suggested earlier, albeit reaching a different conclusion. *The pile of stuff looks deliberate to me, careful, even...*

'A pile of stones to mark a place,' he said, recounting Bennett's theory. 'Like on a hill or mountain. Kate mentioned something about it before, only she thought the pile of beach finds was there to show the killer where they'd left the body. But instead of a personal marker to guide the killer back, you're suggesting it was a marker to everyone passing? A label? A mark of ownership?'

'Yes.'

'And Dr Amara concurs?' Anderson asked.

'She agrees that it's a strong possibility.'

'Fine.' The DI made notes as the theory settled between them. 'A collector. Seeking recognition...' He observed Cora and Minshull. 'If that's what we're dealing with, how the hell do we stop them before they add to their collection?'

—

Minshull still didn't have an answer ten minutes later, as he handed Cora a mug of coffee in Police HQ's faded canteen.

The kitchen had recently been upgraded, much to everyone's surprise, and a shiny new espresso machine had been installed. Which would have been a heaven-sent miracle had the canteen staff accepted the opportunity to make better coffee with it.

The liquid languishing in the mugs before them was hot and approaching an acceptable coffee colour; beyond that it bore little resemblance to a decent beverage. In true South Suffolk Constabulary tradition, nobody had dared raise the issue, for fear that the powers that be would rescind their generosity and take the machine away. Almost-coffee was far better than never-would-be coffee. In this job, you counted your blessings where you found them.

'At least the new machine looks good,' Minshull joked, his smile faltering as he saw it fail to land. 'Cora?'

She looked up, a hint of pink across her cheeks. 'Sorry. Miles away.'

It was as he'd feared, the toll of inspecting the beach finds heavy on her. 'How was it? At the lab?'

'Okay.' It was far from convincing.

'I should have been there.'

'No, you shouldn't. Drew was there and did a great job.'

'I don't doubt he did, but all the same, we found the body together...'

'You were needed here.' A note of irritation edged into her reply.

'What did Rachael Amara say?'

Cora picked up a dishwasher-dulled teaspoon and stirred her coffee. 'She was interested in my process. I think she was impressed.'

'And how was that for you?'

'Good.' She raised her eyes to meet his stare. '*Good*, Rob. I felt like she respected me as a fellow professional. There was no judgement. Just interest. I'll take that over the alternative, every time.'

'She's a star,' Minshull said, his own relief too evident. 'She takes no prisoners and she loves freaking out anyone unaccustomed to her humour, Drew included, although he has a little bit of experience working with her now. But if she's on your side, you know you've an ally of steel.'

'Hmm.'

That heaviness remained, the unseen weight on her back. If she was truly settled with the task she'd just performed, what else could her burden be?

'Cora...' He risked the brush of his hand against hers. 'What's going on?'

'Nothing.' She pulled her hand back. 'I'm just tired...'

'I don't believe you. Talk to me – please?'

Hollow eyes observed him for a beat, flicking first to the left and then the right as if clearing the coast before she replied. Minshull braced himself for what might follow.

'Charlie's back.'

Thrown by the reply, Minshull scrambled to construct a response. 'Your brother?'

'He just arrived at Mum's. His partner didn't even know he'd left Australia until Mum called her.'

'But aren't they expecting a kid soon?'

'They are. But they had a fight and he left home. Bethan assumed he'd gone walkabout.'

'What's he said about it?'

Her stare sought him out, weighing his reaction. 'That's just it: nothing. When I tried asking he just shut the conversation down. That worries me. Scares me.'

'Why?'

Her shoulders bunched. 'Because I've seen it before. And it's never good.'

'He's done this before?'

The teaspoon made slow, deliberate circuits of her coffee, her eyes trained on the trail of bubbles that followed its path. 'He didn't have the best time in his teens. Fought with Dad every chance he got, shut himself away, and every few months he'd disappear. I have vivid memories of Mum pacing the kitchen floor and Dad driving round the country lanes at midnight, looking for him.'

'You think something's made him revert to that behaviour?'

'I don't know. Change on his terms has always been okay, but change he hasn't planned... It throws him.' Her eyes widened and she let go of the spoon. 'I – I have to get back, sorry. I have case files at home I need to get through.'

'No – wait – tell me why you're concerned.'

'I can't. It's just a shock, you know? After he'd told us how settled he was.'

'And you're seeing similar signs? To how he was before?'

'It doesn't matter.' Her feet were restless now, willing her away.

What had he said to spook her?

'It does matter. All of this matters. You don't have to deal with this stuff by yourself...'

'I'm fine.' The steel in her reply shut his mouth. 'Thanks for the coffee, but I really have to go. Keep me updated on the case, okay? And let me know when you need me again.'

Blindsided by the sudden end to their conversation, Minshull could only follow in her wake as she swept out of Police HQ. He saw her to the car park, then watched as she drove quickly away.

'I'll call you,' he said to the tail lights as they disappeared from view.

Twenty-Five

CORA

She shouldn't have run like that.

It was true that she needed to return home, determined to do what work she could during her enforced leave to ease the burden on Tris and her colleagues; true, too, that Minshull couldn't help with her concern over Charlie. But both had been convenient sidesteps for the real issue. The issue she'd only fully understood the gravity of when she'd given it voice.

Change on his terms has always been okay, but change he hasn't planned...

The memory of her brother defending his sandcastle that had returned in the pathology lab had shaken her. Because the compulsion she'd felt as she'd listened to the piles of beach finds mirrored the force of Charlie's possessiveness back then. Something about the timing of his return and the strangeness of the beach murders set Cora's nerves on edge.

One of the times Charlie had disappeared as a teenager, he'd returned covered in cuts and bruises. A friend had confided in Cora that he'd taken against someone on the beach where they were drinking and had lunged for them. *Like an animal*, the friend had said, the fear in every syllable shockingly real. There were never any charges pressed by the other party, nor did Charlie ever admit how he'd sustained his injuries. But it had remained with Cora, an uncomfortable discordant note running beneath everything he said.

He'd retreated to his room then, as he did after every instance of disappearance, busying himself with the task of arranging his belongings with meticulous order. Sheila said she'd know if Charlie was dealing with something just by observing the organisation of his things.

Compulsion. Organisation. Violence.

Characteristics she'd sensed from the piles of beach finds and discussed with Dr Amara and Drew Ellis.

Charlie's sudden return to Suffolk represented a crisis. He'd been staying in Hollesley, close to the beach where Cora and Minshull had discovered Ronald Venn's body. And her mother's friend Edith had been adamant she'd seen Charlie on Buckanay Lane, the narrow track that led from the main road towards the coast at Shingle Street...

She was panicking, she knew. Perhaps it was the shock of the discovery still at work, the repeated phrase from both sets of beach finds that remained in her mind. Maybe she was too close to this investigation: too involved from the outset.

Charlie's sudden return had to be a coincidence.

So why was Cora terrified it might not be?

It was why she couldn't explain her concern to Minshull. Why she couldn't vocalise her fear, however unlikely it was. Why had her mind set these disparate connections sparking off one another? Why was she even entertaining the notion of a link between the beach murders and Charlie's reappearance in Suffolk?

The problem she couldn't get past was that Charlie didn't only have a link to Shingle Street Beach. Slaughden Beach was part of his past, too. It was another favourite place to birdwatch, the hobby the sole connection Bill Lael had managed to forge with his son. Shingle Street Beach was Charlie's favourite birdwatching location, but Slaughden Beach had been Bill's favoured haunt. Could he have returned there, remembering what it meant to his dad?

And might whatever had compelled him to run home to Suffolk also led him to violence, as it had once before?

It was preposterous. She shouldn't even give it a second's thought. But until Cora could fully dismiss it from her mind, she couldn't express any of her worries to Minshull.

'Are you going to tell me what's up?' Dr Tris Noakes asked, next morning. Cora had called him last night, requesting a return from leave. Staying at home with her thoughts was no longer beneficial. Tris, to his credit, had agreed.

Cora stiffened now. 'I don't know what you mean.'

'If you think that answer will cut this line of inquiry, then you don't know me.' His kind smile cloaked a resolve Cora couldn't evade.

They were on the mid-morning coffee run, buying refreshments for their colleagues, Dr Alannah Hope and Dr Ollie Rowan, from the mobile café in the car park of their workplace. Tris had clearly bided his time to ask the question until they were alone. Now his earlier insistence that Cora help him carry the drinks made sense.

Of course Tris knew.

They had been friends for as long as they had been colleagues, and while she could fool most people, Cora knew Tris could read her like a book. It was why he'd let her return to work before her two weeks' compassionate leave was up.

'I'm worried about Charlie.' There was little point avoiding the subject. And Cora needed a sounding post. Minshull was too close to the case – a fact she only realised when she'd started talking to him in the canteen yesterday. But Tris had no such investment in the murder investigation.

'Because he left his partner?'

'Not just that.'

They had reached the back of the coffee queue. Hanging back a little from the people waiting in front of them, Cora lowered her voice.

'He was seen, a few days ago, before he showed up at Mum's. Not far from Shingle Street Beach.'

'You mean...? *Oh*.' As realisation dawned, Tris moved closer, the volume of his own voice lowering. 'And you think he might have seen something?'

'Not like you think. The thing is, everything Dr Amara said about the bodies – and what I heard from the piles of beach stuff found on them – suggests a collector at work. Someone who craves order and attention for their skill.'

Tris frowned as the queue moved forward. 'How does that relate to your brother?'

'Because order and routine calm him when he's low.'

'They calm me, too, but I don't murder people to achieve them.' His smile faded. 'Do you seriously suspect Charlie?'

'No. I mean, it's an impossible jump, right? But I don't know why I keep coming back to the links between Charlie and the murders. Honestly, Tris, I don't know what to think.'

'But you heard a voice, from the beach piles. Was it him?'

'I heard an adult whisper. No tone, just the characteristics of someone older than a child.'

'So it could be anyone.'

'Which means it could be Charlie.'

Glancing at the five people ahead of them, Tris caught Cora's hand and led her from the coffee van to the bench furthest away from the queue.

'You think he's capable of murder?'

'I don't want to. I know it makes no sense. But yesterday, when I was trying to tell Rob, I kept seeing connections I couldn't ignore.'

'Such as?'

'Charlie's been low before. His teens were rough: he broke his leg playing rugby in his third year of secondary school, losing his place on the under-sixteen's squad for Suffolk. By the time it had healed, he was too old to play for the team. Then he failed some GCSEs, got dumped by a girlfriend and lost his way for a while. It was a perfect storm. Mum and Dad were beside themselves with worry. Charlie just shut everyone out.

He started obsessively collecting stuff – beer caps, bird feathers, pebbles he'd found on the beach. And he'd go off birdwatching on the coast and be gone for hours, days even.'

'Lots of teens go through low times,' Tris offered. 'It doesn't mean they're damaged to the point of taking a life…'

'But the collecting, the ordering – it was always a sign that Charlie was troubled by something.'

'Plenty of people use order as a way of regaining control. You know that, Cora. Control is the first thing anyone grasps for when they feel their lives are in freefall. Planning, counting, ordering their environment. It's all part of the same thing.'

He was right, of course. She knew it – and yet the discomforting idea remained. 'I don't want to suspect him. But he was seen near Shingle Street Beach, before Rob and I found the body there, and was staying in Hollesley at first, not far from the beach. And Slaughden Beach is one of his former birdwatching haunts, my dad's favourite place.'

'Coincidence. You're making links where they don't exist. Have you spoken to his partner?'

'Mum has. I haven't.'

Tris regarded her carefully. 'Maybe you should. You could ask her about these details, about his state of mind. If she's been with him for a while, chances are she's witnessed his changes in mood before. My guess is that she'd tell you a lot more than your brother ever would.'

It was a good point: one Cora hadn't considered.

'Maybe you're right. When I asked Charlie why he was back, he avoided the question. And yet he's told Mum he and Bethan are fine. I know he's scared about becoming a dad – and that's valid – but there was more he wasn't telling me. I could feel it in the air around his replies.'

Tris considered this, his brows low as they always fell when pondering a question. 'But have you *heard* it from him? The same voice you've heard from the beach stuff?'

'I told you, I couldn't tell if the whisper was male or female.'

'You couldn't tell if it was Charlie, either.' When Cora looked away, Tris pressed on. 'What I'm saying is that, unless you hear *that* whisper from Charlie or his belongings, all of this is conjecture.'

Slowly, Cora looked back, her next step decided.

'Then I have to see him again. And I have to talk to Bethan.'

Twenty-Six

THE COLLECTOR

The new piece didn't want to be collected. Not like the last one.

It isn't how I planned it. It feels wrong, incomplete. When I think about it, my head buzzes like a thousand bees are trapped inside my skull. I can't consider this exhibit as a successful acquisition, even though I got my own way in the end.

I thought he was asleep, or passed out. I'd watched him for an hour as he drank himself unconscious. I thought he'd stay that way.

RUTHLESS KILLER AT LARGE IN SUFFOLK

I stare at the newspaper clipping in my hand, then let my gaze travel to my open notebook. The report needs to join the others, stuck onto the pages. Primary evidence of The Collection. A properly documented curation. Provenance.

I should be happy: I got what I wanted. Why does it feel like a failure?

I remember the sudden opening of his eyes. His scream before I punched him. The flailing of his arms and legs, disturbing the shingle and sand around his body. His brief escape into the water. The kick that sent him face first into it. My hand gripping the knife, as I rolled him on his back, stabbing and holding the blade in place until his fight was gone.

And then the dragging of him up the beach. How my fingers stung as they pulled his damp clothing, icy-cold beneath my skin.

He should have been the star exhibit of The Collection. But I couldn't show him, not with the damage.

It's why *they* didn't show him, in their papers and TV news reports. Just a pair of boots and an arm beneath that wreck of a boat. It could have been anybody. Not the one I chose.

What's the point of a collection if it can't be seen?

I reach for the glue stick, turn over the clipping and apply the glue with angry stabs. It isn't neat, strands of white adhesive flailing over the edges of the paper. When I slam it onto the waiting notebook page, my fingers smear the newsprint. A mess, all of it.

And the ache remains.

I thought this piece would make it stop. But it's worse. Burning, accusing, twisting inside. It was only meant to be one. One perfect piece to crown it all. But now it's two: the first taken by *them* and the second one spoiled beyond repair.

There's only one thing I can do.

And next time, I'll make sure I learn from my mistakes.

Males don't work. They're too heavy to display. They fight back and damage themselves. So, I'll change my target. Choose a better piece. Change my location, too, somewhere the choice will be better.

I stare at the clipping where it now lives in my notebook. Then I grab a biro and slash through the paper with heavy lines of blue ink, over and over again, until the report is cloaked behind a sea of bitter strokes. The act is a penance, a purging. When I open my palm, my fingernails have carved furious half-moons, deep into the skin.

I watch the pen fall to the ground.

A woman will change everything: will make the ache go away.

I turn the page.
It's white and clean.
Ready for her.

Twenty-Seven

MINSHULL

Cora's strange response was still puzzling Minshull next morning, the thought an irritation that wouldn't leave him alone. No matter how often he swatted it away, it found its way back, disrupting his train of thought, distracting his mind from the tasks of the day.

Why had she reacted like that? She'd practically run from the canteen, just as Minshull was formulating his reply to one of the most personal things she'd ever shared with him. One step forward, five hundred back...

She'd hardly mentioned her brother Charlie in all the time Minshull had known her, bar the odd passing anecdote when she spoke of her childhood in the village of St Just where their association had first begun. He wasn't aware of them being particularly close, her brother being on the other side of the world for several years and traversing the globe before that. Her level of her concern for Charlie Lael now seemed wildly disproportionate to all of that.

So, what had changed?

'Sarge?' Ellis' patient smile tightened a little. How long had he been stood there?

'Sorry, yes?'

'We're ready for the briefing.'

Minshull let his gaze travel across the room. The gathered CID team wore similar expressions to their colleague. At their side, Anderson stood, arms folded, one bushy eyebrow raised.

Great.

'Okay, good. Thanks, everyone.' He snatched up the pile of papers he'd abandoned on his desk and faced the team. 'Let's get a sense of where we are first, and then we'll talk next steps. Dave, Kate, how did it go with Alistair Avebury's next of kin?'

Wheeler and Bennett's faces fell.

'Bloody horrible, if you'll pardon my French,' Wheeler replied, Bennett nodding beside him. 'Mrs Horton positively identified him. She was devastated, as you can imagine. So Kate and I took her over the road for a cuppa. We couldn't let her drive in that state and it gave us a chance for a gentle chat.'

'And was she forthcoming?'

'Once she'd calmed down a little, she wanted to talk,' Bennett replied. 'Turns out she hadn't seen Alistair for a while. They'd had a row and he'd stormed out. Her husband – Mr Calvin Horton – told her not to go looking for the lad, like she'd done countless times before. She was crushed that she'd listened to him instead of following her gut.'

The mood of the team dimmed. Everyone knew what that was like. Bennett, more than most. She'd confessed to Minshull while they were still in Uniform that she'd rowed with her own father before he was tragically killed in a car accident. The guilt of her final, furious words to him would never leave her. Minshull thought of all the heated exchanges between himself and his retired DCI father. There had been so many, and so often: would he feel guilt if John Minshull died without resolving their differences? He couldn't say.

'What did she tell you about Alistair?'

Wheeler flipped some pages in his notebook. 'He wasn't the easiest of kids. Had a lot of trouble at school, pushed people away when he needed them, always got into fights, that kind of thing. He clashed with his mother and, by the sounds of it, she couldn't handle him. He was in and out of care for most of his early to mid-teens. And then, after he'd been settled back with his mum for a year, she threw him out.'

'Did you find out why?'

'Mrs Horton didn't say. But reading between the lines, I think he brought trouble home. And whatever that was, it crossed a line.' Wheeler shook his head. 'I don't get it, myself. No matter what your kids do, you should be there for them.'

'Not always as easy as that, Dave,' Evans said, his rebuke gentle. Everyone in the team knew how utterly devoted Wheeler was to his two boys. But sometimes his own standards for what a great father should be prevented him from seeing any alternative.

'I know. I'm just saying, Les, I couldn't do it. No decent human being should.'

'Yeah, well, people do. My old man gave me a suitcase for my sixteenth.'

The team turned to Evans.

'Oh, Les…' Bennett began, her concern waved away by her colleague.

'He was a bastard. I was better off without him. But that's the thing, Dave, sometimes the kid doesn't have to do anything to warrant the boot.'

Minshull let Evans' revelation rumble around the team before gently moving the conversation on. 'Did Mrs Horton mention any enemies? Anyone who might have wished Alistair harm?'

'I asked that,' Bennett replied. 'She said he had some friends who'd stuck it out with him since primary school, and they squabbled occasionally. Got into fights with each other when they were all drunk. But no real animosity and none of them that would want him dead.'

'Friends that filmed a video of him dead and cared enough to send it to news outlets but not enough to report it?' Anderson asked.

'Maybe they were scared, Guv.'

'And maybe they weren't his friends, Drew. Not friends he needed, at any rate. If they gave a damn about him they would have come forward. But where are they, hmm?' He held up an apologetic hand. 'Sorry, Rob. Continue.'

'Guv.' The sharpness of Anderson's response took Minshull by surprise, as it did the rest of the team. As Ellis hung his head, Minshull quickly regrouped. 'Did Mrs Horton offer any names of Alistair's friends?'

'No, Sarge. She said he had nicknames for them, but she couldn't recall any.'

'Okay. That helps us understand Alistair's home life and the challenges he was running away from. But it takes us no further regarding his killer. The kids who filmed the video might be able to tell us more. We need to track them down. Don't ask me how. Just bear it in mind, okay? So, what does anyone else have?'

'How did Dr Lael get on at the lab?' Wheeler asked.

'Good,' Minshull replied, glancing at Ellis. 'Drew?'

A chastened Ellis looked up from his notes. 'She said she heard the same voice from the Slaughden Beach pile as she did from the Shingle Street one.'

'Maybe it would be beneficial at this point to share what Dr Lael heard,' Anderson prompted, the calmness of his words a contrast with his last.

'Of course, Guv.' Minshull shelved his own concerns about Cora as he shared the details. 'Cora heard an adult whisper repeating the words *I found you… You're mine*. She said it felt like the collector of the beach stuff was claiming ownership. The intent felt strong, jealously guarding what they considered theirs. She thinks – and the Guv and I agree – that whoever killed Ronald Venn and Alistair Avebury was doing it in order to display the bodies to be seen.'

He watched the shudder pass around his team.

'So all that crap in the news is likely to egg them on,' Evans observed, a murmur of agreement sounding from the team.

'Exactly. Which is why we need to find them before they *collect* any more bodies.' Minshull offered a brief smile. 'Anyone have anything else to report?'

Ellis raised his hand. 'I have a call booked with someone from the Ministry of Defence about Hal Jones.'

'Excellent. When?'

'Tomorrow morning, Sarge.'

'Good. Keep me posted. Anything else?'

'More on a possible suspect, Sarge?'

The team turned with surprise to Evans, who was waving the crumpled wreck of his notebook on the back row.

Minshull did his best to conceal his own shock at this bombshell. 'Yes, Les?'

'When we asked Hollesley Prison for names of people who had recently been released and Alfie Gunnersall's name came up? Well, I was chatting to Wilf Caragh from Uniform about it in the canteen yesterday, and he reckoned Gunnersall's a definite contender.'

The news piqued Minshull's attention, alongside his surprise that Evans had taken initiative to make his own inquiries. 'Remind me how you know Gunnersall, Les?'

'I was one of the poor bastards that arrested him for his latest job. Wilf, too. He got sent down for eight years for GBH, four in Aylesbury prison then at Hollesley for the last four. Released just over a month ago and, according to Wilf, has rented a place nearby. No idea why. If I'd just served that long behind bars I'd be out of the county so fast you wouldn't see me for dust.'

'Has Gunnersall been seen in the area recently?'

'Frequently, Wilf says. Likes to get drunk and harangue old ladies walking their dogs. He's been seen on Shingle Street Beach but also one time down at Slaughden Beach, where he tried to start a fight with a bunch of kids. Nasty piece of work, by all accounts. Volatile. Doesn't know when to shut up. But fond of a spot of birdwatching when he isn't being a git, believe it or not.'

'So he could have visited both Shingle Street and Slaughden recently?'

'Wilf reckons so.'

Minshull considered this as he added Gunnersall's name to the decidedly sparse *SUSPECTS* list. 'How old?'

'Fifty-five, fifty-six?'

'Okay, that sounds promising. Can you contact the prison, find out what you can about him?'

'Yes, Sarge.'

A knock at the CID office door caused Minshull to look up, the team turning as one. 'Come in.'

The door opened to reveal Sergeant Erin Hawksley. Newly promoted in the Uniform division, she had shadowed Tim Brinton for a year and, according to him, showed great promise. She offered a brief smile as she walked in.

'Sarge, Guv, we have a situation downstairs.'

'Oh?'

'A woman claiming to be the mother of one the teenagers who posted the viral video is at reception.'

Minshull and Anderson stood immediately, the team instantly energised by the news.

'I'll go,' Minshull said. 'Drew, would you assist?' He caught the stare of Anderson as Ellis scrambled to his feet.

'There's more, Sarge,' Hawksley rushed. 'She says she's brought all of them with her to hand themselves in. Only I don't think they want to be here.'

'No surprise there,' Anderson offered, the deadpan quip a concession after his outburst. 'Hell hath no fury like a mother on a mission.'

Hawksley paled. 'That's the problem, Guv. She drove them here without telling them – or any of their parents – where they were going. She's locked them in her car.'

Bennett stifled a laugh, quickly ducking back to her desk when Minshull glared at her. Wheeler let out a long whistle and Evans swore.

'Right,' Minshull said, the connotations of kidnapping key witnesses racing through his mind as he grabbed his notebook and jacket. 'We'd better get down there.'

Twenty-Eight

ELLIS

Dealing with reluctant teenage witnesses was a test at the best of times.

Extracting them quickly from a large 4x4 parked on double yellow lines at the front of Police HQ in full view of a rabid bunch of journalists was a Herculean task.

Ellis grimaced as he pushed two of the four teens through the barrage of bodies, smartphones and camera flashes blocking their path, all too aware of the gift the spectacle was handing the press. Behind him, Minshull accompanied the oldest of the group, while the woman who had brought them in against their will dragged her screaming, sobbing daughter at the rear. The route to Police HQ's front steps seemed to take an eternity, but eventually the doors closed behind them and they hurried their charges out of sight of the camera lenses pushed up against the glass.

On the way down from CID, Minshull had decided to interview the group together in the largest of the interview rooms. Interview Room 5 was rarely used these days, most often providing a storage space – or dumping ground – for extra chairs and old recording equipment. A swift declutter led by Hawksley and three of her Uniform team had cleared the space while Ellis, Minshull and the furious mother went out to the vehicle. With the clutter gone, the room smelled musty and faintly of someone's ancient Pot Noodle. A world away from the shiny facilities so often shown in TV crime dramas.

Ellis stifled a grin at the thought of a police drama shot here, as he corralled the young people into the room.

'Right, everyone take a seat, please,' Minshull said, any trace of his irritation at the circumstance quickly hidden behind professional calm. 'Mrs Hillyer, too.'

Ruth Hillyer glared at her now sniffling daughter as she sat down. 'I told her, I said, you can't film a body and not report it. It's evil, that's what it is. That poor lad and his family... I hope you realise what you've all done.'

'*Mum*...' her daughter moaned, the two lads and other girl staring back in silent solidarity.

Minshull and Ellis sat on the opposite side of the chipped interview desk. Ellis noted the line of missing laminate along the side where the teenagers and the woman were seated, nibbled edges picked away by nervous fingers over many years.

'Okay, let's all take a moment to calm down. I'm Detective Sergeant Rob Minshull and this is my colleague, Detective Constable Drew Ellis. None of you are under arrest, but I do need to caution you that what you tell us may have ongoing consequences as part of our investigation. However, any light you can shed on the circumstances leading to the death of Alistair Avebury will greatly help us.'

'His name is Ace,' the oldest boy hissed back.

The girl beside him began to sob quietly.

Ellis' heart went out to them. Despite Anderson's response in the team briefing, what Ellis had said was valid. The teens were clearly traumatised by what they'd seen on the beach. Scared. Shocked. Slammed by grief. No kid should ever have to find the body of their friend. Ellis had been faced with the murders of four friends in a case last year and he was still dealing with the fallout from the experience. He wouldn't wish that hell on anyone.

'We want to honour Ace,' Minshull replied, his tone softened, respectful. 'He didn't deserve to have his life taken from him. So we need to find the person responsible for his death. What you saw could make all the difference.'

'It can't bring him back.' The Hillyer daughter eyeballed the detectives.

'No. It can't. But it can stop this happening again. Because until we find the killer, everyone is in danger.'

A chill passed through the cramped interview room.

Minshull waited a moment longer than was comfortable to let the thought sink in. Then he picked up his pen and smoothed the page of his notebook. 'So if you're all ready, let's get started.'

Ellis set the tape to record, introducing himself and Minshull. 'Could you each give your names and ages for the recording, please?'

'Ruth Hillyer, forty-eight.'

'Amelie Hillyer, seventeen.'

'Ross Gainsford, seventeen.'

'Declan Robinson, eighteen.'

'Mia Joseph, sixteen.'

Ellis noted down each name, then looked at Minshull to take the lead. The DS was still, his eyes trained on each of the speakers in turn, hands folded on his open notebook. Ellis had seen this in action many times, but today he recognised it as armour, as a shield between his side of the interview desk and theirs.

After another distinct pause, Minshull began. 'Mrs Hillyer has agreed to act as appropriate adult for the purposes of this voluntary interview. Mrs Hillyer, what led you to believe your daughter and her friends were responsible for the video taken at Slaughden Beach and subsequently shared online?'

'I found it on her phone.' Ruth Hillyer shot a look at Amelie, who glared back.

'You shouldn't have been looking...'

'Good job I did, isn't it?'

'Mrs Hillyer?'

Sighing, the mother returned her attention to Minshull. 'I asked her where she'd got it and she wouldn't tell me. So I made her hand over her mobile and it was there, in a WhatsApp conversation. With this lot.'

'Okay. Who shot the video?'

As one, the teens' heads dropped.

'I can seize your phones and find out for myself, but I don't want to have to do that.'

Another silence. The waiting game was one of the most effective methods in interview, holding your nerve until someone else's broke, sending their words flooding into the painful silence.

Ellis held his expression steady as he observed the group, mirroring Minshull.

Then a hand was raised. Ross Gainsford kept his gaze firmly trained on the damaged edge of the table.

'I did.'

'Did you film it after you found Ace or were you filming when you found him?'

Ross hesitated.

Minshull kept his gaze steady. Ellis followed suit.

'I thought he was mucking around. He used to do this thing where he'd hide and we'd try to find him. We'd film it like one of those true-crime things.' The teen swallowed hard. 'It didn't mean anything.'

'So what we see on the video is you discovering Ace for the first time?'

'Yes.'

'He liked to jump-scare us,' Mia said, her voice shaking as her fingers twisted and pulled at a damp tissue. 'Hide somewhere and scare the crap out of everyone.'

'Hide somewhere like under the old rowing boat?' Minshull asked.

Mia nodded and fell back into silence.

'What did you do when you found Ace?'

'I stopped filming,' Ross replied. 'We tried to find a pulse but... His eyes were open and that pile of shit on his chest was just... We couldn't move him. And then Dec said we should go.'

'And you didn't think to call an ambulance? Or police?'

Ross reddened, turning to Declan for help.

'I just wanted to get us off the beach.' The oldest teen's reply hid nerves behind its defiance.

'But what about Ace? What about his family?'

'He doesn't have any family. Not any that care about him, anyway.'

'He has an aunt. DC Ellis had to accompany her for the formal ID,' Minshull returned, pulling no punches.

Declan's eyes slid to Ellis. 'She isn't his real aunt. And he said he wasn't talking to her.'

'Did he say why?'

'No.'

'Did he tell any of you?'

Amelie raised her hand, ignoring her mother's groan. 'He brought drugs into the house. Nothing major. Just some bags of weed. But his aunt went nuts. Told him he wasn't welcome if he carried on with it. So he left.'

'When was this?'

'Few months ago. He said it didn't bother him, but he was really cut up about it.'

'And it didn't make you think that maybe she'd want to know he'd been attacked?'

'I – I wasn't thinking straight. None of us were.'

Minshull made notes, the scratch of his pen and the nervous breathing of the group the only sounds in the room. Ellis waited, observing the teenagers and the silently fuming woman beside them.

'Okay, so when did you decide to send the video to the content creator Broo Hendricks, known as BrooBreaks, on TikTok?'

'I didn't,' Ross blurted, earning him a line of accusing stares. 'It wasn't my idea. I said we should delete the video and wait for your lot to find him.'

'But presumably someone else here disagreed?'

'I just wanted people to see what happened.'

Ellis was shocked to see the youngest teen make her confession. Mia Joseph kept her chin high, despite the still-twisting tissue in her hands.

'I thought Dec did it,' Ross said, clearly taken aback.

'Like I would ever,' Declan retorted.

'Mia Joseph, I'm shocked at you,' Ruth Hillyer began, but Minshull held up his hand to stop her.

'Why did you think Broo Hendricks was a better person to send the video to than us?'

'Because you never do anything.'

'Mia!'

'No, Mrs H, what do they do? If they'd done their job, the killer would be in prison now and Ace would still be here!'

Would that things were that easy... Ellis didn't know whether to agree with the teenager or dispute her faith in the police. Yes, by rights, they should have found Ronald Venn's killer before another life was lost. Everyone in CID felt it – in Uniform, too. You joined up because you wanted to get dangerous criminals off the streets, to throw them in jail where they belonged. But the reality was far from that. They eluded capture, they relied on solicitors to find legal loopholes to escape conviction, and even when the process brought them to trial, the criminal justice system frequently failed to give sentences commensurate with the impact of their crimes. It was hard not to lose hope when the odds were so fundamentally stacked against you.

But a family discovering they'd lost a loved one – even one estranged in life – via a viral video on a social media network was the worst of a very long line of possibilities.

'You didn't have to sensationalise Ace's death on social media,' Ellis replied, immediately hit by a sudden shock of panic that he'd spoken up.

'I didn't mean to...' Mia began, staring back. 'That wasn't what I wanted...'

'When did you send the video?' Minshull's question cut across any comeback Ellis might have considered making.

'A few hours after we found him. Ross shared it in our WhatsApp group and I sent it to BrooBreaks.'

'Did you tell the others?'

'No.'

'Why didn't you tell them?'

'Because she knew we'd give her shit about it.' Ross slumped in his seat. 'Except everyone thought it was me, so I got grief for it anyway.'

Mia mouthed *sorry* but Ross blanked her. It was fast becoming a finger-pointing match and Ellis felt the mood shift in the interview room. As if sensing it too, Minshull changed tack.

'Okay, so now we know the timeline, tell me what happened on the beach earlier. Were you all there with Ace before he was attacked?'

A wave of nods passed around the sullen teenagers, any fury from the previous topic of conversation snatched from the air.

'When did you go to the beach?'

'About nine?' Declan sought the agreement of his friends.

'It would have been dark then. Why so late?'

He shrugged. 'It's where we go sometimes. To hang out. Nobody else there, just us.'

'What did you do?'

'Chatted. Mucked around.'

'Were you drinking?'

Silence.

Ruth Hillyer rolled her eyes. 'Of course they were drinking. Why else do teenagers go to the beach at night?'

'All of you?'

More nods, this time noticeably more reluctant. Ellis remembered his own teenage years and the many nights he'd snuck out from his family's farm to drink in darkened fields and barns with his friends. He wondered if Minshull had ever done the same. As the son of a domineering then-DCI, it would have been an understandable rebellion.

'Was Ace drinking, too?'

'He brought the bottles.'

'What were you drinking?'

'Cider. Lager.' Amelie caught Ruth Hillyer's disapproval and seemed to shrink a little. 'Ace had bottles of whisky and vodka, too. I told him to go easy, but he just laughed at me.'

'You thought he was drinking too much?'

The teen sighed. 'He wasn't in a good way. He'd had another row with someone. I don't know who. But he didn't want to talk about it. He was... really low. I mean, worse than I'd seen him for a long time.'

Minshull observed the group. 'And were the rest of you concerned?'

'He was necking it,' Ross admitted. 'Like, really going for it. Dec told him to chill but he told us to sod off. He tried to throw a punch... and that's when Dec said we were going.'

'What time was this?'

'About eleven.'

'Did you leave the beach then?'

'Yes.'

'There's no dealing with him when he's like that,' Declan said, regret painting every word. 'If we'd stayed I'd have punched him back and that was what he wanted. No way was I going to play that game.'

'Where did you go?'

'Back to Dec's place. We were supposed to be having a sleepover.'

'Did you know about this, Mrs Hillyer?'

'I did.' Ruth folded her arms, as if a chill draught had passed through the room. 'I wasn't happy about it, but Declan lives nearer the beach and I know his parents. I'd rather Amelie be safe indoors than out at all hours, even if it isn't at my house.'

Amelie Hillyer had started to cry again, soft sobs muffled behind the cuff of her sleeve that she held to her mouth. Ellis reached for the box of tissues on the interview desk and offered it to her. She met his gaze for a moment as she took one, then looked away.

'What made you go back to the beach?' he asked, a nod from Minshull confirming his question was welcome.

Ross and Mia exchanged nervous glances. Declan picked at the skin of his cuticles where his hands rested in his lap. Amelie closed her eyes.

'Did Ace call you? Send a message?'

'We tried calling him,' Ross admitted. 'Several times. The girls were worried.'

'Not just the girls,' Declan muttered.

'Okay, *I* was worried, too.'

'Why?'

'Because we shouldn't have left him. Not with that odd bloke hanging around...'

Ellis snapped to attention. 'What bloke?'

'Ross! You don't know he had anything to do with it,' Mia hissed. The atmosphere in the room had become charged, each one of the group tense and alert, furtive glances being passed between them.

'A man was hanging around?' Minshull repeated. 'When?'

'All the time we were at the beach. He was at the edge of the shingle, where the grass is. Just watching.'

'Can you describe him?'

'It was dark, so...'

'As best you can, please.'

'He was wearing a hoodie and black jeans. Black trainers, too. He had the hood up, so we couldn't see his face. It was definitely a bloke, though. He was muttering away to himself.'

'Could you see the colour of the hoodie?'

'Red. Like this colour.' Mia pointed at the blood-red cover of Minshull's notebook.

'Did you speak to him? Or did he say anything to you?'

'We just ignored him. He was well creepy.' Amelie observed her mother as she spoke. 'Dec stared back for a bit until the bloke moved on.'

'Was he there when you left Ace?' It was the question Ellis would have asked if Minshull hadn't got there first.

'I – I didn't see him when we left. I thought he'd gone.'

'We shouldn't have left Ace.' Amelie's sobs grew louder, her body shaking now. Ruth's arm moved protectively around her daughter's shoulders, her expression set like stone.

'I said we had to go back,' Mia said, her hand resting on Amelie's arm. 'Dec and Ross reckoned Ace was putting it on, looking for drama as he does. So when we got there and he wasn't where we'd left him, we figured he was hiding somewhere, ready to jump out on us. Make us pay for walking off. That's why Ross was filming, so we could use it to mock him later. But...' Her voice cracked. 'Then we found him...'

It was a mess, by all accounts. Underage drinking, disturbance of a crime scene, the leaking of the video that made South Suffolk Police's job a thousand times more difficult. But they had a description of a suspect now, even if Alistair Avebury's friends couldn't provide more detailed information.

It was a start, at least.

Two hours later, after cautions had been issued to the four teenagers, Mrs Hillyer had agreed to talk to Ross, Declan and Mia's parents, and the group had been led discreetly out of a back door to avoid the press, Ellis and Minshull made their way back up to CID.

'Well?'

Anderson, Bennett and Wheeler were waiting for them, Evans hunched over his desk phone on a call.

'There was someone else on the beach,' Minshull stated, walking across to the whiteboard by his desk and writing the description. 'Adult male, age undefined, red hoodie with the hood up, black jeans and black trainers, hanging around the periphery of the beach, watching the teenagers.'

'Who were drinking,' Ellis added, gratified by the eye-roll this elicited from Bennett.

'How old are they all?'

'One sixteen, two seventeen-year-olds and an eighteen-year-old.'

'And Avebury was nineteen.' Bennett shook her head. 'Just another group of daft kids drinking on the beach. Idiots for doing it, but nobody deserved to die.'

'Sarge? Guv?'

Evans had his hand raised, the receiver of the phone tucked between his chin and his shoulder.

'Yes, Les?'

'Just arranged a time to chat to the prison gaffer at Hollesley, tomorrow morning. About Alfie Gunnersall.'

Minshull brightened. 'Great work. When?'

'Tomorrow morning. Eight a.m.'

'Looks like you'll have to break the habit of a lifetime and be in early for work, Les.' Ellis grinned, the chance of a lighter moment a gift he needed.

A single middle finger raised along the phone receiver in reply, Evans returned to his call.

Twenty-Nine

CORA

Bethan Mulroney looked remarkably fresh, considering her partner had gone AWOL and her baby was due any day. Cora, by contrast, struggled to focus on the screen. A four a.m. alarm to wake her for the arranged video call with Charlie's partner was already taking its toll on her body. The two coffees she'd already imbibed had done little to take the edge off.

'How are you doing?' she asked, aware of what a loaded question it was.

Bethan's smile was one of defiance: brief, yet brave. 'We're fine. We have to be.'

'And the little one?'

'Thriving. But she's a fighter, like her mother.'

'Do you need anything? I mean can we send you anything?'

Bethan's raised hand dismissed Cora's faltering question. 'I'm fine, Cora. But thanks. Nice to be asked about myself for a change.' She let out a sigh. 'Sorry. It's just a lot to deal with, and all the questions seem to be about your brother.'

Cora could only imagine. 'Well, you know where I am if…'

'Like I said, we'll be fine. But I'm guessing that's not why you've called?'

'No. Sorry.'

'Don't apologise. What do you want to know?'

Cora had made a list, late last night when sleep she knew she needed refused to arrive. All of it seemed crass when asked to the woman dealing with the most fallout from Charlie's current crisis. 'Did you have any indication that he was low before he left?'

Bethan took a sip of water from a tall glass, her gaze momentarily lifting away from the computer screen. Behind her, shadows of foliage danced across the white walls of her suburban Sydney home. The veranda out of view of the Zoom window was packed with verdant pots, an image Cora had seen several times in Charlie's photos sent home to Sheila. Bethan loved to garden and their small house was a haven for plants. It had been one of the things that brought them together, when they met while volunteering on a nature garden project in a local park. Planting living things calmed Charlie, he'd told his mum back in happier times, and Bethan found inspiration in the way Charlie ordered his own garden.

Order…

Control…

Cora wrenched her thoughts back to her list, glowing blue in the light of her laptop screen in the pre-dawn darkness of her apartment. 'I mean, was he secretive? Absent? Did you fight?'

'Not secretive, as such, but ready to yell at a moment's notice. That wasn't like him, you know? I mean he'll lock himself away for days before he'll ever opt for confrontation.'

'What was he yelling about?'

Bethan blew out a long breath. 'You name it, he was riled about it. Started off as stuff he'd seen in the news, conversations he'd overheard in the coffee shop where he was working… Not anything directly related to us, just stuff that infuriated him. But then it became about plans for the baby's room, or the future of his job, or which of us would take parental leave when she's born. I needed him to make decisions, needed him to step up and bloody do his half. But it was like I was asking him the impossible, every time.'

'That must have been horrible to live with.'

'Well, you know your brother.'

That was the problem, though, wasn't it? Cora didn't know Charlie, not in the way her colleagues talked about their siblings or Minshull talked about his sister and two brothers. She knew Charlie's history and she knew he thought her ability had somehow short-changed his childhood. They were civil to each other during the few short visits he'd made home since he moved to Australia, but beyond that? What did she really know about him?

'Did you notice anything else?' she prompted, pushing aside age-old grievances Bethan didn't need to bear as Cora did. 'How he was in the house, how he organised his stuff?'

Bethan rolled her eyes. 'The organising. The cataloguing. It drove me insane, Cora, and it wasn't just the pregnancy hormones getting ragged.'

'Cataloguing?'

'He started making lists: first of the baby's things we'd bought, which made sense, but then of his books and his music and the clothes in his closet.'

A knot began to tighten in the pit of Cora's stomach. 'Where did he make the lists?'

'In red notebooks. He bought them in packs of three and would only ever use that sort. One time I'd tidied them away and when he couldn't find them he went *off*. Yelling, screaming, accusing me of goading him. It was crazy. Like I didn't even know him.'

'When did that happen?'

'About a week before he left.'

It was as Cora had feared. And she remembered Charlie's near-obsessive preference for red notebooks, begun when Bill would buy them for him from the St Just post office on his way home from work.

'What happened on the day he left?'

Bethan's expression dimmed, the defiant set of her jaw returned. 'He punched a wall.'

'What?'

'In the baby's room. We'd started rowing and he kept saying I wasn't listening to him. Then he put his fist through the wall and stormed out.'

'And that was the last time you saw him?'

Bethan nodded. 'I yelled at him to get out and he did. I went straight over to Mum's and stayed there for a few hours. When I got home, his closet was empty and his travel rucksack was gone. I just figured he'd gone off somewhere to get his head straight, but then he didn't come back. I didn't think he'd gone back to the UK, though.'

'At least you know where he is now,' Cora offered, aware of how inadequate the sentiment was.

'I do. And – honestly – I don't know that I want him back. Charlie has some major shit to sort out and I can't have him doing that when this little lady's here.'

'We'll take care of him,' Cora promised. But even as she ended the call, she was at a loss to know how that was ever going to happen.

The blue light of dawn was creeping into her apartment as she made her way slowly back to bed. She would go to see Charlie in eight hours' time, the information she'd learned from Bethan far from putting her mind at ease about what she might find there. Before that, she had to try to sleep.

Thirty

ANDERSON

'Nice early start for you, was it, Les?'

Evans offered Anderson a wry smile as he watched his colleagues arriving for the beginning of their shifts. 'Actually, I was in just after seven, Guv. Got here in time for a splendid mug of Pete York's coffee.'

'Who are you?' Anderson demanded, a broad smile ruining the effect. 'And what have you done with Les Evans?'

Evans greeted the mockery with a weary eye-roll. 'Don't sweat it, Guv, it's just this once. It feels personal, the Gunnersall thing, seeing as I helped send him down before. Probably won't happen again.'

'There's a comfort,' Anderson remarked. 'What did you find?'

'Plenty. First off, proof he's still a nasty piece of work – not that it's a shock to anyone. Previous for ABH and breach of peace, broke a former girlfriend's collarbone during an altercation, put another bloke in hospital when he objected to our friend chatting up his missus. And all that before the attack that I nicked him for. When he was inside at Hollesley, he spent so much time in solitary confinement after kicking off that the inmates named the cell *Alfie's Place*.'

'Bloody hell.'

'I know. And get this – the gaffer reckons Gunnersall was well known for nicking things and displaying them in his cell for the prison officers to find.'

'Displaying them?'

'Exactly,' Evans replied. 'Like petty little trophies. Spoons from the canteen. Scraps of metal from the workshops. Other inmates' belongings. All kinds of crap. He'd take the rap for it every time, but the prison gaffer reckoned it was a price he'd pay to be able to show the prison officers he could steal anything.'

'What for? Prestige? Recognition?'

'Notoriety, more like. Get one up on the screws, show the others who was in charge. It foxed the prison officers every time. Made Gunnersall a bit of a hero with the inmates. They called him *The Magpie*, for the way he collected shiny things.'

Collecting.

The word immediately struck Anderson.

We're looking for a collector...

Evans consulted his notebook. 'The prison gaffer said, "I always assumed him nicking and displaying that stuff was a middle finger to us to show he could get whatever he wanted into his cell. Just a game to keep us on our toes and make himself feel superior. Weird little violent bloke. He wasn't right, you know." He seemed impressed by Gunnersall, though, despite the hassle he caused for them.'

'The question is, could that behaviour – the collecting – be something he carried on outside of prison, where he didn't have an intended audience?' Anderson asked. 'Might he collect beachcombed finds, too?'

'If they caught his eye, why not?'

The DI considered this. 'Okay, if that was the case, what might be his motive for murder?'

'Who knows, Guv? Thugs like Gunnersall don't need a reason. One thing's for certain, though, he's not afraid to use a blade.'

'How do you know?' Minshull was watching now, the tension in the office rising around Evans.

'They found a makeshift shiv, once, hidden under his bed. Nasty thing, apparently, about seven inches long. Clearly intended to be a weapon. Miracle that he didn't use it on anyone in there. But now he's out, if he's got himself a weapon…'

It was enough.

Minshull underlined Gunnersall's name on the whiteboard, his pulse thudding at his fingertips. 'We need everything you can find on Alfie Gunnersall. And we need an address.'

'Got one,' Evans said, a slow smirk appearing at the reaction of his colleagues.

'That coffee of Pete's must have been good,' Minshull joked. 'Maybe we need to secure a personal supply for Les.'

'Where does Gunnersall live?' Anderson asked, packing away his smile.

'Hollesley. Moved into a chalet on a small static caravan park on the edge of the village. The prison gaffer knows the woman who runs it. Said a few former inmates choose to rent there when they're first released.'

'Brilliant. And we know he's still there?'

'As of a month ago.'

'You bringing him in, Sarge?' Ellis asked.

'I think so.' Minshull looked to Anderson. 'Guv?'

'We'll pay him a visit. See if he has an alibi for the nights in question. If he doesn't – or his story doesn't tally – we'll arrest him. Great work, Les. I'll need to clear the Gunnersall visit with DCI Stephens of course, as all operational detail is now required to be.' He hoped his grimace spoke volumes. 'Shouldn't be an issue. I'll head up to the third floor now.'

'I don't envy you *that* conversation, Guv,' Minshull offered.

'Pray for my mortal soul, Rob! Okay, thanks everyone. Let's keep going and please, for the love of all things sacred, say nothing outside of this office about where we're at. Those press bastards already know too much. Last thing we need is anything else leaking out.'

'Guv.'

'Yes, Guv.'

Minshull remained by Anderson's side while the CID team made their way back to their desks. When all were occupied, he glanced at his superior.

'If DCI Stephens objects…' he began, words pitched below the hum of the office.

'Then I'll appeal to the Super. Fran might be in immediate authority over what we do, but she's still officially on probation.'

'She won't like that, Guv.'

Anderson sniffed. 'Then she'd better get used to occupational frustration, eh? I hear it's an essential part of the job.'

'Absolutely not!'

'But Ma'am—'

'But *nothing*, DI Anderson! We are under enough scrutiny right now without adding police harassment to the headlines.'

Anderson felt every muscle in his body contracting. Had he not been clear enough? He'd followed Stephens' frankly unworkable new rules for the investigation, running their proposed visit to Gunnersall past her before actioning it. The man was clearly a person of interest, on many levels: ex-con, living nearby, history of collecting, previous convictions for violence, the makeshift blade found in his prison cell, reports of antisocial and threatening behaviour on Shingle Street Beach… What part of all that was giving Stephens reason to doubt Gunnersall as a suspect?

'He fits the profile. He has a history of violence, he lives close to Shingle Street Beach. We're looking for someone with the profile of a collector, and he was known as The Magpie in Hollesley Prison for stealing items and displaying them in his cell. By all accounts he's a nasty piece of work…'

'He also has a history of accusing the police of prejudice and harassment. Which you would be well aware of, had you and your team competently investigated Gunnersall prior to this accusation.'

Blindsided, Anderson could only bluster, 'What history? And how did you know to look?'

Stephens sent him a look designed to shrink him to carpet level. 'His name was on the evidence board in CID. Did you think I wouldn't double-check the work of my team?'

Even considering the chequered history of DCIs in South Suffolk Police, this was a first. Anderson couldn't believe Stephens had been doing her own investigations, especially in the light of her insistence that every operational detail be shared with her. Did it not cut both ways?

'You checked Gunnersall, Ma'am?'

'I did. And the other named former inmate – Jude Morris.'

The names had been on the board since the beginning of the investigation, there for anyone to see. But Stephens' actions still infuriated Anderson.

'And you found a press interview?'

'*Three* interviews Gunnersall gave to the press, days after his release. He tried to drag this constabulary through the mud.'

She pulled three sheets of paper from a file on her ordered desk and offered them to him to read.

Anderson didn't have his reading glasses with him and he wouldn't give Stephens the satisfaction of knowing that. Ignoring the reports, he kept his head held high. 'That's as maybe, but my team and I are of the firm belief that he is a serious contender. He has form, location, opportunity.'

'He's too much of a risk. The moment you visit him, he'll run to sell his story. With the current press obsession over this investigation he'll see the perfect opportunity to cash in.'

'But if he's the killer and we ignore him?'

'It's too much of a risk, given his past actions. Unless you have a witness statement placing him at Shingle Street Beach or Slaughden Beach at the time of the two murders, you do not attempt to contact him. Not while lazy journalists are looking for any opportunity to derail us.'

She wasn't going to budge, was she?

Fury searing through every vein, Anderson gave it one last shot. 'If Gunnersall is our man and we miss this chance, more deaths will follow.'

'Enough!' The DCI dropped the papers back on her desk. 'I've made my decision.'

'And if it's wrong?' He didn't care that he was pushing his luck now. His team weren't working their arses off, butting heads against dead-end walls, just so Fran Stephens could play her stupid power games. If they failed – if the killer struck again – she would willingly allow him and the CID team to take the flak.

'Then I take full responsibility.' Insincerity clung to her every word. 'Now, I suggest you go back to your team and get on with your job.'

Thundering away from the DCI's office, Anderson reached the second-floor stairwell before he drew breath. By the double doors that led to the CID office corridor he slumped against the wall, the bare bricks rough through his shirt. How dare she pull rank on his department – on his decisions? How dare she conduct her own investigations below the radar of the team she professed to be leading – and certainly not for their benefit? What kind of message did that send to everyone in CID? And how the hell were they supposed to conduct a murder investigation if fear of the press determined their every move?

Anderson had no answers – and no easy options. If they were forbidden from approaching Gunnersall directly, they could take his photo to the two murder sites and ask passers-by if they'd seen him in the area. But that was far from an exact science – a waste of time and manpower they could ill afford. And if the inquiries got back to Gunnersall, it handed him bargaining power with the media anyway.

Plus, people were staying away. The Uniform patrols still stationed at Shingle Street and Slaughden beaches had already reported a drop in visitor numbers. With a killer at large, fears for safety were understandably high. If anyone had seen

Gunnersall in the vicinity of either beach on the dates in question, chances were they wouldn't venture back until arrests had been made.

It was a complete mess, made more so by the one person who should be doing everything within her power to help Anderson and his team.

Anderson started to reach for the doors, then hesitated. This problem had to be dealt with now, while it was pertinent to the investigation – and while his blood was up. Taking his mobile phone from his trouser pocket, he found the number he needed and dialled.

'Yes?'

'Sir, forgive the short notice, but I need to speak with you. It's urgent.'

'Come right up, Joel.'

He should go back to CID to fetch his jacket, but to do that would mean explaining his plan to his team, and his nerve might fail him. Forget it. He was already going against all etiquette: being improperly attired to meet a superior officer would just have to be another misdemeanour to chalk up with the rest.

–

The fourth floor of South Suffolk Police HQ had the rarified air of power. While the carpet in its corridor had, like the rest of the building, seen far better days, it was still significantly plusher than that of the floors beneath. It was quieter here, too: most of the office space given over to two large conference rooms used for meetings at the highest level. It was a world away from the clamour of the custody suite and Uniform divisions on the ground and first floors respectively and the frantic activity and noise of the CID office on the second. Even the DCI's office, admin, press office, Tech Support and specialist teams on the third floor had more going on than here. If Anderson didn't know better, it would be easy to assume the top floor was rarely in use.

Superintendent Ian Martlesham's uniformed secretary smiled with brisk efficiency when Anderson entered, her slight scan of his unjacketed body the only concession to regular procedure.

'The Super is waiting for you,' she informed him, looking straight back to her work as Anderson quickly checked his tie and smoothed down his shirt. If the secretary was amused by his uncharacteristically scruffy appearance, at least she had the necessary professionalism to hide it.

Martlesham's office was the best appointed in the building, fittingly so for an officer of his high standing. Anderson's shoes envied the thickness of the carpet pile the moment they stepped on it, being far more accustomed to catching the fraying seams of floor covering in his own office.

'Ah Joel. Take a seat, please.'

'Thank you, Sir. Forgive my appearance…'

The superintendent waved away his apology. 'Not a problem. I know things must be fraught down in CID.'

'Like always, Sir.'

'You said you have a problem?'

Anderson took a breath. His adrenaline-charged journey up to the fourth floor had left no room for second thoughts, but here, in the privileged calm of Martlesham's office, the gravity of what he was about to do was unavoidable.

'It's a delicate matter, Sir. And I need you to know that I would not be talking to you if it weren't an absolute necessity.'

'Go on.'

'We have reason to believe that a person of interest, local to Hollesley and therefore both murder scenes, has both proximity and previous to be considered a major suspect. But DCI Stephens has requested every operational decision for Nautilus be run past her before actioning. I did as she asked, but she has expressly forbidden us from questioning this man.'

A frown darkened the shadows beneath Martlesham's brow. 'Did she give any reason for her decision?'

There was no point omitting any of the argument Anderson had endured. If he had any hope of gaining Martlesham's support, everything had to be on the table. 'The suspect has a history of courting the press, accusing this constabulary of harassment and abuse. DCI Stephens believes it would be too dangerous to approach the man for fear that it would attract further adverse publicity for us.'

'And what do you think, Joel? Please, speak plainly.'

There was this, at least. The last murder investigation had brought the superintendent right into the heart of CID, revealing at first hand just what Anderson and the team had to deal with. While Anderson would hesitate to call the Super an ally, Martlesham was certainly more sympathetic to the needs of the team.

Nevertheless, openly criticising a newly appointed DCI when their predecessor had caused so much division and difficulty was a risky move.

Anderson steeled himself. His team were too important to him to back down now. To hell with the repercussions…

'I think the suspect – Alfie Gunnersall – could well be our best bet. I accept it's a risk, but it's our first real lead and to be denied it in the name of protecting public relations is not only short-sighted, but also potentially negligent.'

'Negligent? How so?'

'If Gunnersall is our killer and we miss this chance to apprehend him, he may well claim another life. I don't want that on the conscience of any of us.'

Martlesham considered this, his expression grave. Now it was said, Anderson could only wait for the outcome. Good or bad, at least he'd spoken out.

'It's a difficult situation,' Martlesham began.

'I appreciate that, Sir.'

'We have to support DCI Stephens as much as we can. It's a seismic shift for her, coming from a major force to a rural one. We knew there would be teething problems…'

It was already sounding like a PR exercise in Achieving Bloody Nothing.

'With respect, Sir, preventing a major suspect from being investigated is far more than a *teething problem*—'

The superintendent's raised hand snatched the words from Anderson's mouth. 'I am more than aware of that, Joel. And of the position you find yourself in. I had hoped that you yourself might have been in the running for the DCI role, but as no application from you was forthcoming...' The shrug that punctuated his sentence grated on Anderson like dry gears.

No, he growled inwardly. *Absolutely bloody* not *are you going to turn this around on me...*

'I care about my team, Sir. My brilliant, talented, hard-working officers who are breaking their backs to find the person responsible for the murders. If we are required to have every operational detail rubber-stamped by DCI Stephens before we act, you are setting them up to fail. We don't have time to tick-box every move we make. Because there is a killer at large, who has killed twice already. And, with the greatest respect, if you tie us up in pointless bureaucracy you might as well hand the murderer his next victims. Blood on your hands, Sir. For the sake of DCI Stephens' personal power trip.'

'You speak out of turn about a senior officer, Joel.'

'If it means my team can do their jobs, so be it.'

The two men observed one another, the air in the superintendent's generous office supercharged with tension.

Martlesham kept his eyes on Anderson, but a little of the fight in his stare disappeared.

'What do you need from me?'

'Let us talk to Gunnersall. Visit him at home, establish his whereabouts. If he's in the clear, we leave and make no more of it. But if he isn't...'

'Fine. Do what you have to.'

'And DCI Stephens?'

Martlesham's sigh spoke of more issues than Anderson had brought to his door. 'Leave Fran to me.'

Thirty-One

CORA

St Just sparkled in the early afternoon sun as Cora drove along its familiar streets towards her childhood home. So many memories crowded the pavements, welcoming ghosts and painful spectres, bustling together, undimmed by time. She still expected to see her father, Bill, chatting to people near the ornate stone Meatcross in the centre of the village, waving to her when he spotted her car, despite it being nearly nine years since his passing. Newer memories, too, of the case that first drew her into South Suffolk CID. Of the fear and the frustration, the threat of history repeating and the echoing disappearance of a young girl, seven years after the abduction and murder of a young boy.

Memories of Minshull joined them. Of how he'd fought her in the beginning. Of how they'd been flint on flint. If he hadn't followed her when she'd fled Suffolk at the end of that first case, would she ever have returned home?

In many ways they had progressed a thousand miles from those early troublesome days in each other's spheres. But with her self-enforced silence over Charlie, how far had they really come? The constant back-and-forth between them made the ground unstable beneath their friendship. Minshull had indicated he wanted more: Cora had yet to admit that she did, too. But while they continued to lurch from one crisis to the next, how could she ever trust herself to pursue it?

She should have told him her worries about her brother. Had she and Rob not weathered enough storms to trust how he'd receive it?

But a murder investigation was more than just sisterly concern. If Minshull followed up on Cora's worries, Charlie might become a suspect. And, if Cora was mistaken, what could that kind of accusation do to her brother?

Unless you hear that whisper from Charlie or his belongings, all of this is conjecture…

Tris was right. Cora's fears would remain unfounded until she sought answers direct from the source. Knowing what had happened with Charlie and Bethan only compounded that need. So, the discovery of a free hour between home visits on her work schedule today offered the perfect opportunity to visit her childhood home.

The house was as it always had been: solid, familiar, never changing. Parked outside, Cora took a moment to settle her mind. Whatever awaited her within its walls, she would be further on than she was. That had to be a positive change, even if the outcome proved to be what she dreaded.

Still, her steps felt iron-heavy as she left her car and approached the house. She was reaching for her key when the front door swung open, a pale-faced Sheila Lael gathering her into a tight hug.

'I thought I saw your car,' she rushed, clutching Cora. 'I wanted to ring you but I didn't want your brother to hear.'

Cora gently broke the embrace, pulling back to study Sheila's expression. 'What's happened?'

'He's not himself, Cor. He's in his room all hours, takes his meals at the door. Music blaring from morning till night. And when I manage to coax him downstairs all he does is sit with his notebook, writing pages and pages. Goes off a cliff if I ever ask what he's writing.'

'I've come to speak to him,' Cora stated, stunned by the possibility that her spur-of-the-moment decision might have been a response to her mother's worries, a kind of familial ESP she'd tapped into. It had happened only once before, on the night Bill Lael died. Cora had been out with friends for a drink when she was struck by a sudden, sickening urge to go home. She arrived just as paramedics were entering the house, where Bill Lael had collapsed on the living room floor. Had she ignored the instinct, she would have missed the final, precious yet agonising minutes of her father's life.

Was that what had brought her here, now?

She followed her mum into the house, the usual rush of emotional chatter from Sheila's belongings that greeted her whenever she visited now edged with fear that gripped Cora's frame like a hundred invisible hands. Interwoven with the emotional object voices was a new one: Charlie's thought-voice, seeping between the woodgrain of the stair banister, a sheen of paranoid panic where his hands had made contact.

'Is he in his room now?'

As if in reply, the muffled *thump-thump-thump* of a drumbeat sounded from the floor above. Sheila folded her arms around her body as if a chill wind had blown into the hall, fear-wide eyes fixed on the rise of the stairs.

'I took him breakfast just before nine. He's been there ever since.'

Cora rested a hand on her mother's arm. 'Stay down here, Mum. Pop the kettle on, yeah? I'll go up by myself.'

She had no need of tea, but a simple task for Sheila would distract her long enough to allow Cora to visit her brother uninterrupted. Glad of the invitation, Sheila scurried down the hall to the kitchen, closing the door behind her.

Thirteen steps to the first floor. Three more to Charlie's door, and the answers Cora needed. The smallest journey with the longest time between each step...

Her first knock went unanswered, the stubborn beat of his music the only reply. She waited until the song ended, knocking harder in the silence that followed.

'I'm good, Mum,' his voice insisted through the wooden divide.

'It's me,' Cora replied, aware of a sudden pressure against her torso, as if she were being shoved back by an invisible force. Since she had begun to press into her ability, physical sensations had often accompanied the thought-voices she heard. It was a discomfiting manifestation that she endured rather than welcomed. Feeling it from her brother's audible thoughts was the worst, the familial link only strengthening its effect.

I'm not hiding... Charlie's thought-voice hissed, louder here. *I'm not...*

'I'm busy.' His spoken voice insisted.

'Open the door.'

'Go away.'

The same fierce defiance of his thought-voice characterised his reply. A warning – no, a threat. More than just an annoying younger brother determined to have his way at all costs.

Enough.

Cora was not here to be in conference with her brother through a bedroom door. There were no locks on the inside – despite Charlie whining about not being allowed one as a teenager – nothing to hold Cora back, except her own willingness to respect a boundary. Such polite deference no longer applied.

She twisted the handle and pushed, surprised when the door met heavy resistance. Pushing harder, the scrape of wood on the floorboards of the bedroom protested, followed by a crash as an unseen barricade toppled away from the door.

On his bed, Charlie stared back, pen poised over a red notebook, line upon line of tiny, haphazard scribble covering the pages.

'Get out!'

Nobody understands... His thought-voice hissed from the notebook.

Cora braced herself against the resistance, both vocal and thought. 'No. I need to talk to you.'

I can't tell anyone… Especially not her… My terrible secret…

'Get *out*!'

Charlie's hands scrabbled at the pages, pulling the notebook shut and shoving it beneath the unkempt folds of his bedclothes. The audible fingerprints of his thought-voice continued their protests there, muffled by the sheets.

'I just want to talk to you,' Cora soothed, both hands raised as she carefully stepped over the overturned chair that had blocked the door. 'That's all.'

'You say that to all your patients, right? Before you mess with their heads.'

She let the barb slide. He wasn't going to derail the conversation with tired insults. 'No, I say it to my brother who's scaring me.'

'I'm staying here so nobody has to see me, or worry about me,' Charlie stated, teeth gritted as if he were in physical pain. 'Why can't anyone understand that?'

'But you've been like this for days. Mum's beside herself, Charlie. She can't reach you and it terrifies her.'

'I'm not responsible for Mum…'

'I'm not saying you are. But you have to understand: she's had years of no physical contact with you, just emails and phone calls and video chats from wherever you were in the world. Then you're suddenly back here, in her house, but she still can't reach you.'

Nobody understands… Nobody does…

Pale hands balled into fists, the insistent shove of Charlie's thoughts pummelling Cora as she dared to move closer.

'I have things I need to do.' His words were the wail of an exhausted child, a warning siren breaching the divide across the bedroom floor. 'I have to get this right.'

'Get what right?'

'*This!* You think I came back here because I was scared to be a dad? Or one more jolly before I settle down for good?'

'I don't know, Charlie. You tell me.'

'How can I tell you if I don't even know…' His words were swallowed by emotion, red-lidded eyes unblinking, the swell of resistance so tangible now it was all Cora could do to brace herself against its force.

I'm not *hiding…*

Charlie's thoughts were stronger now, protesting from every object and surface in his childhood bedroom. Myriad repetitions of his pain, fear – and something else Cora couldn't untangle from the mess of the rest.

'Let me help. Talk to me,' she pressed on, struggling to mute the building crowd noise of his thought-voices.

'The writing is helping me make sense of things. I don't need you.'

'Fine, whatever. But you need to talk to Mum. Pass the time of day with her, talk about things we did as kids, talk about anything and everything else. It doesn't matter. The more reassured she is, the less she'll push you about the rest. Be there for her, Charlie. Be the son she's missed for years.'

Cora felt the final sentence leave her like a hammer blow: too hard, too sudden, impossible to retract. She waited for her brother's retaliation, but he didn't move, didn't scream or attack. She saw a slight gasp register in his chest.

'And you'll stop all this if I do?'

It wasn't what she'd come here for – nowhere close to it. But the lull in physical pressure and the cacophonous incantation of his thought-voices were enough to make Cora pause.

'Okay.'

'Yes?'

'Yes.'

Tentatively, Cora reached her hand towards him. 'Come with me now, then.'

'Right now?'

She nodded. 'I have to get back to work. But I don't want to leave you stuck up here. Come down to see Mum. Have something to eat, or a cuppa with her. It doesn't matter what: she just needs to know you're okay.'

Glancing down at the knot of sheets concealing his notebook, Charlie eased himself off the bed. When his cold hand met hers, a sudden memory returned of the young boy he'd once been, happy to be led by his big sister away from the aftermath of a sibling row. Head bowed, feet shuffling, cool and quiet in the sudden absence of their argument's heat.

I'm not hiding... the insistent whispers of his thought-voices repeated.

I'm not.

Driving slowly away from St Just, Cora bit back tears. The exchange had sapped her strength, her head now one dull ache. The reunion between her brother and their mum was the best she could have hoped for. The delight of Sheila as she gathered Charlie into a hug was a step forward, even if every question still remained.

The last thing Cora saw as she left them was Charlie's arms finally encircling his mother, the fight fleeing him.

It made no sense, but she'd heard nothing in Charlie's room that sounded like the voice from the beach. Just his own pain and fear, fighting her attempts to reach them. No possessive whispers, no insistence of ownership. Nothing to suggest any connection between the bodies on the beach or the carefully placed pebbles, shells and sand.

Tris was right: with no direct evidence to link her brother with the voices she'd heard, she had no reason to suspect him of any involvement with the case.

She had to be mistaken, thinking Charlie could be The Beachcomber.

Whatever issues Charlie Lael was dealing with, murder wasn't among them.

Thirty-Two

MID-MORNING NEWS REPORT

[**News anchor**]: Police hunting a suspected serial killer in Suffolk have today been accused by prominent community leaders of dragging their heels. Ben McAra is in Suffolk for us now. Ben, thanks for joining us. What's the latest?

[**Reporter**]: Joanne, this is a community rocked by two seemingly identical murders in the space of seven days. People here are scared. Normally, popular beaches such as Aldeburgh, where we are now, would be teeming with visitors. But today, as you can see, it's deserted. A fact repeated right down the coast. Fear is quickly turning to anger as local people see a real impact on their everyday lives. It's led to an extraordinary statement today from a group of prominent community leaders and councillors, demanding South Suffolk Police take action to apprehend the person or persons responsible for the killings. It is widely believed that a serial killer is at large here. The death of Alistair 'Ace' Avebury, they argue, could have been prevented, had the Force acted swiftly to apprehend the killer of Ronald Venn.

[**News anchor**]: This isn't the first time the constabulary has come under fire, is it?

[**Reporter**]: Far from it. South Suffolk Police have attracted increasingly negative headlines in recent years, dating back to the murder of Matthew Cooper in the village of St Just, eleven years ago, and, more recently, the bizarre case of the quadruple murder in the village of Evernam, six months ago. The feeling here is that the rural, significantly underfunded police force simply isn't equipped to deal with major investigations, and today's statement spells this out.

[**News anchor**]: What does the statement say?

[**Reporter**]: It states that this is now, to all intents and purposes, a community in hiding. It expresses concern that this will impact the tourist trade for the upcoming spring and summer seasons. In an area that relies heavily on tourism to sustain the local economy, the prospect of people staying away is unthinkable. I spoke to the leader of South Suffolk Council, Mitchell Carey, who reiterated the statement's words.

[**Cllr Carey**]: We've taken this extraordinary step because we believe our community is suffering. We've seen a steep decline in visitor numbers since the pandemic and everyone has been working hard to bring people back. But our beaches are no-go areas while this crisis continues. People are staying away. People are scared. South Suffolk Police have said nothing beyond confirming the identities of the two men who tragically lost their lives. No assurances, no suspects named, no clear way forward. We're demanding action to bring those responsible for the murders to justice and save our struggling tourist trade.

[**Reporter**]: We approached South Suffolk Police for comment but so far have received no reply. As pressure mounts on an already beleaguered investigation, the question today is can this community survive further delays while a killer is at large? Joanne, back to you…

Thirty-Three

BENNETT

Whatever had been said between Anderson and Superintendent Martlesham had lit a rocket under the investigation. Within an hour an arrest party had been assembled and briefed: Minshull, Bennett, Ellis and two uniformed officers now all driving out to Hollesley to find Alfie Gunnersall.

Bennett glanced at Minshull as he drove them in the pool car. He'd remained as tight-lipped as Anderson about the set of events that preceded this action, but he seemed energised by it, as much as the DI had been when he'd announced the superintendent's decision to move.

In the rear of the car, his long frame curled up to fit in the decidedly cramped seat, Ellis gave a cough. 'I don't get it, Sarge.'

Minshull gave no indication of his own opinion, his stare focused on the road. 'Get what, Drew?'

'How we're here, doing this.'

'It's quite simple: we all left Police HQ, got into a car and miraculously started driving...' His deadpan delivery was award-worthy, never once cracking a smile.

Bennett, on the other hand, couldn't hide hers.

'That's not what I meant,' Ellis huffed from the back seat.

'I know what you meant.'

'So how did it happen? Why did the Super make the decision? One minute the Guv was off to see DCI Stephens, and the next we're given the go-ahead by her superior. It never worked that way when DCI Taylor was here. Why did he intervene? Is DCI Stephens on the naughty step already?'

'I have no idea.'

'But it's not how things are done.'

'Drew, just accept that there are some things you don't need to know about, okay?' Minshull glanced in the rear-view mirror, the smallest hint of frustration in the movement. 'Point is, we want Gunnersall and now we're going to get him.'

'Ways and means, huh.'

'Exactly.'

'Do we know he's definitely at the address, Sarge?' Bennett cut in, having enjoyed the sport at her colleague's expense but now keen to get back to business.

'We know he's still living there. Local info holds that he's returned to the address several times in the last week. And there's his landlady, who lives on-site. She'll be able to tell us more.'

'And if she can't?'

A thousand contingencies were already buzzing around Bennett's mind, as they always did on a shout. It didn't help to only consider one possible outcome. Preparation for all eventualities was essential. The challenge suited her down to the ground: a natural born strategist, she liked to be three steps ahead of the game, anticipating issues and skirting problems before they arose. Ellis, on the other hand, who could think fast on his feet but seemingly never thought to plan anything before dashing into action, would never relate to Bennett's way of working.

That suited her just fine, even if the laid-back nature of her colleague and friend was a constant source of frustration.

'Then we'll find someone who can, Kate. Look, I know this seems rushed – and contrary to previous operational modes we've followed...' Minshull's emphasis was not lost on either of his DCs. '...but we've planned for eventualities. We've been biding our time waiting for the opportunity to get Gunnersall. Trust the Guv and me, please.'

Trust the process – Anderson's pet phrase for the moments where the tangle of evidence, suspects, motives and crimes appeared insurmountable. Bennett didn't realise Minshull had become a paid subscriber to the notion, too.

Martlesham must have pulled rank on Stephens: it was the only logical explanation. Had that been the Super's idea, or had Anderson gone over his immediate superior's head? And if so, what retribution could he be likely to face as a result? Bennett knew little of the new DCI but she'd already sussed that Fran Stephens was not someone to be crossed. Might there be repercussions once Operation Nautilus was concluded?

As for their intended target today, the evidence certainly existed to put Gunnersall squarely in the frame. A nasty piece of work, according to Evans: someone who wouldn't let conscience or good sense get in the way of what he wanted. Violent, scheming, willing to throw anyone under the bus to protect his own survival, the image of him picking off victims from South Suffolk's beaches didn't require much of a stretch of the imagination.

But did it entirely explain why he'd chosen to kill when he hadn't before?

Bennett wasn't certain it did.

The *Magpie* thing intrigued her, though. Collecting things in prison just to show that he could. Were the bodies on the beaches proof that he'd gone to the next level of his obsession? Unless they found a potential murder weapon in his accommodation, they would need more evidence than a prison governor's gossip to prove motive and method.

'Okay, we're here,' Minshull stated, pulling up on the pavement at the head of a cul-de-sac filled with well-maintained modern bungalows. 'Mallard Way. The caravan park where Gunnersall lives is in a field behind the bungalow down that gravel drive at the end.'

The patrol car that had followed from Ipswich drew up behind them, PC Steph Lanehan and PC Naz Mattu getting out.

'Alright, Sarge,' Lanehan greeted Minshull. 'Where d'you want us?'

'We need to cover as many routes of escape as possible. Kate, you and I will proceed to the front of the property. Drew, take the footpath that runs alongside the field and caravan park. Steph and Naz hang back out of sight around those bushes in case he makes a dash for it.'

'Sarge.'

'Yes, Sarge.'

'What are we arresting him for?' Bennett asked.

'Suspicion of violent behaviour on Slaughden and Shingle Street beaches,' Minshull replied. 'That way we're covered for earlier reports of him being threatening to other beach users and the potential that he's our killer.'

'Anything else we should know, Sarge?' Mattu stepped forward.

'He has a history of violence and isn't our biggest fan. He might come quietly, but my guess is he'll push it. Be very careful of everything you say and do. He's shopped colleagues to the press before: don't give him anything he can cash in on now.'

Nodding their acceptance, the officers moved to their assigned positions.

Bennett walked beside Minshull, her heart picking up pace, as they walked down the gravel drive that led to a large bungalow at the end of the cul-de-sac. She fell into step with the DS, the flutter of nerves and excitement registering in her stomach as they did on every shout.

Reaching the front door, Minshull knocked twice with the dolphin-shaped door knocker. There was a flicker of movement through the obscured glass panels, followed by the shadow of someone approaching the door.

'Yes?'

The woman who answered was a little taller than Bennett, her dyed dark hair blow-dried into soft waves around her face. She could have been anywhere from her late thirties to early sixties, her complexion remarkably free from lines and her choice of clothing giving no clues to her age. The women in Bennett's family were all like that: blessed with good skin and happy to point out the fact to anyone who would listen. It was the one attribute Bennett shared with them, so markedly different in every other regard.

'Mrs Salter?'

'Who wants to know?'

'I'm DS Rob Minshull, from South Suffolk CID and this is my colleague, DC Kate Bennett. We're looking for one of your tenants on the caravan park – Alfie Gunnersall?'

Mrs Salter's enviable features set into stone. 'He isn't here.'

'Do you know where he is?'

'If I did, maybe I'd be three months' rent better off.'

'You haven't seen him for three months?'

'Oh, I've seen him. He just disappears whenever I go to ask for the rent. Problem with having a field and a footpath for him to leg it out to.'

'When was the last time you saw him?'

The woman sniffed. 'Two days ago. Early hours of the morning. He was lugging that massive rucksack of his, off out before dawn.'

'Did he give any indication of where he was going?'

'Birdwatching, he said. Obsessed with it, apparently. He was heading for Slaughden Beach. Walking all the way, unless he could cadge a lift. There's a hide near it that he likes, so he told me. Not that I would believe anything he said.'

'Can I ask why?'

'Proper secretive he is. Won't let me in the chalet for an inspection, even though the terms of the lease say there should be one every six months. And how much stuff does he need for birdwatching? I reckon he has bottles in that rucksack and the only birdwatching he's doing is flat drunk on his back watching seagulls.'

Bennett kept her expression steady but the information lining up made her want to punch the air. Secretive, disappearing for long periods of time, the rucksack too large and bulky to only contain birdwatching equipment... Could his caravan contain items he didn't want to be seen? If the collector theory was correct, what might they find in there?

'If he comes back, can you call me on this number, please?' Minshull asked, handing the landlady his card. 'It's really important we speak with Mr Gunnersall, as soon as possible.'

She accepted the card with a scowl. 'He won't like it. Hates you lot – no offence.'

'Tell us something we don't know,' Minshull said, once they were out of earshot, Bennett, Lanehan, Ellis and Mattu careful to guard their smiles as they walked back to the cars.

'So what now, Sarge?' Bennett asked. 'We just leave? What if he comes back? What if she's covering for him?'

'That's a lot of *whats*, Kate.'

'None of which have answers,' she returned, the frayed edges of frustration showing. Why come out all this way only to be fobbed off at the door?

'Fair point.' Minshull observed the arrest party, gathered around him. 'Well, kids, let's go to the beach.'

Thirty-Four

MINSHULL

He'd styled it out with his colleagues, but Minshull's own frustration burned as brightly as any of them. They had no guarantee of apprehending Gunnersall at Slaughden Beach, with only the testimony of the former prisoner's decidedly unimpressed landlady to guide them.

Bennett was firing pointed glances at him from the passenger seat. She'd made no secret of her suspicion that Mrs Salter was in league with Gunnersall, and clearly thought Minshull had made a grave error in leaving Hollesley. Maybe her theory would prove to be correct. But if Gunnersall was in the wide-open spaces of Slaughden Beach, Minshull needed everyone with him. If Gunnersall ran – or worse, if he were armed as all the intel on the man seemed to imply he could be – they might lose him. He knew the beach better and had vital local knowledge that could facilitate his escape.

Minshull was not about to let that happen. He just hoped his instinct to head there was right.

'Kate, radio Control for me, please. Inform them of our current status.'

'Yes, Sarge.'

Slaughden Beach car park was almost empty when the CID car and patrol car pulled onto it, a startled couple stepping back from the open boot of their ageing Range Rover where three black Labradors were obediently sitting.

'I'll go and have a word,' Ellis said, extracting himself from the cramped back seat with more than a little relief.

'Cheers, Drew.'

Minshull and Bennett left the car and joined Lanehan and Mattu.

'What's the plan, Sarge?'

'We go together,' Minshull said. 'Spread out across the shingle spit but stay in a sweep formation. If he's there, we all need to be able to get to him. Ellis will join us when he's spoken to the beach users.'

It was beginning to rain as they set off along the narrow path, a barrage of cold mist that stung Minshull's face. *Mizzle*, his mum called it. *Too light to need an umbrella but dense enough to soak you.* Why was he thinking of her now? It had been months since he'd visited his parents, communication reduced to occasional phone conversations with his mum after the last row Minshull had with his retired DCI father.

The beach opened out at the end of the footpath, a wide shingle spit stretching off in both directions. The crime scene, over near the Martello Tower, was still cordoned off, the police tape gone, now replaced with bright orange waffle fencing stretched between metal rods driven deep into the beach. Within its confines, the boat where Alistair 'Ace' Avebury's body had been found lay forlorn, abandoned once more to the mercy of the elements after its brief moment of infamy.

Is that why Gunnersall had returned here?

It was well documented that killers often returned to the scene of their crimes, the reason many crime scenes were assigned a patrol to check for returning visitors. Oh that South Suffolk CID was blessed with a budget that allowed for such manpower! Had Minshull the bargaining power, he would have requested round-the-clock patrols of the crime scene.

He glanced to his left, where PCs Lanehan and Mattu were edging out across the shingle, then to his right where Bennett followed the grassy divide behind land and beach. *This* was the manpower he had. What they lacked in numbers they more than compensated for with nous and experience.

The crunch of shingle behind him heralded the arrival of Ellis, who fell into step when he reached Minshull's side.

'Couple said they saw Gunnersall three hours ago,' he reported, a little out of breath. 'Said he was yelling at everyone, causing a commotion.'

'Did they say where?'

'Down by the water's edge initially. Then he was over by the grassy banks, near the cordon.'

It could have been a coincidence, of course. The cordoned area was significant on the narrow beach. Proximity didn't necessarily mean guilt. 'What was he yelling?'

Ellis grimaced. 'Load of rubbish, from what they could make out. They said someone put a call into us, but they can't say who or when for certain. He's been seen here before, apparently. Shouting, swearing, causing a nuisance.'

Could he have been protecting what he considered to be his? Or was he just another angry, alcohol-fuelled person ranting at the world?

'Okay, thanks. Keep looking.'

There were no bird hides here that Minshull knew of and few buildings. The wide, flat landscape bled the land into the slate-grey sea, open as far as the eye could see. The only bodies on the beach today were Minshull and his team, the only footsteps disturbing its shingle their own. The further they walked, the heavier the realisation: Gunnersall wasn't here.

'Sarge!' Bennett was waving to Minshull's left.

He broke the line and jogged over to her, Ellis not far behind him.

'Over there,' Bennett said, when Minshull drew level with her. 'It looks abandoned, but I reckon someone could still get in.'

She pointed to a dark smudge of shadow resting in the long grass that edged the beach. A wooden building of sorts, salt-stained and patched with sections of corrugated iron. Together, Minshull, Bennett and Ellis crossed the wild grass-and-sand border of the beach to reach it.

All was quiet here, the bones of the building providing an effective windbreak from the beach and sea beyond. Even the seagulls were silenced beside the wood and iron walls. It appeared to cast a shadow, though there was no sun in sight. The panels that made up most of its walls had warped in the extreme weather this small section of Suffolk coast endured, gaps appearing between the pieces, making it possible to glimpse inside. If Gunnersall was in there, they would see him.

'Alfie?' Minshull called anyway, regardless of the stillness of the building. 'Alfie Gunnersall?'

Silence met his call.

'It looks empty,' Bennett observed, her face pressed to a jagged gap between the wood panels.

'Can you see anything inside?'

'Just boxes and some old fishing nets piled up in the corner.'

'Any shelves? Cupboards?'

'Not that I can see.' She drew back. 'I don't reckon anyone's been in this place for years. It's falling to bits.'

'Someone has,' Ellis countered, drawing Bennett and Minshull's attention to the rear of the shack. 'Very recently.'

When Minshull and Bennett joined Ellis, he was holding something shiny and silver that appeared to be attached at the side of a long, rusted iron panel bolted to the weathered wood.

'A padlock?'

'A new one.'

'I would've thought one good shove and you could knock your way in,' Bennett remarked. 'Why put a brand-new padlock on this place?'

Minshull stared at it, then looked back towards the land, empty and still behind them.

'Because they have something inside they don't want anyone to see.'

Bennett frowned. 'Or maybe it has a new owner and they just want to keep their stuff safe.'

Minshull had to concede the point. He was grasping at straws, he knew it, denied sight of the person Anderson had fought so hard for them to see. He'd wanted to return to HQ triumphant, delivering their major suspect with maximum expediency and minimum faff. So much for that noble ambition.

'Let's make a note to find the owner. If they're unconnected, we can rule them out of our inquiries.'

'Sarge,' Ellis replied, fetching his notebook before Bennett could find hers. Minshull saw the spark of fun between them: a brief light moment in a day filled with dead-ends and disappointment.

So, what now?

They could return to Gunnersall's address, but how long might they be waiting? And might his landlady have tipped him off to their presence already? Whatever she'd said about Gunnersall owing her money, something about her readiness to distance herself from her tenant irked Minshull.

Getting patrols set up at Slaughden Beach and Hollesley would be time-consuming and budget-challenging. Considering how much DCI Stephens would have had her nose put out of joint by Anderson and Martlesham acting over her head, the chances of her signing off such a costly exercise were slim.

And despite the boxes Gunnersall appeared to tick that matched the traits of the beach killer, they had nothing concrete to connect him to the murders, only proximity, antisocial behaviour and hearsay.

It was another frustrating roadblock in an investigation beset by problems.

The arrival of Lanehan and Mattu brought initial hope, quickly dashed.

'Nothing, Sarge,' Lanehan puffed. 'The beach is empty.'

'You've checked both approaches?'

Mattu nodded. 'Yes, Sarge.'

'Right.' There was nothing else for it but to admit defeat. Minshull couldn't meet the eyes of his colleagues as he called it. 'We're out of luck today. I'll ask the Guv to put an all-patrol call out for Gunnersall, so we have eyes on the ground.'

'But what if he goes back to his accommodation and finds out we've been after him?' Bennett asked.

'We don't have a choice,' Minshull snapped, immediately raising his hand. 'Look, it isn't ideal, I know. But we do this right or not at all. We just have to bide our time. The delay might play into our favour, allow us to get as much as we can on Gunnersall before we bring him in.'

It might, he repeated to himself, the hopeful thought a flickering candle in the vast darkness of uncertainty.

Unless Gunnersall heeded the warning and went to ground...

Minshull didn't want to consider what that might to do to the murder investigation.

'Let's go,' he concluded.

They were losing the light, anyway. And the journey back to Police HQ would afford him time to work out how to break the news of their fruitless search to Anderson...

Thirty-Five

ANDERSON

It wasn't the result he'd hoped for, made worse by the repercussions that were bound to follow from DCI Stephens. But Anderson was not about to let on to Minshull, Bennett and Ellis. Their collective despondency was enough.

'We need a briefing,' he informed them, nodding at Wheeler and Evans to join their crestfallen colleagues. Between Evans' dodgy humour and Wheeler's warmth, the thwarted detectives would likely find some comfort. In a case where steps forward were seemingly rare, anything that boosted morale was essential.

Minshull joined Anderson to face the gathered team, the atmosphere oddly muted.

'Do you want to lead, Guv?'

'Aye, I will.' He let his gaze pass along the row of detectives. 'Now, I know this isn't the conversation we anticipated. But it is what it is. I don't want any of you to think you've failed. Let's be frank: there was always the chance our first attempt wouldn't succeed. The chances of us apprehending him today, when we know he rarely stays at home, were slim. So let's look at where we are now, without recrimination or blame. Rob, what do we know now that we didn't know before?'

'That he owes money to his landlady, that he spends a lot of time away from his accommodation and that he takes a heavy rucksack when he leaves, purportedly for birdwatching.'

'Okay, good. And what about his recent behaviour either at home or out on his birdwatching trips?'

'According to a couple of regular beach users we met at Slaughden, Gunnersall's been seen there as recently as this morning,' Ellis offered. 'They said he was being abusive to people on the beach. And they thought it had been reported, but I can't find any record of that.'

'There have been similar reports at Shingle Street Beach,' Wheeler said. 'Rilla Davis said she'd chatted to a group of joggers who use the beach after work and they said a drunk bloke had been raving at them.'

'So we can place him at both beaches, but we missed him today.' Minshull shook his head, writing the information on the whiteboard by his desk.

Anderson was quick to intervene. 'You weren't to know, any of you. It was always going to be a risk.'

'Is there any chance of getting patrols at the two beaches and Gunnersall's place, Guv?' Bennett asked.

Bless her belief in the budgetary capabilities of South Suffolk Constabulary…

'Would that there was, Kate,' Anderson replied, as kindly as he could. 'But an all-patrol alert has been issued, and Tim Brinton's assured me he'll keep it as top priority until Gunnersall's brought in.'

'Patrols might work against us, anyway.'

The team turned to Evans, slumped in his usual manner in his chair, deliberately placed a little way behind Wheeler as if he were the naughty kid of the class.

'How so?'

'Gunnersall likes to play the victim. He's earned a fair bob or two crying in the papers about police harassment. You have patrols visible everywhere he goes and he'll see pound signs.'

Anderson saw the revelation land with his detective team. He'd kept it from them before, not wanting that detail of Gunnersall's character to cloud their judgement during the intended arrest. But it was something they should be aware of now. Especially if news of their thwarted attempt to apprehend

Gunnersall got back to him and Stephens' worst PR fears were realised.

'Fair point, Les.'

Evans accepted this with a regal sweep of his hand. The gesture brought a much-needed moment of levity to the beleaguered team. It was as Anderson had hoped. They might not have much in terms of resources, but the CID team were rich in camaraderie. That could save lives sometimes, in Anderson's experience.

Besides, they would need all the good humour and strength they could get to see Operation Nautilus to its conclusion. Especially when DCI Stephens got wind of their failed attempt to apprehend Gunnersall, which Anderson was in no doubt would happen soon.

Had he made a mistake, going over her head? Martlesham had given no indication of his opinion of Anderson's actions – would that change if he needed to bypass Stephens again?

He stood uneasy in his boots, as he faced his team. Whatever the consequences of his decision, he would remain proud of one thing: he'd done it for *them*. For the team assembled in the centre of the faded and under-resourced CID office. He'd take whatever might be thrown at him if it meant they could work unhindered.

'Where are we with everything else?'

'No murder weapon found at either crime scene, Guv,' Wheeler said. 'I talked to Brian Hinds and he reckons whoever killed Venn and Avebury took the knife with them. Dr Amara confirmed that the stab wounds on both victims indicated a single type of knife used. The SOCO and Ops teams have done a sweep of both beaches but nothing turned up.'

'Figures.' In a case so hell-bent on foxing them, why would the discovery of a murder weapon be easy? 'Anyone else?'

Ellis raised his hand, as he so often did during briefings. 'I'm still looking into the owner of that net shack on Slaughden Beach – no joy yet. But you asked me to do some background checks with the MoD about Hal Jones? Well, finally I've had a reply. I now have a contact there…' He flipped pages in his notebook. 'Er… Sergeant George Winchcombe. He's looking into army records to find what he can for us.'

'Can you arrange a chat with him instead?' Minshull pushed. 'My experience of email correspondence with the MoD is protracted exchanges with months between them. We don't have that amount of time to invest in this.'

'Okay, Sarge. I'll see what I can do.'

'Cheers, Drew.' Anderson stalked the line of detectives. 'Anything else?'

'Guv,' Bennett replied. 'I've been monitoring coverage in the press and online, to see what theories are being aired there.'

'And?'

'No names, but several of the papers made mentions of men seen with Ronald Venn in the weeks leading to his murder. Only fleeting references, but a couple have been picked up by social media commentators…'

'Vultures,' Evans interjected. 'Picking over the bones of someone else's tragedy just for clicks.'

Ellis smirked. 'That's good, Les. You should write that down.'

'Two good reasons why that will never happen,' Evans replied, holding up the requisite number of fingers to send a not-so-secret message to his colleague.

'Okay, thank you.' Anderson stepped in before the countdown became even more offensive. 'Go ahead, Kate.'

'A man seen on the beach, talking and drinking with Venn. Reported initially by people on Shingle Street Beach the day after the body was found, then threaded through successive social media mentions.'

'Description?' Minshull asked, pen poised by the board.

'That's where it gets weird, Sarge. The reports fall into two camps. One says the other man was older or a similar age to Venn. The other insists he was significantly younger – mid-thirties, maybe.'

'Any idea which is the favoured report?'

Bennett held up her notebook to reveal a hand-drawn tally table. 'It's split down the middle. Initial reports seemed to favour the older man theory, but a rush of online commentators then subscribed to the younger man theory. The anomaly itself has been picked up on social channels, with *YoungOrOld* trending as a hashtag alongside Venn's name.'

'Weirdos, the lot of them,' Wheeler said, shaking his head.

'Can't disagree with you there, Dave,' Minshull replied.

'A couple I spoke to in the beach car park mentioned a younger man,' Evans remembered. 'A younger guy in a red hoodie. Had a dark green rucksack like the one Venn used for his bottles and stuff.'

'Avebury's friends mentioned a strange bloke wearing a red hoodie watching them on the night Alistair was killed,' Ellis said.

'Good shout, Drew,' Minshull replied.

Anderson took this in as Minshull noted it on the board. 'Interesting.'

'Gunnersall's landlady said he carried a heavy rucksack when he went out, presumably birdwatching,' Minshull added.

'Did she mention what colour the rucksack was?'

'Not that I recall. But I can ask her.'

'Do that, please. And see if Gunnersall ever mentioned to her about meeting a friend – at the beach or not. Any mentions of colours of clothing or luggage in the news reports, Kate?'

Bennett nodded. 'Red hoodie is pretty universal across the reports. But not everyone has mentioned a rucksack and even those that do don't state the colour.'

'Keep digging,' Anderson replied. 'Knowing the online lot, someone is likely to mention it. Details are their stock-in-trade.'

'Will do, Guv.'

'Thanks. Okay, that's all for now,' Anderson said. 'Let's keep looking. Any information takes us closer.'

Heading back to the stillness of his office, Anderson allowed himself a small portion of hope. Other avenues of investigation remained open to them, and while apprehending Gunnersall remained first priority, at least they weren't wholly dependent upon a single arrest. In his experience, the smallest detail could blow a case wide open. If he and his team were looking – and not discarding any possible avenue in their search – they would find the answer.

Whether Fran Stephens and Martlesham would be as comforted by this thought as he was remained to be seen.

Thirty-Six

CORA

I found you... You're mine...

The voice was back, louder than it had been on Shingle Street Beach, more multi-faceted than it had sounded from the beach finds in Dr Amara's laboratory. No matter where Cora turned, the sound followed her, twisting and turning to match her frantic movements and always, always remaining in her ear.

Creeping dread blossomed in her chest, her skin clammy and cold as rain began to fall. Greying hands loomed out of the darkness before her, bone-thin fingers grasping, catching her hair, her shoulders, her hands, her neck. Then she was falling, tumbling through stinging showers of shingle and shell, her skin pierced by rain-soaked missiles she couldn't avoid. She opened her mouth to scream, but the wind snatched her words.

And the voice – the hoarse, ragged whisper, grating and cruel – grew louder, viciously engulfing her as the beach beneath her feet gave way...

I found you...
I FOUND you...
You're MINE...

The scream woke Cora from her nightmare. Cold sweat lined her palms where they gripped the edge of the mattress, beading along her collarbone, making her spine damp against the ruckled sheets. Shadowed shapes from her bedroom swam into focus, her thudding heart and ragged breathing filling her ears as she forced herself to look. Noting each familiar shadow, each patch of light where it fell from the small lamp on her bedside table, she gradually found her way back into the tangible reality of the room.

When her pulse had slowed sufficiently, she eased herself into a sitting position, swinging her legs out of bed. The chill of the floorboards beneath her bare feet provided a physical focus, anchoring her to reality. Dizzy from the dream and the sudden waking, she slowly made her way through the apartment to her kitchen.

The dream wasn't the first: in recent nights it had returned, in varying forms, lengths and intensities. But tonight's was the worst by far.

She'd dreamed of voices heard at crime scenes before. Cora had accepted it as part and parcel of her involvement with police investigations. Using her ability meant pushing far into the soundscapes surrounding emotional echoes. It made sense that those experiences would become more deeply ingrained in her subconscious.

This dream felt different, however: the frequency of its arrival, the growing intensity of each repeat, and its rapid development in such a short period of time.

It was beginning to affect her during the day, too. The memory – and the questions it raised – would return at will, without warning or remedy. If she didn't address the issue quickly, it could soon derail her. And as long as no original source was identified for the owner of the menacing thought-voice, the dream looked set to remain prominent and unchallenged.

The only way to prevent it from taking hold was to face it head on.

Later that day, as she worked on her caseload in the Educational Psychology Team office, a plan began to form. Seeing the director's door open, Cora left her desk and headed over.

'Cora! Save me from endless admin of doom!' Tris exclaimed, his huge smile the warmest welcome. 'Come in, come in.'

'Mind if I pick your brains?' she asked, perching on the chair opposite his cluttered desk.

Tris chuckled. 'Most of them have seeped out of my ears dealing with this paperwork. But if you can scoop any usable scraps from my desk, you're welcome to try. What's up?'

'I had the dream again, late last night.'

'The voice on the beach? How was it?'

'Far more detailed than before. And it seemed to last longer.' A chill passed over her as she recounted it. 'It's every night now. Last night I woke myself with a scream.'

Tris' smile faded into compassion. 'And it's a similar form and structure each time?'

'Same location, same emotions.'

'Shingle Street Beach?'

Cora nodded. 'It's always that beach.'

Tris considered this. 'Have you been back there since you and Rob found the body?'

'We've had no reason to.' Why did her reply sound defensive? 'I mean, *I* haven't…'

'Maybe you should.' When he saw her reaction, Tris spread his hands wide in appeal. 'Humans often link experiences to places, whether we intend to or not. Not always, but I do and I suspect you do as well. Places, sights, sounds, smells. They imprint on our subconscious as groups of stimuli, a linked file that plays whenever we recall or revisit a certain place.'

Cora knew this, but reminded of it now she found it offered a possibility she hadn't considered. 'So, if I go back to Shingle Beach, I'll address the links my mind has created with it and what happened there?'

'Yes. Or you'll be able to create new links to lessen the impact of the current ones.'

It made sense in theory. But would it work in practice?

'I'll try that, thanks,' she said, making to leave.

'I could come with you, if you like?'

It was unexpected, not least because Tris was a confirmed non-runner.

'That's kind, but I'll be fine.'

'I mean it. I'll even bring my trainers and try jogging.' He offered her a pink-cheeked smile. 'The pathetic sight of which might take your mind off what else happened on that beach.'

Cora smiled. 'I thought the purpose of going back was to make me think of what happened, not take my mind off it.'

'Or be further traumatised by my efforts,' Tris agreed. 'Good point.'

'I should do this one alone. But thanks. One day I will get you running.'

'I'll look forward to it – I think?' His wry grin lasted a moment before concern usurped it. 'I'm here for you, is what I'm clumsily trying to say. Don't do this alone unless you feel it's necessary. Maybe you could ask Rob...?'

'No.' It was too strong a reply to pass under her friend's radar.

Tris narrowed his stare. 'Problems there?'

'No. It's just... Rob has enough to deal with at the moment with the double murder investigation. The last thing he needs is to go back to Shingle Street.' Spoken aloud, it sounded as weak an excuse as it had in her mind. She couldn't explain why Rob shouldn't be there, other than that she suspected he had his own demons to contend with. And the thought of revisiting trauma with Minshull as a concerned spectator was worse than the prospect of the nightmares returning.

At least Tris understood, even if his own thoughts on the matter were carefully guarded.

'Best to do it by yourself, then. And call me, the moment you do.'

'I will. Thanks.' Remembering her running shoes and gym stuff were in the boot of her car, she decided to push her luck. 'I couldn't finish here a little early this afternoon, could I?'

'Be my guest.' Tris eyed the pile of paperwork still demanding his attention. Compared to the stack of files on

Cora's desk, it was mountainous. Was he making that comparison now? Cora would make up any time she was granted and Tris was well aware of this – a result of several years working closely together. It was such a fundamental characteristic of Cora's work ethic that it no longer needed to be said. 'Head off just after three p.m., if you like. And if you need to talk to someone while you're on the beach, I'll be here till at least seven tonight.'

'Thanks, Tris.'

The opportunity was too much of a serendipity to ignore. The benefits of facing her trauma head on and preventing another disturbed night were plain to see. Still shaken from last night's rude awakening – and the sleepless hours that followed – Cora found the prospect of a better night's sleep ultimately compelling.

She was going back.

–

The beach was cold when she arrived, the weak afternoon sun already giving way to the incoming dusk. Visibility was greater than it had been on the morning they'd discovered Ronald Venn. Cora followed the sweep of the shingle towards the sea, the ripples across the silvery waves under the defined line of the horizon. The movement was calming, the sting of cold air as it entered her lungs a tangible sensation upon which to anchor her thoughts.

She bent to adjust a shoelace, damp already from her warm-up walk from the car park across the shingle. Then she stood, fixing her earbuds in place. She'd considered making this visit with no music, but as she'd neared Shingle Street her building nerves had called for a little more comfort. Now her plan was to run to her usual playlist until she reached the part of the beach still cordoned off with police tape, turning off her music to experience the traces of sound that remained there.

The familiar beat of the first song surrounded her as she broke into a run, ankles and knees a little stiff from the drive out from Ipswich. She pushed through the ache as she always did, the satisfying stretch in her calves and thighs more than compensating for the effort.

Keeping close to the shore gave her another shot of confidence, the taking of a slightly different line across the shingle a new memory to challenge the old. The breeze chilled her skin, as refreshing as a cold-water dip. It was beautiful here, she reminded herself. Quiet and dramatic, subtle colours in the shingle contrasting with the pale afternoon sky and the deep green of the natural lagoon at the beach's heart. Her heartbeat settled to the rhythm of her steps, the knots across her shoulders beginning to unravel as she moved.

Shingle Street Beach was where Bill Lael had brought Cora and her brother as kids, and where he took Charlie alone during his difficult teenage years. Their visits here became so frequent that the name of the beach fast become a byword in the family for tough times. If Charlie 'needed to go to Shingle Street' it was their father's attempt at helping his son the only way he knew how. They would visit at first light or twilight, accompanied by Mars bars and flasks of tea packed in a hurry. Cora was never party to what they discussed here, or what their visits entailed, save for the token premise of 'birdwatching'. All she knew was that Charlie would return exhausted but calmer, Bill happier, and the change would last for several days.

A sudden pang of loss assaulted her at the memory.

Grief meant that even harder times and less-than-perfect aspects of life became as heart-achingly reminiscent as happier moments. Cora missed *everything*. It had been years since she'd lost her dad, but memories of him still possessed the power to stop her heart. Maybe in the end that was what memory boiled down to: sudden bursts of old emotion; glimpses of the past given as gifts to the present.

Dad came here with Charlie…

Charlie came here…

Cora's thoughts swung back to her recent concerns.

Her brother had come back here recently, too. His admission at Sheila's house confirmed it.

Things were hard for him once more, the old shadow of trouble returning to summon him across the world to this place.

What might he have done here to combat the darkness this time, without the intervention of Bill Lael?

Cora's playlist flipped to a faster dance track. Her feet picked up pace in reply. Kicking her fear and pain, memory and loss into her steps, she pushed further up the beach. Soon she would reach the point where police tape danced in the strengthening breeze, where she would have to part with the comfort of her music and allow the hidden soundscape to engulf her.

She set her focus on the beach ahead, blinking away water from her stinging eyes. A few more steps and she would be there…

'Oi!'

Ignoring the new sound, Cora pressed on. The blue and white tape was just visible on the horizon. A group of people were standing nearby, facing the sea, a collection of assorted dogs playing around their feet. Their conversation was carried by the sea breeze, bursts of laughter and chatter blowing around Cora.

'Not talking to me, are you?'

The voice came again, competing with the dance beat in Cora's ears. She slowed a little, easing one bud from her left ear.

'Not good enough to notice, am I? What do you know?'

A sudden, hot sting registered on her arm. Shocked, she raised her hand to touch the skin, her fingers pulling immediately back when two more blows followed. She turned to the direction from which the missiles had come, only for more tiny blows to register.

'Stop!' she yelled, as the bulk of a man stepped into view. He was unkempt and unshaven, a baggy once-black T-shirt hanging over muddied grey joggers, a grubby red hoodie tied at his waist. In his hands were piles of pebbles scooped from the beach, now aimed at her.

'I just wanted a *hello*. That too much to ask?'

'Go away,' Cora shot back. Whoever this man was and whatever he wanted, she was not going to stop for him. She turned back towards her intended destination but a sharp pain at her knee made her stumble, the shingle of the beach suddenly rising up to meet her as she fell.

His hands were upon her in seconds, grasping at her feet and legs, attempting to pull her back towards the grassy edges of the beach.

Cora screamed, kicking out and scrambling out of reach. But the man launched himself at her, pinning her legs down.

The fall knocked her remaining earbud from her ear, a rush of noise, breath and voices flooding in. Intense fear gripped her core as she flailed, disoriented by the rush of voices both hidden and real. The urge to escape welled within her, powering her body with white-hot resolve.

And then, the shouts were around her, other arms reaching for her as the man crashed to the ground, face down, inches away. Cora was lifted upright as another body dropped across her attacker, followed by the frantic barks and growls of several dogs.

'Get your hands off her!' a new voice yelled, male and breathless.

'Someone call the police!' a woman shouted.

The dog walkers formed a cordon around the prone man, two of them pinning him down now, ignoring the foul tirade that poured from his mouth as he squirmed beneath them. Two older women flanked Cora on either side, their hands comforting as they supported her.

Shaken, she fought to regain her breath, beset by the hidden voices of the group and the man they guarded.

He came out of nowhere...

Men like him shouldn't be allowed here...
Not like the police will do anything...
BITCH! Bastard do-gooders!
I found you... You're mine...

The voice from the body, from the piles of beach finds, from the recurring nightmare, snaked between the louder thought-voices of the people around Cora. She pushed past the immediate noise to catch its tail. Still a hiss, although lessening in velocity and volume, but still present on Shingle Street Beach.

She turned her attention to the swearing, spitting wreck of a human pinned to the beach. The shingle he'd touched when he'd fallen now bore his thought-voice – the audible fingerprints Cora could read. Words, curses and hate spilled out around him like an invisible slick, repeating with each new area his body touched. Was the original voice from the crime scene part of it, or an echo from before still playing nearby?

Cora tried to separate the strands of sound, but as soon as she freed one, it would twist with another, joining and melding together until it was impossible to tell them apart.

'What's your name, love?'

The layers of sound collapsed in on themselves as the older woman's question pulled Cora's mind back to the beach.

'I'm Dr Cora Lael,' she managed, disoriented from her sudden aural journey.

Her name was relayed to a younger woman the other side of the group, a mobile phone pressed to her ear.

The woman on her right patted her hand gently. The care and concern in her voice and gesture brought hot tears to Cora's eyes. 'Police are on their way, love. You're safe with us now.'

Heart thudding hard, Cora closed her eyes.

Thirty-Seven

MINSHULL

'Minsh, wait!'

Wheeler scurried in his wake, the DC's breath-starved words lost on Minshull. The moment Cora's name had been relayed from Control, there had been only one thing on his mind. Reaching her.

A fresh attack at the scene of a murder was shocking enough. But in broad daylight, at a time when there were others on the beach? It didn't make sense.

And worst of all: Cora was the victim.

Cora, who'd found Ronald Venn's body when it could so easily have been missed.

Had the attacker seen her that day and plotted revenge? It didn't bear thinking of. But if so, what was the significance of the second murder at Slaughden Beach? Why strike there and then return to the scene of the first attack? And how long had he lain in wait, hoping Cora might return?

'Give me the keys,' Wheeler panted, drawing level with Minshull as they emerged at the ramp overlooking the car park.

'I'm fine to drive,' he snapped. They would get there a whole lot faster if he was behind the wheel, and Dave Wheeler knew this well.

'The keys, Minsh. *Now.*'

It wasn't often Wheeler utilised his commanding voice. The sound of it shocked Minshull to a halt, staring at his colleague's outstretched hand. 'But I've got to – *we* have to get there—'

'And we will. But you're not killing us on the way. *Keys*.'

He could argue the toss. Pull rank on his colleague. But it would waste time that they could be using to get there. Against his instincts, he handed the keys to Wheeler.

To give him his due, Wheeler rose to the challenge, cutting through the building rush-hour traffic with surprising speed. Was Cora's involvement in the beach attack urging him on, too? In a few short years, Cora had become an invaluable member of the CID team, winning over even her most vociferous opponents. Wheeler, true to his nature, had loved her from the beginning, so the prospect of Cora under attack would shock him as much as it did Minshull.

They spoke little on the frantic journey out of town and on through the Suffolk countryside: Minshull monitoring the police radio for reports from the two patrol cars already nearing the scene; Wheeler's brow furrowed with concentration on the road.

There had been no confirmation of Cora's condition, only that the attack had been successfully impeded by the swift actions of a group of dog walkers. Minshull would shake every single one of them by the hand when he met them. But the calling of an ambulance to the scene and the frustratingly sparse information surrounding Cora's injuries did nothing to allay Minshull's worst fears.

When he arrived, he would be the picture of professional calm.

But here, in the car with his long-time colleague, Minshull could be a scared wreck of a human.

Because Cora Lael was so much more than a friend and colleague. Even though he'd only ever admitted this to himself.

They had danced around one another since they'd met, never just colleagues and never quite more than friends. Despite knowing comments from Anderson and Wheeler, Minshull couldn't bridge the gap that remained between them. All he knew was that he cared deeply for Cora. That the thought of her not being in his world was inconceivable.

He hadn't been able to protect her on the beach when she'd found Ronald Venn. He hadn't been able to protect her now. And while common sense assured him that he couldn't have known Cora would return to Shingle Street Beach, he still wished he could have been there. He hated the powerlessness he felt in the face of the juggernaut of events, standing wide-eyed as a rabbit before the headlights of a thundering oncoming vehicle, unable to run…

This investigation. It might be the end of him.

Maybe he needed time away. Use some of the leave he'd accrued. He could visit his brother Ben in Cornwall, finally get round to seeing his nephew and niece, stand by the wide blue Atlantic Ocean and get some damn perspective…

'She'll be fine,' Wheeler muttered.

Was he trying to convince Minshull or himself?

'We don't know that.' He would admit this here and nowhere else.

'People were there, Minsh. They stopped him.'

'But the ambulance…'

'A precaution, mate. You know that.'

'But still…'

'Hang tight. You'll see her soon.'

Wheeler's kind words did nothing to allay Minshull's fear.

The patrol cars were parked across the entrance to the beach car park, blue lights operational, with two Uniform officers stationed at the start of the path leading to the shingle spit. Beyond them, the ambulance was parked. Minshull couldn't see if anyone was inside. A crowd of onlookers watched from the grass bordering the beach, the buzz of scandal carried on the wind.

Wheeler swung the pool car into a parking bay a little further away from the main car park and Minshull jumped out, powering away towards the patrol. He could hear the hurried crunch of his colleague's footsteps behind him.

'Where are they?' he demanded of the officer guarding the beach path.

'Just up on the beach, Sarge,' PC Naz Mattu replied. 'Patrol have apprehended the attacker. They're bringing him down.'

Minshull relented, forcing a smile. 'Cheers, Naz.' It wasn't Mattu's fault that Minshull was frustrated and battling fear.

'She's okay, Minsh—' Mattu rushed, quickly correcting himself. '*Sarge*.'

'Right.' Minshull hoped his nod conveyed the strength of his gratitude before he took the beach path towards the ambulance with the group of bodies surrounding it. It wasn't often police officers broke protocol regarding names, especially not between Uniform and detective ranks, but in times where colleagues were in the thick of it, familiarity was solidarity: a mark of police family.

Wheeler arrived at his side as Minshull neared the ambulance. Its doors were slightly ajar, a light visible within…

A sudden commotion from the beach caused Minshull to turn, in time to see four uniformed officers wrangling a tall, broad male along the shingle towards them. The bulk of a man was kicking and struggling between them, his vicious vehemence drowned out by the shouts of the arrest party.

'*Pigs!* Get your stinkin' hands *off* me!'

'Stop kicking, sir!'

'I in't coming with you! Bastards! Let *go*!'

'Watch him! Grab his arms!'

The man gave a roar that sent a pair of seagulls flapping angrily into the air. He twisted his body, kicking out, his mud-smeared boot making sharp contact with the leg of one of the arresting officers.

'You stop that bollocks now, sunshine!' a familiar voice commanded.

PC Steph Lanehan caught Minshull's eye, her grim, gritted smile the most gratifying sight. On the other side of the arrested man, PC Rilla Davis did the same. If Lanehan and Davis were in the arresting party, the attacker stood no chance.

'Dr Lael's with paramedics on the beach, Sarge,' Lanehan called, as the officers edged past Minshull and Wheeler. 'Shaken, but okay.'

'Cheers, Steph. You taking this one in?'

'Soon as we can get him into a vehicle.'

Minshull peered at the furious man held between the officers. A red hoodie hung limply at his waist, the knotted sleeves almost come undone. At that moment, he raised his head – and everything became clear.

Alfie Gunnersall locked eyes with Minshull, a sneer giving way to a gob-full of spit, aimed at the detective's shoes.

Minshull side-stepped, holding Gunnersall's furious stare, until the ex-con was wrestled past him, towards the waiting patrol car.

'Gunnersall,' Wheeler breathed. 'We were bloody right.'

'I know you came sniffin' round after me,' Gunnersall hissed back, over his shoulder. 'Went on a jolly to the wrong beach, didn't you? Shame you were too shit to find me.'

'We have you now, though,' Minshull returned. It wasn't how he'd wanted to apprehend the man they'd sought, but this was proof of Gunnersall's ability for violence. And this time, they had a group of witnesses to corroborate the charge.

If Alfie Gunnersall was willing to attack a defenceless woman in broad daylight with onlookers present, he was more than capable of murdering two men under cover of night on deserted Suffolk beaches.

They'd got him.

But what of his victim?

Fear swelled again within Minshull, kicking speed and fire into his steps. He emerged on the shingle of the beach, Wheeler keeping step with him, heading for the hi-vis jackets and green suits of the paramedic team. They were crouched around a seated woman, her back to the approaching detectives. But there was no mistaking her identity: the rich auburn of her hair glowing against the cloud-dull beach.

Cora…

It was all Minshull could do not to race to her side.

He forced his attention instead to a group of around eight or nine people, an excited gaggle of dogs at their heels, talking to a Uniform officer, who was taking notes. The group looked up as one when Minshull and Wheeler approached.

'DS Rob Minshull,' he said, receiving the relieved smile of the young PC and the concerned smiles of the group. 'And this is my colleague, DC Dave Wheeler.'

'PC Lizzie Nevin, Sarge,' the young officer rushed. 'This is the group who apprehended the assailant. This gentleman performed a citizen's arrest and they held the man down until we got here.'

Minshull offered his hand to the bearded man who stepped forward. 'Thank you for your efforts, sir.'

'My pleasure. I'm Jim Greene. This is Frank O'Shea, Maureen Holness, Viv Bristow. Then there's Pat Yates, Laurie Duncan, Thom Gibney, Sue Cottesloe and Mary Keats-Duncan.'

One by one, the group acknowledged their names, Minshull and Wheeler shaking hands with all of them.

'Can you tell me what happened?'

'We heard a bloke shouting, but paid it little notice. You get drunks here occasionally, mouthing off at people. But then there was a scream. It spooked the dogs, so we all looked over – and that's when we saw him attacking the lady.'

Minshull's stomach knotted tighter. 'How was he attacking her?'

'He'd knocked her to the ground and was pulling her legs, trying to drag her up the beach.' Jim Greene winced as he spoke. 'It was horrific. The poor woman was kicking and screaming, but he wouldn't stop.'

'*He was dragged a short distance, concurrent with the marks we found in the shingle leading to the body…*'

Minshull remembered the report from Dr Amara, noting that both bodies showed torn clothing and marks to suggest being dragged up the beach. Was this what Gunnersall had done with Ronald Venn and Alistair Avebury?

'So, you intervened?'

'Of course we did! We all dashed over. I knocked him down and sat on his back, then Frank held his legs and Thom and Laurie grabbed his arms. I informed him I was performing a citizen's arrest, while Maureen, Viv and Pat kept him away from the young woman. Sue called 999.'

'He looked like he was going to kill her,' one of the women said, the others in the group murmuring their agreement. 'No way was that happening on our watch. We couldn't help poor Ronnie Venn, but we could stop that man killing again.'

'You think the man we arrested killed Ronald Venn?' Wheeler asked, a note of caution in his question.

'If he attacked that poor love in broad daylight, he'd have no trouble killing Ronnie at night.'

Minshull caught Wheeler's concerned glance in his direction. 'Have you seen that man here before?'

'Several times in the last two weeks,' Jim Greene confirmed. 'Always three sheets to the wind, frequently aggressive if he catches you looking. We've called your lot about it on more than one occasion. He threw stones at the dogs two days ago. I said he was capable of injuring someone then.'

'Has he ever given you his name?' Minshull asked.

'Never been willing or *compos mentis* enough. But I heard from another walker last week that he's recently done time inside. I hope you'll send him right back there.'

'We'll do our best, sir. Would you all be okay to come into the station in Ipswich to give your statements?'

'Happy to,' another woman replied. 'We'll come in together, if you like.'

Minshull thanked them and left Wheeler taking contact details while he headed back over to the circle of paramedics. He had delayed seeing Cora long enough.

She was pale, a blue blanket draped across her shoulders. Small cuts and blueing bruises peppered her calves, the skin visible beneath the cropped running leggings she wore. One of her palms was bleeding, an attending paramedic cleaning the wound with gentle strokes. Smears of sand streaked her hooded jacket where she must have fallen onto the beach.

'DS Rob Minshull,' he announced, crouching down beside them. 'How is she?'

'She's fine.' Cora lifted her head slowly. 'I'm fine, Rob.'

'But your legs...'

'He threw pebbles at me then knocked me over.'

'Superficial cuts and grazes,' the paramedic closest to Minshull said. Her smile was kind, her words economic. 'It could have been a lot worse, if the group over there hadn't intervened.'

'We've got him,' Minshull said, his eyes fixed on Cora. 'He can't hurt anyone else.'

'There you go, Cora.' The paramedic attending to her hand fixed a bandage and smiled. 'Try not to put pressure on it for the time being and change the dressing daily. It won't need stitches, but it's likely to be sore.'

'Thank you.'

'Ready to stand?'

Cora nodded and the paramedics gathered around to support her as she rose shakily to her feet. Minshull stood back, powerless to help.

'Will you take her in?' he asked.

'I think it would be wise, although it's likely to be a bit of a wait, knowing A&E.' The chief paramedic, a broad, bearded man, grimaced. 'We need to make sure you're not concussed and get you checked over, okay?'

'My bag...' Cora began. 'My car...'

'Give me your keys and I'll fetch your things,' Minshull offered. 'We'll follow you over. Dave can drive your car to the hospital.'

Cora made to argue, her words replaced with a resigned sigh. 'Okay, thanks.'

'We'll take good care of her, DS Minshull.' The bearded paramedic beamed, clamping a hand on Minshull's shoulder, a gesture that revealed just how much he understood. How many frightened friends and relatives did they deal with daily? Could the paramedic see Minshull's real fear for Cora? 'We're heading to Ipswich A&E so we'll see you there.'

Cora unzipped a pocket in her jacket and handed a set of keys to Minshull. He held her fingers for a moment before her hand fell back to her side and the paramedics assisted her away from the beach.

'She okay, Minsh?' Wheeler returned to his side, concern as clear as day.

'Shaken up. Cuts and bruises. They're taking her to A&E.' His reply sounded mechanical, devoid of emotion.

'Those her keys, are they?'

Minshull looked down at them in his palm, the tips of his fingers buzzing from where they'd held Cora's. 'Uh... yeah. Can you drive her car over to Ipswich Hospital and I'll follow you in the pool car? We can get her statement there.'

'Maybe we should ask one of the Uniform bods to do it and I'll drive us to A&E,' Wheeler countered. 'No offence, Sarge, but I don't trust you behind a wheel.'

The urge to dismiss Wheeler's argument vanished as a cold shiver traversed Minshull's spine. He was bone tired all of a sudden, weary from the investigation and the shock and the unplanned return to this place that had unsettled him beyond logic or reason. What he wanted more than anything was to be close to Cora – and away from this place.

'Fine,' he breathed, glancing back at the silver-grey sea. 'Let's get out of here.'

Thirty-Eight

ANDERSON

'Alfie Gunnersall.'

Anderson hissed the name through gritted teeth, ignoring the scowl from his immediate superior. Stephens could think what she liked: if she'd taken his team's suspicions seriously and acted quickly, the team might have been able to apprehend him earlier, meaning Gunnersall might have already been in custody and Dr Lael would be unharmed.

If Stephens felt any shred of remorse for her baseless objection now, she hid it well. 'What's the charge?'

'He attacked Dr Cora Lael on Shingle Street Beach, an hour ago. Uniform are bringing him in.'

'Was she badly injured?'

What kind of a heartless, idiotic question was that? Was she about to dismiss it if Cora's injuries were minor? 'Her injuries, Ma'am, are beside the point. She should never have been put in danger of attack…'

'Was she at the location on police business?'

'No.'

'Had she gone there as part of the investigation?'

'No, but—'

'Then I fail to see how you think any of us could have prevented this.'

That was her best shot, was it? Anderson felt the ice-cold steel of indignation fortify his spine. 'We knew Gunnersall had a history of violent behaviour and that he had chosen to stay near the prison after his release. We have had several reports in recent weeks of him being aggressive and threatening to harm other users of Shingle Street Beach – a beach that remains partially cordoned off after a murder. The signs were there, as I told you at the time.'

'The *signs* were circumstantial, DI Anderson. And you were well aware of the potential problems with us going after Gunnersall...' The smallest hint of uncertainty danced at the edge of her tone. Had her armour revealed a weak spot?

'We should have brought him in.'

Stephens said nothing, staring back with flailing defiance.

Anderson readied another shot... but hesitated. They could argue the toss all day. But the fact remained that their now chief suspect in a double murder investigation was under arrest and heading for Police HQ. Regardless of how it had occurred, it was the step forward they so desperately needed.

Besides, he'd heard the rumours flying around Police HQ. Not that he was one for station gossip, but his own suspicions about Stephens' move from Essex Police to South Suffolk made this one topic he'd make an exception for. A bungled drugs bust that left two officers on life support and the flagship Serious Crimes Unit publicly disgraced. It had been her operation, so she'd fallen on her sword. Or had been pushed sideways across the border to South Suffolk... Any way you looked at it, Fran Stephens had become a liability for her former Force. Or a scapegoat.

Anderson knew all too well how that felt.

His parry became a sigh, all of the frustration and fury of the past few days borne upon its back.

'Permission to speak candidly, Ma'am?'

Stephens observed him warily. 'Go ahead.'

'Fight with us, not against us.'

'Excuse me?'

'You want to put your stamp on CID. Make your mark here. I understand that, more than you realise. But we are in this up to our sorry necks, Ma'am, and if we don't pull together now we could be our own undoing.'

'Is that why you deliberately disobeyed a direct order from me and went running straight to Superintendent Martlesham?'

'For pity's sake, you gave me no choice, Ma'am!' When Stephens didn't respond, Anderson pressed on. If she was going to have his hide for this, he might as well make the injustice worth the punishment. 'I don't want to fight every decision with you. If we're not united in this, we will lose. We don't have time for power games.'

'You think this is a game?'

'No, Ma'am, but I think you do.'

That stung. Stephens looked away.

'I don't know what went on in your last posting,' he offered, because, officially, he didn't. 'Frankly, I don't want to know. But here, we're a team. It's the only thing South Suffolk CID have going for us. We've not had strong, compassionate leadership for this division for many, many years, and yet my team has overcome every bloody obstacle chucked at them. They've done it without the help of a DCI for far too long. But you can change that.'

'How, exactly?'

'By trusting them. Trusting *us*. And giving us the support we need. You're the bridge between CID and the higher ranks and we bloody need you on our side.'

'I need to be kept informed…'

'…and you will be. But you have to let us get on without every decision passing to you first.'

'Is Dr Lael badly hurt?'

'No. But she could have been. She's a valuable member of this team, Ma'am, and she deserves your support. We all do. The simple truth is, if you work against us and persist in butting into every decision in this investigation, we will fail.'

The DCI moved to her desk, standing behind it as if seeking a barrier from Anderson's verbal barrage. 'I don't appreciate your tone.'

Great. So much for extending an olive branch. The woman was impossible…

'But I hear you. I – I didn't expect to be given this posting. I didn't expect to leave Essex Police, either.' She gave a cough, and began rearranging a pile of papers on her desk as she spoke. 'I was not first choice for this position, as I'm sure you're well aware. I am more than likely expected to fail.'

Any response Anderson could make was stolen by the DCI's candidness.

'I don't expect you to understand and none of that is to leave this office, clear?'

'Ma'am.'

'I have to make my mark here. Quickly. And this investigation could ruin any chance I have of that before I even start.'

'Tell me something I don't know,' Anderson risked, raising a hand in apology. 'You've seen the headlines, Fran. Go back to any of our major investigations in the past five years and you'll see the same rubbish, regurgitated every time. *They* expect us to fail. So let's not give them the bloody satisfaction, eh?'

She blinked. 'It's DCI Stephens.'

'Of course, Ma'am. My mistake.'

The slightest smile passed between them.

'I'll need a full report of Gunnersall's interview,' she said, turning her attention back to the papers.

'You're welcome to sit in if you want?'

'I think your team can handle that well enough without me, don't you?'

It was the smallest concession, an unexpected sliver of light in the murky gloom. But to Anderson it was seismic. How long it would remain was anyone's guess. But he had her cooperation for now. That was more than he'd ever hoped to achieve.

'We can, Ma'am.' With one last nod, Anderson turned and left the office.

Thirty-Nine

CORA

Nothing broken. The news did little to counter the pain that beset Cora's body, but it was one consolation, at least.

'We won't admit you,' the young doctor smiled, 'but you need to rest. You have some serious bruising and that's going to hurt for a while until it recedes. I'll give you a prescription for some painkillers which should take the edge off.'

'Thank you,' she replied. 'So I can go home?'

'You can.' He looked exhausted. Cora wondered if the doctor wished he'd been given permission to head home, too. 'Keep that ankle raised as much as possible and take it easy for the next couple of weeks.'

Cora nodded, fully aware that rest was the last thing she intended to do. With Charlie still in crisis and her involvement with the murder case, rest wasn't an option. Minshull and the team didn't have that luxury: why should she?

All the same, she'd been shaken by the attack, shock only now beginning to set in. What might have happened if the group of dog walkers hadn't been there to intervene? If the beach was empty and no one had heard her cries for help?

She had become accustomed to danger during the years she had worked with South Suffolk CID, her body bearing the scars of previous cases. But this felt different. More personal. Maybe because, when she went to Shingle Street Beach, she was going for her own peace of mind, not expecting to encounter anything except the ghost-echoes of Ronald Venn's killer.

She hadn't been with Minshull and the police team, running towards danger. If she had, maybe she would have felt better prepared to face an attack.

But could you ever really prepare for that?

Minshull, who had always given the impression that he took the rigours of the job in his stride, had visibly struggled with this investigation. Cora had caught it in his unguarded body language, in the tone of his voice and in the snippets of thought-voice rising from the neatly placed belongings on his desk. He was careful not to reveal too much around her, knowing what she could hear, but with this case he was slipping.

Was it the same thing? That discovering Ronald Venn's body on their morning run was an eventuality he hadn't prepared for?

Whatever it was, Cora resolved to listen closer the next time they were together. Without realising it before, she'd come to rely on Minshull's carefully constructed steadiness. It worried her that he might be enduring a battle alone. Whatever else they might be to each other, he was a good friend. She intended to be there for him, no matter what.

Leaving the A&E department, Cora headed for the pharmacy. She chose a route that went outside, skirting the exterior of the hospital that allowed her space and fresh air, finally bringing her phone into an area of reception it hadn't had inside. Two messages and a voicemail from Minshull awaited her. It was both reassuring and frustrating. It must have been a shock for him to see her in the state she'd been in on the beach, but that would mean weeks of his panicked concern during her recovery, checking her every move. The prospect was exhausting before it even began.

'Hi, Cora, it's Rob. Give me a call when you can, okay? And if I can't answer, leave me a message. We've taken your car home, on the advice of the paramedics, so I'll arrange transport for you when you need it. Just let me know...'

Tempted though she was to find her own way home before she called Minshull, Cora reluctantly dialled his number. Better to inform him as soon as possible than keep him on tenterhooks. Life would be easier if she took preventative action now.

'Hey, how are you?' Minshull sounded breathless, answering on the second ring.

'Nothing's broken. I'm picking up painkillers at the pharmacy and then I'll head home.'

'How long will you be? I'll get someone to pick you up.'

'Don't worry, I'll get a taxi.'

'Seriously, it's no problem.'

'Rob, I'm fine. You have more important things to think about.'

There was a pause, the sound of a creaking door and footsteps taking the place of Minshull's voice. 'Fair point, we do. If you're sure?'

'Completely. I'll call you this evening and you can ask me anything.'

'Message received. Sorry.' The rueful smile in his reply was as clear as if Cora had seen it in person. 'We have him in custody, by the way.'

'Who?'

'Alfie Gunnersall. The man who—'

'Oh, okay,' Cora rushed, not wanting to think about him.

'We've been looking for him, actually. We've good reason to believe he's our man for the beach murders.'

Cora stopped walking. 'You think he's the killer?'

'He's our primary suspect now. He has everything: proximity, opportunity, past history. Matches our profile as closely as it's possible. Plus, he's been seen on both beaches in recent weeks. We have eyewitnesses placing him at Shingle Street and Slaughden Beach.'

If they'd found the killer, it put Charlie in the clear, and Cora's fears for her brother to rest. The flood of relief was immense, the pain from her injuries fading a little in the wake of it. 'That's great news.'

'It is. I'm just so sorry we didn't get to him before he...'

'That's okay. You have him now. I hope you can get a charge against him.'

'Me too. Right, I'd better get back. Are you sure you're okay?'

'Better than okay,' Cora replied, meaning so much more than Minshull knew.

Forty

WHEELER

Alfie Gunnersall looked like a killer.

Wheeler didn't often make snap judgements on people he encountered in the job, acknowledged by his colleagues for being the one most likely to give someone the benefit of the doubt. But this bloke... He gave Wheeler the creeps.

There was no acknowledgement that he'd done anything wrong, despite a crowd of witnesses who'd seen his attack. He sat, imperious, as he heard the details of the evidence against him, an irritating smirk on his face. Beside him, his solicitor eyeballed Wheeler and Anderson, his mouth held in a grim, tight line.

Of all the criminals Wheeler had met over the course of his police career, he had only encountered a handful he would class as actually evil. Most ended up on the wrong side of the law by misfortune, dreadful life choices, bad associations or greed: few could chill your bones with their attitude. This guy was a thug, pure and simple, but a clever thug, which was the worst of all. He knew exactly what he'd done and was proud of it, justifying his actions to himself in a way that nobody else on Earth would accept.

It didn't bear thinking of what might have happened if Cora had been alone on that beach. Gunnersall displayed no remorse, no thought for the welfare of the woman he'd attacked.

What concerned Wheeler most were the statements from the people who'd intervened: Gunnersall dragging Cora across the shingle; the sudden, unprovoked violence meted out seemingly at random. There had been evidence that Alistair Avebury had been dragged. Ronald Venn, too. So had Gunnersall dragged both men before or after he'd dealt the fatal blow?

There were anomalies, too, that Wheeler couldn't ignore, much as he wanted to. The first being no knife used in the attack – a blessing for Cora but a detail that bothered Wheeler. He'd mentioned it to Anderson as they walked down to Interview Room 2, but the DI hadn't seen it as an issue.

'He attacked Cora. That's what we focus on.'

This summarily dismissed, Wheeler voiced the next concern. 'And there was no sign of a rucksack, or bags of beach stuff.'

'Maybe he stashed them somewhere. Maybe the attack on Cora wasn't planned.'

Wheeler hated to make the point, but the differences were impossible to miss. 'Doesn't it strike you as odd, though? When the other two murders were so similar? So organised?'

Anderson had stopped, a little way from the interview room door, his face flushed with irritation. 'Dave. I know you always think the best of people, but this guy isn't someone you save. He attacked one of our own. He's guilty as hell and we'll throw the book at him.'

Maybe Anderson was right. Maybe Gunnersall was interrupted by the dog walkers before he'd had the chance to pick up his weapon. Perhaps the knife was stored wherever Gunnersall was dragging Cora to. If he'd hidden it – or the rucksack his landlady said he always carried – in the rough grass at the edge of the beach, the uniformed officers left at the scene would uncover it.

But what if they didn't?

'Why were you at the beach?' Anderson asked now, working slowly down his list of prepared questions.

'It's a free country, ain't it?' Gunnersall replied, smirking at his solicitor, who didn't respond.

'Were you there to drink?'

'I had cans, so…'

'Do you often drink at the beach?'

'None of your business. Maybe you should try it, though. Get that stick from out of your arse.'

Anderson didn't flinch, moving on. 'When were you first aware of the female runner?'

'I saw her running along the beach, so I watched. No law against that, is there?'

There should be, Wheeler thought.

'Did she see you?'

'You'd have to ask her.'

'Did you try to speak to her? Initiate a conversation?'

'Too busy minding my own business.'

Gunnersall's solicitor made unhurried notes, glancing back at the detectives between the strokes of his pen as if keeping watch of an animal he didn't trust.

'So, you saw her running along the beach and then what?' When Gunnersall didn't reply, Anderson continued. 'I think you tried to attract her attention.'

'So what if I did?'

'But she didn't respond.'

A pause. 'No.'

'That annoyed you, didn't it? Pretty young woman ignoring you?'

'Is that what you think?'

'I don't know what to think. This is your opportunity to tell me.'

'Maybe you like chatting up young women in random places, DI Anderson. I don't.'

'Then why did you call out to her?' When Gunnersall made no reply, Anderson pressed on. 'I think it annoyed you when she didn't respond. So you approached her.'

'Nice story you've worked up there, detective. One might call it *fabricated*.' His emphasis of the word wasn't lost on Wheeler and Anderson.

Is that what this whole charade was leading to? Wheeler knew Gunnersall had form with selling stories to the media, but how could he claim this here? There were eight or more witnesses who saw exactly what happened. How could he refute what they'd seen? He'd attacked Cora, tried to drag her to the edge of the beach and caused her physical injuries, with a crowd of witnesses who had intervened to stop him. No news outlet could twist that into a tale of police harassment.

'We have witnesses to your attack,' Anderson replied, as cool as ever. 'They've agreed to give statements. Every single one of them. Given your history with violent attack, I can't see how that will work in your favour.'

Gunnersall made to speak, then shut his mouth.

'Why did you attack the woman?'

'You'd love me to tell you, wouldn't you?'

'That's why we're here, Mr Gunnersall. So you can tell us your side of the story.'

'Stories are made up. A bit like this interview.'

'Here are the facts, then, to refresh your memory. You attacked a woman on the beach, in broad daylight, metres away from the site of a recent murder,' Anderson stated, his tone cool and steady. 'A site which is still cordoned off. Tell me, why did you choose to drink there? Out of all the parts of Shingle Street Beach?'

'It's my usual spot.'

'The beach is many people's *usual spot*, but unlike you they've decided to stay away. Because a murder took place there. Why didn't that deter you?'

'I like the view.'

Wheeler only just managed to contain his disgust. Gunnersall was clearly enjoying this game of back-and-forth with Anderson, as if the seriousness of his crime were no more than an inconsequential detail. Was the attack on Cora so justified in Gunnersall's own thinking that it didn't warrant proper consideration here? Did he realise how bad he was making things for himself?

'Why did you attack the woman?'

'I'm not saying I did attack her.'

Anderson pulled several loose sheets out from the back of the folder, his elongated exhale the only indication of his frustration. Wheeler knew a molten fiery core burned beneath his cool exterior. The DI selected one of the sheets, running his finger down the paper until he found the right place.

'*I saw him call out to her. When she ignored him he launched himself at her, knocking her to the ground. Then he started dragging her up the beach. She was screaming, kicking, trying to fight him off. But he was too strong for her...*' Anderson looked up from the sheet. 'You knocked her to the ground and dragged her across the beach, despite her fighting back.'

A quick glance from his solicitor seemed to embolden Gunnersall.

'No comment.'

If Wheeler had been a betting man (and Les Evans had thought to run a sweepstake on the outcome of this interview), he would just have won a considerable prize pot for seeing this coming. What surprised him was how long Gunnersall had held out before utilising it.

'So, I'll ask again, Mr Gunnersall: why did you attack her?'

'No comment.'

'And why did you choose that location on Shingle Street Beach, so close to a cordoned-off crime scene?'

'No comment.'

'Is it your favourite spot on the beach for a reason? Beyond the view?'

Gunnersall glared back, the first glimpse of indignation since he'd arrived at Police HQ. 'No comment.'

'Did you return to that spot because you'd attacked someone else there, a week ago?'

'No comment.'

'Was it a man last time? A man who didn't have the strength to fight back? Or who didn't have a crowd of beach users to come to his aid?'

'What are you saying?'

'Is that why you attacked him at night, when the beach was empty?'

'DI Anderson, my client is not here to answer for previous events at the beach…' The solicitor locked eyes with Anderson. Wheeler knew who his money was on to prevail.

'On the contrary, your client chose to wait at a location where a body was found nine days ago in order to attack a female runner. We have every right to ask the question.'

'You're accusing me of murder?'

The solicitor's arm reached across Gunnersall, coaxing him back to his seat. His client reluctantly complied, face flushed and breathing pronounced. A nerve had been hit and Wheeler felt the power shift in the small interview room.

'I wish to request a break at this point,' the solicitor stated. 'In order to fully brief my client.'

Anderson slowly placed his pen down on his notes, eyes trained on Gunnersall and his brief. 'Of course. Interview suspended at…' He consulted the clock on the recorder. '…18:56.'

'You're not pinning that on me,' Gunnersall hissed. 'You've got no evidence.'

His solicitor raised a hand to calm him, but his client was clearly rattled.

Good, Wheeler thought. About time the cocky bastard was scared. Maybe if Gunnersall took this seriously they might get somewhere.

'You'd love to nail me for this one, wouldn't you? As if you haven't done enough.'

Anderson didn't so much as raise an eyebrow as he and Wheeler stood, blanking Gunnersall completely to address his legal representative. 'Given the hour and the need to brief your client, I propose we reconvene in the morning.'

'Agreed.' Gunnersall's solicitor rose from his seat. 'But we will expect a charge or release within twenty-four hours.'

They swept out, a uniformed officer accompanying them back to the custody suite.

'Good luck with that,' Anderson snarled, once the door had closed.

'Overnight stewing in the cells should do him good, I reckon,' Wheeler quipped, secretly relieved that he was no longer in the same space as Gunnersall.

'Let's hope so.'

'So, what's the plan?'

'We've got him as far as the attack on Cora is concerned. But I want him on more than assault. We just have to hope that CPS is amenable to an extension to press for murder.'

'Do you think he did it?'

Anderson eyed Wheeler. 'You don't?'

'Oh, he's capable of it, all right. Creepy bastard wouldn't know remorse if it jumped up and bit him. But he didn't have a knife. Or any sign of beach finds, like the piles we found on Venn and Avebury. And the attack happened in broad daylight, when he could see others on the beach.'

'That didn't deter him from attacking Cora.'

'No, but it feels different...' Wheeler shook his head, not wanting to attribute any portion of innocence to Gunnersall. 'Ignore me, Joel. I'm probably just tired.'

'If you have doubts, Dave...'

'I don't. Not really. I'd just be happier if we'd found a knife.'

'You and me both, pal.' Anderson clamped a hand to Wheeler's shoulder as they left the interview room. 'Go home. Get some rest. Then tomorrow, we'll nail the bastard.'

Wheeler wished he felt as confident as Anderson did.

Forty-One

MINSHULL

The call woke him. He hadn't intended to sleep, not on the sofa. He couldn't even remember closing his eyes.

Pushing his stiff limbs upright, a shower of pins and needles in his fingers as he reached for his phone, Minshull answered. 'Guv?'

'Rob, it's Joel. You're needed here.'

Blinking away sleep, Minshull pulled the mobile phone from his ear, squinting to read the time in the glare of its too-bright display. 2:52 a.m. 'What's happened?'

Anderson's pause was agonisingly long, Minshull picturing his superior auditioning words for his reply. 'Another attempt. Felixstowe Beach.'

'Attempt?'

'The victim fought back. She's alive. And she saw the face of her attacker.'

But they *had* the attacker in custody. Didn't they?

Minshull was already pulling on his shoes. 'I'm on my way.'

—

Two teenage girls huddled together in the family room, a liaison officer seated beside them. Minshull and Bennett waited for the nod from PC Janey March to begin.

The room's ambience was as far removed from a family atmosphere as it was possible to be. A saggy sofa the colour of marzipan, a pathetically small and threadbare rug laid beside it, a low flat-pack square coffee table that dipped a little on one side and a sad-looking potted palm that leaned hopelessly towards the high, narrow window as if vainly seeking escape. There had been several attempts to soften the edges of what was essentially a small office in recent years. None had succeeded.

Minshull couldn't imagine what it must be like to be ushered into this sad, unwelcoming space, carrying the weight of the most horrific, nightmarish experiences. An insult added to unimaginable injury. Ghosts of previous pain clung to the depressing grey walls, staring bleakly at the latest occupants with hollowed-out eyes. Horror and hurt were infused into the very fabric of the room, offering the worst surroundings for the delicate discussions that needed to happen here.

But it was all South Suffolk Police had.

All the same, Minshull noticed Bennett wearing the same look of apology he knew he was offering. Nobody in Police HQ liked being in this room, from PC liaisons to the highest-ranking detectives. No easy words were spoken here, no peace delivered.

Even less when the identity of the assailant was suddenly in question.

Alfie Gunnersall had been in custody all night. Which meant either the attack on the two girls now seated beside Janey March had been a copycat assault, emboldened by the growing urban myth of The Beachcomber, or that Gunnersall wasn't the killer they'd been seeking.

Neither eventuality filled Minshull with hope.

March was talking in hushed tones to the two teenagers, her hand gently placed on the back of the girl nearest to her. She was the best FLO in South Suffolk, her steady, gentle nature calming the most distraught witnesses and families of victims. The girl was crying, dark hair falling like a veil over her tears as she held a tissue to her mouth. Beside her, a distressed young woman with vivid red hair stared at her friend, fury pulling at the muscles of her jaw.

Anderson had briefed Minshull as soon as he arrived, sharing what the Uniform officers attending the scene had managed to glean from the victims. Abi Quigley, nineteen, and her friend Georgie Kelsall, eighteen, had been down on Felixstowe's South Beach with friends, drinking. When the rest of their party called it a night, a little after one a.m., Abi and Georgie had remained on the beach, a bag of cans from an off-licence to keep them company.

Just over an hour later, a hysterical Abi had called 999, screaming that her friend had been grabbed by an assailant wielding a large kitchen knife.

What happened in the intervening sixty minutes was what they had been brought into Police HQ to share, the shock of which was only just beginning to sink in.

March looked to Minshull, her slow nod his cue to begin.

'Thank you both for agreeing to come in,' he began, hoping his professional tone conveyed all the respect and welcome he wanted the victims to hear. 'I'm Detective Sergeant Rob Minshull, and this is my colleague, Detective Constable Kate Bennett. We won't keep you long. Your families are on the way, so they'll be able to take you both home when we're finished.'

A sob came from Georgie. Beside her, Abi stared back.

'I know you've told my uniformed colleagues on the beach what happened, but we need to go over the details with you now. It's important you tell us everything you remember, so we have the best chance of catching the person who did this. PC March will remain with you both for as long as you're here. If it's easier to direct your answers to her, please do.'

March offered the girls a smile of encouragement. 'Take your time, sweethearts. We'll do this at your pace, okay?'

Minshull realised he was gripping his notebook. He forced his hand to relax. Despite his sudden race to Police HQ and the interminably early hour to be working, his questions had to be clear, concise and targeted to glean as much information from the shaken young women as possible. And what he said here had to be free from the crushing revelation he now had to accept: that they'd been mistaken in suspecting Gunnersall; that while he was responsible for the assault on Cora, the killer of Ronald Venn and Alistair Avebury was still at large, planning more attacks…

'Georgie, can you tell me what happened?'

Georgie shook her head, another sob escaping.

'We were down on the beach, kicking about with some friends from college,' Abi interjected, keeping wary watch over her distressed friend. 'Drinking, and that.'

'Who was there with you?'

'I gave a list to the copper who picked us up.'

'Great, thanks. How long did your friends stay on the beach?'

Abi shrugged. 'Couple of hours. They wanted to go to a mate's house, but Georgie and me didn't fancy it.'

'So they left. And what did you and Georgie do?'

'We moved along the beach, to be away from some lads from college who were down there, being dicks. We drank some more, mucked around a bit, had a good chat. Then Georgie said she was tired, so we found a place by the rocks to crash.'

'You slept on the beach?'

Abi fell silent, a hurried look at her friend piquing Minshull's interest.

'We just wanted to rest for a while,' Abi replied. 'I mean, there's no way we'd have stayed there all night. But I think we must have dropped off. Next thing I know, Georgie wasn't next to me and I could hear her screaming further down the beach.'

Minshull glanced at Bennett, who accepted his invitation.

'What happened, Georgie?'

'Someone grabbed me.' The teenager's fingers worked the tissue in her hand, damp twists of paper falling to the threadbare rug at her sand-encrusted boots. 'He pulled me up off the rocks and started dragging me towards the sea.'

'Did you fight back?'

'I – I tried to...' Georgie gritted her teeth against the memory. 'But he was too strong. He yelled at me to shut up. My arm hurt so much where he was gripping it. And then I saw the knife...'

Abi stared at her friend as heavy sobs began to shake Georgie's body.

'I'm so sorry that happened to you,' Bennett offered, the gentle compassion in her words a surprise to Minshull. 'Can you describe the knife?'

'A big one, like a kitchen knife. It had a brown wooden handle and the blade was about this long...' She held her hands about eight inches apart.

Minshull remembered Dr Amara describing a weapon with a blade around that size when he'd asked what had likely been used to inflict the fatal injuries on Venn and Avebury. There had been no mention of the type of knife used in any of the press reports, meaning that this was either a coincidence or a worrying sign for the investigation.

'What did you do when you saw he had a knife?'

'I – I was so scared. I let him drag me. But when we'd gone a little way, I waited till he was looking at the sea before I kicked him. He shouted as he fell and I screamed as I started to run.'

'That's when I heard her,' Abi agreed. 'I went running after them. I could see him, getting up from the beach. He was yelling at Georgie to come back. She started running towards me, screaming. But he was faster than she was. I saw him grab her hair, then yank her backwards. She lost her balance...'

'What did you do?' Minshull asked.

'I saw a rock on the beach. A big one. So I grabbed it.' Abi's voice cracked. 'I didn't think about it. There was no time. He was waving the knife around, screaming at Georgie to stay down. I thought he was going to kill her. I ran towards him and slammed the rock into his head.'

As she spoke, she held out her right hand. The cuff of her jacket revealed deep red smears soaked into the dark blue denim.

The bloodstains could be a breakthrough. In the absence of a knife, the potential of the attacker's DNA on Abi's jacket sleeve could not be underestimated. Was there enough in the smeared stains to build a profile? It was a bright spark in the horror. Minshull wished it weren't so, but practicalities of the investigation remained.

'We'll need to hang on to your jacket,' he said, as kindly as he could. 'It could help us find the person responsible.'

Abi nodded blankly. Georgie sobbed again.

'What happened then?' Bennett asked, moving the conversation away from the blood.

'I grabbed Georgie and we ran up the beach to the prom. I didn't stop. I thought he was going to chase after us. But he was just lying on the beach. I – I thought I'd killed him…'

Bennett made careful notes. March reached across Georgie to squeeze Abi's shaking hand. Minshull wrangled his thoughts into order.

'You ran onto the promenade. Where did you go then?'

'We just kept running until we reached the houses on Buregate Road. My nan lives there. She was in bed already, so I used my key and we ran inside. That's when I called 999.' Abi's wild stare sought out Minshull and Bennett. 'Is he dead? Did I kill him?'

'No.' At least there was some comfort Minshull could deliver. 'When our officers went down there, the beach was empty. There was no sign of him.'

He watched relief play out across Abi's body, her friend less comforted by the news.

Minshull, however, felt no relief. If the attacker had been knocked unconscious, they would have him now. But he'd escaped. It was conclusive: the man they had in custody wasn't the killer. There were too many similarities with this attack, too much that a wannabe attacker couldn't possibly have known.

'Can you describe the man who attacked you?' Minshull asked, when Abi and Georgie's initial reactions subsided.

'He was older than us,' Abi replied.

'In his forties? Fifties?'

Abi shook her head. 'Thirties, I'd say.'

'Whereabouts in his thirties, would you say?'

'Early thirties? Dark hair, no sign of grey. Taller than me and Georgie. A sort of a beard, patchy in places. He had a red hoodie on with the hood pulled up and was wearing black jeans.'

'Could you see how long his hair was?' Bennett asked.

'It was hard to tell. He was wearing a grey beanie under his hood. But I could see a bit of dark fringe underneath. The hood slipped when I hit him with the rock.' She fell silent again, staring at her stained jacket cuffs.

The blood was something at least. But Alfie Gunnersall wasn't The Beachcomber.

So, who was the man who'd attached Georgie Kelsall? And how would Minshull and the team find him now?

Forty-Two

ELLIS

'We're looking for a white male, dark hair, between five foot ten and six foot two inches tall, age early to mid-thirties. Red hoodie with the hood up over a grey beanie hat, black jeans. No mention of the type of footwear. But he was carrying a large knife, described as having a wooden handle and a blade around eight inches long.'

Minshull looked both beaten down and fired up by the revelations from the two survivors of the Felixstowe Beach attack. The push-pull of this case was keenly felt by everyone, not least Ellis. A sense of helplessness as new developments happened, coupled with a blazing determination to find the killer.

Ellis glanced at Bennett, who had been in as early as Minshull, summoned by Anderson's call. She stared back at Minshull, lips pressed together. He wondered what words she was imprisoning behind that firm line. Knowing Kate Bennett, plenty.

She, like Ellis, Minshull and Evans, had been convinced Alfie Gunnersall was the killer they were looking for. Everything had pointed to him – hadn't it?

Now the investigation was further back than ever. A main suspect with no name, no face and no clue to where he might be found. And another attack for the ravenous jaws of the media to savour. Because they would find out, wouldn't they? They always did.

Ten days since the discovery of the first victim. Two dead, a third alive only thanks to the desperate actions of her friend.

Was The Beachcomber ramping up his campaign? Had he been emboldened by the incessant media coverage of his crimes? And if he was changing locations now, where might he strike next if he wasn't apprehended?

In Felixstowe, too. Ellis felt a chill at the thought. No longer a deserted coastal location frequented only by a select group of visitors, but a hugely popular beach at the heart of a busy town, much loved by tourists and locals alike. If people stayed away from Felixstowe's beaches, the accusations against police for killing the tourist trade by failing to apprehend a murderer would only gain traction.

Ellis stifled a yawn. He hadn't been called in as early as Minshull and Bennett, but still two hours before his shift was due to begin. He felt a little resentment that Bennett had received the call before him, but he understood why: as the only female detective on the team, Bennett was first-call when women or girls were involved in an investigation. It was only right. But it didn't stop the sting of being left out that never quite left Ellis alone.

'Could there be CCTV from the prom, Sarge?' Ellis offered, keen to be at the heart of things now, despite his body protesting the early hour.

'Good point, Drew, thanks. The scene of the attack isn't covered by any cameras, but our attacker may have passed some when he left the beach. Can you contact the council and request the files, please?'

'Yes, Sarge.'

'One of the girls hit him with a rock, so he'll have sustained a head injury. Kate, can you check with hospitals, doctors' surgeries and walk-in clinics, please? See if they've treated anyone for that kind of injury within the last few hours?'

'No problem, Sarge.'

'Appreciate it, thanks.'

'Reckon we'll get any DNA from Abi Quigley's jacket?' Bennett asked.

'It's gone to Forensics, so we have to hope,' Minshull replied. 'Guv, any chance we can get it fast-tracked?'

Anderson shrugged. 'As much of a chance as there ever is.' He had a dark shadow of stubble across his chin, clearly roused from his bed before he could shave. 'I'll see what I can do.'

Ellis stuck up his hand, ignoring the wink Evans sent him for it. 'Sarge?'

'Yes, Drew?'

'The girls said Georgie's attacker was wearing a red hoodie, right?'

Minshull glanced at the list he'd written on the whiteboard. 'Correct.'

'The kids who were with Alistair Avebury said the strange bloke watching them had a red hoodie on, too. Black jeans as well.'

'That's right.'

'I'm just thinking, if the killer is methodical with everything else – the knife blow, the pile of beach pebbles and stuff displayed on the victims, it would follow that he might choose a uniform, too.'

He saw the look that passed between Minshull and Anderson, gratified that his theory had hit home.

'Good call, Drew. Dave, can you ask Tim Brinton to check the statements his Uniform team took at the beaches, please? See if anyone else has mentioned a male wearing a red hoodie and black jeans.'

'No problem, Sarge.'

'Cheers.' Minshull offered his team a weary smile. 'So, forget our former theories. Let's focus on what we have. The bloodstains might provide a lead, the perpetrator's chosen attire, too. But the threat is greater than before. We know this person is willing to kill, multiple times. And being unsuccessful on this occasion is only likely to increase their need to kill again. We have to find them, before they can do that. I know I'm not telling you anything you don't already know, but I must state, as strongly as possible, how vital it is that we get ahead of them. We've been on the back foot for far too long.'

'Sarge.'

'Yes, Sarge.'

'Okay, thanks, everyone. Now, you'll be glad to know the Guv has ordered bacon rolls for us all, to compensate for the criminally early start.'

This was met with a rush of appreciation, a sudden lifting of the tension in the office. A small moment of positivity that might just sustain them through the long morning ahead.

Ellis pushed his chair back to his desk, revelling in the brief buzz around him. Food could do that in this job, especially when it was free.

As he settled back to work, Minshull joined him.

'When's your call with the MoD?' he asked, lowering his voice.

'Nine a.m., Sarge.'

'Okay, good. Can you see if they have a photo of Hal Jones on file, please?'

Ellis frowned. 'Won't his sister have one?'

'She will,' Minshull replied dryly, 'but the longer we can leave it before the senior reporter at the *Suffolk Herald* learns we have a description of The Beachcomber the better.'

Ellis kicked himself for not seeing the blindingly obvious point. 'Right. Sorry.'

'Don't sweat it.' Minshull patted his shoulder. 'We're all a bit fuzzy-headed from the early hour. Keep me updated on that call, yeah?'

A boxful of bacon rolls duly arrived, half an hour later. A grateful mob of detectives descended upon them, hands quickly warmed by steaming, foil-wrapped packages. Coffee arrived, too, much to the delight of everyone in the room.

Anderson joined the breakfast throng, accepting good-natured jibes about the treat with his usual gruffness.

Wheeler nudged Ellis. 'I'm going to buy a lottery ticket tonight.'

'Why's that, Dave?'

'Because a Scot parting with his money has to be lucky.'

'Should've had a sweepstake on it, Les,' Ellis joked. 'You would've cleaned up.'

'Not even a hardened bookie could have put odds on that.'

'Glad to be of service to you all,' Anderson said, shaking his head at the attack on his Caledonian nature. Ellis suspected the DI was glad of it today.

One thing was certain: there would be precious few lighthearted moments ahead for them all.

Nine a.m. took an age to arrive, Ellis clock-watching until it did. The earlier joviality amongst the team had given way to studied quietness in the office. It was necessary, of course. But the muted atmosphere only heightened his nerves.

When the time arrived to make the call, Ellis picked up his notebook and pen and headed for one of the small meeting rooms down the corridor from CID. Minshull blessed him with a nod as he left.

The call was answered on the second ring, a brisk but polite secretary putting him through to his contact.

Ellis had already exchanged several emails with Sergeant George Winchcombe and had built up an idea of the man to whom he now spoke. But the voice on the other end of the line surprised him – sounding much younger than he'd envisioned when picturing the MoD official.

'Good to talk at last,' Sergeant Winchcombe said, his tone brighter than Ellis felt. 'Email is so impersonal, don't you think?'

'It is, sir,' Ellis replied. 'Appreciate you taking the time for this call.'

'Pleasure, DC Ellis. Now, to Private Henry Jones. What was it you wanted to know?'

'We know he was discharged from the army eight years ago, on medical grounds. I was wondering if you could shed any light on the circumstances regarding that?'

'Of course. I have his service record here. Can I ask why you need to know?'

Ellis had been warned the MoD was famously cagey about sharing army personnel files, even to the police. But there was an edge in Winchcombe's question that caught his ear.

'He is a person of interest to us in a murder investigation,' he replied. 'His sister told us he'd been discharged from the army on medical grounds.'

'And it isn't possible to ask him yourself?'

'No, sir. He appears to have gone to ground.'

There was a pause, a shuffling of papers, a bark of a cough.

'I see. Did Private Jones' sister define the medical reason for discharge?'

'She told us he was let go due to mental health issues.'

'Right.' Another pause. 'In that, she is correct. However, the discharge was not a medical one.'

'Oh?'

'Private Jones was dishonourably discharged for attacking a fellow soldier while on operation.'

Ellis looked up from his notes. 'What kind of attack?'

'Fists, boots and attempted strangulation. Pretty frenzied, by all accounts.'

'Was a reason given for the attack?'

Winchcombe sniffed. 'A mental health episode linked to PTSD was mooted as the cause. Looking at the notes it seems this was his chosen line of defence. But a medical examination found him mentally fit to face trial, and the military court ruled that the attack bore the hallmarks of premeditation. During the trial, another soldier in his patrol testified that Jones had spoken openly of attacking the squaddie in question for weeks before the attack. And a knife was found among his personal effects. Like I said, ample evidence that the attack was planned.'

The mention of a knife made Ellis sit up. 'Do you know what type of knife?'

'Not specifically, I'm afraid. But a smaller knife – a paring knife, perhaps? Private Jones denied it was his, but the evidence was damning. He was dishonourably discharged by unanimous decision.'

'Was this passed to police?' Ellis asked.

'Should have been. But Jones accepted a nine-month stint in a secure mental health unit in lieu of a prison sentence, prior to his discharge. It was arranged before he left.'

'Do you know where he served that?'

'I don't, sorry. But I know it was where he went directly after leaving us.'

Had Maggie Jones mentioned any of this to Minshull? Ellis would lay odds that she hadn't. But was that because she didn't want the details known or because her brother hadn't informed her of the full facts?

'Any chance you could send us a copy of the discharge records? And notes from the proceedings, too?' he asked, aware he might be pushing his luck with the latter.

'Discharge records are not a problem. Some of the information will be redacted of course. As for the rest, it isn't usual protocol to release them, even to the police. But I'll see what I can do.'

'If you could, please. It's vital we know as much as we can.'

'Has he attacked someone?' The question was a surprise.

'We're investigating two murders and an attempted murder,' Ellis replied, heart thudding. 'All involving a large knife. We have reason to believe they're linked and that the person or persons responsible may be planning to strike again.'

'The beach murders, eh?'

'I really can't—'

'I watch the news, DC Ellis. Have nieces and nephews now, living near Hollesley. I hope for your sake Jones isn't involved. The way he left that soldier, the total lack of moral and physical restraint – it doesn't bear thinking about what could happen if he were provoked again.'

'In your opinion, sir, is Hal Jones capable of murder?'

'Indubitably,' Winchcombe replied. 'If Jones is involved, I would advise extreme caution if you approach him. His stay at the mental health unit might have calmed him. He could be a completely altered individual, but in my experience people rarely change. In my opinion the army is well shot of him.'

'Thanks for the warning,' Ellis said, battling to keep excitement from his reply. It felt like a huge breakthrough, despite any suggestion that Hal Jones might be the beach killer still being conjecture. 'One more thing, sir: do you have a photo of him?'

'There's one on file. I'll send it over. Bear in mind it will be several years out of date now.'

It didn't matter, Ellis thought. Anything was better than where they were at present. 'Thank you so much, sir. This is really helpful.'

'You're welcome, Detective. I hope you find him. But be careful when you do. Dishonourable discharges are not issued lightly. If we don't want him in the army, you certainly don't want him on your patch.'

Forty-Three

CORA

Despite her protestations of being well enough to work, Cora found herself back on official leave for a week.

'I insist,' Tris Noakes said, ending Cora's appeal with the nicest of intentions. 'You need time to rest and recover. Ollie and Alannah are happy to cover your schedule until you return.'

'But they're snowed under, too,' she countered. 'I can't ask them to do that.'

'It's done. Ollie said I should fight you if you tried to refuse.'

Cora had to smile at that. Her colleague, Dr Ollie Rowan, in contention with Tris for the title of Nicest Bloke in the Educational Psychology Team, was the least likely to fight anyone, let alone encourage his colleagues into battle. Their care for Cora meant a great deal — yet another reason why she loved working alongside them.

Not being able to go to work was frustrating, though. Being at home gave her far too much time to think. With everything that had happened since she and Minshull had found Ronald Venn's body on the beach, together with the host of unanswered questions regarding Operation Nautilus, too many conflicting thoughts already beset her mind.

She'd heard the voice from the crime scene when Alfie Gunnersall had attacked her. But had the voice come from him as he'd been grabbing her or from the cordoned-off crime scene, a few feet away? The question had bothered her last night and had woken her this morning, before the call from Tris that laid her week wide open for speculation.

Maybe a walk would do her good. It had rained first thing but now the slightest hint of brighter light edged the grey clouds over the sea. Despite the beach being minutes away by foot, she hadn't ventured down there since she and Minshull had found the body on Shingle Street Beach. And while Felixstowe's South Beach was a world away from the two beaches where bodies had been discovered, the link between the sandy shingle and the sea was impossible to ignore.

She missed the sea, even though she had a wonderful view of it from her apartment in the old Bartlet Hospital, up on Undercliff Road East. Walking along the shore represented peace for Cora, the rhythm of the waves and sound of the ocean a white noise that calmed her mind and obliterated all other voices competing for her attention.

If it rested her mind, it counted as rest, surely?

Decision made, she changed out of her work clothes into jeans and a sweatshirt, put her book and a bottle of water into her bag and left her apartment. She'd take a walk and then head for her favourite coffee hut on the promenade, sitting at its outside tables to enjoy a drink and a read. Her earlier annoyance at being denied her planned workday dissipated as she considered the morning ahead, invigorated by the blast of sea air that met her as she walked down to the promenade.

She should make more time for herself, she decided, surprisingly relieved not to be called upon by either her day job or her police consultant work with Minshull and the CID team. She'd worked at full pelt for as long as she could remember, her body only now reminding her of the physical toll such demanding hours took, not to mention the emotional cost of pushing the boundaries of her ability. Somewhere, at some point, something had to give.

Until now, her semi-regular runs with Minshull had offered her a break. But their off-duty exercise would be intrinsically linked with a body on the beach, at least for the foreseeable future. Maybe she should suggest to Minshull that they head inland for a change, exploring Suffolk's impossibly lovely charms away from the sea. It might help Minshull, too.

She was worried about him; about how he appeared to be struggling to deal with the particulars of the case. At least with Gunnersall in custody awaiting charge, Minshull could rest easy in the knowledge that the killer was no longer on the streets.

The killer.

Cora braced as a shiver passed over her.

Alfie Gunnersall wanted to attack her. Had he planned to kill her, like he'd killed Ronald Venn and Alistair Avebury? How close did she get to becoming his third victim?

I found you... You're mine.

No. I'm not thinking about that today.

Pushing the memory of the voice away, Cora kept walking.

The road fronting the sea seemed busier with cars this morning. Perhaps it was because she was visiting at a time when she'd normally be at work. But as she neared the section of beach beyond the pier, something felt wrong.

The air was stilted, an odd tension around the space. Sounds from the ground were muted, the usual chatter from litter blowing along the promenade strangely absent. Despite the brightening sky and the salt-sweet billow of breeze from the sea, a deep chill settled in Cora's bones; a shroud of emotional shadows covering everything where none could be seen.

Something had happened here – *was happening* here.

The temptation rose to turn tail and race back home, but intrigue called to her. She would only wonder what it might have been if she left now. So she pressed on, following the invisible pull that drew her closer.

And then she saw it, opposite Sea View Gardens: a police Support Unit van. And the unmistakable flap of blue and white police tape, cutting the promenade off from the beach. Was Minshull there, too?

There was no sign of the CID pool cars, but she had long since learned that didn't mean the team weren't present. As she approached the cordon, a uniformed officer raised his hand.

'Morning, Dr Lael.'

'Sergeant Brinton, how are you?'

'Oh you know,' Tim Brinton replied, his ever-present smile as bright as ever. 'Keeping busy. And yourself?'

'Officially off work for a week,' Cora replied, the weight of it registering again.

'Ah. Sorry to hear about – you know.'

Of course he would know. News like that spread around Police HQ quickly. It was oddly comforting, despite Cora's natural reticence for being in the spotlight. Her police family – a term she'd heard her CID colleagues use regularly – now felt as real as her own. They looked out for one another, took each blow against one of their number as an insult to all. To belong to such a team meant more to Cora than she would ever be able to express.

'Thanks. I'm okay, just a few bruises.'

'We all know about those. Mark of a true copper, that.'

'Glad to bear them, then. What's happening?' Cora asked, the privilege to do so and expect an answer another part of the belonging.

'Another attack. Last night.'

'Another one? But I thought...'

'We all did,' Brinton conceded. 'Thankfully, the victims got away. They're shaken, but they're alive.'

Cora felt the light around her dim. 'Same MO?'

'Looks like it, although the change in location is new. Guy had a knife. Tried to drag the victim across the beach. Teenage girl this time. Her friend heard her screams and came running. She hit the attacker with a rock, which has gone off for testing, along with the jacket she was wearing when she clobbered him. SOCOs reckon there's a decent blood sample to be got from them both.'

'Were the girls able to give a description of their attacker?' Cora asked.

'White male in his thirties. Red hoodie with the hood up, black trousers, beanie hat. That's all we know for now, but we're sweeping the beach for anything else we can find.'

'Thanks for letting me know. If you need me...'

'I'll make sure the message gets passed on.' A shout from the beach made Brinton raise his hand, a hurried smile sent back to Cora as he started to leave. 'Good to see you, Doc. You take care, yeah?'

Numb, Cora watched Brinton rejoin his team.

The revelation made the ground beneath her feet uncertain, the place she knew so well suddenly alien, cold. Why Felixstowe Beach? It didn't fit the profile of the previous two attacks. Could it be a copycat, out to grab attention from the journalists now buzzing around the case? Or had the killer altered their MO, shifting gears as the need to kill grew stronger?

She turned away from the beach, all plans for her morning gone. She couldn't stay here, neither could she find somewhere to rest and take the news in. Home was the only option: the only place she felt safe to consider it all.

Cora was aware of little else as she retraced her steps. The thud of her quickened heartbeat obliterated all other thoughts, the need to be in her own space urging her on. She could feel the questions she would inevitably wrestle being restrained at the edges of her consciousness like a riotous crowd pushed back behind a fragile cordon.

It was as if she was back at Shingle Street Beach, kicking and screaming as Alfie Gunnersall dragged her body, shot through with panic, unable to escape.

It was shock, the rational part of her mind knew, a delayed response to the attack that had, until now, lain dormant. But it was more than just reaction: it was confirmation that the relief she'd felt at Gunnersall's supposed identity as The Beachcomber was now meaningless. The killer was still at large, the memory of their voice she'd hoped to dismiss once and for all now given licence to remain in her mind.

Almost level with her apartment building as she climbed the hill, the sound of her phone cut through the noise of the rest.

> MUM calling

'Hi Mum, can I call you back? I have to—'

'It's Charlie.' Sheila Lael's sob stopped Cora in her tracks. 'He's really bad, Cor. I need you here, right now.'

Grabbing her keys from her bag, Cora ran for her car.

Forty-Four

THE COLLECTOR

The glass shatters where it hits the wall.

Anger rages in me, blocking my ears with a high-pitched wail that obliterates every other sound. The buzzing is back, but this time I only feel its reverberation in my head, the sound lost behind the scream.

I can't think straight. I don't even remember throwing the glass, the only proof I did the shards of it where the floor meets the wall and the dark stain of wine running down the cracked plaster from the point of impact.

I should have seen it through. Taken both of them, if I could.

Why did I run?

I hate my stupid self for failing *again*.

But it wasn't in my plan for them to fight back. And outside of the plan, I can't operate. I had nothing to combat it. Even my knife was useless. Why am I getting worse, not better, at this?

A woman was meant to solve the problem.

But two of them made it worse.

I didn't see the other one. I was too focused on the blonde. My head still hurts where the redhead hit me. I should have picked up that rock before I ran, but I was dazed from the blow and the fall. Now my blood is on the beach when it should only ever have been hers there. It's all so messy and not how a skilled collector operates.

I wanted a clean acquisition. A perfect pick.

Now the way forward is muddied again. Like it was at the beginning, when I left.

You think you know what you want. You fall into it and you're comfortable. You think you'll stay there forever. And then you lose the way, lose sight of the plan. The world crowds in, making demands, making your ears ring, until the only solution is escape.

Collecting makes it better. Ordered. Clean. Make a plan, execute the plan, enjoy the calm that follows.

There's no calm now.

There won't be until I can succeed.

One clean, simple collection will make all of the other stuff go away. Something more personal, more of a sacrifice.

I failed this time.

I won't fail again.

Forty-Five

CORA

Charlie Lael lay motionless on the old green sofa in Sheila Lael's living room, his skin blanched by the sunlight from the bay window. Dark purple shadows circled his eyes and hollowed his cheeks, curls of unruly beard clinging to his jaw like shipwreck survivors. He was a ghost of the brother Cora knew: little more than a shell.

His dark blue T-shirt was stained with sweat, no sign of the red hoodie he'd seemed to live in since his return. A salt tide edged his black jeans, a sight that reminded Cora of their father, Bill, who would often return home from a day's walking with sea-soaked hems on his trousers. Is that where Charlie had been, following in his late father's footsteps?

A grey beanie-style hat covered his hair, flecks of sand visible between the peaks and troughs of the rib knit. The side nearest the light bore a dark red-brown stain: dried now, flaking a little at the edges.

'He won't tell me where he was last night,' Sheila whispered, gripping Cora's arm as they approached. 'Came home an hour ago in a right old state. I think he's hurt his head, but he won't let me look.'

'Mum, stop fussing. I'm fine.' Charlie Lael's words were flat and slurred, as if someone were speaking through him. Was he drunk? Under the influence of something?

As Cora approached, the physical force she'd experienced in his room returned: a shove to her core, a warning sign. She braced against it, as swirls of her brother's thought-voice rose up before her like an angry tide.

I'm not hiding…
I don't need them…

The voices had an edge to them this time, weakened a little but desperate now, skeletal fingers clawing at anything that approached her brother. Fear and terror frayed the edges of every frantic repeat, swelling as Cora forced her way through.

'Did you hit your head?' she asked, her voice sounding far away behind the wall of noise and hurt.

'Leave me alone…'

'Charlie, I need to know what happened. Do we need to get you to hospital?'

'No-oo-oo…'

As she reached the edge of the sofa, a strong waft of stale alcohol met her.

'Were you drinking?'

'Go away.'

'I'm not going away until you tell me what happened.'

'I don't *know*…' The last word was a wail, a cry that summoned the thought-voices like an enchanter casting storms on the sea. 'Let me sleep. I just want to sleep…'

'Close your eyes, sweetheart,' Sheila rushed, her hand resting on Cora's shoulder, anxiety painting her words. 'Me and Cor will make you a nice cuppa.'

Cora let herself be guided away, the onslaught of noise ebbing as they left the room. Her mind bruised from the experience, with her own physical injuries smarting as she moved, she emerged into the hall. Sheila's chattering thoughts echoed around her as Cora made for the kitchen.

What's wrong with him?
It's my fault, I know it is.
I don't recognise my boy…

'He's been like it since he got in,' Sheila whispered as she fussed around the kitchen. 'Didn't want to say where he'd been, whining like a kid, pale as death. I think he might have taken something...'

'He's been drinking,' Cora replied, wanting to comfort her mum while battling questions of her own. Charlie had been drunk before, but she'd never seen him like this. Was another substance involved?

'But if it's drugs...'

'We don't know that, Mum.'

'But what if that's what's caused all this trouble? He always said he was happy in Australia and I believed him, but what if he has a problem he didn't want us to know about? What if Bethan chucked him out because of it? And she didn't tell you or I because she was so disgusted by it? She doesn't want that rubbish around when she has a baby. She doesn't need a druggie for a partner...'

She was flapping now, her fears dragging her away to the direst eventualities. Cora caught Sheila's arm and drew her into a hug.

'Mum – *Mum* – just slow down, okay? Take a breath.'

She mimicked a slow inhale until Sheila joined suit, leading her mother in a studied breath exercise usually reserved for her young charges at work. Slowly, Sheila's breathing calmed, her eyes filling with tears as her panic subsided.

'I'm scared,' she breathed.

'I know, Mum. But he needs to work stuff out in his own time. He might need help...'

'Which you could do, right? I mean, that's your thing...'

'It isn't the same. And it would be unethical for me to do that. I'm too close.' Seeing her mum's crestfallen expression, Cora added, 'But I know people who could. We just need to get him to a place where he'll accept help.'

The crescendo of steam and the click of the kettle called Sheila's attention back to tea-making. Cora watched, trying to process all she'd seen. Charlie had struggled before but he'd never been in a state like this. Whatever Sheila's fears for the reason he and his fiancée had argued, Cora was certain Bethan would have told her about a drug issue when they'd spoken. She'd been candid enough about everything else. She cared about Charlie, even if she couldn't live with him right now.

What was different with her brother this time?

And why did Cora feel such resistance to her presence there?

The blood on his hat was worrying. It had dried, so it must have happened some time ago. But what had caused it?

She hit the attacker with a rock... there's a decent blood sample...

Tim Brinton's words made a sudden, unwelcome intrusion into her mind.

No. It couldn't be that.

She refused to believe Charlie could be responsible for the murders and whatever had happened on Felixstowe Beach last night.

But the blood...

And the voices...

She helped Sheila with the tea and followed her back to the living room, the crush of emotion and barrage of thought-voices hitting her the moment she crossed the threshold. Charlie hadn't moved, his eyes still shut tight. Sheila placed the mugs she was carrying on the coffee table and knelt by her son's side, reaching out to rest her hand on his arm.

'Oh sweetheart, you're freezing!' She glanced up at Cora. 'He's so cold.'

'Is his hoodie around?' Cora asked.

'It's probably up in his room. Fetch it for me, would you, love?'

Relieved to be out of the living room, Cora headed upstairs.

The same whispers of Charlie's voice lay on everything in his bedroom like an invisible sheen of dust, quieter now without her brother's presence. The bed had been made but Cora remembered Charlie's hastily stashed notebook when she'd entered the room before. Might it be there now?

She needed answers, faster than her brother was ever likely to surrender them. While he was indisposed downstairs, she could search his room without fear of being discovered. It was an invasion of privacy, but she already knew so much of his hidden life from the echoes of his thoughts all around. Really, what was the difference between listening to them and reading his words?

Pulling back the duvet, she found nothing but empty sheets. The pillows revealed no notebook hidden beneath them. Nothing in any of the three drawers in the unit opposite Charlie's bed; no sign in the bedside cupboard, either. The wardrobe remained empty, Charlie never a fan of hanging up clothes from his earliest days, where a pile on the floor or a bundle stuffed into a bag would suffice…

His bag.

He'd arrived home with only his large green rucksack, the kind he'd used during the years where he travelled around the world. It was leaning against the wall in the far corner of the room, the flap on top unclipped. It was the only place that remained where the notebook might be, save for the pocket of his red hoodie which didn't appear to be in the room at all.

Cora moved to the rucksack, one ear trained on the sounds from the landing beyond the door, in case either Sheila or Charlie came upstairs. Her fingers found the frayed nylon strip around the edge of the flap. She lifted it up and…

I FOUND YOU.

YOU'RE MINE!

The force of the voice sent her backwards, grasping the edge of the bed to prevent herself falling. Breathing hard against the shock of pain the sound caused, she forced herself to return to the rucksack, reaching inside to locate the source of the thought-voice.

The voice from the beach.

The voice she'd done everything to get away from.

Not peripheral, as it had been on Shingle Street Beach when Gunnersall attacked.

Not controlled, as it had been in the sterile surroundings of Dr Amara's lab.

But angry. Present. Shockingly close.

Her hand closed around cool plastic, weight registering in her palm and wrist as she pulled the object out.

A clear plastic bag, bulging with pebbles and sand.

And attached to it, repeating with vigorous menace, the voice she'd heard from the pile of beach finds left on the bodies of Ronald Venn and Alistair Avebury.

Not the panicked mutterings of her younger brother, still resonating around the space. Not a cry for help.

But the possessive, malicious thought-voice of a killer.

Forty-Six

CORA

'For someone on paid leave, you're awfully keen to keep working...' Tris Noakes' cheery greeting on speakerphone cut through Cora's panic as she drove out of St Just.

'No, Tris, listen. I heard the voice. The thought-voice from the beach.'

'Where?'

'In Charlie's rucksack.' A sob stole her words, the reality only just setting in.

'Your brother? But how...?'

'There was a bag filled with pebbles and sand inside his rucksack. The same kind of collected beach finds that we found on Ronald Venn and Alistair Avebury. And it looks like Charlie has a head wound – there's dried blood on his hat that he refuses to take off. The attacker on Felixstowe Beach was hit on the head with a rock by a young woman trying to save one of his victims—'

'Okay, slow down. An attacker on Felixstowe Beach?'

Cora forced breath into her lungs, willing her thoughts into some kind of order as she fixed her focus on the road. 'A teenage girl was attacked last night, on Felixstowe Beach. The assailant had a knife. But her friend hit his head with a rock so they could escape. I saw the police there this morning. They're treating it as another attack by The Beachcomber because of the similarities to the first two murders. And Charlie has a wound to his head that he refused to let Mum or I look at. Tris, I think Charlie could be the killer.'

'Cora, no...'

'I don't know what to do. I was concerned before, but then Alfie Gunnersall attacked me and Rob was so sure he was the beach killer. So I figured I'd got it wrong. But the attack happened last night, and Gunnersall is still in custody at Police HQ for the attack on me. He can't be the person who killed Ronald Venn and Alistair Avebury.'

'Have you told Rob?'

'Not yet. What do I do, Tris? If I tell him what I know, Charlie could be arrested for murder. And if I'm wrong? I don't know what that could do to my mum. Or to him. But if I don't say anything and he kills again...'

She could hear the click of her colleague's pen down the line, a habit he had whenever he was thinking. She'd hesitated to even call him, but she needed advice and, of all the people in her life, Tris was the one most likely to think of a way through the issue.

She'd faked a work call as an excuse to leave Sheila's house. While Charlie slept she'd hugged her mum and told her to keep her son as warm and calm as possible, promising to return soon. Had Sheila bought the story that Cora was being summoned back into work on an emergency call? She couldn't say.

'Okay, back up for a moment. Is there any other way that bag of pebbles could have ended up in Charlie's rucksack? Could he have found it on the beach? Might one of his mystery friends have given it to him for safekeeping?'

'Maybe...'

'I know it seems like there's only one explanation, but it might be a case of coincidence and really crap timing. Is there anything in Charlie's past behaviour that could indicate potential for violence?'

The counterpoint slammed the brakes on Cora's racing mind, sending her reeling for a moment as she tried to consider a different outcome to the one that had seemed so obvious a moment ago.

Charlie had his demons from the past, but had he ever exorcised them with violence? There had been that one time, when he'd come home injured, his drunken attack on a friend described as being *like an animal*. He'd been sixteen, then. A one-off in teenage years remarkably free of such fights. Could that be different now he was an adult, the place he found himself in mentally far bleaker than it had been before?

It had been years since Cora had spent any real time with her brother. How well did she know the man he had become?

So much had changed for him lately: the row that led to him fleeing back home; the notebook he guarded, covered with obsessive, tiny handwriting; his secretive nature and unbound fury when it was challenged. All of these things could be indicators of a seismic mind-shift, one where violence might present itself as a justifiable response. If he were experiencing some kind of breakdown, could violence be his response?

But wielding a knife, piling beach detritus on recently murdered victims, attacking young girls on Felixstowe Beach – was Charlie really capable of that, even when circumstances were playing with his mind?

'I don't know,' she replied, the truth stark as it hit home.

'Talk to Rob.'

'I can't. What if he drags Charlie in and accuses him of it all?'

'That's a risk you have to take. It may be as simple as a blood test to see if his blood type matches that found on the rock the victim hit her assailant with. Eliminating him from their inquiries would mean peace of mind for both of you.'

'But Charlie would know I suspected him of murder. If I'm wrong and he's in the clear, he's always going to know his sister thought him a killer.'

'If he has an alibi for last night, it won't be a problem.'

'And if he doesn't?'

A sigh met her question. She was going round in circles, she knew. Tris was right: the only way to know for sure wasn't to hide away, hoping her fears weren't justified. It was to face them at the first instance – and trust Rob and the CID team to find the right person.

'What if he knows someone who is close to the real killer? That beach stuff might have been a gift, or something Charlie found when he was birdwatching. It could be evidence. What if something he knows could lead Rob and the team to the murderer? Charlie could be the link that saves lives. Have you considered that?'

Maybe that was the answer that solved it all: that Charlie was the link rather than the person of interest. Helping police bring the killer to justice might bring Charlie the peace he so clearly needed.

'I hadn't thought of that.'

'I think you should. Ask yourself this: if you say nothing and someone else dies, how will you feel then? Knowing you could have prevented it?'

It was enough to make up her mind.

At a crossroads, where one way led home and one to Ipswich, she opted for the latter.

She had to talk to Minshull. Immediately.

Forty-Seven

CORA

The CID office was quiet when Cora arrived, missing the usual bustle and chatter that met her. Minshull's desk was unoccupied, Wheeler's too. Bennett's chair was pushed back as if she'd just left, the neighbouring chair where Ellis sat pushed carefully under the desk. Their thought-voices remained, as they always did, but the absence of their owners felt strange. Only Evans was bodily present, working at his typically messy desk, the usual grumbles from the overflowing wire bin beneath it strangely comforting.

'Afternoon, Les. Where is everyone?'

'Doing more interesting crap than me.' Evans flashed a brief smile that might have been read as a grimace if Cora hadn't known better. 'It was ever thus. You looking for Minsh?'

'I am.'

'He's with Joel, down in the interview suite. Got that bastard Alfie Gunnersall in for a final interview before charging.'

Cora stiffened at the name. 'They're pressing charges?'

'Of course.' Evans' smirk softened. 'He doesn't attack one of ours and get away with it.'

His remark meant more than Cora would ever let on. She and Evans had endured quite the journey to reach where they were now, from his initial scepticism and mistrust to a point where his life had depended upon her ability. 'Good to know.'

'You're welcome to wait, but I reckon they'll be down there for a good while yet. Gunnersall's playing silly beggars with them. Winding down the clock for as long as he can, the slimy git.'

It wasn't what Cora wanted to hear, but what choice did she have? If she left now, she would lose her nerve. Waiting was the only option. Taking the seat next to Minshull's desk, she pulled out her phone, the need to keep busy overwhelming.

A message from her mother was waiting on the screen, typed in Sheila's trademark ALL CAPS style:

> CHARLIE'S NOT IN HIS ROOM. HIS
> RUCKSACK'S GONE.
> I'M WORRIED. CAN YOU FIND HIM? MUM XX

Fear rising, Cora found Charlie's number and called it.

> User busy. Call back?

She cancelled the call, her fingers shaky as she fired off a text. If he didn't want to talk, perhaps a message would be less threatening? She'd found it to be effective before, Charlie far preferring written communication to phone conversations.

> Are you okay?
> Mum's worried. You don't have to call, just message me ASAP.
> C xx

Another delay. Another frustration, when Cora's fears surrounding the bag of pebbles with its persistent thought-voice were already at fever pitch. No sign of Minshull, no indication of how long it may be before he returned to CID. And now Charlie missing, when he'd promised Sheila he'd stay at home…

No, wait...

She forced her speeding thoughts to halt.

Following her fears would solve nothing. She needed perspective, a changed view to allow her to think proactively. Summoning all of her mental strength, Cora forced positives into the panic, as Tris had led her to do during her drive here.

Charlie might just have needed some space. Sheila's concern could often stray into cossetting: smothering and claustrophobic as her own fear blinded her to anyone else's needs. Maybe he'd gone for a walk to clear his head, his rucksack his regular companion. It didn't mean he'd left the house permanently. Minshull would return as soon as he could and Cora was confident he'd listen to her concerns. As for the beach finds...

The sharp trill of Cora's mobile rescued her thoughts from the shadowy path they were bound for. Could Charlie have replied so soon? Or might it be Minshull, on his way back to the CID office, unaware Cora was waiting there?

> Gone where I can think. With a friend. I'll be okay. Don't look for me.

Attached was a photograph – one that stopped Cora in her tracks.

Shadowy and taken in low light, of two pale faces. A stranger who looked to be in his thirties, his arm around Charlie. Both men wore red hoodies, their hair hanging just shy of their shoulders, grey beanie hats, straggly beards and haunted expressions almost identical.

White male in his thirties, Tim Brinton had told her at the beach in Felixstowe. *Red hoodie with the hood up, grey beanie, black jeans...*

Cora stared at the image and the message below it, the words and tone unlike her brother. *Gone where I can think?* Did that mean the beach? Or the bird hides he used to visit with their father? And was the *friend* the same person he'd told Sheila he was spending time with?

The last line was what stuck in Cora's gut. *Don't look for me…* Did that mean he was even where he said he was? Or that he was planning to leave for good?

'Problem, Doc?'

When Cora raised her head, Evans was watching her from across the office.

'I don't know, Les. I—'

A sudden commotion out in the corridor cut off Cora's words. She and Evans turned to see the door to the CID office crash open, a short, smartly dressed woman marching in, a uniformed officer scurrying in her wake. Evans struggled to his feet. Cora could only look on.

'…and if they think they can omit me from my own investigation – DS Minshull? DI Anderson?'

'They're not here, Ma'am,' Evans offered, earning him a withering look from the DCI.

'I can see that, DC Evans. Where are they?'

'DI Anderson and DS Minshull are conducting a final interview with Alfie Gunnersall, Ma'am. DC Ellis and DC Bennett are taking statements from another eyewitness who's come forward following the Slaughden Beach attack.'

'And DC Wheeler?'

'He's out on inquiries.'

The female officer turned to Cora. 'And you are?'

'This is Dr Cora Lael, Ma'am,' Evans rushed, before Cora could reply. 'She's our consultant expert, working on the investigation. Dr Lael, this is Detective Chief Inspector Fran Stephens, who's recently joined us from—'

'Lael? You were attacked by Gunnersall.'

Cora stood. 'Yes, I was.'

'You can't be here.'

'Ma'am, Dr Lael is—'

'I don't care why Dr Lael is here,' DCI Stephens retorted. 'She is a witness to an attack from a suspect not yet charged. She can't be here.'

Tension fizzed from Stephens, an armour-like shield of fury surrounding her words. Cora felt it, sharp as metal.

'With respect, DCI Stephens, I'm working on this investigation.'

'On whose authority?'

'DI Anderson requested my assistance, as he has for the last three years...'

'On what grounds? What kind of consultant are you?'

'Psychological indicators. Behavioural patterns—'

'We have in-house psychologists. Why would we require outside assistance?'

'Ma'am, Cora – Dr Lael – is part of our team.'

'Not when she is a witness to an attack by a chief suspect in a multiple murder investigation. I would have expected a better understanding of police procedure from you of all people, DC Evans.'

'Ma'am.' Evans slunk back, his face reddening as he bowed his head.

'DCI Stephens, if I could just explain,' Cora offered, despite nothing within her wishing to explain anything. She had been employed by South Suffolk Police for longer than the new DCI had been in her post. She'd more than proved her worth to the CID team and was widely acknowledged as a key member of the unit. Stephens could think what she liked: the time when Cora might have doubted the legitimacy of her appointment was long gone. She was meant to be here.

If the rest of the team were here, they would attest to that fact.

But Evans was her only ally in this conspicuously empty office, his own retaliation swiftly silenced by Stephens, who now bore down on her.

'I don't require explanations. I want you gone.'

'But—'

'Let me put this in words you'll understand, Doctor: *you can't be here.*'

'I'm waiting for DS Minshull.'

'*I* am in charge of this team. You are a witness to an attack and therefore incapable of contributing anything extra to this investigation. Please leave.'

'I'm here on the authority of DI Anderson.'

'And *he* is under *my* authority. Out. Now.'

'But I have information pertaining to the case!' It left her in a hot rush, impossible to catch before it had been said. What was she doing? If Charlie was The Beachcomber, was she really ready to sell him out without knowing the facts? Or what if he had encountered the killer and was with them now, completely unaware of the danger?

Either way, why should DCI Stephens have this information?

'Which is precisely why you can't be here. Hand me your pass.'

'No!'

'Excuse me?'

'DI Anderson appointed me. I can only surrender my pass to him.'

Stephens rounded on Cora, every word a threat, every gesture a promise of worse. 'I don't care what you have given this department in the past, or who you assume has authority over your retention within the team. I am the superior officer here. And your involvement with this and future investigations is under my discretion and jurisdiction.' Her palm was thrust at Cora, manicured nails like talons extended like a cordon. 'Your pass. Now.'

Evans could only offer a helpless shrug over the DCI's shoulder as Cora removed her lanyard, depositing it in Stephens' hand.

I will not be refused, the DCI's thought-voice hissed, as her fingers caught Cora's.

Fear edged the words, defiance layered deep around it, the bedrock beneath secretly unstable, a sense of history cracked through its foundations.

She's been hurt before, Cora realised, the truth of DCI Stephens' power hidden from all but her.

But what use was the insight, when the DCI was clearly intent on ejecting her?

Charlie was missing, photographed with a man who could have been his brother. Dressed the same. Staring unsmiling straight into the lens. Either one could be The Beachcomber. And they were together – somewhere dark and forbidding, somewhere unknown to Cora. Minshull needed to know – but the DCI was already walking her out of the office.

At the door, Cora turned to Evans, who was staring blankly at her from behind his desk.

'Tell Rob I need to talk to him,' she managed. 'It's important. Please!'

She barely caught sight of Evans' hurried nod before she was bustled out into the corridor.

Forty-Eight

THE COLLECTOR

I've found a new place for The Collection. One where I won't have to hide it.

The net shack has been at the edge of the beach for years but nobody knows who owns it. I found it a week ago. The padlock on the front was so rusted it came away as soon as I pulled it. I bought a new one and put it on, to keep it safe. Now I'm finally ready to move The Collection in.

Today is the day my plan becomes reality.

It's dark inside, the gaps between the vertical planks allowing just the right amount of light to be able to see. The old nets I found here when I took it over are now folded into neat piles around the wooden walls, a space in the middle of the sand-covered concrete floor the perfect size for my needs.

I told my friend about this place and he agreed to come with me when I needed to use it. I said my collection had to live somewhere out of the elements, where it could remain undisturbed. Not like the beach. I won't make that mistake again.

Now, it's time.

The final piece of The Collection, collected with his help.

I called him this morning. Told him it was urgent. He arrived at our meeting point and I paid the taxi to drop us off here. Birders, we told the driver. *Crazy people*, he muttered as he left us in the car park.

It's colder than I expected it to be. But the thought of what lies ahead makes me warm inside.

'Let's take a selfie,' he says to me.

'In here? It's too dark.'

'Exactly,' he says, clearly loving the game. 'Two shady blokes in a shady place. It'll be a laugh.'

He poses beside me. We take two photos – my hand shakes too much with the first. It wasn't what I planned, but it will work.

I'm not used to sharing this with anyone. It's only natural to find it alien. I think about what my sister would do in this situation, force her smile onto my lips, and keep it there while my friend fusses with his mobile. He's so set on getting his photo, as obsessed as I am with The Collection. That's a good thing, I think. Kindred spirits, working for a common good. I'll support him in this like I expect him to support me in what lies ahead. It will play in my favour when I reveal the full extent of the plan to him.

When the selfie is done, he sends a copy to my phone. Then he goes back to picking through the old fishing floats we found piled under a tarpaulin at the back of the shed.

I find her number.

Copy the message I planned in my notes app late last night, when I knew the final acquisition was near, every word fighting for its place in line.

Add the photo as a final flourish.

And press *SEND*.

Forty-Nine

CORA

How *dare* she?

Cora stormed away from the CID office, fury and hurt powering her steps. After everything she'd endured during this investigation, how could she be so roundly dismissed?

She hadn't expected much contact with Fran Stephens following the new DCI's appointment. The little interaction she'd had with Stephens' predecessor had been mostly via Anderson's furious recounting of his fights on her behalf. But Stephens' attitude shocked her. How dare she discount Cora's contribution to South Suffolk Police, when the DCI had so little knowledge or experience of the work she'd done?

That Stephens had ejected her when both Minshull and Anderson were otherwise occupied spoke volumes. This was the moment they needed Cora most. What would they think when they discovered she'd been sent away?

She could appeal – and would – but time was not on her side. And her own fears surrounding Charlie were too strong to be dismissed. Where the hell was he? And what if the beach litter she'd discovered among his belongings was concrete evidence that he'd killed and planned to kill again?

She could call Minshull, knowing it would go straight to voicemail. But how long would it be before he was able to listen to her message? Would it be too late to prevent another death?

Charlie was missing. His belongings bore the emotional echo of the bodies discovered on the beaches. And the notebook –

the endless lists in handwriting so angry and spider-like that she barely recognised it. What if the notes were plans, either of his own or on behalf of someone else?

Was the killer planning to add more bodies to their collection?

Or might he be working with someone else?

The *friend*. The shadowy figure who dominated Charlie's ramblings, holder of the *terrible secret* he refused to share. An accomplice?

Two faces in the photo. One of them could have taken two lives and tried to take a third. Either way, the evidence could be the breakthrough Minshull and the team needed – if only Cora could have got it to them.

But was Charlie the one the police were searching for?

Or might Charlie be protecting the real killer?

Don't look for me…

Why say that if he had nothing to hide?

'Dr Lael!'

Cora kept her head down, ducking around the gaggle of journalists as she made her way out of Police HQ. Why her name had been called was a mystery – had someone made the connection between her and South Suffolk CID?

After three years working with Minshull and the team, it was a minor miracle that a link hadn't been uncovered before. But the possibility of it now unsettled her.

'Dr Lael!'

The voice was following her, away from the others. She reached the junction where the path to Police HQ met the street beyond, hoping to dissuade whoever was trying to get her attention, but the stab of heels remained as insistent behind her.

'What do you want?' she barked, turning to find a woman in her wake. Maggie Jones. She'd seen the journalist's photo on the cover of the *Suffolk Herald*, the weekly paper Cora's mother read at home.

'My brother is in trouble. And so is yours.'

'Sorry?'

'My brother Hal says he knows Charlie.'

Cora froze. 'How does he know him?'

'They met on Shingle Street Beach, a few weeks ago. They've spent a lot of time together.'

Was that where Charlie had been? Was Hal the other man in the photo Charlie had sent? 'How do you know this?'

Maggie put a hand to her lower back, her words made staccato by the shortness of her breath. 'He told me. He's been talking about Charlie a lot.'

'It might not be my brother. Charlie isn't an uncommon name.' Even as she said it, Cora knew she was grasping at straws. The evidence was there, wasn't it? The two men in the photo Charlie had sent, the possibility that Maggie might have seen the same picture.

'Do you know where Charlie is, Cora?' Maggie followed, step for step, as Cora powered on, walking out of Police HQ's site.

'Please, leave me alone.'

'Right now, I mean? Do you know exactly where Charlie is, right at this moment?'

'I wouldn't tell you if I did.'

'Because my brother just sent me a message to say they're together in an old fisherman's shed on the dunes at the edge of Slaughden Beach.'

Gone where I can think. With a friend. I'll be okay. Don't look for me.

Cora dismissed the words of Charlie's text from her mind. 'I shouldn't even be speaking to you.'

'I'm not lying – look! *Look*, Dr Lael!' She shoved her phone in front of Cora, causing her to stop. 'I am begging you to help me.'

Gone was the attitude, the accusation. In their absence, Cora saw intense fear staring back at her, mirroring her own. When her gaze slipped to the phone Maggie was brandishing, her blood turned to ice.

The same photo Charlie had sent her.

'You need to tell DS Minshull about this,' Cora stated, numb as she stared at the image.

'Minshull won't see me,' Maggie returned. 'As far as he knows, Hal is still missing. I haven't told him Hal came back a week ago, or that he's been sending me messages every day since. And these two are together, right now, hidden away on a remote beach, an hour's drive from here. I know you're worried, Cora. I am, too. My brother – he's had issues. He doesn't make good choices when it comes to making friends. He's been burned before...'

'Are you suggesting Charlie is The Beachcomber?'

'I'm suggesting that either of them could be, and neither of them should be there. A source told me Charlie has had issues lately—'

'I'm sorry, what? A *source*? What source? Who have you been talking to about my family?'

'Sorry – don't take offence, that's not how I meant it.'

'You said my brother is bad company for yours. How the hell am I supposed to take it?'

'I'm scared.'

Cora's wrath cooled on impact. 'Why?'

'Because I know there's been another attack. In Felixstowe. Because I think they may be working together. And I think they're in danger. From each other.'

'You need to tell DS Minshull.'

'There's no time! We need to go there. To Slaughden Beach. Right now. Hal and Charlie have an hour advantage on us already. We don't have time to clear it with the police. Besides, you are working with the police, aren't you? I know you're a consultant expert.'

Not anymore...

'That's none of your business.'

'I think Hal and Charlie are in a bad place, mentally, and they could be a danger to others. And I can't sit by and wait for the worst to play out. I have my car, just over the road. We can be there in an hour. Quicker, if the traffic is in our favour.' Maggie dared to step closer to Cora, a deep chill of fear exuding from her, Hal's name repeating over and over in her thought-voice, a shrinking, twisting, python-like creature around her spoken words.

Cora tried muting the repeated name, pushing back against the physical sensations registering around her own frame, but the journalist's emotional voice was too strong.

'We could talk to them,' Maggie urged. 'They might listen to us. Can you honestly say you're willing to leave them alone in that place? Together?'

The final volley hit its target. Wasn't this what Cora had secretly feared for days? That Charlie might be hiding a terrible secret? And if she was wrong and Hal Jones was The Beachcomber, bringing Charlie into his confidence, the thought of her brother alone with a potential killer was enough to make her act.

'Okay,' she said. 'But I'm calling Rob on the way.'

The voicemail might take hours to reach Minshull. But it was a chance Cora had to take.

'Fine, yes, whatever,' Maggie rushed, racing towards the car park. 'Let's go!'

Fifty

MINSHULL

'I think my client has been more than forthcoming with the information he has given.'

Really? The snivelling solicitor was pushing that angle?

Minshull wrestled the urge to retaliate, his steady expression a razor-sharp weapon. '*Your client* was seen attacking a woman by eight witnesses.'

'Eight *aggressors*, who attacked my client with unnecessary force.'

Beside Minshull, Anderson was a smouldering lump of coal. Minshull glanced at his superior to offer him the floor, but his long, slow blink refused it.

'Alfie, this is your last opportunity to give us your side of the story,' he said, blanking the furious legal brief beside Gunnersall. 'There won't be another interview after this. And we are ready to charge.'

Yellowing teeth were revealed by a slick of a smile. 'I've said all I want to.'

'Why were you on the beach at Slaughden?'

'No comment.'

'Did you go there to attack someone? Why did you choose the woman?'

'No comment.'

'Did you want to kill her?'

'DS Minshull, we've gone over this…'

'And your client has failed to give any kind of answer.' Minshull turned back to Gunnersall again. 'Last chance, Alfie. We will be taking this to the CPS for a charging decision.'

'It's a mistake. I'll sue the backsides off you.'

'Why did you attack the female runner on Slaughden Beach?'

'No comment.'

'Did you intend to kill her or just scare her away?'

'No bloody comment.'

'If you have a reason for the attack, tell us now. It won't help you if you stay silent.'

'You're making a mistake.'

'Oh? How so?'

Gunnersall met Minshull's stare. 'When this is proved to be a set-up — which it will be — I'm sure the papers would like to know about the persistent police harassment I've suffered.'

It was bluster, a pointless show of resistance for a clear-cut case of assault. But that Gunnersall even considered it necessary spoke volumes about the man. Minshull was weary of it — an hour going round in circles, prodding apparent gaps in his replies, doubling back on small points of order to trip him into a confession. An hour wasted when they should have been searching for the real killer.

He knew Gunnersall couldn't have killed the others, not after the testimony of Abi and Georgie. That knowledge made it no less aggravating to undergo this rigmarole of interviews before a charging decision could be applied for. Anderson expected a confession, Minshull knew, his superior's quickly frustrated goal only adding to his fury.

'I think we're done here,' Minshull announced, catching the raised eyebrow from Anderson in his peripheral vision. What was the point of extending the interview any longer? Gunnersall had more than made his position clear. He would waste as much time as they gave him, so it was time to call it. 'Unless there's anything else you wish to add?'

The defiant smile of Gunnersall's solicitor badly concealed more than a touch of relief that the ordeal was reaching its conclusion. One thing the snide little man and Minshull could agree on: the sooner they ended this charade, the quicker he and Anderson could return to the real work of the case.

'I wasn't the only bloke on the beach,' Gunnersall growled. 'Plenty of others were hanging around. You should be chasing them, instead of harassing me.'

'Which others?' Anderson broke his silence to eyeball the man.

'Plenty. Ask the busybodies who attacked me. I wasn't the only one there.'

'Names?'

Gunnersall leaned across the interview desk, leering at the detectives before turning his head to the recorder. '*No... comment...*'

—

'Bastard!'

Anderson powered along the corridor to the stairs, trailed by Minshull. He'd been anticipating the outburst, but it made it no easier to endure.

'I know, Guv.'

'He knows we've got him for the attack on Cora, so what the hell was that hour all about?'

'Wasting time, Guv. It's the only power he has.'

'Well, good bloody luck to him if he thinks the press will come within fifty feet of his sorry arse when he's convicted. I hope they laugh in his face.'

Minshull just managed to catch the door as Anderson sent it flying open towards him. 'Are we taking it to CPS now?'

'Aye, as soon as we get back to CID. Can you get the team together for a briefing, please? Once they've all returned from the four corners of the county.'

'Will do, Guv.'

Anderson had reached the stairs and was now taking them two at a time. Minshull kept in step, but only just: his recent run of sleepless nights doing nothing to help his stamina or his mood.

He hated that Gunnersall had attacked Cora. That he hadn't been able to keep her safe. Even though logic assured him there was nothing he could have done, guilt refused to leave him alone.

He'd promised to keep her safe, four years ago, when he went looking for her in the aftermath of their first investigation together. Not to her face, of course, but to himself. Everything he had done for Cora stemmed from that decision, made on a shingle beach in South Devon, where he'd found her hiding from the world. There had been countless missteps and misjudgements since, their journey together as colleagues and friends far from smooth. He still had far to go – and the terrain between them remained uncertain.

He would call Cora when they returned to the office: check to see how she was. Tris Noakes had talked about giving her some time off to recover, but Minshull had been too preoccupied by the investigation to enquire whether or not Cora had accepted. Knowing her, he suspected she hadn't. Cora wasn't one to rest, not even when she'd endured an attack. Keeping busy seemed to heal her in a way that no rest could. As if consistent action fed directly into her energy supply, a rechargeable power unit requiring constant attention. Rest seemed to get in the way of where she wanted to be: *rest-less* in every sense.

Still, Minshull needed to know she was okay. It mattered to him to find out, even if it was days later than he'd intended.

As Anderson reached the top of the stairs and threw open the double doors, Minshull remembered his mobile, turned off for the duration of Gunnersall's interview. He let his superior storm off down the corridor towards CID, switching his phone on and taking the time it needed to power up as a much-needed moment to breathe.

The missed call and voicemail notifications from Cora appeared on the screen at the exact moment a roar went up from Anderson – a loud expletive most of the offices in Police HQ would be able to hear.

Pocketing his phone, Minshull ran.

Fifty-One

CORA

Maggie Jones drove like a woman possessed, white-knuckled hands gripping the steering wheel, making sharp swerves as she overtook vehicles with inches to spare and displaying scant regard for anything resembling a speed limit. Cora clung to the passenger seat, her body thrown about by every sudden jerk of the vehicle. She'd felt safer in speeding police patrol cars, blues and twos in full flash and blare. Would the journalist get them to Slaughden Beach in one piece?

She tried her phone again, frustrated when the screen advised no service.

'Did you call him?'

'There's no signal.'

'What's the deal with you and DS Minshull?'

'There is no deal.'

'That's not what I heard.'

She was bluffing: she had to be. Throwing out hooks of potential information in the hope of attracting a bite. Nobody from Police HQ would be talking to a journalist, especially not from CID. It was a lucky guess at best.

'Well, you heard wrong.'

'I heard you're more than a consultant. That you've been involved in active duty.'

'You vastly overestimate my capabilities. I'm flattered.'

'Have it your way.' Maggie slumped behind the wheel, eyes fierce on the road ahead. 'Can't blame me for trying.'

Trying what? To gain personal information from Cora when they'd barely met? Irritated, Cora twisted in her seat. 'Do you ever just have a conversation with someone for its own sake, or are you always seeking a story?'

That earned her a frown. 'I don't know, Dr Lael. Do you ever have a conversation with someone for its own sake, or are you always psychoanalysing them, playing mind games and tripping them over their own words?'

The question was meant as a biting comeback, but the words revealed more to Cora than the journalist could have intended. So, Maggie Jones had encountered a psychologist in one form or other during her life. A counsellor? A therapist? That part was unclear. But her hatred of those using psychology to help others hissed and spat through every word. That level of vitriol only came from first-hand experience of unwanted intrusion.

People often revealed so much to Cora without ever realising an exchange had taken place. She was used to the unspoken thoughts, hidden emotions and deep-buried fears of relative strangers presenting themselves to her. If she'd ever wished to capitalise on what she heard, sensed and understood, Cora would have untold power at her disposal to destroy those she encountered. But she had never approached her ability that way – and especially not now she had a deeper understanding of her mind's capabilities. The 'Spider-Man clause', as Tris jokingly referred to it: the greater the power, the greater the responsibility.

She muted the defensive whispers now clinging to the journalist, sending their unbidden secrets back to silence. Maggie Jones would not be a victim of Cora's insight, however frustrating a travelling companion she was.

'How long until we're there?' she asked, the tense air between them easing a little in response.

'Twenty minutes. Call your detective again.'

'The signal isn't good.'

'*Try*. Please.'

The call took a while to connect, then went straight to voicemail, Minshull's familiar tone cracked and burred by the poor signal.

'Rob, it's Cora. Charlie is with Hal Jones, Maggie Jones' brother, in a fisherman's hut on the edge of Slaughden Beach. I'm on my way there now with Maggie. I think...' Her voice broke, not wanting to speak the words out loud for fear of them proving true. '*We* think they may be involved in the beach murders. I found something in Charlie's belongings, something with the voice from the beach attached to it. Come here, please. Hurry.'

Maggie glanced across. 'What did he say?'

'Straight to voicemail.'

The journalist's expletive split the air.

'We should call 999,' Cora said, hating what that might mean for Charlie.

'No. DS Minshull will bring them.'

'If he gets the message. We don't know what we're dealing with, Maggie. We need them here.'

'No uniformed police!' The knuckles whitened to bone on the steering wheel.

'But if he's... If *they're* involved in the beach murders...'

'We can't! I don't know what Hal will do if police cars turn up. That's why I want DS Minshull and the CID team there. Hal can't cope with uniformed officers. He's not been well. Dishonourable discharge from the army, the worst time with the military police. It messed with his head. I don't know what he's capable of.'

Hal and Charlie. Charlie and Hal. Both struggling young men, both forced to the peripheries by demons they couldn't share. The bag of beach finds in Charlie's rucksack. The strange uniform of red hoodie and grey wool beanie hat. A million heart-stopping questions Cora needed answers for, terrified of what she might find.

She saw the same fear in Maggie as they drove towards Slaughden. The thoughts she couldn't bear to entertain. The terror that *her* brother, not the other's, was the killer. That they might be planning to kill again.

A *collection*.

That was what Maggie had said Hal talked about. But hadn't Cora sensed the same urge in her brother, the need to gather things around himself to soothe and to protect? The frantic lists in his notebook he didn't want anyone else to see? If Charlie had killed – if the knowledge of that was what was keeping him in Suffolk, away from his partner and unborn child – how would it ever end? And if Hal was The Beachcomber, what would bringing her brother into his confidence mean for Charlie?

Had they bonded over loneliness? Over collections? Or over a need to control?

And could they bond over the need to kill again?

It was too much. She needed Minshull here, and the team she had come to view as police family. What was she even doing here, now, hanging on to the passenger side door as Maggie Jones threw the car around narrow, twisted country lanes? Was she trying to prove her worth in the wake of DCI Stephens' dismissal?

'I'm scared.' Maggie's confession was tight, small, a terse whisper reluctant to find a voice.

'Me too.'

'Things he's said lately, the way he flies off the handle whenever I've asked about where he disappeared to, or what he's doing – it terrifies me.'

'Maybe they're just friends.' Cora didn't believe it any more than Maggie, but the words were out before she could keep them captive.

Maggie was already shaking her head. 'No, no you don't understand. Hal's point-blank refused to tell me where he goes. Until now. Why send me that photo and state exactly where he is when he's been so adamant it was none of my business?'

Don't look for me… The phrase from Charlie's text itched like a gnat bite on Cora's skin.

'Charlie told me not to look for him,' she said aloud, her need to hear actual sound greater than her concern to keep her thoughts locked away.

'When?'

'In a text, just before I left South Suffolk Police. But that isn't something he'd ever say. I've always gone looking for him, ever since he was little. I reckoned as his big sister it was my job to keep him safe, whether he accepted it or not. Why tell me not to look for him now?'

'They're together. Hal sending me a photo and location, Charlie telling you to stay away. Two things they wouldn't usually do. Why?'

'Because they want us there.' Cora's stomach twisted at the realisation. 'They require an audience…'

Both women fell silent as the accelerator roared.

Fifty-Two

ANDERSON

There was no time for recriminations, or a face-to-face challenge of his superior.

Despite the rage blurring his vision, Anderson ran with his team.

To his right, Minshull, pale-faced and silent, trying and failing to call Dr Lael.

To his left, Wheeler, concern etched into his expression.

Behind them, Ellis and Bennett. Evans reluctantly holding the fort, left behind to co-ordinate with Uniform patrol units already racing to the scene.

No question of a proper course of action. No hesitation, or consultation with higher authority. One of their own had been dealt a great disservice and was willingly placing herself in danger for a cause their superior should have concerned herself with.

Dr Lael deserved better. She was as much of a copper as any of them.

Not on my watch.

Evans had told him of Cora's undignified dismissal at Fran Stephens' hand. And just as Anderson was turning the CID office air blue with his response, Minshull had raced in, a message from Cora in hand. She was with Maggie Jones, speeding towards a location where both their brothers were. She believed Charlie or Hal could be The Beachcomber. Putting herself in danger because Fran bloody Stephens had dismissed her…

Verbal battles would happen at the proper time. And they *would* happen – Anderson was resolute about that. He would hold Stephens to account and to hell with the consequences. After all her promises to work with the team, to be part of the push and not the opposing force, she had forged ahead with her own agenda. Proof, if it were ever needed, that Fran Stephens had much to learn if she were to prove to them all that she was worthy of wearing the uniform. When this was all over, Anderson would go straight for the jugular.

But that could wait.

'Where?' he barked, as Minshull replayed the voicemail while they ran.

'The line is bad… The message is breaking up. But she mentioned the beach.'

'Which beach?'

Minshull frowned as he listened to the message. 'Shingle Street – I think.'

'Thinking isn't enough.'

'Shingle Street, Guv.'

'You're certain?'

'I think – yes.'

Was he certain? Anderson couldn't tell. But how could anyone think clearly in the circumstances? He nodded. 'Lead the way, then. Dave, you and I will take Rob. Drew and Kate, take another car.'

The detectives burst out of the fire doors at the bottom of the stairs, scattering down the ramp to the car park beyond, the line of pool cars and patrol vehicles glistening in the sunshine as an older man in a blue boiler suit washed them.

'Bloody hell, what's the rush?' Oz Synett yelped, yanking the hose away just in time as Ellis vaulted the bucket of soapy water beside the mechanic to reach the nearest pool car.

'Shout,' Wheeler panted, heading for the driver's side of the car next door.

'But I only just cleaned 'em…' Synett moaned, watching his newly washed vehicles about to be made filthy in the line of duty again.

'Appreciate it, Oz,' Bennett rushed, disappearing into the passenger side of Ellis' car.

Anderson didn't wait for Synett's reply. He didn't need to hear the words to get the gist. They'd be in Police HQ's chief mechanic's bad books for months now…

Minshull was already in the back seat, Wheeler having insisted it was better for him there. Anderson was inclined to agree, even though he wished he'd grabbed the keys instead of Wheeler. Jumping into the passenger seat, he slammed his hand against the dashboard.

'Go!'

Both pool cars sped out of the car park, lights and sirens ablaze as the sluggish town centre traffic reluctantly parted to let them through. The beach Minshull had identified was forty minutes away in regular conditions – too long to have Dr Lael and Maggie Jones alone with potential murder suspects.

Anderson kicked himself for not pursuing the connection sooner. Maggie had raised concerns at the beginning of the investigation, all but dismissed by Minshull and himself. Why had they been so convinced Gunnersall was the killer? It galled him to think of the time wasted on him and his weasel-faced solicitor when they could have been out looking for Hal Jones.

Why hadn't they ascertained Jones' whereabouts as soon as Ellis had talked to the MoD? Or called Maggie Jones to ask if Hal had returned home?

And now Charlie Lael was in the frame? How was Anderson only just learning this from his DS in the back seat? Why hadn't he been flagged before?

Both men in their thirties. Both with a history of mental health concerns.

'Cora told me she was concerned about her brother being home,' Minshull confessed. 'She wouldn't tell me why, but when we arrested Gunnersall she didn't mention Charlie again. I figured she'd talked to him and found out why he'd left Australia. But she says she found something in his belongings that has the voice from the beach attached to it.'

'Found what?'

'I don't know – that part of her message is garbled. I'm replaying it, but it isn't making sense.'

He could hear the panic in his colleague's voice. Minshull had taken this harder than anyone else, for reasons Anderson couldn't yet make out. He knew his DS and Dr Lael had some kind of history beyond the job – a tension between them neither had yet acted on. Was that enough to warrant Minshull's uncharacteristically emotional response to the investigation?

'Keep listening. Maybe it will become clearer.'

'Why were we so dead set on Gunnersall?'

Wheeler's question stung.

'He had the history, the location, the motive…'

'But did he, Guv?' Wheeler's suggestion caused Anderson and Minshull to fall silent. 'He's a bastard, for sure, and violent. We've got him bang to rights for attacking Dr Lael. But what would have been his motive for murder? There was no knife, no rucksack at the scene. Did we put him in the frame because he fit or because it was close enough to get a result?'

'If he hadn't been stopped from attacking Cora, he could have killed her,' Minshull shot back. 'You know this, Dave.'

'But right at the start, when we were talking to people who'd seen old Ronald Venn on Shingle Street Beach, they said about a younger bloke chatting with him. What if that was Hal Jones? Or Charlie Lael? And we missed him?'

'There's no point in going over this, Dave,' Anderson snapped, guilt and fury barely contained. 'Just drive.'

Minshull's phone gave a sudden beep. 'Guv.'

'What is it?'

'Cora just sent this.'

He passed his phone through the gap between the driver and front passenger seats, Anderson squinting to bring the photo on the screen into focus.

Two men. Both dark-haired and bearded. Both dressed identically: a red hooded sweatshirt and a grey wool beanie. Almost indistinct from one another, Hal Jones bearing a mole in the centre of his left cheek, where Charlie Lael had none. But both could be a match for the photofit reconstruction of Abi Quigley's attacker she had helped a police artist recreate.

'Where was this taken?'

'It's from Maggie Jones. Hal sent it to her to say where he was. And Charlie Lael sent the same photo to Cora.'

Why were the two men together, now? Where was the darkened space in which the photo was taken?

And who else might be in that place with them?

Fifty-Three

CORA

'Did it send?'

'I think so.'

'What did you say?'

'Just that Hal sent it to you just like Charlie sent it to me, and so that's where we're heading.'

'Has he replied yet?'

Cora shook her head, the *no signal* symbol appearing on her phone screen again. 'Do you know where the fisherman's shed is?'

'I think so.' The blare of a horn sounded behind them as Maggie overtook another car, the journalist glaring at the driver in her rear-view mirror. 'Well, don't drive so slowly if you don't want overtaking!'

'Please be careful.'

'We don't have time to be careful! I know what I'm doing.'

'Do you?' It seemed to Cora that the closer they drove to Slaughden Beach, the more reckless Maggie's driving became.

'Your nagging won't help.'

'I'd just quite like to stay alive long enough to get there.'

'Do you want to get to them or not?'

A sharp turn led to a narrow country lane, the landscape opening out around them, flattening towards the sea. What was Charlie doing there with Hal Jones? What could they be planning? And why had he told Cora not to look for him? Fear gnawed at her as the coast came into view. Was Charlie trying to prevent another killing, assist in one or mastermind it? Try as she might, Cora couldn't reconcile the image of her brother, sad and struggling as he was, with the vicious, calculated Beachcomber, displaying his victims like a curator preparing exhibits for a public show. But how well did she actually know her brother?

Since his return, it had been abundantly clear that Cora could trust nothing Charlie had told his family in recent years. Had he ever been happy in Australia, as his phone calls, texts and emails home led them to believe? Or was all of it a smokescreen for the cold, lonely truth?

Bethan said they'd had problems for a while. How long for?

Personal struggles were one thing. Murder – calculated, coldly premeditated murder – was another thing entirely. Why had Charlie returned home to kill, if that had been his plan? Might there be more of his victims scattered across the world?

No. She couldn't think like that. She wouldn't know anything for sure until they were in the same place together, where she could sense the hidden voices around him knowing what she now did about his state of mind and the company he chose to keep. Might the added context unlock his secrets at last?

He'd told her not to look for him.

But could that have been code for a cry for help, knowing Cora was unlikely to heed his request?

'What are we going to do when we get there?' she asked, aware that the time for formulating any kind of plan was quickly running out.

'We get inside. And we talk to them.'

'We can't let them know we suspect them of murder.'

'And how do we do that?' When Cora looked at Maggie's expression, she understood this as a genuine question, not sarcasm. Maggie was as lost as Cora – the knowledge of that both comforting and concerning. 'They've summoned us there. There's a reason they want an audience.'

'So, we play along,' Cora said, her training coming into play. *Be open, don't challenge, allow them to talk. Gain their trust by listening first...* 'We listen and we don't give them a hint of our worries or opinions on what they want to show us.'

'But if they're planning to kill—'

'—then they will regard it as if their plan is above reproach. As if it's the most logical, most reasonable course of action.'

'But – it isn't.'

'I know that. But we have to pander to their egos. Just like you would with someone obnoxious you have to interview...' Her breath caught as the answer presented itself, just as Maggie turned the car onto the rutted, rough gravel track leading to Slaughden Beach. 'That's it. *Interview* them, Maggie. That's what we have to do. Retain objectivity. Report the facts as they see them. Allow them to dig the hole, while hiding our own response.'

'I – I don't think I can do that...' Maggie began, fear strangling her voice.

'When you see Hal, tell yourself he isn't your brother. He's just a witness. A source for your news report. Your job is to allow him to speak, to provide information that builds a case. I'll do the same with Charlie.'

Could she do that? Cora dismissed the question. If they were to have any chance of talking Charlie and Hal down from what she feared they were planning, she and Maggie would have to play it straight. No emotion. No reaction. Just facts, gathered with as little ceremony as possible.

The journalist's eyes welled. 'Our brothers—'

'—need us to be there. For whatever reason. And the only way we can help them is to play along. Be calm, listen. Gain their confidence. And pray the police reach us before we have to do anything with what we hear.'

Was it possible? If she learned the worst about Charlie, could she hide it long enough to gain his trust? And would Maggie be able to do the same?

The track came to an abrupt end, a patch of rough grass passing as a car park. Beyond, a sandy path snaked away across flattened dunes towards the sea. Leaden grey clouds hung low over the beach, a storm ready to break. The wind had been steadily building as they'd neared the coast; now, as Cora and Maggie left the car, it buffeted their bodies, whipping their hair around their faces, the almost-whispers of previous visitors swirling ghost-echoes around them.

In the low light beneath the clouds, this was a lonely place. Stark, forbidding, at the mercy of the elements and the whim of the wind. To choose this as a location for whatever The Beachcomber wanted attention for revealed a darkly ominous intent, one that chilled Cora to the bone.

She shivered as she and Maggie picked their way around rocks and tough hummocks of grass, the way ahead twisting here, obscured there. Just like the unfolding situation, there was no clear way ahead; each step revealed just a little more.

'Where is the shed?' Cora asked, drawing level with the journalist.

'At the end of this path. We turn right and follow the edge of the beach for a while.'

'How do you know it? Have you been here before?'

'Yes.' Maggie couldn't quite meet Cora's stare. 'A long time ago.'

A tightness registered at Cora's chest as soon as Maggie spoke – a tight fist of fiercely guarded emotion. What had happened here in the past? And why would Hal Jones choose to return here now? Was its significance to whatever Maggie held tightly the reason Hal chose it?

And was Maggie even telling the truth? Now she was here, miles away from anyone who could help, Cora realised how vulnerable she was. What if Maggie was part of whatever her brother had planned? And could Charlie be in on it, too?

It was too late to turn back now. So many questions would be answered when they reached the fisherman's shed. But was Cora ready for what awaited her there?

Fifty-Four

MINSHULL

'How long?'

'Twenty minutes at least.'

'Too long.'

'I'm doing the best I can, Minsh.'

Wheeler's wounded reply brought Minshull up short. 'Of course. Sorry, Dave. I'm just—'

'Worried, yeah, we all are,' Anderson cut in. 'What do we know about the two men?'

Struggling to pack away his frustration, Minshull checked his notes. 'Hal Jones, thirty-five. Former soldier. Dishonourably discharged eight years ago for an attack on a fellow squaddie. His sister said he'd suffered a mental breakdown and would take off alone for long periods. She raised it with me earlier, but we were so set on Gunnersall—'

Anderson muttered something unintelligible, waving away the comment. 'And Charlie Lael?'

'He's thirty-two, resettled resident of Sydney, Australia. Works for a travel company after years of backpacking the world. Cora told me he'd suddenly returned to Suffolk, leaving his partner who is expecting their first child.'

'When did he turn up here?'

'Shortly before Ronald Venn's murder.'

'Did Cora hear anything from him that might put him in the frame?'

Minshull's stomach twisted. 'She'd come to CID to tell me something this afternoon. The things she's found with the voice from the beach. Les said she was looking for me when DCI Stephens dismissed her.'

The three detectives fell silent, the shock and injustice of Cora's removal still sinking in.

'What can we do about Cora?' Minshull rushed, when the tension became too much. 'She's one of us, Guv, you said so yourself.'

'Nothing for now.'

'But Guv...'

'She's about to place herself in untold danger with one or both of those young men. That has to be our priority.'

'Fran Stephens can't just dismiss Dr Lael, can she?' Wheeler asked, eyes firmly set on the road ahead as vehicles pulled to the side to let the car pass.

'She can do whatever she bloody well likes,' Anderson bit back. 'We'll deal with it when we're back.'

'And when she finds us all gone from the office?'

'Oh, I'm sure Les will keep her entertained.'

Minshull's phone, which had been frustratingly out of signal since the photo arrived from Cora, suddenly burst into life.

He answered, praying Cora might be at the end of the call. 'DS Minshull?'

'Would you care to tell me exactly why the majority of my CID team are AWOL with only one DC present?' Stephens' fury burned Minshull's ear.

'We've had a tip-off, Ma'am. We're heading to Shingle Street Beach.'

He felt the air prickle around him as Anderson and Wheeler realised who was calling.

'I did not sanction this. I was not consulted.'

'It's an emergency. We had no time to consult anyone.'

'Then I should have been informed immediately, not told by DC Evans. Who is with you, DS Minshull?'

'DI Anderson, DC Wheeler, DC Bennett and DC Ellis.'

'You were all required to respond?'

'No, Ma'am. We all chose to respond. We have reason to believe one of our team is in danger.'

'Who?'

'Dr Lael.'

She wanted to know, so Minshull had no qualms about informing her. To hell with the consequences: maybe their combined action would confirm just how vital Cora was to the team. If Stephens failed to appreciate it, it would be a unified act of defiance. Either way, she would be in no doubt of the CID team's commitment to Cora.

'Dr Lael is no longer required by this division.'

'With respect, Ma'am, Superintendent Martlesham would disagree.'

'How do you know?'

Minshull lifted his chin, as defiant away from the DCI's glare as he would be facing it in person. 'Because he gave her work with us his personal seal of approval after the last major case we worked on.'

The silence this was met with registered a direct hit. Martlesham knew what Cora had risked in the line of duty: how she had put herself in danger for the sake of the last investigation. How she ran towards the challenge to support her police colleagues, putting her own safety on the line for the service of others.

'Give me the phone, Rob,' Anderson said, his voice low below the scream of the engine.

Minshull didn't hesitate, passing the device to his superior.

'Ma'am, it's DI Anderson.'

'I was talking to DS Minshull.'

'Well, now you're taking to me. We are minutes away from the location. We don't have time to debate this. One of my team is in danger and we are going to assist her.'

'But I—' Stephens spluttered, before the line went dead.

Calmly, Anderson handed the phone back to a stunned Minshull. 'That solves that problem.'

'Guv?'

'We don't have time for arguing the toss. We focus on the job at hand.'

The detectives lapsed back into silence, the country miles passing the windows as they sped towards the beach.

From the back seat, Minshull observed the shoulders of his DI, set resolutely straight. Anderson's actions were noble, but dangerous, too. He'd already overstepped the mark with DCI Stephens in this case: defying an express order and deliberately disconnecting a call with a superior officer could land him in a world of trouble. Was he regretting his own reticence to apply for the role of DCI? Everyone in the car knew he was made for the job, despite no one daring to say it aloud. He might loathe the change in hands-on policing, might battle the inevitable pressure from the high-ups, but none of the crap they'd faced with Fran Stephens or any of her predecessors would happen under Anderson's control.

What would happen to him after this was over?

Minshull was surprised by how much the answer mattered to him.

They may have butted heads on numerous occasions, but they had one another's backs. Infuriating though Anderson might be, he'd supported and rooted for Minshull since the first six months of his promotion to DS. He might not have supported the appointment at first, concerned that Minshull lacked the necessary experience in CID to be fast-tracked to such a role, but Minshull knew the DI looked out for him like a grumpy, sweary mother hen.

In turn, Minshull had grudging respect for the DI whose support for him never wavered, who had stood by him when investigations questioned Minshull's capability for the role. And his respect for Cora was impossible to ignore. Anderson had put more on the line for the sake of his team than anyone else Minshull had encountered in his police career.

If his very public defiance of DCI Stephens had repercussions for Anderson's career, Minshull vowed to do everything in his power to stand in the gap for him. He suspected his colleagues would do the same.

'We're here,' Wheeler announced, swinging the speeding pool car hard right to bump and crash over the rough track leading to Shingle Street Beach.

Minshull steeled himself for whatever they would find. Was Cora hurt? Could her brother be the killer that had eluded them until now? If that was the case, what would it do to his friend and colleague – and what might it mean for her ongoing association with South Suffolk CID? Or were Maggie Jones' worst fears real? Could Minshull have saved Abi and Georgie from the attack on Felixstowe Beach if he'd followed up on Maggie's concerns? Could he have spared Cora her ordeal by making an arrest earlier?

The car came to a halt beside the path that traversed the dunes to the beach. Wheeler, Anderson and Minshull leapt out, turning to hear the squeal of brakes on gravel as Bennett and Ellis arrived in the second pool car.

'We're looking for a shack,' Minshull informed them, when the team had gathered around him. 'I couldn't hear all of Cora's message, but she insisted her brother and his friend are in some kind of wooden building – a fisherman's shed, a mackerel bothy, any kind of structure where fishing equipment might be found.'

'On Shingle Street Beach?' Ellis asked.

'Clearly, as that's where we've been sent.'

'I don't remember seeing any buildings on Shingle Street Beach.' Ellis shrugged. 'Except the café at the end of it.'

'Well, look for one,' Minshull snapped, instantly relenting. 'You might not have seen it on previous visits, but that doesn't mean it isn't there.'

'Sarge. Sorry.'

'No time for that. Let's find Cora.'

Fifty-Five

THE COLLECTOR

This time feels different. The anticipation. The promise.

My friend agreed to come without ever asking why. He trusts me.

Maybe he shouldn't.

I haven't told him why we're here yet, only that I have my eye on a new piece for The Collection. He isn't as impressed with the shed as I hoped he'd be. Only a fraction of my pieces are in here, space being at a premium. I couldn't bring it all with me, just what I could fit in my rucksack.

'What is all this stuff?' he asks.

'The Collection. Every piece curated by me.'

He's watching, as I unwrap each item. I daren't look up from my work for fear of catching his response too early. I need to see how he reacts when everything is laid out before him.

Trophies, I call them. Tokens that promise greater things. Stolen or snatched, taken by force – it doesn't matter. All part of the necessary acquisition process. One by one, they will be exchanged for the real Collection. And now I have a kindred soul to help me, my stupid mistakes will stop.

He doesn't know about the message I sent her. That's part of the surprise. When she arrives, we can get to work.

My sister.

The ultimate piece my Collection needs.

Every curator knows the more personal the piece, the greater its potential. My sister as an exhibit will be the closest I can get to adding a piece of my own flesh.

She will be the perfect sacrifice. The piece it hurts to donate. If I give it my all, people will see how much it matters.

I know she'll be on her way. The message was out of character enough to get her running here. I don't mind admitting a sense of pride about that. I know her better than she knows me.

The knife is in my rucksack, with the bag of finds. My friend hasn't seen that, either. Before, I thought it all should be done alone. Now, the theatre of it appeals to me. An audience – of two at first, then one.

Contained here, in this place nobody knows but us. Where interruptions can't happen. Where her body can be protected.

Prepared. Beautifully arranged.

A thrill passes through me at the thought, my hand shaking as I unwrap the final pieces to add them to the display.

I look up.

And my friend is staring at The Collection in awe.

It's perfect.

Now, we wait.

Fifty-Six

CORA

The wind had sprung up from the sea, sending pale green waves dancing through the rough grass that edged the shingle beach. Cora wrapped her arms around herself as she followed Maggie, the low-lying landscape seemingly endless before them beneath a cloud-strewn sky.

No sign of a structure of any kind, wooden or otherwise.

'Are you sure it's here?' she called, repeating the question when the sea breeze stole the first.

'Yes. I've been here before,' Maggie replied, forging on.

'When?'

'A few years back.' There was a flatness to her tone, a held breath of emotion cloaking it from the world. Cora sensed a sadness Maggie shrank back from entertaining, a loss synonymous with the shack. What if it had followed the fates of many a seaward-facing building on this coast, by falling into disrepair and eventually being demolished? Where else would there be to look for Charlie and Hal?

They rounded a curve where the grass-edged path navigated a large rock – and there it was. A small wooden construction that had clearly seen better days, its exterior cracked and salt-stained by years of exposure to the salt, wind, sun and rain.

Rusting sheets of corrugated iron formed the roof and patched some parts of the wooden walls where the original building material had worn away. At the front of it, the remains of an upturned rowing boat: skeletal slats like ancient, salt-baked ribcage bones reaching in vain to an unforgiving sky. Cora tried to imagine how the shack had appeared when first constructed: when the structure had stood proud and new, surveying the wide sweep of sea that it gazed out upon. The fishermen who considered it their workplace, long gone now, their only ghosts the scraps of construction that once formed a thriving business along the wide, sweeping coast.

'We go in, we talk to them, we get them out.' Maggie stood by Cora's side, the two women observing the place that had drawn them to Slaughden Beach. 'Right?'

'Yes,' Cora replied, firm in her response even if privately she doubted the exchange would prove so easy.

'I just want to get my brother home.' The journalist's jaw was set with resolve, her eyes fixed on the broken, battered building. 'To *my* home, not that mould-infested hovel in Hollesley he insists on renting. It isn't good for him, being out here. He needs family around him. Always has, even though he'd kill me for saying it…' She fell silent, blanching a little.

'I need Charlie back at my mum's,' Cora conceded. 'I don't know what he's going through at the moment – nobody does. But if he's there, I can find him help.'

'Perks of the job, eh?' Maggie's smile didn't quite reach her eyes.

'Something like that.'

It felt odd, joking at the moment they were about to visit their brothers in this hostile, lonely place. A moment of camaraderie with a relative stranger, united only in fear. Cora drew comfort from it as a glimpse of warmth from a shared candle flame, before the cold reality of the task ahead of them returned.

'There's a door on the other side,' Maggie said, resolve setting steel into her words. 'We'll go in there.'

'First sign of trouble and I call it in.'

Maggie observed her, a cluster of frown lines gathering between her eyebrows. 'Fine. But I'll lead. Hal will be expecting me.'

'You're sure of that?'

'Yes,' Maggie breathed, the weight of her acceptance surprising. 'He shared information he never has to summon me. He knows I'll come running.'

'What information?'

She blinked, a rush of repressed tension surrounding her. 'He told me he knew about the uncle who abused me.'

'Maggie, I'm sorry—' Cora rushed, but Maggie raised her hand.

'We should go.'

The journalist set off again, Cora hurrying to keep up with her.

They began to cross the final curve of wild-grass-edged bank, careful to keep to the softness of it instead of straying onto the shingle, where their approach would be announced immediately. Only the last few steps onto the beach were unavoidable, both Cora and Maggie stepping as lightly as possible. Better to give as little warning as possible to whoever they'd find inside.

Hal Jones expected his uncharacteristic message to immediately summon his sister. Was Charlie's warning to Cora not to come looking for him calculated to do the same? Was her response so predictable that he could guarantee she'd come looking for him?

She had no time to consider this as Maggie raised her hand to the patched and splintered blue door and knocked.

When no movement sounded beyond it, Maggie leaned her face against its time-bleached surface. 'Hal, it's me. It's Maggie. Let me in.'

A dull thud came from within, like something heavy being pulled back and dropped. Then the door slowly swung open.

With a final glance at each other, Cora followed Maggie inside…

Fifty-Seven

ELLIS

There was nothing on the beach. They'd scanned the long shingle spit as they'd walked alongside it, looking back across the flatlands and saltwater wetlands to search for anything that may have once been a structure.

Nothing matched the description.

Ellis had already visited the café further up the beach, the owner confirming that the only visitors he'd had all day had been the dog walkers who had come to Cora's aid when Alfie Gunnersall had attacked her.

He had a bad feeling about this, a sense of *déjà vu* after their failed attempt to apprehend Gunnersall when they'd come here looking for him. Different beach this time, same outcome: nothing.

Somewhere, Dr Lael and Maggie Jones of the *Suffolk Herald* were chasing after their brothers, both fearing the worst possible news. But if they believed their siblings capable of murder, how wise was it to go after them, especially to such remote locations?

What was the link between the two men? Ellis had seen the photo Cora sent to Minshull's phone. It was creepy: a freakish costume play with two haunted young men staring out of the photograph. Neither looked in any state to make rational decisions. And they were in an old fisherman's shack? For what purpose? The shadowy backdrop to their strangely hollow-eyed selfie looked anything but welcoming. Definitely not the place Ellis would head to meet a potential murderer. It made no sense. But little in this case had so far.

Bennett pressed ahead a few steps ahead of him, her shoulders tensed in dogged determination. She wouldn't give up until the beach surrendered its secrets, so neither would he. Ellis admired her spirit, even if it was relentless in its pursuit of the truth. It mattered to her that right be done and wrong be stopped – as it should for any police officer – but with Bennett everything was magnified. For someone who protested so much when asked to step into the spotlight, she had no idea of the strength of her influence. If she caught the scent of trouble, she was off like a shot. All you could hope was that you had the energy to keep up.

As Minshull, Anderson and Wheeler headed off across the hummocks of wild seagrass and sand, Ellis jogged up to Bennett's side.

'Something's wrong,' he confessed. 'Whatever Cora told Minsh she must have made a mistake. There's *nothing* here. Not even the foundations of an older building.'

'This is where Cora said they were,' Bennett returned, her own frustration for their fruitless search evident in her reply.

'I know. But I can't understand it. Maybe she got it wrong. That would be understandable, right? She can't be thinking straight: panicking about her brother, scared he's done something stupid. It would be easy to make a mistake.'

'Do you think she suspects Charlie of murder?' Bennett faced him now, eyes enquiring, gaze intent on him.

'Either that or she thinks Maggie's brother is a killer and she wants to protect Charlie.'

It doesn't bear thinking about what could happen if he were provoked again...

Ellis recalled the words of Winchcombe, the MoD sergeant, and shuddered.

'This is ridiculous. I'm going to double-check with Minsh.' Bennett powered away from him in the direction of Minshull, Wheeler and Anderson.

Checking behind him one last time for any sign of a building, Ellis reluctantly gave chase.

Minshull looked sick when Ellis and Bennett reached him, his eyes wide beneath a deep frown as he scanned the horizon. Anderson and Wheeler walked four paces apart, eyes fixed on the unfolding landscape before them.

'Any sign, Sarge?' Ellis asked, already guessing the answer.

'Not here.'

'Did Dr Lael definitely say Shingle Street Beach?' When Anderson glanced back, Ellis moved to cover any offence his question might have caused. 'I'm just wondering if the message actually said that. You said the signal was breaking up when you were listening to it.'

Wheeler joined them. 'He makes a good point, Sarge. What did you hear?'

'Exactly what I told you. The reception was patchy, but I heard enough.'

Instinctively, Ellis pulled his own phone from his pocket, heart jolting when he saw the screen. 'I've full reception here. Play the message again. You might hear more of it.' When Minshull stared back, he quickly added, 'Sarge.'

The detectives gathered together as Minshull produced his phone, moving a few steps away to call his voicemail service. Ellis exchanged looks with Bennett as Anderson kept his eyes on Minshull.

'Where else could she be?' Wheeler asked quietly. 'Cora knows these beaches as well as any of us. That's why she brought the Sarge here for their run. Even if she was scared, even if she wasn't thinking straight, I reckon it's unlikely she'd get the name of the beach wrong.'

Relieved not to be the only person on the team doubting the chances of a mistakenly named beach, Ellis nodded. 'That's what I was saying, Dave. There's only the café here and that's open. Nobody hiding out there. The only place I've seen a fisherman's shed is...' The revelation hit like a thunderbolt. 'Slaughden! It isn't Shingle Street, Sarge, it's...'

'Slaughden!' Minshull shouted. 'She said Slaughden!'

'The shack we saw when we went looking for Gunnersall,' Bennett cut in.

'Exactly! That fits the message. And someone had put a new padlock on it.' Ellis looked up, but Minshull was already running.

Kicking up showers of shingle, Ellis and the others ran after him.

Fifty-Eight

CORA

Boxes everywhere.

Across the sand-strewn floor. Balanced on top of piles of old nets and coils of frayed blue rope. Stacked against one of the wooden walls. Each one numbered with a yellow sticker. Some of the items had been laid out on small lengths of black velvet, more numbers accompanying them. Like in a museum.

A collection.

Stones. Broken necklaces, spiky lengths of hair tangled around the fastenings. A line of single shoes, from a man's boot and a woman's red patent high heel to a scuffed Mary Jane shoe a toddler might wear. Mirror shards. Muddy shoelaces. A family photo, its glass fractured in an explosion of angry cracks. Torn pages of books, the paper yellowing at the edges. A small plastic doll, naked, hair half-ripped from its head.

The noise hit Cora the moment she entered the fisherman's shack: wails and cries, muted as if gagged. Fear and loathing, shock and terror. Here and there, indignation, fading in volume with each protest. And breath, heavy and ragged; dragged from the deepest place, expelled into the dusty air. Sinister and unsettling, the antithesis of a museum collection preserved for observation and delight.

'Charlie?'

In the shadows behind the macabre display, Charlie stood, red notebook in hand, his stare locked on her while his pen dug hurried lines of tiny writing into the pages. His pale face a monochrome against the darkness of the shack's peripheries.

'You came,' he said, his voice cracking.

'Of course I did. What's going on?'

'I'm cataloguing.' His tone was completely devoid of emotion, a flat-line facsimile of the voice she knew to be her brother's.

'What the hell?' Maggie's horrified stare passed from the collection to Charlie, then across the room to the opposite corner, where Charlie Lael's doppelganger watched from the gloom.

In the photo there had been little to set the two men apart from each other. Here, the similarities were overwhelming.

Hal Jones said nothing, a strange half-smile his only expression.

'Come home, Hal,' Maggie entreated. 'I've no idea what this is, but it doesn't matter. You'll be safe at home…'

'Safe? Nowhere's safe.' Hal's voice sounded strained, as if he hadn't slept for days. 'Why do you think we needed this place?'

'Is it yours?'

The smile switched from Maggie to Cora. 'It is now.'

'Charlie, come back with me. Mum's worried.'

Charlie blinked in reply, the list growing on his notebook page.

'What is all this stuff?' Maggie walked into the centre of the floor.

'My collection.'

The discomfiting symphony of voices swelled in reply. Cora couldn't tell who had answered her question, the peripheral thought-voices too numerous to control.

I found you.

You're mine!

The whisper from the beach rose above the other sounds, harsher now. Crueller. Covering every strange and random object in the collection, as if smothering the voices of the people each one had been stolen from. It chilled Cora's blood.

'Why the collection?' she asked, forcing the words through the cacophonous din.

The word snatched the other voices from the air, a sudden silence that almost knocked Cora over.

'Because it's mine. I found it.'

She saw horror register in Maggie first. When she turned to look at Charlie, tears were now staining his deathly pale cheeks. How had this happened to her brother? What twisted thoughts had claimed his mind? She hardly recognised him. Fear swelled all around her and within, a choking, crushing tide.

'We're leaving,' Maggie said.

'No.'

'Hal, we need to get out of here.'

'I can't leave.'

'Then I'll come and get you.' She stormed across the shack, sending objects tumbling to the ground as she crashed through the crude displays. Velvet trodden beneath her boots, plastic trinkets skittering across the ridges of the rough concrete floor, the smash of mirror shards in her wake.

'*NO!*'

The scream split the dank air, Hal launching his body at his sister. They collided with a force Cora felt, Maggie falling to the ground where her head met the concrete with a sickening crack.

Cora rushed to help the journalist, but a heavy blow caught her under her chin.

The last thing she saw before darkness stole her vision was a bearded man in a grey beanie hat and red hoodie leering over her...

Fifty-Nine

THE COLLECTOR

Why didn't my friend help me?

Must I do everything by myself?

This wasn't how it was meant to play out. She was going to arrive, meet The Collection and then join it. No mess. No drama.

No *noise*.

I clamp my hands to my ears, but I can still hear the crack of her head. She's damaged now. I needed her intact. Why can't the pieces do as I want?

He's just standing there. I told him the plan before the women arrived. I explained what we were here for. It's simple enough for a child to understand. It should be no problem for him.

She isn't moving. I check the back of her head, relieved there's no blood to stain her. The other woman is out cold, too. At least she won't get in the way.

'Help me,' I growl at my friend, reaching for a coil of rope. I'm ruffled by the mistakes but maybe it can play to my favour. I'd expected crying, pleading, screams. She always was one for tantrums, for commanding attention from everyone in the room – like she was special. Like I wasn't. It would have been fitting for her final sounds on Earth to match the pattern.

But maybe silence is better.

No struggle, just collection. Simple death. And calm display.

The best collections lie in buildings where quietness is required. Reverence. Respect. Full attention paid to the art of the curator and the beauty of his gatherings.

My friend isn't helping, just staring at me like he's forgotten what to do.

I set to work, binding her wrists and ankles, careful not to break the skin with the rough rope. Her hands and feet should be as perfect as possible. I can't do much about the head. Still, I take one of the fallen velvet lengths and force it between her open lips, tying it tight around the back of her head.

'I wish you could see this,' I whisper, close to her ear, as I tie the knot. I hope she can hear me. That her final lucid thoughts are of my gentle words, not the knife that will end her.

I stand to admire my work, then move to the other woman, tying her wrists and ankles, too. I don't gag her, though. It will be good to discuss the finished Collection when the job is done. My first visitor to view it.

Now I'm here, I'm strangely emotional. That's a surprise. Maybe it's pride that I've done what I set out to do. Or relief that The Collection will at last be complete.

It isn't perfect, though...

I tense.

NO. I won't listen to you now. Go away.

It didn't follow the plan. She won't be the unblemished crown of The Collection...

'No!' I say out loud.

The other woman stirs.

I have to act now, before the voice condemns me.

I hurry to my rucksack, the one that's accompanied me on every journey I've made since my teens, and pull out the knife. It's reassuringly heavy in my hand. I let it rest there for a while, drawing strength from its familiar bulk. A damn good knife, Dad used to say, when he carved the roast every Sunday.

Why am I thinking of Dad now?

I take a breath, force all other thoughts out of my mind, steady my hand. This has to be perfect. A single blow, right in the centre of the heart. One entry wound, no ragged edges.

I turn – but he comes out of nowhere. I cry out as he slams into me, red-faced fury blocking my vision. The roar is animal-like, unearthly. It winds me, screams in my ears, wrecking the peace that was going to work for me.

And then the roar becomes a gurgle, the whites of his eyes showing when the pupils disappear up into his head.

I feel warmth flood my hand where it holds the knife.

Too much warmth…

Disgusted, I force his body away. He skids across the floor from his stirring sister and doesn't move.

'You shouldn't have done that, Charlie,' I hiss at his crumpled body, hot tears blurring my vision as the knife slips from my hand. It clatters against the concrete, soiled and sticky, totally unworthy now of the task I'd assigned it.

It's not perfect, the voice taunts me. *You've failed again!*

I curl up in a ball, as small as I can be, slamming bloodstained hands over my ears as a frantic wail goes up from the woman who *isn't* my sister.

Sixty

MINSHULL

'All units to Slaughden Beach,' Anderson barked into the radio as Wheeler slammed his foot on the accelerator, siren blaring and blue lights ablaze.

Minshull gripped the seat, furious with his mistake. Why hadn't he made the connection between the fisherman's shack and the ramshackle building that he, Ellis and Bennett had encountered during their fruitless search for Gunnersall? Why had he missed the obvious parts of Cora's message?

The patchy phone reception had stolen the beach's name. But Minshull should have remembered the building they'd seen on Slaughden Beach.

Eighteen miles in the wrong direction. Cora and Maggie having at least forty minutes' advantage on them for arrival at the shack. What if they were too late? Both Charlie Lael and Hal Jones fit the description of the assailant on the beach at Felixstowe. Both had a history of mental health issues. Either one of them could have a knife. Hell, they could even be working together.

Cora was out there, believing her work was no longer wanted by South Suffolk CID, terrified for the welfare of her brother. And where was Minshull? Eighteen miles in the wrong direction, a delay that could prove catastrophic.

'You weren't to know, Minsh,' Wheeler soothed, glancing back in the rear-view mirror.

'I should have known. I should have worked it out.'

Anderson snorted. 'You're not solely to blame, Rob. Dave and I both listened to Cora's voicemail: we missed it, too.'

'But the delay...'

'Aye, Rob. I know.'

'I'm doing everything to get us there,' Wheeler reassured them both, speeding past a line of motorists who had graciously moved aside to let them through the traffic.

'Cheers, Dave. I'm just worried for Cora, you know? Either one of those men could be a killer.'

'Control to DI Anderson, over?'

'Go ahead.'

'Guv, there's a patrol close by. We're sending them over now. ETA ten minutes, over.'

'Excellent, thanks. Out.' Anderson twisted in his seat to look back at Minshull. 'Boots on the ground, son.'

Minshull nodded. It *was* good news. But Minshull wanted to be there, getting to Cora first. He'd created the situation by not properly listening to her concerns – or Maggie's. Now he needed to right that wrong. The thought of Cora locked in a shack – with a murderer who'd already stolen two lives and attempted to take two more – was too horrific to consider.

The buzz of his phone dragged him back into the speeding CID car.

'Yes, Les?'

'Bit of a development, Sarge. There's a link between Hal Jones and Ronald Venn.'

'What? How?'

'Drew's contact at the MoD sent through a number for an armed forces charity Jones was involved with. So I spoke to Aubrey Peters, a retired army major. He organises yearly get-togethers for ex-servicemen and serving soldiers. To build morale, share knowledge, support each other, that kind of thing. Turns out Venn was just about leaving the army when Hal Jones arrived, so they shared a battalion for around six months.'

'So Jones knew him? How well?'

'Not well when they served together, but over the years they both became leading lights of the yearly reunion. Thick as thieves, according to the major. But a year ago they got into a fight at the event. Proper nasty, apparently. Jones made fun of Venn's reduced circumstances, calling him a failure and a loser and that. Venn retaliated by calling Jones a scam artist, using his former connection with the army to curry favour with everyone, despite the fact he'd been dishonourably discharged. It caused such a fuss that Jones was barred from attending the reunion party.'

'Could Hal Jones have sought revenge?'

'I reckon that's the most likely outcome.'

'Great work, Les. See if you can find any link between Jones and Alistair Avebury. If we can prove a connection it might shed new light on the murders.'

'Will do, Sarge.'

Minshull ended the call, staring at the phone for a few seconds as he let it all sink in. It was the missing piece that had eluded them: the fact that made sense of everything else. He'd been at the point where he'd started to think it might evade them for good.

Despite all his experience, Minshull never took this moment for granted. It could so easily be missed in the flood of information that surrounded every case.

If Ronald Venn was far from an indiscriminate target and a link was proved with Alistair Avebury, intent could be demonstrated. But if killing Venn had unlocked a compulsion in Jones, Avebury's murder and the attempt on Abi Quigley might have been opportunistic attacks to feed that need. Either way, a picture could be formed of what had caused Hal Jones to become a killer.

But what did that mean for Cora's brother? Was he an accomplice, an accessory or a helpless individual caught in the crossfire? Had Jones sensed a kindred spirit in the young man battling his own demons? Or a troubled soul that could be easily led? Was Charlie Lael an unfortunate bystander or a carefully recruited right-hand man?

Either way, Cora and Maggie had no idea of what they were walking into.

'Hal Jones is the one we're after,' he said aloud, witnessing the impact the news had on Anderson and Wheeler. 'He knew Ronald Venn through an army connection, and he has the skills, anger and opportunity necessary to carry out the other attacks.'

Anderson received the news with grim determination. 'And Charlie Lael?'

'I don't know,' Minshull admitted, wishing he knew for certain. Wishing any of it had made sense sooner. 'My guess is he connected with Jones because of his own current struggles and Hal saw a ready recruit for his plan.'

'Unless they knew each other before,' Anderson offered.

'It's possible. They're of a similar age. Do we know where Hal and Maggie Jones grew up?'

'We can find out,' Minshull said. 'I'll text Les, ask him to do some digging.'

'What was Hal's plan?' Wheeler asked, his tone grim.

'*So they're looking for attention?*'

'*Not just any kind of attention. Recognition. Acclaim. For their keen eye and their skill at curating.*'

A collector.

A cairn to remind them where the body was…

The Beachcomber adding to his gruesome collection…

Minshull remembered Cora's words, Dr Amara's observation, Bennett's theory about the stones on the dead men's chests, even the media's overdramatic title for the beach killer. Suddenly, sickeningly, it all made sense.

'To collect what he felt he was owed.'

Sixty-One

CORA

The scene that met her aching eyes when consciousness returned was a nightmare. Maggie Jones, bound and gagged, lying motionless on the floor a few feet away. Her own wrists and ankles lashed together with plastic rope that dug into her skin as she tried in vain to free her limbs. Hal Jones crouched into a ball, red-stained hands pressed to his ears. A bloodied kitchen knife on the floor between them, caught in a shaft of light from the weathered boards of the shack.

And Charlie slumped in the corner, his breathing ragged, a dark stain spreading across the fabric of his red hoodie, glistening and wet.

'Charlie!' she cried out, the full impact of what she saw body-slamming her like Hal had done when she'd rushed to help Maggie. 'Charlie, speak to me!'

'It's too late,' Hal Jones stated, the timbre of his voice a perfect match for the whisper Cora had heard from the beach finds. 'It's all too late.'

'Let me get to him,' she entreated Jones. 'He needs me.'

'I needed *him*.' The indignation became a wail, the cry of a child denied their desires. 'But he made it not perfect. He didn't help me.'

A rush of condemnatory voices rose from him, a thousand pointing fingers, accusing him of failure. Cora felt it as if the digits were prodding her own skin. Sharp, hate-filled self-loathing, personified as a crowd of invisible accusers.

'Let me help him,' she insisted, slower this time; more deliberate. The childlike voices around Jones and his own injured words made Cora shift her approach to one she often used to reach the children she worked with. Small steps, gentle words, a careful omission of blame or anger.

'He took the knife. It wasn't meant for him.'

'Who was it meant for?' She swallowed back the bile that accompanied the thought. Had Hal summoned his sister in order to add her to his collection? And why the switch to victims he knew, after the unprovoked, seemingly random attack on the two girls at Felixstowe Beach?

You failed.

No...

It isn't perfect.

The accusatory voice battled with Hal's own thought-voice, the squabble as audible to Cora as if it were happening between two figures in front of her.

Had Minshull received her message? Was he heading here? Or had the demands of his job kept him from checking his phone? What would happen if they were truly alone, in this dark, discarded, unloved place?

Jones cowered beneath the weight of the voices. 'Maggie was supposed to have it.'

Have it. As if a murder weapon was a gift given to his victim.

Sickened, Cora pressed on. With each question so far, she'd sensed Jones opening a little further, revealing more. Battling her own fear for her brother, Cora forced her focus on the conversation. If they were ever to get out of here, she had to keep the lines of communication open.

'Is that what you planned?'

'It doesn't matter what I planned. She ruined it.'

'She's hurt, Hal. But you can help her.'

'She didn't help me. She made it worse.'

'Maybe this is a different plan. One you can't fail.'

Hal flinched at the word, repeated out loud from the words aimed at him by his thought-voices of which Cora could now sense several. His hands left his ears, leaving behind ugly red smears across the sides of his face. 'I don't want to fail. That's all I've done since I started The Collection.'

The word shone like a beacon between them. Cora's theory proved. Not just a description, but a title, designed to be writ large over it. She glanced at the scattered remains of the display Hal had laid out prior to their arrival, now littering the floor.

'Tell me about The Collection,' she cajoled, ensuring the proper weight of the name.

'The Collection is ruined.'

'It wasn't when we arrived. That was what you wanted us to see, wasn't it?'

She spoke as if to a child, coaxing confidence with tiny scraps of connection. With each tentative verbal step, Cora felt a slackening of Hal's defences. If she could engage him in talking about The Collection, it would buy her time – and give Minshull more time to receive her message.

Danger remained within this damp and murky place. Her life, along with Charlie's and Maggie's, depended upon keeping Jones distracted from his stated purpose for as long as possible. The knife was within grabbing distance if Maggie's brother chose to reach for it: Cora couldn't risk him returning to his original plan.

'I told Charlie what it was. It was meant to be a surprise for him. But all he wanted to do was spoil it...'

'Charlie was protecting Maggie,' Cora offered, pulling back when the voices around Hal Jones swelled in response. She had to keep him on side. 'He was trying to stop you making a mistake.'

Jones stared at her. 'She made the mistake, not me.'

'She didn't know. You didn't tell her what The Collection was for.'

A slow moan came from the corner of the room. Jones scowled in its direction.

'I'm here, Charlie,' Cora rushed, relief and terror pulling the words from her. She forced her attention back to Jones. 'Tell me about The Collection.'

'He'll die, you know. That much blood.'

Not today, Cora vowed. *Not like this.*

Where was Minshull?

'He'll join The Collection, even though I failed.'

'Maybe he'll live and that will be your achievement,' Cora countered, fighting back tears. 'Maybe you can you make a living collection, not a dead one.'

Another moan, this time from the bound and gagged woman beside Cora – and Jones shaking his head as the hidden voices of accusation rose again.

You failed. You always do…

His attention was slipping, the punishment of hidden voices stealing his focus. If they swelled too far, they could drag him back to his intended plan. Cora couldn't let that happen: for Charlie and Maggie's sakes. For her own survival.

The knife was too close to Hal; too far from Cora to kick it aside. Her only option was to keep Jones distracted, talking.

Praying help had already been summoned, reinforcements racing across the county to get here, Cora forced her own horror aside and gave all her attention to Jones.

'Tell me about The Collection, Hal. I want to know it all…'

Sixty-Two

EVANS

'Where are they now?'

DCI Stephens glared at the map on the CID office whiteboard. Evans was glad it summoned the full force of her scrutiny: when it was aimed at him it was terrifying.

She'd rushed to CID when Control had appraised her of the live operation, spitting feathers at the actions of Anderson and the team. Since then, she'd been demanding updates seemingly every minute – at least, that's what it felt like to Evans.

'On the way to Slaughden Beach, Ma'am. There's a Uniform patrol closer to the scene. Should be there within the next ten minutes.'

'And the others?'

'I'm awaiting a status update from Control.'

'Good. Keep pressing them. We need to know exactly what we're dealing with.'

I know exactly what I'm dealing with, Evans retorted in his mind. *A DCI who's crapping herself because she made this happen.*

He'd encountered any number of Fran Stephenses in his police career. Ambitious, self-important tossers, more concerned with saving their own skins than serving their teams. The Force was littered with them. They picked up and dropped postings at will, squeezing whatever they could for themselves before sodding off somewhere shinier. *Stepping-stone people*, his old mate Sid Vardy used to call them. The old-timer had mentored Evans when he joined the Uniform ranks, wet behind the ears from police training college, not really certain if the job was even for him.

You watch out for them, Lesley. They'll lead you a merry dance in the name of leadership, promise you all kinds of crap to get you onside, then drop you like a hot rock the moment something better comes along. You don't need their rubbish. Avoid the bastards, son. Don't give them what they want – or if you have to, give only the bare minimum...

That mantra had served Evans well – until the attack that took him out of action for months. Now, the gratitude he felt for the team that had saved him refused to let him stay at arm's length.

It also meant dealing with the ultimate stepping-stoner herself – or, at least, making her think he was.

Like it or not, Fran Stephens had brought this situation to their door: interfering in every decision, dismissing Dr Lael like she didn't matter. If she'd let the team get on with it, they might have discovered the information on Hal Jones that Evans was finding now. Or they would have had the space to think beyond the top-line investigations instead of tripping over red tape.

Either way, Stephens needed to learn from this if she were ever to prove she was better than the last DCI. The jury was out on whether she would.

Bloody well done to Joel Anderson for hanging up on her. Evans had to admit even he was surprised at the act from his DI, Anderson always erring on the right side of the road in all decisions – to the high-ups' faces at least. His sardonic humour out of earshot was a joy when shared with the CID team. At the end of the day, he was one of them, and he made no attempt to disguise the fact.

But he'd risked more than a dressing-down when he'd ended the call to Fran Stephens. Already on dodgy ground after going over her head on the Gunnersall decision, Anderson had nailed his colours firmly to the mast now.

At least she was on the back foot for the time being. Panicked, barking orders to Evans as if the rest of the team were in the room, pacing the threadbare carpet so different from the new floor covering in her third-floor office. While she'd never admit it to Anderson, she was clearly terrified. Evans would take great pleasure in relaying this information to his superior when they returned.

But the thought of what his colleagues were heading towards tempered any joy Evans might feel.

Every copper knew the dangers that could jump out at any moment: the possibility that your next shout could be your last. And it didn't matter which division you served in, anyone could fall foul of fate. Only a few years ago, a friend of his in the Traffic division tragically lost his life when a routine road-check led to a driver pulling a gun from the passenger seat and shooting him at point-blank range. He'd seen colleagues leave the Force after scuffles that injured them for life, more breakdowns and burnouts than anyone should encounter and colleagues taken too young by suicide.

His own brush with death, still painfully fresh in his memory, had felt at the time like his luck had finally deserted him. So while a part of him envied Anderson, Minshull, Wheeler, Bennett and Ellis racing across the South Suffolk coastline to help Cora, Evans felt a huge sense of relief that he wasn't among them.

All the same, he worried for them. As DCI Stephens continued to yell and pace and wring her hands, Evans kept his eyes on the screen, searching for anything that might help his colleagues.

Sixty-Three

THE COLLECTOR

I know what she's trying to do. Keep me talking so I don't threaten her. She thinks she's helping her brother and my sister, but she's only delaying the inevitable.

Perfect or not, The Collection needs completing.

I have the advantage still, despite so many mistakes littering the shack around me, and the voice denouncing everything I do. I can reach the knife when I need to – which none of the others in this place can. And unlike the rest of them, I know how to use it.

Because I've rehearsed the blows for months.

There's an old fake leather sofa, abandoned in woods at the back of my digs in Hollesley. I found it when I was walking one day. Dumped in a thicket of trees, half-hidden by ivy and grass. When I was planning my first kill, it proved useful. I knew Venn was a big man, that the crapness of his existence after leaving the army meant his frame was well padded, all instance of muscle tone gone. Picturing his bloated body where the cracked pleather sagged over its broken frame was easy. Stabbing over and over, the edges of the wound becoming less ragged, the best training.

Charlie is bleeding more now. It won't be long before he's done. I'm disappointed in him: I thought he'd help me. Believed he'd understand my mission. When we met on the beach he was writing in that notebook of his – the obsessive scribble that covered page after page. I complimented his commitment. It made him smile. We got talking then, and it only took two beers before he finally told me why he wrote in it.

'I note down everything I see, everything I think, everything I feel, as they're happening, as I'm aware of them. If I document it, I have control. No surprises. Nothing I'm unprepared for.'

The planning impressed me. And I knew then that we thought the same.

It calmed his mind, he said. Like counting or humming or organising do for others. Like indexing finds and the procural process of each piece do for me. It talked him down from panic attacks and gave him something steady to focus on. I knew immediately that he would catalogue The Collection for me. My handwriting is a mess — hardly worthy of a curator. He would be the difference I needed to be great.

'Tell me about The Collection, Hal. I want to understand it.'

Charlie's sister says it like it's easy: like the items I've gathered over the last year are some simple, childlike hobby I can explain in a sentence.

'You wouldn't understand.'

'Try me.'

She's casting glances at Charlie when she thinks I'm not looking. I should be touched by her concern for her brother — more than my sister has ever shown me. Too obsessed with her own career, her own life and ambition, to ever really care about my existence. Our parents acknowledged it, too, over and over. *Maggie will go places. You only have to see her work to know that.* No such glittering predictions for their son, of course. Just concerned whispers as I left the room; pitying glances when weighing me up against *her*.

It's why knowing what our uncle did to her makes her important to me.

He discarded her: thought her worthless.

I will make her a beautiful exhibit to be admired again. As she should always have been. Precious things like her should be preserved. Adding her as my star piece will bring The Collection the renown it deserves.

Charlie and his sister will be the surprise additions nobody was expecting. Always good to have a few pieces not in the catalogue. To delight the viewer with something else. Charlie as an easy acquisition when his time runs out, his sister collected as soon as she thinks she's won.

I'll let her have her victory before I claim mine.

'It's my gift to the world,' I say, my sight set on the knife, one swift movement away.

Sixty-Four

BENNETT

They reached Slaughden Beach first, Bennett and Ellis spilling out of the pool car and racing along the path they'd taken when looking for Alfie Gunnersall, days before.

Bennett wasn't certain how they'd got ahead of Anderson, Minshull and Wheeler, but she had to admit to a small sense of pride that she and Ellis were first on the scene. Ellis led the way, his steps powered by his own chagrin at not making the connection between Cora's message and the dilapidated building they'd previously encountered. He'd spoken of little else as Bennett had driven through the slowly shifting traffic.

It was clear from what they now knew about the inhabitants of the shack that Cora and Maggie were in grave danger. Whether Charlie Lael was an innocent victim too remained to be seen. But as far as Bennett was concerned, he had to be counted among those needing to be rescued. Anderson had called Bennett and Ellis from the other car as they sped towards Slaughden Beach to tell them what Evans had discovered, the news delivered via speakerphone. Maggie Jones' brother Hal, the one dishonourably discharged from the army, likely armed and ready to kill.

She edged ahead of Ellis, glad her recently resumed early morning runs were paying off. Ahead, the fisherman's shack crouched on the horizon like a looming storm cloud. Bennett remembered the conversation they'd had beside it during the search for Gunnersall, its entry point not immediately clear.

Had Hal Jones prepared the shack for what he planned today? Was the new padlock on the side door his?

Nearing the shack, Ellis raised his hand to signal for them to slow. Bennett joined him in the hummocks of wild grass, a little way from the building.

'How do we get in?' she whispered. 'The main door?'

Ellis shook his head. 'Too direct. I reckon we need another way in.'

The sides of the shack were cracked and weather-damaged, gaps between the planks wide enough in places to see between them. But for all its age and weathered appearance it seemed structurally sound. The roof wasn't an option, impossible to gain access without alerting those inside of their presence.

'Where, then?'

Ellis raised a finger to his lips and indicated the back of the shack. They moved silently over the grass banks, careful not to disturb any of the shingle that edged the shack.

'There,' Ellis whispered, pointing at the single panel of corrugated iron they'd seen before. 'I reckon that's another door they've bolted the panel over.'

Bennett stared at him. 'How does that help us?'

Ellis grinned and pulled a silver object from his pocket. 'Because I have this.'

When Bennett saw what it was, it took all her self-control not to laugh aloud. *The Pocket Pal Chrome* – a metal multi-tool on a key ring that his mum had bought him from a shopping channel for Christmas last year. It had been the source of much hilarity among the CID team, Ellis' initial pride at his über-gadget lost in the breathless amusement of his colleagues.

'You're not serious,' she whispered.

'I am,' he returned, selecting a screwdriver from the many-tooled gadget. 'I reckon I can unscrew the panel. The iron is okay, but I noticed the screws holding it in place are already loose.'

'Is that going to work?'

'Of course. Just sometimes, Kate, I wish you'd trust me.'

There was a definite edge to his reply. Bennett observed him as if unsure what she was seeing. 'I – I do trust you.'

'Because I have the ability to surprise you. If you'll let me.'

A sound from inside stole any answer Bennett might have offered, both detectives instinctively dropping to the ground. A shout – followed by the urgent murmur of a woman's voice.

Dr Lael.

Was she talking Jones down?

Bennett and Ellis crouched beside the panel together, ears trained on the shifts of sound coming from within the shack. A low moan, another frantic yell, the sound of sobbing, with the steady, deliberate flow of low-spoken words soothing the space between.

What was being said in there? Was someone in pain?

The not knowing was the worst, Bennett and Ellis inches away from the people inside, unable to help.

'We should wait for the others,' Bennett whispered, close to Ellis' ear.

'We wait for the sound to stop, then we carry on,' he countered.

Usually she would fight Ellis for her own way, determined not to surrender ground for anyone. But the sounds from inside the shack scared her. If Hal Jones felt cornered, if someone inside was injured – or worse – there was no time to wait for the rest of the team.

The sobbing subsided, all other noises gone. Bennett nudged her colleague, mind made up.

'Do it.'

Sixty-Five

CORA

Maggie Jones was terrified and in pain. Her eyes bulged over the velvet gag as she struggled against the restraints at her wrists and ankles, her gaze flicking between her brother and the large, bloodied knife on the floor.

'Stop crying,' her brother barked. 'You should be flattered I wanted you here.'

'Bound and gagged?' Cora asked. 'What kind of a way is that to treat your sister?'

What do you know? Hal's thought-voice hissed.

'All I've heard for weeks is her banging on and on about what I'm doing, where I spend my time, why I hide things from her. Incessant questions, constant nagging. It's why I went away. I needed peace. Because of her.'

A sob came from Maggie. Further across the dusty space, Charlie lay, worryingly still. Cora did her best to suppress her own panic at the sight of her brother, forcing herself to remain in the conversation with Hal. Her best hope of helping Charlie was talking Hal down. Tension sparked around him, the dissenting voice still front and centre, answered by Hal's own defiant thought-replies.

You failed…
I have a new plan.
It won't work. You'll fail there, too.

'Stop crying!'

'Hal, calm down,' Cora rushed, the sudden peak of his anger scaring her.

'But she's spoiling everything! You wanted to be here, Mags. You wanted to know the truth. I'm willing to let you be a part of it, but you have to embrace it or it won't work.'

'Embrace what, Hal?'

'The *honour*…' Exasperation was carried by every syllable, as if his reply was the most reasonable explanation.

'The honour of seeing The Collection?'

'The honour of *being* in The Collection!'

Truth, sickening and abhorrent, dawned for Cora. Hal had summoned his sister here to join Ronald Venn and Alistair Avebury as ultimate trophies. Where he'd failed to add their bodies to the rest of his macabre collection before, he intended to succeed now. Were Charlie and Cora to be afforded the same honour? Or would Hal consider them as acceptable collateral damage and dispose of them here?

Maggie's sobs became soft whimpers, tears streaking her face as she squeezed her eyes shut against the reality in which she found herself. Cora felt her stomach twist, her breath constricted by emotion.

Were they going to die here?

'Let me get to Charlie,' she said, not caring now about rocking her carefully constructed approach to talk Hal Jones down. If she was to die in this broken, unloved place, she intended to be as close to her brother as possible when it happened. Her poor, troubled, scared little brother, battling against a world too big and complex for him to comprehend.

She'd been wrong to suspect him in all this. He'd been reaching out, trying to find peace amidst the turmoil. He'd found it on Suffolk's beaches before, back when Bill Lael could offer space and light and life to meet his son's needs. Bird-watching and blokey chat, beers when he got older, and mile upon mile of wide-open space in which to frame every other concern.

Fatherhood was approaching, a new chapter that terrified him. Without a touchpoint, or the kindness and wisdom of his own dad to lean on, the shadows had become too big, the answers invisible. He'd returned home to find the spirit of Bill Lael, to attempt to tap into the certainty, kindness and space only his father had ever afforded him.

He couldn't take a life, any more than Cora could.

Instead, he'd found Hal Jones: a deeply scarred and dangerous man. He'd mistaken beach conversations for connection, a twisted view of controlling an uncertain world for a strategy to cope. In turn, Hal had found what he believed to be a trusting acolyte, ready to assist in the perfect acquisition of the ultimate piece: his own sister's body.

It would have been easily dismissible as melodrama, an unrealistic pantomime that surrounded a killer, had it not been for the voices only Cora could hear. The condemnation of one, the call to arms of another. And in the middle, tossed like a fragile rowing boat in a gale, a damaged man using any means necessary to forge a reason for being.

'Let me go to Charlie,' Cora pleaded again. 'He's badly hurt, Hal. I need to check on my brother.'

'He'll join The Collection when he passes. Think how beautiful that will be!'

'No, Hal. Charlie is mine. My brother, my family. He's not yours to take.'

Hal Jones lifted his chin, cruelty scratched into his smile. 'But I found him. On the beach. That means he belongs to nobody except the one who discovered him there.' He stabbed a blood-covered thumb at his stained chest. '*Me.*'

Sixty-Six

ELLIS

The gap beside the iron panel looked wide enough to afford a glimpse of the interior. Holding his breath, Ellis pressed his face against it, squinting to see inside.

What he saw caused every nerve to twist.

One body slumped against a side of the shack. A woman lying in the middle of the floor, her hands and ankles bound. Ellis could hear Cora Lael's voice, steady and insistent, but he couldn't see her. And the rise and fall of a male voice, staccato stabs where Cora's remained consistent. In the centre of the floor, a large knife, its blade and handle blood red...

Shocked, Ellis dropped to his knees and started to work on the screw that secured the bottom right of the panel, turning it in small increments, careful not to make a sound. Bennett had walked a little way inland across the grass and sandbanks that edged the beach, placing a call to Minshull, Anderson and Wheeler. How far away were they? And would Ellis be in trouble for beginning a rescue attempt without his superior officers?

There was no time to consider protocol. From the rise and fall of the sounds inside, Ellis feared the situation had escalated. He kept going, pausing occasionally to check the sound levels from within, willing them to remain steady. If Cora could keep Jones calm, there would be less chance of Hal Jones lashing out.

Bennett had wanted to storm the shack from the main door, but the presence of the knife made that too dangerous a choice.

The knife Ellis had glimpsed, while currently not being held, was threat enough to negate an attempt to rush in. Jones might be able to grab it from wherever he was – and they were well aware of what he was capable of when armed.

By removing the panel, they could sneak in from the rear of the shack, giving them the advantage of surprise, from a direction Jones would not expect. The bodies Ellis had been able to make out had all been facing the main door. That could prove vital to the rescue attempt.

The first screw suddenly came loose, Ellis fumbling with it before it tumbled to the ground, hitting the broken concrete base with a high metallic clatter. Ellis froze: Bennett, too, standing in the middle of the wetland grass.

Ellis held up his hands in apology, earning a sharp look from Bennett. Heart thudding hard, he resumed his task. When he next looked back, Wheeler, Minshull and Anderson were standing beside a relieved-looking Bennett, a line of support officers edging across the grassy bank towards them.

Minshull began to cross the divide, gently arriving at Ellis' side as he worked the fourth of six screws loose. Ellis didn't dare stop, for fear the released panel would swing open or drop down. The moment Jones realised the building was surrounded, he could panic.

'Wait until the team are in place before you take out the last one,' Minshull whispered against Ellis' ear.

Ellis nodded, supporting the weight of the panel as the screws were removed. All that remained now was the final fixing, in the top right corner. He prayed it would hold until the time was right.

Beside him, Minshull scanned the periphery of the shack. Hands were raised as, one by one, the support team took up positions. If Jones tried to run from the front door, he would instantly be caught by the support officers. If he pushed past Ellis and made his escape through the section where the metal panel had been, he'd be met by Ellis, Bennett and half a dozen more officers.

'There's a knife,' Ellis whispered back. 'It's close enough for someone to grab it.'

'Where's Jones?'

Ellis indicated the right side of the building, then mouthed, 'Two bodies,' placing his free hand first at the left side and then at centre back, and 'Dr Lael,' waving roughly at back right.

Minshull nodded and began to stand – just as Ellis raised the multi-tool to be ready for the signal to remove it. His elbow collided with Ellis' hand, sending the tool crashing against the wooden wall of the shack, the noise sending a wading bird flapping away in fright.

The police teams froze – as a banshee-shrill scream sounded inside…

Sixty-Seven

CORA

Hal Jones was upon his sister in a heartbeat, the bloodied knife in his hand. Cora called out in shock, twisting her body so that she could kneel instead of lie on the floor.

'I told you to be quiet!' he hissed in Maggie's face, spittle spraying her features as she sobbed and shook. 'You *have* to be quiet!'

Cora had heard the clang from outside, followed by the swell of terrified and condemnatory thought-voices that swirled around the man with the knife.

Failure!

They're coming for me…

They'll laugh at you. Incompetent!

Maggie Jones wrenched her head from side to side, her brother realising too late that she was using the curve of his shoulder to push the velvet gag away from her mouth. 'This stops *now*,' she rasped, her voice thick with emotion and fear. 'Charlie needs help.'

'Charlie betrayed me. Now he'll join The Collection as compensation.'

'What are you even saying? You're insane!'

'And you'll join him, silent or not!'

Suddenly the knife was in the air, Maggie screaming out as her brother embedded it deep in her thigh.

Cora screamed, too, the sight of fresh blood and Maggie's horrified expression too much to bear. Behind her, Charlie slumped to the side, one hand cradling his wound, blood oozing thickly between his fingers.

It was all wrong.

It should never have come to this.

Minshull and the team were outside, she knew now. Nothing else would have made such a noise. But what use were they when two people were lying in their own blood inside the shack?

Hal Jones' fury had gone, his bloodied hand against his sister's head, making slow, deliberate strokes from her crown to her neck.

'Ssh, it's done now,' he cooed, gazing at her as if she were shining. 'You'll be my pride and joy, Maggsie. The star piece. I'll make sure they honour you like no other.'

'I... *hate*... you...' the journalist gasped, shudders passing through her body as she bled out on the floor.

'You don't mean that. You're in shock, like Ronald was. I placed a cairn on him while his heart was still pumping. I told him it was better this way. It's better, Maggsie. You know the time of death. You know you'll be admired. This—' he held up his hand, dripping with her blood '—this is *beautiful*...'

Cora couldn't watch any more. White-hot indignation seared through her body, disgust and injustice and hate melding together, gathering pace.

'FAILURE!' she yelled, the sound a war cry from another world.

Jones' hand stopped stroking Maggie's hair.

Failure! the angry thought-voices concurred.

'No. I did what I came to do!'

Cora gathered up the scraps of thoughts surrounding Hal, repurposing each one as a sharpened weapon aimed squarely at him. She forged a molten steel channel of words and thoughts direct from Jones' own neuroses and fired them back in a barrage of hate.

'You failed! You failed and everyone will know it. The Collection is broken, smashed and sullied. You can't crown it with your sister because there's nothing else left.'

'No! I won! She's bleeding!'

'*No blood*,' Cora repeated, taking each thought-voice and amplifying it with her own, shocked at the stream of consciousness that revealed so much of Hal's inner monologue. 'You said, *no blood*. A single wound with no overspill, no ragged edges. A perfect death. This isn't perfect!'

Look at the mess you've made!

A new voice joined the flood, one Cora hadn't heard before. A woman's voice, haughty and dismissive, every word laced with stinging venom.

Cora mimicked it, matching the tone and threat. 'Look at the mess you've made!'

Hal's mouth dropped open. 'No…'

She repeated the line directly after the emotional echo had spoken. 'Mess, Hal. Disorder…'

'Shut up! Stop talking! I'm not listening!'

Maggie whelped as he raised the knife again.

'Say it one more time and she dies!'

'Hal Jones! This is the police. Open the door!'

Joel Anderson's voice caused a sob to sound from Cora. They were here, just the other side of the wooden walls.

Hal froze, eyes trained on the door.

'Come out!'

'It's over,' Cora said, her voice deliberately soft. He still held a knife and his sister was bleeding beside him. 'We can get Maggie out. Charlie, too. You can leave, Hal. This can finally be done.'

'It isn't done. The Collection can't be seen – it's not perfect.'

Cora surveyed the carnage inside the shack with desperation. The collected pieces were broken, scattered and unrecognisable from how they'd been when she and Maggie arrived. It couldn't be reassembled now even if they had hours to make it happen.

But she sensed that Hal wouldn't leave unless his work was viewed.

And then, it struck her. A way forward.

Sixty-Eight

MINSHULL

'DS Minshull, we need you!'

At the front of the shack, a line of support officers behind him, Minshull's breath caught.

Cora. Calling him.

When he'd heard there was a woman down inside the shack, he'd feared the worst. Leaving Ellis and Bennett at the rear of the building, he'd moved to the front, ready to storm the door. The sound of Cora's voice both allayed his fears and set his nerves on edge.

'I'm here,' he called back, resisting the urge to shoulder his way in to reach her.

'Hal wants you to see his collection. You've come to see it, haven't you?'

Minshull turned to Anderson for help. His shrug did nothing to aid him.

'Haven't you?' she prompted, the smallest hint of worry in her words.

He remembered the conversations around the beach killer being a collector, a curator of things. If that was how Hal Jones talked about his activities, Cora was using it now to open the door to the shack, both psychologically and physically – a key Jones wouldn't even realise was being utilised until it was too late.

'Yes. I'm excited to see it,' he replied, ignoring the mystified looks from the uniformed officers surrounding him. 'I'm a big fan.'

Anderson stood beside him. 'Ellis has the panel ready to go. He'll go in with Kate and Dave from the rear.'

'Collection, Guv?' Minshull asked, a moment of panic gripping him.

'Just act interested,' Anderson replied. 'Distract him long enough for the others to get in.'

'DS Minshull *only*, come to the front door,' Cora instructed.

Minshull took a breath, set his frame, and approached the shack. Why was he doing this? He felt sure Anderson, Bennett, Ellis or Wheeler would make a better job of it than he would. Acting had never come easily to him, truth and facts the only things he really understood. Wheeler was the talker, the gentle negotiator, the natural crowd-pleaser. Anderson, while gruff, could have a party in stitches with his dry humour and stories. Ellis could charm anyone with a pulse; Bennett was believable no matter what she said, and possessed an air of calm confidence that put everyone at ease.

Why him?

'Let me know when you're at the door.'

Cora's voice reminded him of why he'd agreed to this. Her trust in him. Her faith, sometimes erroneously placed when Minshull inevitably made a mistake. She'd once told a witness that she trusted Minshull with her life. He didn't think he'd ever fully get over the magnitude of that.

He was doing this for her. He'd do whatever she asked.

'I'm here,' he called.

The door of the shack slowly opened, revealing a bloodied hand on the handle.

Hal Jones stepped into the gap.

Minshull felt the officers behind him tense as one.

'I'm here to see The Collection,' Minshull declared, hating the sound of his own voice.

Jones observed him for a moment, then pulled something from behind his back. Smeared with blood from blade to handle, some of it very new. The shape and size of weapon concurrent with Dr Amara's estimation. The murder weapon used to end the lives of Ronald Venn and Alistair 'Ace' Avebury.

'Just you,' he stated, pointing the knife at Minshull. 'Or I'll kill everyone inside.'

Sixty-Nine

CORA

She could see him in the doorway, hands raised as if he were being arrested. Had she done the right thing, bringing him inside? If Jones got wind of a deception, he had the means and experience to kill them all.

Minshull would be hating every second, but Cora needed someone who kept his cool in a crisis. Ellis might lose his temper; Bennett, too. Wheeler would come across too softly and reduce the assumed gravitas of the occasion. Anderson would likely throw himself headlong into the fray. She couldn't risk anything that might reveal to Hal Jones that he was being duped.

It was good to see Minshull, too. For him to be at the door of the wooden building Cora feared might never be located. This investigation had thrown them together like never before, binding them tight. The only way Cora had come through the experience of finding Ronald Venn's body – followed by Gunnersall's attack – was to lean on Minshull. And while it was clear the case had dredged up personal trauma for Rob, it had made him lean on her in the same way.

'Slowly,' Jones commanded, the tip of the knife too close to Minshull's back as they entered. The door closed them in with a thud, Cora's fear churning in reply.

She saw the sweep his eyes made of the carnage inside: of Charlie's lifeless body, of Maggie, bound and bleeding, of Cora's own tied hands and ankles. Shock registered in his eyes, in the tensing of his jaw. He gave a long, slow blink – his effort to bring everything under control.

Jones was staring at Minshull, his eyes glazed a little as if dissociating from the moment. Cora needed him fully distracted so that the police team had a chance to formulate a plan.

'Tell Rob about The Collection, Hal,' she prompted.

Jones hesitated, the knife still aimed at Minshull. 'It needs rehoming. It isn't in perfect condition.'

'That's okay,' Minshull replied, his gaze locked with Cora's, taking his cue from her. 'Show me what you have.'

Cora watched as Hal began to describe the items that had covered the interior of the shack when they had arrived, detailing where he'd found them and why they were chosen.

'I like things nobody else treasures. Things people take for granted. They might never think about the bottlecap they discarded on the beach, but I find it and clean it and give it a place of honour. Lost shoes, cracks of glass from a mirror, broken jewellery. I know what it's like to be written off, thrown away like a piece of rubbish.'

'That's a great collection,' Minshull replied. 'So why the bodies?'

Jones appeared taken aback. Had Minshull pushed too far?

'People get thrown away, too.'

'The people you tried to collect didn't.'

What was he doing?

'But I still collected them. I gave them a purpose. And then, I found more.'

A gentle scratching sounded from the iron panel in the back wall behind Cora. Minshull and Jones were facing into the shack – the wrong direction to distract the collector from the sound.

'You should check Charlie,' she blurted, her own fear shuddering through her voice. 'If he's joining The Collection.'

Minshull understood immediately, stepping in front of Jones so that he shifted position, his back towards Cora. They knelt down beside Charlie and Cora saw Minshull's hand rest against her brother's neck before she looked away.

Charlie hadn't moved for a long time. There was no sign of breath in his chest. The dark stain had travelled across the front of his hoodie, and down across his right thigh, a small puddle converging beneath his knee. There were many things she would never understand about him – about the choices he made and the life he lived – but when it mattered, he'd thrown himself onto a knife to save someone else.

If Cora got out of here – *when* she got out – this fact alone would bring some consolation for her mother.

It broke her heart, but she couldn't save him this time. Years of looking out for her younger sibling, ended in the cruellest way. Hearing Jones talk about discarded things gave her a glimpse of what might have drawn Charlie to Hal. If he'd felt seen, at his lowest ebb, by someone with no history of friendship with him, might that have seemed providential?

His thought-voice remained, fading now, but still present. Cora had experienced the phenomenon before with the death of her father. Weeks after his physical passing, the final scraps of his emotional voice faded away – a profound moment that drew a fresh line beneath her loss.

A wash of tears distorted her view of the shack. She bowed her head…

…as the back wall of the shack imploded.

Seventy

CORA

Ellis burst through the hole where the steel panel had been, followed by Wheeler and Anderson. The shack was filled with shouts and movement, confusion and noise.

Minshull elbowed Jones hard in the ribs, causing the knife to topple from his hands. Jones kicked out, catching Minshull hard on his shin. He staggered back, only just bracing himself against the shack's wall to stop himself from falling on Charlie Lael's slumped body.

Jones scrabbled for the knife, but Ellis reached him, pushing him bodily backwards. But somewhere between the contact and the stumble, Maggie's brother found it again, bringing it up between them.

Cora cried out as the air expelled from Ellis' lungs, the DC crumpling over, sinking to his knees. Her wrists and ankles still bound, she was powerless to help, watching in horror as her colleague and friend collapsed to the floor.

'Drew! No!'

'Bastard!' Anderson and Wheeler piled on Jones, a metallic crash sounding as the knife finally fell to the floor, wet again with blood. Cora kicked her bound feet to send the weapon skidding across the concrete and beneath a stack of old fishing nets.

A yell from behind her heralded Bennett's arrival, stumbling through the crush of bodies to land at Ellis' side.

'Okay, it's okay,' she rushed, pulling him to her. 'We need an ambulance!'

'On the way,' one of the support officers called back.

All around Cora, officers were crouched beside the injured, a rush of concern and love replacing the fear and horror this place had become synonymous with. Jones was muscled out first, leaving the crush of Cora's colleagues tending to the fallen.

Her police family – as real and vital now as it had ever been.

Minshull half-staggered, half-fell to Cora's side, his fingers tangling with the frayed rope binding her hands and feet.

'I'm sorry,' he rushed. 'I'm just so sorry…'

'You got here. It's okay.'

'We didn't get all of your message. We went to Shingle Street, got it completely wrong… We could have prevented so much…'

The bonds fell at last, fire-red welts left in their place. Cora reached down to rub them, losing her breath when Minshull gathered her into his arms.

Pain and betrayal, fear and hatred sounded all around Cora, the last vestiges of her ordeal playing out amidst the relief and concern of her police colleagues. But held against Minshull, Cora found a well of peace. Soft rhythm of breathing. Strong reassurance of heartbeats. The noise from the physical and emotional layers of the building muted around this sacred space; a sense of warmth and a boundary and a promise of safety enveloping her body.

Instead of fighting, Cora let herself be held.

And in that moment, she could breathe.

Seventy-One

ANDERSON

'By rights, I should throw the book at you.'

'Sir.'

'All of you racing off like TV cops, with no arranged back-up, no plan... What were you thinking? I don't need to tell you how unprofessional that looks. When we are at a crucial time for police and public relations, and trust in the Force is at an all-time low. The press could have had a bloody field day with the details – if we'd let them have any.'

The ghost of a smile Superintendent Martlesham allowed to appear gave Anderson the smallest hint of hope.

Not that it made his solo-summoning to the superintendent's fourth-floor office any more comfortable.

It had been a hell of a twenty-four hours since the CID team's return to Police HQ. Hospitals, interviews, arrests, recriminations, and all before the inevitable questions began to be asked.

Martlesham released a sigh as he sank into his chair. 'Sit down, Joel. I imagine your body will thank you for it.'

Jokes, it seemed, were inevitable, too. It had been a while since Anderson had been involved in so hands-on a shout and news of his stunt-like intervention to overpower Hal Jones had spread across Police HQ like wildfire. Wheeler, too: now nursing a pulled muscle in his back for his efforts.

'How are your officers?'

Where to start? Earlier today, Les Evans had joked that he would need to cover all of South Suffolk CID's physical police work for the foreseeable, being the only team member not injured.

'So it's light duties for you lot and all the exciting stuff for me, eh? Reckon I'll enjoy that...'

'Drew Ellis is being kept in for observation. We have to be thankful that the injury was sustained in his forearm, not his chest as we'd feared. He's likely to be out of action for a week. There was talk of an operation initially, but the doctors are happy that he won't have any permanent nerve damage.'

'A lucky escape.'

'Indeed. Dave Wheeler is just aching, which goes for me, too. Rob Minshull has been given compassionate leave, at my insistence, to allow him to fully process the events on Slaughden Beach and the discovery of Ronald Venn's body at Shingle Street. Kate Bennett sustained some cuts and bruises during the arrest. I've managed to persuade her to accept a couple of days off but she'll be straight back to active duty at the first opportunity.'

'And Dr Lael?'

Anderson hesitated. Without Cora's intervention, Hal Jones might never have been apprehended. But she'd endured injustice and physical attack before she even accompanied Maggie Jones in search of their brothers. That was a wrong that required righting.

'In shock, as you would expect, but remarkably strong considering her ordeal. Permission to speak plainly, Sir?'

Martlesham waved his hand. 'You've never waited for it before. Why break the habit now?'

Anderson appreciated the superintendent's light-hearted reply, but what he wanted to say deserved a sober audience. 'Dr Lael willingly put herself in danger because she felt discarded by South Suffolk Police. Dismissed, by DCI Stephens, when neither I nor my team were present to fight her corner. She made it possible for us to capture a serial killer who would have killed again, and facilitated the rescue of herself and two other civilians. She is more than just a civilian consultant, Sir. And she deserved better from us.'

Martlesham nodded, his expression grave. 'Mistakes were made...'

'Mistakes that almost cost two lives,' Anderson snapped. He wouldn't stand by and let anyone paper over the injustices dealt to his team, of whose number he counted Cora. 'We need clear, actionable working practices, Sir. Ones that value and honour our detectives. We need protections for consulting members of the team. And we don't need any more operational red tape than is already foisted upon us.'

'I hear you. I do, Joel. And you have my word that recent mistakes won't be repeated.'

Anderson would believe it when he saw it. *If* he ever saw it...

'How is the journalist?'

'She lost a lot of blood. But she's stable and awake. For now, that's all we know.'

'And Dr Lael's brother?'

A sudden memory of Charlie Lael's body and the flurry of activity to try to save him returned, making Anderson's blood run cold. The events at Slaughden Beach would take some time to process. With everything that had occurred in the twenty-four hours since, he knew he hadn't even begun.

'His heart stopped at the scene. But paramedics were able to revive him. He's likely to be in hospital for some time, then he'll convalesce at his mother's home. It doesn't look like he'll be heading back to Australia this year.'

'I see. Joel, you have my word that Dr Lael will receive a full apology, from both DCI Stephens and myself. I hope she can come to feel she is a valued member of this force once again.'

In our office, Anderson retorted, *she already does.*

Seventy-Two

CORA

The stillness of the Critical Care ward was at odds with the battles going on in every bed. Voices were hushed, information delivered in low tones, while monitors flashed and counted, observing life at the edge of its limits. But the frightened, bewildered and frustrated thoughts of the patients here hummed restlessly around each bay.

Sheila Lael was dozing in a regulation green vinyl armchair beside her son's bed when Cora arrived. Standing by the curtain that edged Charlie's bay, Cora paused for a moment, watching her nearest relatives in their relative slumbers. Both looked peaceful now, at least. The horrors of Slaughden Beach and the nerve-shredding aftermath of the following hours seemed a world away from here. Cora hoped it could remain at a distance, giving her mum and brother space to heal.

Charlie had died in the bloodbath of the shack. Cora had yet to come to terms with the full horror of that. His heart had stopped for just under a minute, but that was fifty-eight seconds too many. If Minshull, Ellis and the CID team hadn't arrived when they did...

She dismissed the thought.

It was immaterial. Charlie was here, now, still in a critical condition but conscious and breathing and ready to fight. It would be a long time before he would be able to return to Australia – if Bethan would have him back. His partner knew what had happened, but with the birth of their baby now days away, she was relying on friends and close family to help her, the focus of the mother-to-be necessarily commanded by her imminent arrival. But further down the line, when Charlie had recovered and Bethan and the baby were settled in a routine, who knew what might be possible?

Sheila stirred, blinking sleep away. 'That you, Cor?'

'Hey, Mum.' Cora edged into the curtained bay. 'You need to go home and sleep.'

'Oh, I'm fine here, love. The nurse made me a lovely cuppa and found me a pillow and a blanket.'

'It's not the same as your own bed.'

'Yes, I know, but—' Her gaze drifted across the tightly tucked white sheets to Charlie's pale arm where it lay. 'I want to stay.'

There would be no arguing with her while Charlie was here.

Cora smiled at her mum. 'At least go and get yourself something to eat. The café's open downstairs and they do a lovely bacon roll.'

'That does sound nice...'

'Go. I'll sit with Charlie.'

Sheila hesitated for a moment, but the promise of breakfast proved too strong. Slowly, she rose from her chair, pausing to embrace her daughter before stiffly edging past her. 'You're a sweetheart, thanks. I won't be long.'

'Take as long as you need, Mum.'

The chair was warm where Sheila had been, when Cora sat down, the blanket woven with audible worries. She loved that her mother wanted to take care of Charlie, but was concerned for her, too. Medical staff had warned that Charlie's route to recovery may be extensive: it would be a considerable amount of time before he could live independently. How prepared was Sheila for that kind of commitment?

Cora would help, of course, where she could. But questions still remained about her brother. Questions not easily dismissed by the relief of his still-beating heart. Why had he befriended a killer? And when he knew what Hal Jones had planned, why didn't Charlie stop him?

She watched the steady rise and fall of his chest beneath the sheets, the lights on the monitor screen over his bed marking every peak and trough of his heartbeat. She had believed him capable of multiple murders. Had framed him as a killer. It would take time for her to reconcile that with the brother she wasn't sure she still knew.

'Sis?'

The voice was little more than a croaked whisper, Charlie's eyes open now, watching her.

'Hey.' She reached for his hand, aware of the coolness of his skin beneath hers. The last time she'd held it was moments before paramedics took him away from the broken remains of the Slaughden Beach shack.

'I didn't think... Mum wasn't sure you'd come...'

Cora didn't reply, willing the words that wouldn't arrive into the smile she gave in their stead.

I'm sorry.

His thoughts spoke from the sheets, from the contact points of his body in the hospital bed. They hurt to hear, but Cora didn't mute them. Truth would be what got them both through this: she couldn't ignore it.

'Where's Mum?'

'I sent her down to the café to get some breakfast. I think she slept here last night.'

His bruised eyelids gave a slow blink. 'I can't get her to go home.'

'Neither can I. Let her do it, Charlie. She thought she'd lost you.'

'And you?'

The question was a knife to her, dragging her straight back to the stink and terror of the Slaughden shack. 'I watched you die in there. I can't ever forget that. I just wish...'

'I didn't know, Cor. What Hal was doing.'

Stunned by his rushed confession, Cora stared back.

Charlie coughed, his neck straining as he tried to swallow. 'He said he was collecting stuff. I watched him picking pebbles and rubbish from the beach. I didn't think...'

'Why did you tell me not to look for you?' It had bitten at her since their ordeal ended: proof, it seemed, that Charlie had been in on Hal's plan and was warning her off.

'Because I knew you'd do the opposite. You wouldn't be told by me. It was the only way... He was watching me when I sent you the message. There was no time to say what I needed.'

'I thought you were involved.'

'I know. I shouldn't have been there.'

'No, you shouldn't.' Cora fought hot tears back as she faced her brother.

Charlie's eyes slid to the lights of the monitor screen. 'His sister, is she...?'

'She lost a lot of blood, but she's alive.'

He was quiet for a while, his attention fixed on the screen.

I didn't mean to be there.

I'm sorry.

I thought he understood me...

Cora caught the thought-confession and held it captive. What made Charlie believe that of Hal Jones?

'Why were you with him?' she asked, aware of the tricky path this could be. 'Why put your trust in someone like that?'

'I thought he was a friend. Lost. Like I feel. He understood the need to collect things to calm his head. I collected bird photos to do it. He collected pebbles and beach stuff. I just wanted someone who didn't judge me for it. Who didn't know me from before.'

'But he was killing people. And he planned to kill his sister.'

'I know, I know...' He raised a hand to his pale features, his hospital bracelet scratching his cheek, the cannula tube bending where it entered his skin. 'I couldn't stop him. He thought I agreed with him — I don't know why. But then he just said it. *I need her to crown The Collection. The closest thing to a piece of me…*'

Cora baulked at the words, at the memory of Hal's thought-voice, the screaming compulsion at war in his mind. 'You need to tell the police what you know.'

Charlie nodded, a stream of saltwater stained blue by the dimmed light of the bay as it fell from his closed lids. 'Call your friends. I'm ready.'

Seventy-Three

WHEELER

Team briefings were proving tricky in CID when half of their number were currently on leave. Ellis off for a week, Minshull off for three. Bennett persuaded to take a couple of days off, but due back in tomorrow. Thank goodness for Pete York, who had gamely stepped into the breach – and unfamiliar daylight hours – and PC Steph Lanehan, who was on her way up to CID to play detective for a few days.

Wheeler, York and Evans grinned at Anderson as he observed the depleted ranks of his team.

'Morning all. Or *few*.'

'Morning, Guv.'

'Bet you wish you'd taken a week off now, Guv,' Evans joked.

'And leave all the fun? Never!' Anderson assumed his favourite briefing perch on the edge of Minshull's impossibly tidy desk. 'Besides, they don't award compassionate leave for old codgers' backs. Even though this bastard is killing me.'

'Steph offered her apologies,' Wheeler said. 'She's been held up for an hour, sorting out the rotas for Tim Brinton. But she'll be here by ten.'

'Excellent. We might make a DC out of her yet.'

Good luck with that, Wheeler thought. He'd been trying to persuade Lanehan to take her detective exam for years, with no sign of her relenting. Although her new shifts in CID would certainly keep her busy.

'Right, let's get started. So, Hal Jones has had a medical assessment and been deemed fit to answer questions…'

Anderson paused while the detectives welcomed this. It had been three days since the events of Slaughden Beach and Jones' legal brief had done everything possible to delay his client talking to them. 'So Dave, if you'd assist me on that?'

'Sure, Guv.'

'I've just had a call from Dr Lael – she's fine, but her brother is awake and asking to talk to us. Pete, I wonder if you'd mind heading to Ipswich Hospital to do that? Take Steph with you.'

'Guv.'

'Les, if you could cadge a lift with Pete and Steph? Maggie Jones is ready to give her statement, too.'

'If Pete brings coffee, I'm there.'

York gave a cheery salute in reply.

'Cheers. So, news from Dr Amara. The knife used by Hal Jones in the incident three days ago fits the wound profile of those found on Ronald Venn and Alistair Avebury. And notebooks found at the scene on Slaughden Beach list details of their murders. His handwriting, his prints... a solid body of evidence to support us. But if we can get a confession or information from Jones it'll make it watertight.'

'What about Alfie Gunnersall, Guv?' Wheeler asked.

'Court date still to be confirmed, but he's being held in custody.' Anderson gave a wry smile. 'No doubt penning his latest tell-all to whichever news rag will take it.'

Evans clapped a hand to his heart. 'Hope I get a mention in his memoirs, Guv.'

'Yeah, wouldn't that be something? Okay, thanks everyone. Dave, shall we?'

—

Hal Jones made startling eye contact from the moment Wheeler and Anderson took their seats in Interview 3. His solicitor, by contrast, stared only at the copious notes in his file. Wheeler started the recording and, the formalities thus completed, focused on his own notes as Anderson began.

'Mr Jones, your legal brief informs me you have been declared fit for interview. Therefore, this is your opportunity to give us your side of the story. I want to understand what led you to this course of action.'

'Of course, DI Anderson.'

'Thank you. Let's begin with the attack on Ronald Venn, on Shingle Street Beach, four weeks ago. Did you know Mr Venn previous to that day?'

'He's a former squaddie. I used to see him at regiment reunions.'

'You went to those even after being discharged from the army?'

Jones' eyes narrowed. 'It was a family thing. A necessity, no matter what your service record was. They had no problem with me being there.'

'And yet a former colleague told us you fought with Venn?'

'I did.' His stare didn't flicker. 'So when I saw him on the beach it was a serendipity.'

'So you could get revenge?'

'So I could heal the past. Make him part of something lovely again.'

'Did you talk to him on the beach?'

'Only afterwards.'

Wheeler's throat caught and he reached for his mug of tea to stop himself coughing. It wasn't what he'd expected to hear. After the wrangling over Jones' fitness to attend an interview, Wheeler had anticipated evasive answers, if any. The confidence and candidness of Jones' reply was a shock.

'Afterwards?'

'When it was done. I told him he had a home. Something I expect he'd always wanted.'

'When you say *done*, what do you mean?'

'When his heart had stopped.'

Anderson made notes – and Wheeler wondered if his superior might be using the pause to process what he'd just heard. Wheeler already felt sick and he thought he'd experienced pretty much every horror in the job.

Another surprise was that Jones' brief, so combative regarding the need for an assessment for his client, didn't move to challenge him or request that his reply be ignored. What had changed?

'Why did you kill Ronald Venn?'

'I *collected* him. Very different from killing.'

'How, exactly?'

Jones maintained his unnerving gaze. 'Killing is the wrong term. Anyone can kill something. Spontaneity. Opportunity. Lashing out. I studied my piece. Watched him. Familiarised myself with his movements. Like I learned in the army. He wasn't killed. He was collected. Chosen specifically for a purpose.'

'What purpose was that?' Wheeler couldn't help asking the question, despite every shred of human decency within him not wanting to know the answer.

Jones switched his attention to Wheeler. 'To be seen. He'd been ignored, like me. Written off. Forced to sleep on the beach because nobody wanted him. I made him a spectacle. I made people look. The kid, too. Abandoned by his friends like he didn't matter. People know his name now, don't they?'

'And your sister?'

Wheeler tensed as Anderson asked the question.

The defiance in Jones' stare flickered for a moment. 'A piece of me. She was meant to make up for the others. The biggest sacrifice. The perfect exhibit.'

'But she wasn't, was she? Because you failed, Hal. She's alive. Not part of your collection.'

'That's because she refused to comply! I gave her a beautiful chance and she didn't want it.' Hands balled into fists on the interview desk, Jones' retort hissed through gritted teeth.

'I request a break,' the solicitor interjected, finally finding his voice.

'We're almost done.'

'I *require* a break in order to brief my client,' the solicitor returned, firmly, 'in light of new information he has revealed during this interview.'

With more relief than irritation, Wheeler paused the interview recording. He felt sick, his own memories of the scene Hal Jones had caused in the Slaughden Beach shack threatening to return. He'd lost a few nights' sleep to it already and didn't welcome the reminder.

Anderson leaned on the wall of the interview room after Jones and his solicitor had hurried out. 'Bloody hell, Dave.'

'I know. We have him, though, don't we?'

'He near as damn it confessed to killing Ronald Venn and Alistair Avebury on tape. And we can prove prior intent, so they can't argue for manslaughter.'

'But if they go for diminished responsibility? A lesser charge?'

'Then we have to hope what we've got is enough to dismiss it.' He rubbed the back of his neck, and Wheeler wondered if the DI had caught any more sleep than he had. Knowing Anderson, he suspected not.

He'd get his wife to call Anderson's missus later. Sana and Ros knew more about the rigours of the job than any civilian should. If Ros was watching her husband, at least Anderson had a hope of finding rest.

Wheeler thought of Alistair Avebury as he and Anderson made their way back upstairs to the CID office. Nineteen years young and feeling like the world didn't give a shit about you. No kid should feel that way.

One thing was certain: when he got home tonight, Wheeler was going to hug his two boys for as long as he could. They'd protest loudly, of course, as they always did. But it didn't matter. They might think their old man was a soppy git, but they would always, *always* know they were loved.

The CID office was eerily empty when they returned, the desks revealing so much about his colleagues, even in their absence. Cora Lael had told him once that she could hear the thought-voice of each detective, floating up from their desks. Wheeler could almost hear them now, laughing and bickering: Ellis with his hand up like a kid, Bennett rolling her eyes, Evans running some questionable bet or other, Minshull hard at work unless they could all jolly him out of being a copper for once. His team. His people. The sound they filled CID with daily something he couldn't wait to have back at full strength.

Three weeks before Minshull came back.

Ellis due back in one.

Bennett returning tomorrow, likely in before anyone else, the strain of even a few days' admission that she needed a break evident in her determination to get on with the bloody job.

Then Wheeler could relax. As much as anyone could in this place.

'It's a yes from CPS,' Anderson said, striding into the office from his own. 'Two counts of murder, four of attempted, two of abduction, ABH on Drew. Full house.' He drew level with Wheeler, a hand clamped warmly on his colleague's shoulder saying more than the gruff DI would ever admit. 'Let's go and charge the bastard.'

'Yes, Guv.'

Seventy-Four

CORA

The sea had always called to her, no matter where in the world she found herself. The absence of all other voices in the presence of its vastness and sound a gift. A place of calm, of grounding: a place of peace.

In the days following the events on Slaughden Beach, she had wondered if this long-held sanctuary would be barred to her. Would memories of Ronald Venn's body piled high with beach finds and the pain of Alfie Gunnersall's attack mar Shingle Street for her? Would the horrors of Slaughden keep her from ever walking its coast again? Even Felixstowe Beach – the one she saw every day from her apartment window – could no longer just be the location of her early morning run because of the attack Abi Quigley and Georgie Kelsall had survived.

And what of her involvement with South Suffolk CID? What did the future hold for her there?

'Don't overthink it,' Minshull said, taking a bite from a freshly made doughnut, wincing as the steam stung his lips. 'Or maybe always visit with me.'

Cora jabbed an elbow into his side. 'I'm serious, Rob.'

'I know. Sorry. But this is good, right?' He relaxed back on the bench, stretching his legs out towards the edge of the promenade. 'I mean, food helps.'

'Four doughnuts is excessive,' Cora observed, laughing despite the flurry of nerves she'd experienced since arriving at the beach. 'Even for you.'

'Cheek,' he grinned, sugar crystals studding his lips. 'I'm on official leave: how else am I supposed to make the time pass?'

His humour was a shield, of course. He knew it as well as Cora did. Whatever had triggered his response to Operation Nautilus, he needed time to address it. He still hadn't expanded on what had shaken his usual steadiness. Maybe he'd never be able to articulate it. A single event, a past injustice, or just the combined pressure of a career filled with hastily hidden issues – whatever it was, at least he was allowing himself space to acknowledge it now.

Spending time together away from the CID office was helping, too.

They sat in amiable silence, watching the seagulls stalk the beach for discarded treats and wheel and cry above in the startling blue arc of the sky. Soft grey waves lapped the shore. Sun danced on the incoming tide. And the tang of salt filled Cora's lungs as she breathed it all in.

'I've been thinking,' Minshull began, tipping the grease-stained paper bag towards Cora for her to take another doughnut.

'Always dangerous.' She smiled at her own joke, at the lightness in her spirit she could finally enjoy.

'I have two more weeks of leave.' His eyes fixed on a point far out to sea. 'I'm thinking of visiting Ben and the kids in Cornwall. Play Uncle Rob for a bit. Catch some waves. Eat my body weight in ice cream.'

'That sounds good.'

'Come with me?'

When she turned her head, he was looking at her, the shield of humour gone.

'Why?'

'Because there's something going on with us. And we can't talk about it here.'

She remembered the embrace, sudden and strong, in the hell and confusion of the fisherman's shack; the brief space of sanctuary she'd found there. Of the days they'd spent in each other's company since being granted compassionate leave from their workplaces; the natural gravitation towards one another on days they could spend however they wanted.

Perhaps a different coast would bring answers that had eluded them.

Or offer them a glimpse of peace.

It was a moment of honesty Minshull rarely offered. A briefly opened door.

And Cora Lael had no good reason to refuse.

The voices from the promenade stilled; even the sea hushed a little.

Cora's own voice took centre-stage.

'Yes.'

A letter from MJ White

Dear Reader

This is Cora's sixth case and what a journey she's had to get here! More than anything, I'm so proud of this series and blown away by the support and love for Cora, Minshull and the detectives of South Suffolk CID. Thank you!

No book goes out into the world without a team working their socks off to make it happen. My thanks to my editor, Keshini Naidoo, and the Hera team, for believing in Cora and bringing her adventures to the world. Thanks to Phil Williams for copy-edits and Ross Dickinson for proofreading.

Thanks, as always, to my agent, Hannah Ferguson, for championing Cora and my writing. For authorly cheerleading, my thanks to AG Smith, Craig Hallam, Kim Curran, CL Taylor, Chris Callaghan, Mick Arnold, Ian Wilfred, Dorothy Koomson, DV Bishop, Mari Hannah and Julia Chapman. Special thanks to Katy and William Baldwin of Tea Leaves and Reads, for their tireless and vital support of this series. It means the world to me.

Huge love to Team Sparkly and to my brilliant viewers of Fab Night In Chatty Thing, for all your love and excitement about everything Cora does. Special thanks to Alan Gillies, Angi Plant, Katie Harris, Catherine Clapperton and Carol Lesley. Thanks also to supporters of my Sparkly News and WriteFoxy substacks.

The Stolen Dead is dedicated to the memory of Tony Crooks, who loved this series. With my love and thanks.

And all my love to my lovely Bob and fabulous Flo. I love you to the moon and back and twice around the stars xx

This book looks at the challenge of mental health and how it affects so many young people in the UK. If you need to talk, here are some fantastic organisations who are there for you.

Mind Support Line: 0300 102 1234 (Lines open 9 a.m. – 6 p.m., Monday to Friday)

Samaritans: 116 123 (Free from any phone, lines open 24 hours a day, 365 days a year)

Switchboard: If you identify as gay, lesbian, bisexual or transgender, you can call Switchboard on 0300 330 0630 (10 a.m. – 10 p.m. every day)

Follow Miranda:
Website: www.miranda-dickinson.com
Twitter: @wurdsmyth
Instagram: @wurdsmyth
Facebook: MirandaDickinsonAuthor
YouTube: youtube.com/mirandawurdy
Threads: @wurdsmyth
Bluesky: @wurdsmyth.bsky.social

The Stolen Dead *book playlist*

For every novel I write, I compile a soundtrack playlist that captures the emotion and atmosphere of the story I want to create. Here are the songs and pieces of music that inspired *The Stolen Dead*. Happy listening!

Main theme of *The Stolen Dead*:

A' CHUTHAG (THE CUCKOO) – Valtos & Julie Fowlis

TARANSAY – Elephant Sessions – *For the Night*

NÍU – SKÁLD – *Vikings Chant (Alfar Fagrahvél Edition)*

CREATURES OF THE SUN – Dotter – *Creatures of the Sun (Single)*

STARS – Dubstar – *Disgraceful*

SHOULDA – Jamie Woon – *Mirrorwriting*

OVERCOME – Skott – *A Letter from the Universe*

LUST – RURA – *In Praise of Home*

GIANTS – Dermot Kennedy – *Giants (Single)*

ORDINARY WORLD – Duran Duran – *Arthur Dent's Playlist*

HEAVEN – Cian Ducrot – *Victory (With Choir And Strings)*

REBIRTH – Elephant Sessions – *For the Night*

SKYWORLD – Two Steps From Hell – *Skyworld*